Last Train to Polmouth

JOHN TRETHEWEY

authorHOUSE®

AuthorHouse™ UK
1663 Liberty Drive
Bloomington, IN 47403 USA
www.authorhouse.co.uk
Phone: 0800.197.4150

Published by AuthorHouse 03/21/2016

ISBN: 978-1-5246-3017-1 (sc)
ISBN: 978-1-5246-3018-8 (hc)
ISBN: 978-1-5246-3016-4 (e)

Contents

Last Train to Polmouth

Decline and Fall of Polmouth

The Polmouth Legacy

Ost-West Express

The Polmine Project

Sunset over Polmoor

Polmouth Sunrise

Polmouth Council Map

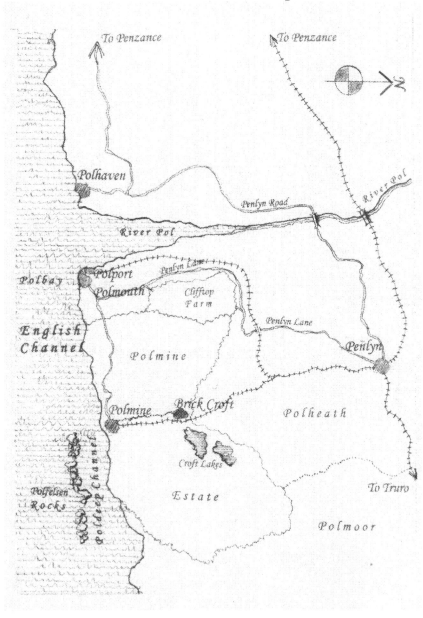

Map produced and provided by Brooke Fieldhouse,
with sincere thanks from the author

Decline and Fall of Polmouth

Decline and Fall of Polmouth
1964

Chapter One

Monday, May 24th, 1964

The sun was scarcely above the horizon, casting long shadows through narrow cobbled streets. Out at sea, a group of trawlers was approaching the mouth of the river Pol. The two smallest fishing boats separated from the group of eight, veered to starboard and headed for Polport in the estuary, while the other six proceeded in convoy towards Polhaven to the West.

Harry Pengarth, the Polmouth village postman was striding down Harbour Lane to Polport to collect the mail from the Polhaven ferry's first visit of the day. As he made his way down the steep lane from his home to what had once been the village centre, he joined a group of adults also heading for the ferry, going to work in Polhaven or Penzance. The hoot of a steam engine's whistle as it slowly drew a three coach train into tiny Polport Station heralded the appearance of a dozen children in school uniform, merging into a group outside the station entrance. Aged between eleven and eighteen, this was their daily pilgrimage to the nearest seat of learning, the eighteen mile journey over the heath and the moor to Penlyn Grammar School. None of the youngsters was accompanied by an adult; there was no risk of abduction or molestation by sexual predators in 1964.

Pengarth recognised several among those passing into the ticket office. He espied fourteen year old Colin Penpolney, tall for his age, and beside him Margaret Wells, the music teacher's daughter. Straggling behind the group were two young girls, Henrietta Carrington, who lived in the decaying Polmouth Manor House, and her friend Petra Zabrinski, daughter of a Polish fighter pilot in World War 2. At the very end of the gaggle of those catching the train to school was a much taller passenger, an adult, Felix Ingram, the Latin teacher at Penlyn Grammar. It was eight o'clock. The postman continued his downhill walk to Polport harbour.

Some distance away from the passengers waiting for the white ferry, he sat down on a low wall, not relishing the daily long trek through the maze of narrow streets, and even less the climb up the cliff path to the farmhouse at Polmine Estate. Even before the ferry had moored, an elderly lady approached. It was Mary Talbot, the Village Council secretary.

'Morning, Harry.' She was carrying a sack of mail. 'Have to add this to your round. One to every household. They're important, so make a note of any that you don't manage to distribute. Very important. There's even one with your address on the envelope. Have a nice day...' And she was gone.

As the morning train from Polmouth to Penlyn Junction was puffing and wheezing out of Polport Station and Pengarth was loading three sacks of mail onto a wheelbarrow for sorting at the minuscule village Post Office prior to delivery, many miles away in a grimy rented one room office in the London Inns of Court a corpulent dark haired man with jaundiced eyes was browsing through the inside pages of the previous day's Sunday Telegraph. He turned a page and saw several columns of small print with a headline: **Beeching Cuts**. He glanced cursorily down the lists of planned railway closures, the "Beeching Cuts" to the rail network destined to reduce the British Railways deficit with lasting economies. Doctor Beeching's remedy was to be drastic, the closure of numerous unprofitable branch lines across the United Kingdom. The lists were divided by region to make them more comprehensible. Too much so, for this man's liking. His eye settled on Cornwall and he stiffened, then blenched. He reached across the dusty mahogany desk and called his brother.

'Zacharias, come down immediately... No, I mean now. It's urgent, and we're in difficulties. Get down here!' He rang off, consulted a tatty address book and dialled his friend Miles Hendricks at the offices of Fiduciary Agents and Liquidators "Barnes, Todd and Hampton". Time had run out, as had the fortunes of "Chronos Investments".

Zacharias Chronos, sitting opposite his brother at the desk, pushed the newspaper away and stared blankly at the far wall.

'That's our last asset,' he started, 'Father thought it might be ripe for housing development one day. But without the railway, and only a country lane across the heath from Penlyn... What are we going to do?' he asked Leonidas.

'We're finished.' Leonidas' voice was hoarse. 'Father should never have bought it back then, in '45, from the Ministry. I had a bad feeling about it even then, but he shouted me down, pooh-poohed me as an ignorant young know-all. And Polmine Estate is our last asset. I've called Miles, at "Barnes, Todd and Hampton".'

'So it's come to that? Christ! What am I going to tell Helena? And the children? And who'll want to buy a derelict, run-down estate at the ends of the earth with a defunct mine that closed years ago, a Brick Croft without clay, and nine square miles of land on crumbling cliff tops?' He stared at the wall again. 'And now no rail service to civilisation? That village, what's it called... Polmouth, is finished! No developer will ever build houses down there, not in a million years.' He wiped his swarthy face in desperation. 'What did Hendricks say?'

'He's coming over. Get the file on Polmine Estate, will you? It'll be in the archives. We'll need the 1945 Land Registry extract.' Leonidas felt in an inside breast pocket and pulled out a hip flask, took a long draught then offered it to Zacharias, who shook his head. 'Best Hungarian *Barack Palinka*,' insisted Leonidas, 'apricot brandy.'

'Go on like that, you'll meet the same end as father. The mortuary.' Zacharias was impatient. 'I'll search for the file. Call me when Hendricks gets here.' He left. Leonidas stared at the columns of tiny print, then lifted the hip flask to his lips again.

Two hours later Hendricks left the two dejected, bankrupt brothers and crossed the Inns of Court to return to his office. He was carrying a slender file of "Chronos Investments" assets and creditors. There was only one asset, and numerous debts. He also carried the file on Polmine Estate, the original Land Registry extract, plans to the grounds and a heavy bunch of unlabelled keys.

In his office he cast the two files aside and opened the Land Registry extract and the plans. After a brief study of both it was clear that he would have to go to Polmine Estate for a valuation. It was more than extensive: nine square miles of land and buildings. And the assets file was slender because the only asset was, or had been, the Estate. Any properties on the Estate also looked distinctly meagre, not to say bleak. Mine workings, disused since 1945 and now probably in disrepair, as would be the five adjacent miners' cottages. A Brick Croft two miles to the North, where the clay reserves were long since exhausted, which explained why the rail head for the branch line spur from the main railway line from Penlyn to Polmouth was also defunct. The two extensive, deep pits excavated for clay over decades were now indicated as tranquil lakes. Hendricks saw that a railway extension from the Brick Croft railhead all the way to the mine workings on top of the cliffs had once been functional.

He leaned back in his chair and stared at the wall, visualising how things must have been before the war. Frequent trains, flatbed cars and freight coaches drawn by gleaming steam engines pulling out of Truro and branching south at Penlyn Junction, heading for Polport, and then onto to the Brick Croft spur and the extension to the mine. God knows what state those tracks would now be in. Yes, he would have to pay a visit. His eye fell on a property adjacent to the Estate, a separate Land Registry parcel, not part of the liquidation. A farm. He grimaced. The closure of the railway line from and to Penlyn would not bode well for the farmer, but Hendricks had enough on his hands with the "Chronos" file. He reached for the phone and dialled Directory Enquiries.

Shortly before lunch the phone rang in Penzance Tourist Information Office. Trainee Matthew took the call, then turned to the Office Manager Dennis Latimer.

'Mr. Latimer, there's a surveyor in London or something, asking whether we know anyone from Polmouth. He wants information about Polmine Estate, whether there's anyone who could take him round the place on Thursday. D'you know this place? I've never heard of it.' Dennis nodded.

'I do, grew up close by as a lad. Used to play in the farm next door, and when I was older collect eggs and milk the cows with the farmer. Yes, I know it. I'll take the call...'

Hendricks put down the phone in satisfaction, crossed the office to a bookshelf and consulted his Bradshaw's for the times of the Tuesday night sleeper train to Penzance. He steeled himself for his third call, to his wife. Four nights away from home...

Chapter Two

The tiny Primary School in Polmouth only had eighteen pupils aged between seven and ten. No sooner had they left the building at the end of afternoon school than the Caretaker made a telephone call. By four o'clock there were three men setting out chairs retrieved from the Council depot in rows in the school hall. The Village Council was about to hold court.

A mile away on the clifftop plateau farmer Jake Blackitt was in the farmyard in front of the barn. Using a winch and pulley he lifted a heavy milk urn into the air then swung it round and lowered it in the back of a farm cart. When all four shining urns were aboard, he secured them and walked to a stable. The only way to get his milk to civilisation, and hay and chicken feed in return, was the farm cart. A dairy and poultry farm has no need of a tractor, and Blackitt, who ran the entire enterprise single handed, did not even have a Land Rover. He opened the door of the one horse stable.

"One horse" was a gross euphemism for the sole occupant of the stall, Jasper. It was a monstrous animal, dwarfing any conventional equine breed. Jasper was a Great Horse, a nearly extinct derivative of the Shire horse, with distinctive feathering of long tufts of black and white hair from the fetlocks down to the hooves. In 1964 there were only 50 Great Horses in the entire UK, and half of those were in a little known equine sanctuary deep in the New Forest owned by Blackitt's brother who bred a couple of foals each year.

The Great Horse stands well above eight feet in height and is as long. Jasper, as tame as he was elderly, stood nine feet tall and weighed more than one ton. He docilely followed Blackitt out of the stable towards the farm cart, where Jasper obediently backed in between the cart shafts to be attached to his load. This was a daily ritual.

No rider could ever have mounted the nine foot monster, not even with a mounting block. Blackitt always walked alongside the friendly giant, using a loose rein. He led the way to the gravel track that led one mile downhill to the village and the station.

Even had it been allowed, there was no way that Jasper and the farm cart could reach the platform through the ticket office, nor was it necessary. Blackitt walked the horse to the harbour end of the platform where it sloped down to allow wheeled vehicles to reach the train. Jasper effortlessly pulled the four milk urns up the slope and halted where the rear coach of the train that was even now slowly approaching would stop.

The guard, standing in the goods wagon, slid open the door and started to push a second cart off the train onto the platform. It held two empty milk urns, four bales of hay and six one hundredweight sacks of grain and corn for the hens. Blackitt assisted him, and they then pushed the milk cart into the freight car. The guard slammed the door, the two men shook hands, and Blackitt hitched the new cart to Jasper's leather straps. A daily ritual indeed, but today there was a variant. As Blackitt, Jasper and the cart reached the tiny Station Square, Mary Talbot approached, sent by Percy Teague, the President of the Village Council.

'You got the letter this morning?' Blackitt nodded glumly.

'Dunno what I'll do. And I can't make the meeting this evening, you know I can't...' Mary Talbot cut him off.

'We know you can't, that's why I'm here. Mr. Teague will come up tomorrow to talk it through with you. The Council's made plans, as far as possible, to cover the railway thing.'

'He sent you?' Blackitt's eyes widened. 'Nice of him. Good to see the Village Council sees how serious this is going to be. Thank him for me, will you?'

He moved away, leading his Great Horse and the day's supplies through the narrow village streets to the gravel track.

The last ferry of the day from Polhaven moored at seven o'clock, by which time the school hall was already filling with anxious villagers. Monday's letter from the Council announcing the closure of the railway to Penlyn affected every single inhabitant. Among the few passengers disembarking from the ferry, a group of three, none young, made their way through the village to the school; the Village Council comprised three elected members and these were they. President Percy Teague, flanked by Rupert Tredinnick and Monica Polnay, was not looking forward to the evening meeting.

At 7.30 Teague opened proceedings. Over and above the one hundred seated citizens there were more than twenty standing at the rear.

'Good evening.' His voice was a resonant baritone, his silver hair brushed back from the forehead and his tall stature commanding attention. 'Well, we all know why we are here, and I shall not mince my words. The Beeching decision to terminate rail services from Penlyn will have dire consequences. It is the Council's responsibility to mitigate, as far as is possible, those consequences. We have drawn up three plans so far, namely the transport of school pupils to Penlyn, the transport of farm produce and essential supplies for the whole village, and public transport. I shall now outline these, and then take questions.

'I'll start with the school matter. Pupils who currently travel by train to and from Penlyn will now join the 8 a.m. ferry to Polhaven, with the Secondary Modern children who already use it to Polhaven School. Ferry transport for all pupils aged up to 16 will be free. A free bus service leased from West Cornwall Transport will run between the harbour and Penlyn Grammar School, returning at 4.00 p.m. for the 5.00 p.m. ferry to Polmouth.'

'Free, my eye!' called a derisory voice. 'You'll just hike the Council Tax to cover the costs...'

A buzz of conversation was humming through the crowd, and a man stood up to interrupt. Teague held up his hand imperiously.

'I think I know what Mr. Williams...' the standing man sat down, '... is going to ask. Penlyn Grammar has classes on Saturday mornings. Transport will be provided.' The buzz died down, Williams nodded.

'Concerning Clifftop Farm, and essential village supplies, the Council is still finalising details, but I can assure you that adequate means will be found. All villagers will be notified by letter as soon as possible. The same goes for public transport, additional ferry services.' He paused. 'Now I'll take questions.' He had carefully omitted informing the assembly of even worse news, the decision by "Chronos Investments" to sell the valueless Polmine Estate. A stout woman stood up, the village grocer.

'Is there any chance of West Cornwall County Council widening and improving the road link to Penlyn? Right now it's a disgrace! You couldn't even get Farmer Blackitt's horse cart along that lane! Road? It's a disgrace!' There were calls of "Hear hear!" from the hall. Teague shook his head regretfully.

'I asked them that today. There are no plans to improve the road link between Polmouth and Penlyn.' The grocer sat down disappointed, and now a slender middle aged man rose to his feet.

'Michael Tomlinson, Pharmacist.' He introduced himself. 'That company that bought Polmine Estate back in '45, from the Ministry of Defence... Wasn't there talk of them developing it with housing, and a small commercial shopping centre? What's the position there? Surely if they went ahead, West Cornwall would have to improve the road?' He sat down. Teague sighed. His hand had been forced.

'Sadly, the Council has learned that the owners of the Estate, "Chronos Investments", is going into liquidation, and Polmine Estate, its only asset, will be sold. It is considered worthless, has not even venal value.' He reached for his glass of water as the assembly voiced noisy consternation. In the hubbub, one man was not looking unduly concerned, on the contrary a strange look of anticipation mixed with a sudden excitement crossed his face. Percy Teague held up his hand to quell the hum of conversation.

'The Village Council really has done all it can in the last 48 hours. As long as the farm can continue, and the fishing boats are kept in good repair, Polmouth can at least be self-sufficient...' He was interrupted by a raucous, hollow laugh from a man in the front row. Victor Polwhele stood up.

'Self-sufficient?! On eggs, milk and fish? You wish! You're delusional! How can the shops stock groceries, washing powder, fruit, veg, even toilet paper? Hm? And the Chemist? The butcher? You have the nerve to say "Polmouth can be self-sufficient"! Not one of you even lives here! No chance of Polhaven stagnating, which is where you live! But Polmouth is doomed, condemned. Everything comes by train... until when? What date is the last train to Polmouth?' Teague consulted a document. Bleakly he said:

'This Friday, May 28th, the start of half-term for the schools. The 7.00 p.m. to Penlyn. We are still making contingency plans...' Polwhele seemed to be about to erupt again when the man seated next to him stood up alongside, touched him on the shoulder. It was the lone individual who had not shown consternation at the liquidation of "Chronos Investments", Felix Ingram, the Latin teacher at Penlyn Grammar.

'Victor… may I say something?' He addressed the Council. 'Felix Ingram…'

'Mr. Ingram, good evening.' Teague was suddenly unctuous. 'Ladies and gentlemen, I'm sure many of you know Mr. Ingram, our local historian and intellectual, Polmouth's answer to Einstein, but best known for his seemingly never-ending philanthropic generosity…' Ingram held up his hand in mild protest.

'Too kind. I just wanted to share this with the community… I shall be brief…'

Several of those present, former pupils of erudite Felix Ingram at Penlyn Grammar School, winced. They knew that "brief" was not one of Ingram's attributes.

'Over recent years I've been conducting some research for a book that I intend to write, a "History of Polmouth".' There was a murmur of approval; everyone was listening. 'The closure of the railway is the last nail in the coffin in the 4,000 year history of Polmouth. I really do not want to change the title to the "Decline and Fall of Polmouth". So let us examine our options, pitifully few as they are.' He slipped off his spectacles and polished them industriously on the tails of his jacket. There was one option in his mind which he had no intention of sharing with the Village Council or the villagers.

'Now, with the railway to be closed, we are cut off from the outside world, not only socially but also economically. This four thousand year old village is condemned. Our only assets are the climate, the fruits of the sea and… the potential locked up in Polmine Estate on the clifftop plateau. "Locked up" since its purchase in 1945 by these "Chronos" creatures. And do we really want a housing development of Val Doonican "Little boxes" maisonettes owned by Yuppies, and…' he imbued his voice with a strong, bitter inflection of sulphuric acid '… a commercial shopping centre? Everything now hangs on what the purchaser of "Polmine Estate", the new owner decides to do with it. Without adequate rail or road connections, who would

buy it anyway? I shall be watching developments very closely.'
It was evident from the faces of those around him that he had
spelt out very clearly what every villager had been grappling
to grasp: the destiny, or the destruction, of Polmouth.

'I should add that there is one potential asset. The
railway track from Penlyn Junction was laid, including the
embankments and cuttings through the heath and across
the moor, in 1890, and it only happened because the Village
Council of the day funded it. British Railways has the franchise
to provide train services and maintenance, but the track and
the infrastructure, right down to the signal boxes, the land,
belong to Polmouth village. To us all. So Dr. Beeching may
close the service, but he will not be lifting any railway tracks to
sell as scrap metal. They stay. And will simply rust over future
decades. Unless...

'I suggest that for the moment we support the Village
Council in its efforts to maintain the essential lifeline, and we
watch what happens to the Estate.' He sat down to scattered
applause. Shortly afterwards Teague closed the meeting, and
he and his two councillors made their way to the village pub
"The Crab & Lobster", obliged as they were to spend the night
away from home in Polhaven. The pub was the only hostelry
with rooms.

In the 1960s a Labour politician accepted an invitation
to tour the USSR where a mixture of wishful thinking and
Russian propaganda blinded him. He returned to Britain like
Chamberlain waving a piece of paper proclaiming "Peace in
our time" with Hitler. The words this time were: "I have seen
the future, and it works!" History was to prove him wrong.

Blackitt had seen the future and it was bleak. He was no
longer young but he was not indecisive. No point crying over
spilt milk. His lips twisted in a bitter smile. "Over a future
without milk". He was on the telephone to his brother Roy in
the New Forest, and had been for half an hour.

'The road from Penlyn is fine for a lorry as far as Polheath. But then it suddenly stops and is an overgrown narrow lane with high embankments on both sides. You couldn't even drive a car from Polheath to here... What? Oh, about six miles, a two hour walk. Can they manage that distance?' He listened for a moment then gave a hollow laugh. 'The cows certainly can. Hang on a minute...' He reached across his paper-strewn table and picked up the "Farmers' Monthly". 'I'll check...' He studied the back page. 'Ah, there's an auction on Friday in Penlyn. I know the auctioneer. I'll call him, he has a holding pen. I'll reserve for a dozen. But are you free on Thursday for the round trip? Only your driver?... Be a pity not to see my brother after all this time... You will? So you'll bring four and four, and I'll put the herd up for auction, dairy farm or abattoir, they've got to go. More's the pity.' A few minutes later he rang off. His face was bleak. He had seen the future, and it did not work.

Chapter Three

With trainee Matthew Parkinson holding the fort in Penzance Tourist Office, Dennis Latimer took a leisurely breakfast before strolling to Polport station to meet Hendricks. The ten o'clock train from Penlyn wheezed to a halt and Latimer held up a large white card with the text "HENDRIX". There were only five passengers, which served to underline Dr. Beeching's decision to close the line. Hendricks introduced himself.

'By the way, it's spelt like STICKS.' He looked at a slip of paper in his hand. 'I've taken a room at the "Crab and Lobster". Can you give me directions?'

'I'll walk there with you, it's only a hundred yards, down by the harbour.'

They walked down a cobbled street and turned onto the Esplanade overlooking the harbour. A trawler sounded its horn as it entered the port, returning from the night's fishing. They arrived at a sixteenth century, low-roofed building of stone walls and inset black beams. Suspended over the door was a rough-hewn wooden sign: "Crab and Lobster", and engraved in the lintel was the date 1576.

'Good Lord!' Hendricks was staring at the quaint little building, then turned to look out over the tranquil blue waters of the port, the headland across the broad estuary catching the morning sunlight. 'What a charming place.' But he was thinking that he really did not want to do what he was paid for, what he had come for, the sale of what was probably the village's only asset on which to build, to survive. 'Are you sure that you can spare me three days? And I should say, I really wish I was down here under happier circumstances.'

'You mean the sale?'

'So you know about that?'

'The whole village knows. It's a death knell for Polmouth. But no-one will blame you, you're just doing your job. Anyway, this is the "Crab and Lobster"... Shall I come in with you?' Hendricks shook his head.

'No, no, no need. Will you join me for lunch, though? Provide some background?'

'Willingly. The catch of the day is always excellent.' Latimer grinned. 'No-one eats meat in Polmouth!'

'Suits me. Say... midday, here?'

'I'll see you then.' They parted company.

Up on the clifftop farm Blackitt completed his morning collection of eggs laid overnight from under the hen huts and inside the coops, then went to his living room. He picked up the phone and called Mary Talbot, Secretary of the Village Council, to postpone his meeting with Teague to a later date. That done, he sighed and went sadly outside for the morning milking, the last time that he would ever milk a cow, after forty years on the family farm. For by this time tomorrow, the cows would all be gone.

Latimer and Hendricks were sitting at table in the small restaurant of the "Crab and Lobster". Hendricks looked expectantly at Latimer.

'Well?'

'Hmmm... I grew up here, but the real expert on the Estate, on Polmouth in fact, is the village historian, Felix Ingram.' Hendricks made a note of the name in his pocket book. 'I only know about the place in my lifetime. In 1936 my best friend at Primary School was Jimmy Blackitt… the farm next to the Estate is Blackitt's Farm, they've had it for generations. Anyway, we used to play up on the farm, Jimmy and I, and they let us collect the eggs that had rolled out of reach for an adult, from under the huts, and to milk the cows. At that time there was a stile in the fence between the farm and Estate. I believe it suffered very badly in the Great Depression in the '20s, and the mine closed. The Brick Croft was running out of clay, but the baking tower was operational and the trains still came to collect the bricks. The mine was sealed off, and by the time I was nine, when war broke out, the entire Estate was overgrown and derelict. But a perfect playground for little boys whose imagination could run wild…' Latimer seemed to be reliving his childhood. A waiter served a lobster starter, and there was a brief silence.

'So that's how you come to know the place. And in the war?' Latimer wiped his lips.

'In 1940 things changed. The Estate was sequestered by the War Ministry. The trains from Penlyn Junction to the Brick Croft brought soldiers to the mine workings. Jimmy and I had never seen a great big steam engine pulling a train across the Estate on the old track to the mine. They put up a solid fence around the entire perimeter so the stile was blocked. But boys of eleven are resourceful, we still got into the Estate whenever we wanted, hiding in the dense undergrowth. When they were building the fence the train left every night and came back next morning. Then they started to clear out and renovate the miners' cottages… have you seen the plans? There are five terraced cottages.' Hendricks nodded. He was surprised by Latimer's detailed knowledge. 'But now the train didn't leave every night, the soldiers moved into the cottages, lived there. The train only seemed to go and come back in the daytime, with a lot of heavy mechanical equipment. One day, Jimmy and I noticed that the sloping entrance to the Phoenician mine

– a shaft cut on a slope that goes down to the workings – had been opened. And then the lift over the modern vertical shaft was operating. We hadn't a clue what was going on, of course, and by now the whole village was buzzing with conjecture. But no-one ever told the villagers what it was all about.'

'Fascinating. Did they, I mean you, ever find out?' Latimer shook his head.

'The most probable theory was that the Army was carving out a space underground for a possible evacuation of the War Cabinet from London, in the event of a German invasion.'

'Good God! But of course it never happened. Go on.'

'No, by 1943 the risk of invasion seemed to have passed. So the village gossips were stuck for any other reason for the War Ministry to be active. Some thought it might be a firing range, like Salisbury Plain. But not a shot was ever fired. And yet, far from reducing activity, not only did the train stay overnight, but it had brought two First Class sleeper coaches, you know, like for the night train from London to Penzance... And now the whole mine workings were teeming with men and heavy machinery. I guess they slept in the train.' The waiter brought their John Dory and chips. This time there was a longer silence.

'I don't know if this is of any use to you?' Latimer looked embarrassed.

'More than you might think.' Hendricks reassured him. 'It means that the Polmine Estate had some value for someone as recently as the 1940s. And my job is to get the best price possible for it, to set against "Chronos Investment" debts. Did this activity continue after the war?' Latimer shook his head.

'Only a month after VE day they took down the fence, the sleeper carriages left, and so did all the soldiers. The mine shafts were sealed again. The only difference in '45 was that the mineshaft lifts were in working order, as was the pump and Pump House, and I suppose that underground at least part of the tunnels and shafts had been made accessible. And logically the cottages, at least back then, must have been inhabitable.

19

The gossip in the village was the whole caboodle had been "mothballed", in the event of nuclear war...'

'I'll look at the cottages and the mine workings tomorrow. I have the keys. I think I know the rest.' Hendricks interrupted. 'In 1945 my clients, "Chronos Investments", bought the Estate from the War Ministry as a long term investment that might one day attract a housing developer. Now, twenty years later, with the railway closing, that'll never happen.' The dessert was served. 'Coffee?'

'Not for me. I don't think there's a lot more that I can tell you that wouldn't be better done on our visit tomorrow. Do you have plans for the afternoon?'

'Well, it's a lovely day. I think I'll wander around the village, get some sea air and my bearings. Oh, one question... if I want to walk up to the Estate today to have a look around... how do I find the track up to the clifftop?'

Half an hour later they parted.

In a tiny village the size of Polmouth news travels fast, and gossip even faster. But as yet the only people who knew that the liquidator of Polmine Estate was in the village were Latimer and Hendricks himself.

Given that Penlyn Grammar School had classes Monday to Friday and Saturday mornings from nine to midday, every teacher was timetabled with one free afternoon. Felix Ingram had Wednesday afternoon off. He particularly disliked eating school lunch with the boys, and hurried to catch the 12.30 train back to Polmouth. But hunger was not what drove him, at least, not hunger for food. By a quarter past one he was in his bedsit on the telephone to London. His first call, to "Chronos Investments" gave him the number of the liquidators "Barnes, Todd and Hampton". On the 'phone to them he noted the name "Hendricks" on a sheet of school file paper, and then "Crab and Lobster" and finally "until Friday afternoon". No sooner had he rung off, still omitting to eat any lunch, than he took a sheet of his headed notepaper and scribbled a few lines. After sealing this in an envelope he left his tiny apartment and walked down to the "Crab and Lobster". On his way to the bar with the envelope, he actually walked past Hendricks who was finishing his coffee at a distant table.

Felix returned to his ground floor flat and finally prepared some lunch. Then he sat down to wait, re-reading Virgil's Aeneid. He had no doubt that Hendricks would telephone, but this was going to be a waiting game. It was to be a two hour immersion in Virgil before the phone rang. Hendricks had returned from his exploration of the quaint village to find Felix's message. Hendricks was intrigued.

'I know your name,' he said, 'your reputation as village historian. I'd really value your in-depth information, not just to assist my valuation... it's an unusual village, Olde England to the core. I'm going up to the Estate tomorrow, with a man called Dennis Latimer...'

'Dennis?' Felix interrupted him. 'I taught him Latin, at Penlyn Grammar. I thought he was in Penzance now. I think I have a little more... ah... depth. When might we meet?'

'Perhaps after I've done a tour of the grounds, the buildings? Say, tomorrow evening, here at the pub? I can stand you dinner, if you accept?'

'I never refuse good food,' chuckled Felix, 'and I'm certain I can provide you with a mine...' he chuckled again, 'of information. But I also have some other information, not historical but current, which you really should hear. Today. Or tonight? How are you placed for dinner tonight?' Surprised, Hendricks played for time.

'Uh... does it concern my eventual valuation?' Felix grinned.

'Most definitely. So tonight, then?'

'Beer, or wine?' They were at the bar in the "Crab and Lobster".

'Let's see a menu.' Felix brushed chalk dust off the lapel of his tweed jacket. They opted for wine, sat down and ordered. Hendricks opened the unexpected meeting with what he wrongly believed to be an innocuous start. It opened a floodgate.

'Young Latimer mentioned something about a Phoenician mine. He had me foxed by that. Phoenicia?' Felix licked his lips and launched into a comprehensive history of Polmouth.

'Well, thousands of years before Christ, in the Iron Age and the Bronze Age, the Cornish had discovered vast reserves of tin and copper in the form of ore, and had mastered open-cast mining. In no time, the Gauls from northern France were frequent visitors, traders, merchants, to buy the ore. No money existed back then of course, so it was barter.' Hendricks was unwise enough to revert to his original query.

'But Phoenicia?'

'The Gauls were not the only visitors! Incredible as it sounds today, a regular flotilla of indestructible, wooden sailing ships set sail from ports in the Eastern Mediterranean, Phoenicia, the area of Jordan and Palestine today, and headed West the length of the sunny Mediterranean. On passing the Straits of Gibraltar, they would turn right and head North through the dreaded storms of the Bay of Biscay, finally crossing the English Channel and arriving at their destination. Cornwall. Numerous English villages and towns exist today solely because of trade thousands of years ago. One such is the tiny village of Polmouth.' Felix sipped his wine. Hendricks was wondering how to quell the flood of enthusiasm. He glanced at his watch. Oblivious to this, Felix continued unabated.

'Entirely dependent on foodstuffs and essentials from elsewhere, Polmouth relied on frequent deliveries by boat across the estuary of the River Pol, and the goodwill of the citizens of Polhaven. And yet... Polmouth's precarious existence only continued because of the huge deposits of iron ore and copper, much of it in veins extending deep underground down to two thousand feet below the cliffs and even out under the sea. However, while Polmouth's miners became proficient at ore extraction, they had neither the means nor the expertise in smelting it to useful metal. This presented a seemingly intractable problem: how to get the ore to those who desperately wanted it?'

Felix had warmed to his pet topic, he was unstoppable. If Percy Teague had described him as philanthropic, Felix was no less generous in didactic material.

'Polmouth's blessing was the Pol estuary; its sheltered, broad deep water channel was ideal. The creation of Polport harbour was the result of the influx of large sailing vessels. Against all probability, then, little Polmouth flourished and grew. Its population peaked at 800 souls around 1930, more than four thousand years after it was created, but then declined rapidly. Today the population has dwindled to a paltry 176 households, the result of a constant flight of the young to greener post-war pastures.'

To Hendricks' relief, the waiter was approaching with a huge tureen of "Symphony of the Sea", a veritable repast. At least this should keep the erudite historian quiet for a while he thought.

'Well,' he said with heavy irony that was lost on Felix, 'that certainly covers the Phoenician business.' He seized the ladle and served from the tureen.

Later, and not without trepidation, Hendricks moved to pastures new.

'You mentioned some... ah... current information?' Felix pushed back his chair and looked Hendricks in the eye.

'In a word, I want to buy Polmine Estate, and I'm in a position to pay cash.'

Hendricks dropped his fork and spoon in his astonishment. His experience in disposing of property in liquidation was extensive, but he had never encountered anything like this. His next question was decidedly risky, given Felix's philanthropy with words.

'So maybe you know something that I don't? I mean, I haven't even seen the property yet...' Felix shook his head.

'Not at all! It's a decaying wreck as I'm sure you'll agree on inspection. It's like this... The mine has no value, British tin prices are far too high, no-one'll buy our ore when they can get it cheaper elsewhere. The Brick Croft is finished. No clay. And as for the miners' cottages, when I last saw them, they were still standing, but the interiors have probably weathered badly with the salt from the sea. There's a large house at the Croft, and that could be renovated. At a cost. I don't think you'll have difficulty in valuing the Estate.'

'I'll be the judge of that.' Hendricks was firm. 'So if, as you say, the place is "a wreck", why on earth would you want to buy it?' There was a pause while both men advanced with their "Symphony of the Sea". He's playing for time, Hendricks thought, still thoroughly taken aback. But Hendricks was wrong.

'I live a very frugal life.' Felix Ingram said inconsequentially. 'But by inheritance I possess a considerable fortune. I would never play the stock market, no, my assets are in sound investments. And although I spend practically nothing on myself, I will go to great lengths to support Polmouth, and more importantly all those who live here, with what wealth I have. I have no children. I suppose you could say that Polmouth is sort of my baby, my child...' His voice tailed away in embarrassment. Hendricks was now even more perplexed.

'So... let me get this straight. You're a Latin teacher, local historian, and... you give financial support to the local community?' Felix was still looking embarrassed.

'Well, I suppose you could put it like that, yes.'

'And may I ask what kind of price you envisage for the entire Estate?' Felix lifted a clean paper napkin from the bundle on the table, took out a biro and wrote a figure on it.

'Take that with you when you inspect the place tomorrow. And if you think a further discussion might be useful, you'll find me here at seven o'clock. Oh, and if you do join me, dinner will be on me.' A smile flashed across his face. 'I'm a rotten cook, and this is the only good restaurant in the village.'

Hendricks was as excited as he was confused. He had never sold a property before even valuing it. And he wasn't about to now. But...

'If you're in good faith, would you sign this and date it?' Felix Ingram pushed his chair back violently, looking deeply affronted.

'I have never in my life acted in anything other than "good faith"!' He seized the napkin and added the words "Preliminary offer for Polmine Estate", then signed it and added the date. He pushed the napkin back to Hendricks. Encouraged by the word "preliminary", Hendricks realised that he had offended a possible purchaser.

'I'm so sorry,' he started, 'that was extremely tactless of me. I'm afraid that in my profession... and you completely wrong-footed me with your offer.' Felix nodded.

'Liquidators are not known for their sensitivity.' Hendricks laughed.

'Touché!' He folded the napkin and put it in his wallet. 'In any event, I'll be delighted to dine here with you tomorrow evening.' Relieved, Felix Ingram reached across the table and shook Hendricks' hand.

'I look forward to it.'

The two men finished their meal discussing world affairs.

Chapter Four

Thursday, May 27th, 1964

The night sky was tinged with royal blue on the horizon heralding imminent dawn. It was seven o'clock when three transporters pulled onto the verge of Polheath and cut their motors. The three drivers had been on the road since leaving Tuke House Farm three hours previously, at four in the morning, and now they were only six miles from their destination. However, all three knew that those six miles would take nearly as long again, a two hour trek on foot. In the front lorry Roy Blackitt pulled a large picnic box from behind his seat, then opened the passenger door for the two other drivers. He pulled out thermos flasks and a large pack of corned beef sandwiches.

Half an hour later the three men released their equine cargo, marshalled the animals into a 2-4-2 formation and set off down a narrow lane towards Polmouth. Roy saw that his brother had been right. The lane was so narrow and the embankments on either side topped with hawthorn hedges so steep as to make it impossible for even a car to travel this route.

At eight in the morning Latimer walked from his home to the outskirts of the village and the track up to Clifftop Farm, a bulging knapsack on his back. He reached Blackitt's farm to wait there for Hendricks' inspection of the Estate. A dozen cows were ruminating in the meadow. He found Blackitt in the cow shed, sluicing down the walls and floor. A large pile of broad planks and a set of heavy duty tools lay beside the wood.

'Well, well, Dennis.' Blackitt cut the water to the hose pipe. 'You never could stay away. There were evenings we had to call your mum to drag you home and to bed!' The two men shook hands warmly.

'Old habits die hard.' remarked Latimer with a grin. Blackitt suddenly looked bleak, his eyes directed at the wet ground.

'Wish you hadn't said that.' he said. He dropped the hose nozzle on the ground. 'Come into the farmhouse for a cuppa. I'm afraid there are changes on the way, needs must. Not sure you'll like them. I sure don't.'

In order to be up on the Estate at nine to meet Latimer, Hendricks was on his way. At the outskirts of Polmouth where the redundant lane from Penlyn reached the village, he stared up the gravel track to the clifftop, then at his shoes. Not ideal. He wished now that he had followed his initial instinct, to take a look the previous afternoon, but had found himself captivated with the unique Olde Worlde charm of this tiny village. Now he was filled with curiosity. Ingram's surprise offer, written on a paper napkin, was not only highly original, it also set him a bench mark. But it also put him in a quandary. If he valued the Estate at a higher price, and if Felix Ingram proved to be the only buyer... Having a buyer ready to sign would obviate the need for expensive nationwide advertising and a perhaps fruitless auction, but how high could he push Ingram without losing him as potentially the only buyer?

His thoughts were interrupted by the clip-clop of what sounded like the Royalist army advancing on Cromwell's Roundheads. And in its own way it was indeed an army. Hendricks stared in disbelief. He saw heading towards him a short, stocky man holding two long, loose reins in one hand and to either side of him two equine giants the like of which he had not known existed. All three were marching determinedly, inexorably, towards him. And to the track up to the Estate. Behind this unrecognisable vanguard he saw a second man accompanying four smaller versions of these prehistoric monsters and behind them, a further two of the beasts. The tallest easily stood nine feet high. They were immense. Uncertain as to their intentions, Hendricks hastily started his walk up the track. He had only gone a hundred yards when he became aware that the equine Royalist army's clip-clop advance was close behind. He looked over his shoulder and saw the convoy only fifty yards away. He hastened his step.

Hendricks was no fool, but this had him stumped. As he walked up the track he was grappling with a series of improbabilities. The men and the unknown breed of what he assumed to be horses had entered the village from the allegedly unpassable lane from Penlyn. So did this mean they grazed up on Polheath or Polmoor? But if so, surely they would be brought back to the farm in the evening, not early morning? There was no doubt in his mind that they were bound for Clifftop Farm, they had no place on the Estate, and no right to be there. An unwelcome thought crossed his mind. The Estate had been deserted for twenty years. Had the farmer perhaps taken to allowing his horses to wander the Estate at will, roaming across a vast area, at liberty?

Determined to question the unknown farmer, he quickened his steps.

On reaching the top he sat down on a bench and took his bearings. To his right was the cliff edge and a stunning view of the English Channel. He started to write a note on his clip board: needs fence at cliff edge. The eight Great Horses reached the top of the track and were led towards the neighbouring farm and its extensive outbuildings where he saw a dozen black and white cows grazing in a meadow. There *were* fences on the estate, however, for he now saw an iron gate and wire mesh around a sloping path that led steeply down to an iron door set in the cliff. This must be the Phoenician mine. More notes. One question was constantly forefront in his mind: why did Ingram want, apparently urgently, to buy the Estate?

He saw a neat terraced row of white cottages. On the plan they were marked as two-up two-down dwellings, and they looked in remarkably good repair, but as a surveyor Hendricks knew that appearances can be deceptive. Looking around the vast expanse of the overgrown estate he saw in the distance a tall brick structure and beside it what he assumed to be the Brick Croft house. He was joined by Latimer.

'Sorry I'm late, I was chatting in the farmhouse.'

'No matter. What's with the horses? Do they graze on the estate, or only on farm land?' Latimer looked sombre.

'It's complicated. They've only just arrived. And they'll be on farm land, over five acres of it. Plenty of space. I'll tell you about it as we go round. Where d'you want to start?' Hendricks unfolded the plan on the ground.

'We're here, right? And I assume that ramp and iron door are the Phoenician mine?' Latimer nodded.

'Let's start with that, then the cottages and work round from there.' They approached the metal gate. Seeing a heavy padlock on a chain, Hendricks pulled the bunch of keys from his briefcase and selected one. It opened the padlock at the first attempt.

'How did you do that?' Latimer asked in admiration. Hendricks shrugged.

'Only key that isn't for a door or a building.' They eased open the high gate, passed into the enclosure and Hendricks carefully closed the gate, having locked the padlock shut on the loose end of the chain. Vandalism was unheard of in Polmouth, but it would only need one joker to close the padlock and lock them in...

They strolled down a sloping gravel path until they reached the huge rusty iron door set in the mouth of the tunnel behind it. This time Hendricks had to try four keys to find the right one. The lock squeaked fiercely but he was surprised at how easily the door swung open on giant hinges.

A wave of cold, damp air enveloped the men, misting Latimer's glasses as the moisture met the warmth of sunlight. There was a strong, bitter odour in the tunnel and Hendricks stiffened. He knew that smell from the war, his time in the military.

He paused to inspect a hinge in the dim light; it was well greased. From the door the tunnel sloped sharply downwards and rapidly became invisible in the blackness.

'I don't think we want to hang about here.' His voice was sharp and clipped. 'And we're not going down there.' He pointed to the steep, sloping, rough-hewn tunnel. 'Let's get out of here! And for God's sake don't light a cigarette!' He almost pulled Latimer out of the tunnel mouth into the sunlight and eased the heavy door shut, locked it. Latimer was confused.

'I don't understand… is there a problem?'

'The problem is that smell. You couldn't miss it.' Latimer nodded.

'Very strong, and very bitter. What is it?'

'It's cordite. And sulphur.' Latimer was no further forward.

'And that means?'

'Explosives. If the smell is that strong, after all this time, they're probably still in there. You said the army used this ramp in the war?' Latimer nodded.

'And the Pump House, and the lift down the deep shaft over there. I still don't understand.'

'Right now, neither do I. But I'm wondering what the army was doing down there for so long, and what I *do* know is that there's no way they'll tell me. I want to see the Pump House and the lift housing next, and then the cottages.'

Mystified, Latimer accompanied Hendricks past the white cottages. At the Pump House Hendricks again got through several wrong keys. Once inside he inspected the hinge on the door. It was thickly greased, which explained why the door had offered no resistance, even after twenty years. The machinery was massive, fully two storeys high and some of the casing rusted. Hendricks moved to a huge shiny piston where it entered a cylinder. It too was thick with grease. The conclusions that Hendricks was drawing disquieted him. They went outside.

'I'll give the lifts a miss, after all. I need people from the Camborne School of Mining down here to inspect the whole installation, and whatever's going on underground. But that'll cost a bit, they don't come cheap. Anyway, Ingram assures me that whatever they find down there, market prices make it completely uncompetitive.' Latimer looked surprised.

'Ingram? You've met him, then?'

'Yes,' said Hendricks thoughtfully. 'Yes, I have. Now for the cottages.'

An hour later they were outside in the sunshine again.

'Well?' Latimer asked. 'What do you think? I mean, are they structurally sound?'

'They're more than structurally sound. If you dried them out for a day, people could move in tomorrow. They're even furnished downstairs, right down to kitchen fittings. All that's missing are mattresses on the beds.' He looked at Latimer quizzically. 'Yesterday you used the word "mothballed". I think you were right. Doors greased that open at a touch, the pump idem. Cottages that are sound and semi-furnished. I think you were right…' he repeated. 'But why? And why leave them, and the mine, empty for twenty years? And that stench of cordite and sulphur reeks of the word "military". Which is the quickest way to that Brick Croft place?'

'I guess straight along the railway track.' Latimer pointed to the dirty, overgrown rails that ended between the Pump House and the mineshaft lift. The two men set off along the track, walking on and between the wooden sleepers. Weathered by rain, sun and salt from the sea, they were in surprisingly good condition. Hendricks stopped walking and stooped to inspect a wooden sleeper. Now he was certain he had been right. The wood was thickly impregnated with tar. He wiped a fingertip over the wooden surface and showed it to Latimer. His skin was brown and sticky with the tar.

'Mothballed for certain. But why?' Leaving the question unanswered the two men proceeded along the track until they reached the platform at the railhead between the Brick Croft house and the lakes.

'Are you hungry?' Latimer gestured to his right and the extensive blue lakes. 'I've brought a picnic.' Seated on the grassy bank by the lake Hendricks spent some minutes making notes on his clipboard while Latimer produced a selection of drinks and sandwiches.

Half an hour later they returned along a different, narrow gauge rail track from the clay pits and arrived at the Croft House and the buildings. Hendricks was not surprised after their inspection of the house that the only faults were superficial damp in the walls and a thick coating of dust on everything.

"Five bedrooms, three large ground floor rooms and a huge kitchen." he wrote on his clipboard.

'It's bizarre.' Latimer remarked as they approached a rusting skeleton of metal ramps that had once been a conveyor belt from the clay trucks on their rail track to the top of a high building. 'As if we'd taken a time machine back to the war, and nothing has changed. I guess they used this...' he gestured at the now defunct conveyor belt, 'to get the raw clay up and into this building to compress it and cut the bricks.'

'I'll give the baking tower a miss.' Hendricks gestured to a broad, circular building with several doors in the sides. 'One more thing here, and we're done.' He moved to the standard gauge railway track and followed it as far as a solidly locked metal gate. The line continued into the distance to the North.

'Where does, or did this lead, I mean come from?' Latimer looked solemn.

'"Did" is right. It's a spur from the main line Penlyn to Polmouth across Polheath. But it stops tomorrow. Beeching cuts.' Hendricks nodded.

'And that's why I'm here.' He made more notes. Then: 'You say you know the farmer. I'd like a word with him. Do you think he'll accept a brief visit?' Latimer looked at his watch. Two o'clock.

'We'll have to hurry. He'll be moving his cattle any time now.'

'Moving them where?'

'I'll tell you as we go. It's a sad story.'

When they reached the stile over the fence into the farm, Hendricks gripped Latimer's elbow and restrained him. He had seen three men corralling the twelve cows and herding them along the path towards the track and down to Polmouth. A solitary elderly man was standing forlornly in the farmyard, his shoulders slumped, head looking at the ground.

'If he's losing his lifetime's herd, and his livelihood, I don't think this is the time.' murmured Hendricks. 'I'll come back tomorrow morning.'

'As you wish. Shall I come too?' Hendricks shook his head.

'No. Join me for lunch, though, say midday at the pub?' Latimer nodded and the two men made for the gravel track to Polmouth. Latimer was thinking that the liquidator had shown a high degree of sensitivity towards old Blackitt. Hendricks was now even more anxious than ever to meet Ingram again, to pursue the meaning of the folded napkin in his wallet. The two men walked all the way down to the village without exchanging a word.

In his impatience to see Ingram again, Hendricks arrived at the bar early. He ordered, then asked:

'What's the catch of the day today?' Helena, the barmaid, beamed.

'Line caught sea bass.' She looked at Hendricks' diminutive stature. 'If you're eating with Mr. Ingram again, I reckon one sea bass will satisfy the two of you. They're huge. We're eating ours later.'

'Good enough for me,' said Hendricks. 'But I'll let Mr. Ingram decide.' It was not only the decision on what to eat that Hendricks was referring to. There was another "catch of the day" to be snapped up, and it was in his hands. And Ingram had already bitten for it, hook, line and sinker. All Hendricks had to do now was reel him in. And the last thing that he wanted was to throw the dead fish back into the water, for he knew that, such was Ingram's devotion to this tiny, dying village, a refusal would kill the man. He sniffed, and wiped his eyes. It was a novel sensation, the hard-nosed liquidator succumbing to the pastures of emotion. Ingram joined him. Unaware of Hendricks' unwonted sensitivity, he said:

'I've reserved for half past. What'll you have?'

'Sea bass it is, then.' They ordered. 'Well, what did you make of the Estate?' Ingram was impatient to advance with his proposal, his long term notion of which he had no intention of speaking to anyone, least of this vendor of all that he could one day hold dear. Hendricks stared at the glass in front of him. He cleared his throat, but when he spoke his voice was still hoarse. The two men were facing each other across the small table, neither of them tall or portly in stature, two little figures on the face of the earth, each with two arms, two legs, a head and a limited life span. Hendricks had never felt so small in his life.

'I hardly even know you,' he started obliquely, 'but I know that however hard I press you, you will never tell me why you so desperately want to own the Estate.' Before he could continue Ingram interrupted him.

'True. But I sense that I am not the only one who is desperate. Or am I wrong?' This gave Hendricks the leeway that he had been seeking.

'If that were true, not at any price. I am not some Greek landowner who goes in for land-banking, I think you know that. I have to find a purchaser, yes, but not at any price. And your offer is... too high.' He looked away, feeling in his pocket for a handkerchief. Then he pulled out his wallet and crossed out the figure that Ingram had written on the paper napkin, and wrote above it a lower price, lower by five thousand pounds. He turned the napkin so that Ingram could read it. Ingram's eyes widened, but before he could speak, Hendricks retrieved the napkin. 'And I know why you want it so badly. It's for this, isn't it?' He underlined the words that Ingram had written at the top: "Polmine Estate" and added three words in capitals. Now he turned the napkin so that Ingram could read the text. Ingram swallowed.

'How did you know?' But at that moment a waiter arrived with a trolley carrying a huge grilled sea bass sand started to fillet it expertly into two immense portions.

'We can discuss the payment details afterwards.' Hendricks' voice was still husky. 'Right now would be to demean a fine meal.' Ingram nodded.

'But first...' the waiter was putting the finishing garnish to the plates, '... this.' Ingram extended his right hand towards Hendricks and they shook hands solemnly. 'You have a deal...' murmured Ingram and then, looking at the overflowing plates, 'and we have a great deal, right here.' Silence ensued. The waiter stared surreptitiously at the two middle aged men and retreated to behind the bar. He turned to Helena.

'You know what? I reckon they're gay!'

Chapter Five

Friday, May 28th, 1964

The air was cool and fresh, a perfect dawn on a sunny day in May. A peewit's distinctive cry was the only sound to break the silence of lonely Polmouth. It was climbing ever higher above Hendricks' head, a solitary black dot set in the azure velvet of the sky. Hendricks was striding up the track to Clifftop Farm.

He found Blackitt among the hen huts, lying flat on his face and reaching with one arm under a coop to retrieve eggs that had rolled there. Hendricks had thought long and hard about this meeting. He crouched down beside Blackitt.

'Can I perhaps help you?' Blackitt rolled over to stare at the unknown man.

'And you are?' Hendricks introduced himself.

'So you're with those Chronos bastards!' Blackitt was aggressive. He pulled himself to his feet. Hendricks shook his head.

'With them, no, of them, no. But they're bankrupt and…'

'Good!' Blackitt's voice smacked of satisfaction. 'So you're a winder-up, so to speak?' Hendricks nodded. Blackitt grinned suddenly and extended his right arm in greeting. 'I guess it'd be unfair to shoot the messenger. All right, help me collect my eggs, then I'll get you a cuppa. But I'm warning you…' the grin returned, '…if you break one and it's got a double yolk, I'll sue!' They shook hands and completed the morning collection.

36

'What kind of outfit'd want to buy the Estate now, anyway?' Blackitt asked Hendricks. They were sitting in the cosy farmhouse living room. 'Now the trains have stopped running, and no road connection... I wouldn't want to be in your shoes, trying to find a buyer. Have a biscuit.' He stood up and fetched a tin from a cupboard.

'Actually, that's why I'm here.' Blackitt looked puzzled. 'I don't just have a buyer, it's practically sold. And you should be the first to hear the news.' Blackitt put down his cup carefully.

'Very decent of you. Obvious question...'

'Do you know Felix Ingram, down in the village?' Blackitt failed to make the connection.

'Everyone knows Ingram, bit of a celebrity in Polmouth. Resident local historian. But what's he got to do with it?'

Hendricks told him what Ingram had to do with it, and there was a long silence. Then:

'Can I pass this on, I mean to others? Or is it still "pending completion"?'

'If I have my way, completion will be today, before I leave for London. But I guarantee it will go through, and the deal is signed and sealed. How d'you feel about that?'

'Well... coming out of the blue like this... I'm shocked. But pleased. What will he do with it, d'you know?' Hendricks smiled.

'Any more tea?' he asked. 'And yes, yes I do.'

While the two men were drinking tea, Felix Ingram walked from Penlyn station to the Grammar School. On arrival he went straight to the Secretary, Susan Baxter.

'Any chance of seeing the Head today? Preferably lunch hour?' Susan consulted the Head's diary.

'Nothing marked in yet. Wait, I'll check...' She called the Headmaster, Temeritus Tennent.

'Is he there with you now?' Tennent asked her. 'Put him on then, please. Felix... we're long overdue for a chat. Join me for lunch in my quarters. You know how I detest eating with the boys in the canteen, and you're an excellent excuse. Come straight over after Period 6.' Relieved, Felix left the office. This would provide him with the time he needed.

Meanwhile, Farmer Blackitt had come to a decision. He picked up the phone and rang his brother Roy at Tuke Farm in the New Forest.

Temeritus Tennent, full title Colonel Tennent, DSC and Bar, was a thoroughly military man, even 20 years after the War. Slightly older than Ingram, he welcomed Felix and offered sherry. His housekeeper, Mary, brought in a steaming pie.

'Game pie, Headmaster.' she announced. 'Piping hot, so take your time, sir.' The two men sat down. After the sherry, wine was served. Unthinkable now, many teachers went to the pub in the lunch hour and downed a couple of pints before afternoon lessons. Colonel Temeritus Tennent's social habits were on a higher level.

It was a good ten minutes before Ingram finally put down his knife and fork, his ambitious plan now aired.

'My word!' Temeritus took a long draught of his wine and rang a hand bell, summoning Mary. 'Well, Felix, I commend the plan! I commend it wholeheartedly. But it's hugely ambitious, may take years to come to fruition. And I can see what you're after. I know you have a certain fortune on which to call, but even it is not infinitely elastic. And I really would counsel against...'

'On all that, we agree Headmaster.' Ingram was grave. 'So, yes, I need to seek funding, financing...' This time it was Tennent who interrupted.

'I realised that. Unfortunately, the school's budget is fully committed. But I'm getting your drift. You're thinking of education authorities to chip in to...' he smiled, and gestured to Mary to place the dessert on the table, '...let us call it, "The Felix Ingram Foundation".' Felix shook his head.

'Yes, to the first part. But that's not a name I would choose. I was wondering whether you could point me in the right direction of a name or two to contact in the Local Education Authority, and even better, in London, the Department of Education and Science...' Tennent's face cleared.

'Well, I can suggest Malcom Campbell at the LEA, but as for the DES, no. I'd be thinking of the Professor of History for the DES. But you know, Felix, the crucial element to all this will be that confounded rail link to Polmouth, and to the Estate. And with British Railways making drastic economies, those damned Beeching Cuts, they won't be as philanthropic as you.'

'I know. I was thinking of contacting the West Cornwall Light Railway Society, you know, they run a tourist train in summer down to Falmouth.' Tennent laughed.

'Well, you're certainly tenacious, not to say persistent! Listen, contact Campbell, and the DES, and keep me informed. It's a phenomenal idea. And if it takes off, you can call on the school's CCF team for any heavy work on the Estate, the Combined Cadet Force, and that young hothead from the Art department, Sub-Lieutenant Matthews.' They turned to the dessert of trifle. 'By the way, I'm still waiting for your nomination of the Junior Latin Prize, for Prize-Giving Day.' Felix looked sheepish.

'Apologies, Headmaster. No question about that, it's Petra Zabrinski in Form Four.'

'Fine, drop it in to the office this afternoon. Any plans for half term? Pompeii again, or Herculaneum?' Ingram's lips twitched in a semblance of a smile.

'No, Headmaster. I shall be moving into the Croft House, on...' the smile broadened, '...my estate.'

At four o'clock Blackitt was on the single platform of Polport station, waiting for the afternoon train from Penlyn. His mind was made up. The closure of the railway, the demise of his herd of cows and income from the Milk Marketing Board called for radical solutions. If the addition of the eight Great Horses was a start, it was only that. In the distance the archaic steam engine was approaching, wheezing and puffing as if on its last legs. As this was its penultimate journey ever, it was probably an accurate appraisal.

The train disgorged its school pupils from Penlyn Grammar, home for half term, and a few shoppers back from an expedition to civilisation. Blackitt intercepted Ingram as he climbed down from his compartment.

'Mr. Ingram, sir, I'm Blackitt, the farmer.'

'Of course. Blackitt. My dear chap, so sorry to hear about your cows. A tragedy, absolute tragedy.' Blackitt nodded.

'It's about that that I wanted to see you, sir. If you can spare me the time, would you accept a cuppa in "Polly's Tea Room"?' Intrigued, Ingram nodded.

Blackitt finished outlining his dire financial situation, present and future and there was a long silence. Then:

'I can see that there's no obvious solution,' commented Ingram. Blackitt was diffident.

'Well, I thought… you might be the solution, sir.' Ingram was astonished.

'Me?' His face cleared. 'Don't tell me you want me to buy the farm?!' Blackitt shook his head vehemently.

'No, no, sir. I want to *give* you Clifftop Farm!' Now Ingram was speechless. Blackitt went on rapidly, 'I hear you're buying the Estate. So I was thinking I might transfer the Deeds of the farm to you, making one single Land Registry parcel of Estate and farm, if you'll give me lifelong tenancy, free of rent, with – if I can find one – the same for a farm hand, for me to run the poultry farm as best I can.' He stopped, feeling awkward and uncertain how Ingram would react. Ingram had not become an outstanding classicist without being endowed with a first class brain. He saw what had happened.

'May I ask who told you I might be buying? On second thoughts, don't answer that. I'll wager it was the man from London, Hendricks. And I'll wager, too, that he let on about something else, didn't he? That's why you'd like to maximise my potential if I can get this thing off the ground.' Blackitt nodded.

'Do we have a deal, sir? I can go to the Land Registry on Monday with you, and we can sign the transfer of the parcel to you. And all I need for assurances is a signed, legal document.' Ingram laughed.

'Strike while the iron's hot, eh? Oh, Blackitt... do I divine that you may be envisaging allowing the Great Horses to roam over the entire Estate?' Blackitt swallowed.

'That would be a bonus, sir.' Ingram extended his right hand.

'We have a deal.' he affirmed, and the two men shook hands.

Two hours later Ingram was back at the station, and this time it was he who was waiting for a passenger. He saw Hendricks approaching with his suitcase. Hendricks caught sight of Ingram and joined him.

'You waiting for someone?' Ingram nodded, and without speaking pulled out a cheque, handed it wordlessly to Hendricks.

'Immediate possession?' he asked. Hendricks laughed.

'You can move in tomorrow, if you like. But I'd get the place cleaned first. And I can see that, as no removals lorry can get up to the clifftop and across the Estate, furniture will be a problem.' Ingram shook his head.

'Logically, yes, you'd be right. But I've found a solution to that.' Hendricks stared at him.

'You're a strange man, Mr. Ingram.' Ingram shook his head.

'Me? Good Lord, no! I'm just a Latin teacher.' The train from Penlyn sounded its whistle as it approached. 'Well,' said Ingram, his voice tinged with regret, 'this is it. The last train to Polmouth.'

The Polmouth Legacy

The Polmouth Legacy
1974

Chapter Six

The Inheritance

1974 was not an auspicious year socially for the United Kingdom. Indeed, the word "United" seemed frequently to be in doubt. Petrol rationing meant that fuel could only be bought using coupons issued to every driver, a penury of oil the result of the Arab-Israeli Yom Kippur war. A bitter coal miners' strike, with power stations violently picketed, reduced the country's industry to a three-day working week to minimise consumption. Households suffered rolling power cuts for weeks, and there wasn't a candle to be bought anywhere in the British Isles. And yet life went on as best possible.

Over the ten years since the last train to Polmouth the village's fortunes had remorselessly declined. It had always been a village without motor cars, as none could ever have arrived there; the Polhaven ferry only carried passengers, and the road link to Penlyn in the North was still no better than an overgrown track. Supplies for Polmine Estate and Clifftop Farm could only get up the mile-long track pulled on a farm cart by a Great Horse.

Blessed with a clement microclimate, daily life in Polmouth was idyllic, but the village owed its very existence now to the ugly, black flat barge that made two crossings a day to Polport, six days a week, from the affluent little town of Polhaven across the estuary. With the closure of the railway, Polmouth Village Council had leased the barge and it now brought every conceivable product for the Pharmacy, the butcher's, the baker's and every other retailer down to the candlestick maker. It was not, however, a car ferry.

In theory the Council paid for the service, but in practice an increase to every householder's Council Tax covered this essential lifeline. Everyone rued the day that the railway service stopped in 1964. Any prospects of finding work and a future life lay over the estuary, in Polhaven. For that reason, the only lawyer in Polmouth, Derek Carruthers, had transferred his office to Polhaven, where he now had Chambers.

Carruthers' legal assistant Petra Zabrinski, who doubled as secretary and factotum, popped her head round his office door.

'Just going for the post, Mister Carruthers. Five minutes.'

On leaving the majestic Victorian building on the High Street, Petra paused, squinting in the warm, bright June sunshine, before crossing the road to stroll down a short, narrow alley that led to the Esplanade, and the Post Office. Petra Zabrinski was a bubbly, invariably cheerful young woman in her twenties. Although it was unfashionable, she always wore her blond hair tied as a ponytail, giving her a school-girlish appearance that belied her true age. In the lawyer's PO Box she found three bills and a sizeable package in brown paper tied with string. Back at the office she slipped into Carruthers' room with the package.

'Just three bills, sir, and this.' She placed the bulky parcel on his desk and left. Carruthers picked up the heavy dossier; it was from the Justice of the Peace. He opened it, to find a note on top of the bundle of documents.

"Death certificate and related documents. As Executor of the Will, you may proceed to probate. I suggest you read the dossier annexed. It is germane to the inheritance." Carruthers pressed a button on his intercom.

'Petra, bring in the Ingram file, please.' He opened the pile of documents but had only read a few lines of the Land Registry extract when Petra arrived with the file. 'Thank you.

Do I have any appointments this morning?' She shook her head and returned to her office. Disregarding the advice from the Justice of the Peace to read the dossier first, Carruthers opened the Ingram file and took out the man's Last Will and Testament which he opened. As he reached the middle of the first page he stiffened, his eyebrows involuntarily rising. Now he realised that he should have followed the Judge's advice. In a quandary, he stared at the names of the heirs to Ingram's estate, then decided that, as he had no appointments, he would postpone the reading of the Will to the legatees and instead turned his attention to the Judge's folder. But it was not the Judge's, it was detailed documentation of the hopes, aspirations and efforts of Ingram over the last ten years before his recent untimely death. Carruthers, who lived in Polmouth, had known Ingram only slightly, but then no-one seemed to have known the man well. He had ended his days a sad, lonely and bitter man, his grandiose plans had never come to fruition, as Headmaster Tennent had feared. Shortly after Ingram's retirement in 1972, he had suffered a stroke. Handicapped by a certain degree of incapacity, he had only been able to continue his solitary life in the Croft House with the daily support of his housekeeper. This much Carruthers had known. What he was now about to discover kept him reading for a full hour.

When he had absorbed the contents of the weighty documentation, he turned to the Will again, sat staring at the names of the legatees. His eyes lifted to the clock. It was eleven. He pressed the intercom button.

'Petra, my dear, please make a pot of tea and come in with two cups. And switch on the answerphone. We don't want to be disturbed.' Petra did as he asked, but her able mind was grappling with the oddity of Carruthers asking for two cups when he was alone. Nor had he ever before used the expression: "**We** don't want to be disturbed." Intrigued, she carried the tray into Carruthers' office.

47

'Please sit down.' Carruthers gestured to the chair across the desk from him. He poured two cups of tea, pushed one across to her. 'This is highly unusual.' A hint of a smile touched his lips. 'Right now, you are not only my prized Legal Assistant, but you are also a client. And you could not possibly have expected this...' He gestured to the Will lying open in front of him. Petra was lost.

'I don't understand...' she started, but Carruthers cut her off.

'Do you know a man called Colin Penpolney?' he asked. She nodded.

'Slightly, not well. We were at school together, at Penlyn. He was a year above me, he was Head Boy in the Upper Sixth when I was in the Lower Sixth. I never knew him well. I remember he was into the Arts. Played the violin in the school orchestra. And acted in all the school plays. I never really knew him, but he was nice. Oh, and we acted together in the School Play when I was in the Lower 6th. He was Pantalone, and I was his daughter Clarice. "A Servant of Two Masters",' she explained. 'Goldoni'. Where is this leading, she wondered. 'Why?'

'And do you know where he is now?'

'Actually, I do. He works at the Polhaven book shop, just two doors away. I only remember him because I sometimes see him on the ferry, or when we pass in the High Street, and say "Hello". And that's all I know about him. Why?' she asked again.

'Wait. And drink your tea, it's getting cold.' Carruthers was leafing through the local telephone directory, picked up the phone and called the book shop. He switched on the speaker for Petra's benefit. The owner, Rodney Hastings, took the call. After a few exchanges to which Petra was a party but of which she understood nothing, Hastings said:

'He's here now, and he's on holiday next week. D'you want to speak to him?'

'No, no. It's like this… I have some urgent legal business to discuss with him, and if he's away next week, it really should be today, I don't suppose…?'

'That's fine, we only get any real custom in the High Season. He can start his holiday this afternoon. Are you sure you don't want to speak to him?'

'No. Just ask him to come to my Chambers after lunch, two o'clock. It *is* important, you can tell him that.' He rang off, swivelled to face Petra. 'I really should wait until you're both here, this afternoon,' he started, 'but on this occasion… did you know Mr. Ingram?' Petra was growing increasingly impatient. She was in a maze, but it felt like a forest. 'We're getting there,' murmured Carruthers encouragingly, 'just answer that first. Ingram?'

'He was my Latin teacher. I studied Classics at York because of him, really. He was outstanding as a teacher, a nonentity of a man outside the classroom, but an intellectual giant in front of a class.'

'And you got a First, I seem to remember. Well, this is highly unusual in more ways than one, because legally speaking Mr. Penpolney should be here as well. And I think you might need a second cup of tea, my dear, because I'm about to read you Mr. Ingram's Will.' He put on his reading glasses and bent his head to the text.

'Here we go then: *"This is the Last Will and Testament of blah-blah-blah, replacing all previous blah-blah-blah… I hereby bequeath my entire estate and fortune, comprising the following:*

Polmine Estate including all properties and possessions on and in the Estate;

My financial assets and investment portfolio;

to Miss Petra Zabrinski of Harbour Lane, Polmouth, and Mr. Colin Penpolney of Cliff Rise Mews, Polmouth, in equal halves, with the stipulation that…"'

There was a crash from across the desk and when Carruthers raised his eyes from the text he saw that Petra's teacup was lying on its side and the liquid running over the desk and onto her skirt. She was shaking, and had gone white. A strange emotional snort had her raising her hand to her mouth, it was half laugh, half sob.

'My God!' she gasped. 'Oh, my God!' She started mopping up the spilt tea with paper handkerchiefs.

'That was rather my reaction.' said Carruthers. 'I can understand your surprise. Listen, go and compose yourself, and then I'll treat you to lunch. The least I can do for a...' he grinned, '... valued client! Go on, shoo!'

Seated at a table for two in the Harbour Restaurant with stunning views over the harbour and to the cliffs of Polmouth beyond, Petra was grappling with the enormity of the surprise, unable as yet to evaluate what it meant, what would be the consequences.

'I suppose that, putting on my cap as Legal Assistant, I should ask what the stipulation is?' Carruthers signalled to a waiter for menus.

'You'll need to read, or rather I need to re-read that bundle of documents that you brought this morning, but it seems that Mr. Ingram absorbed Clifftop Farm into the Estate, guaranteeing that lifelong tenancy of the farm free of rent, including any family or employees, and any proceeds from the farm, eggs I suppose, accrue to the tenants. That's all. A detail, really. It's in a Servitude, an easement in the Land Registry. So it's binding. But you must be reeling from this. Remind me, how old are you?' He stared at her girlish appearance, she looked like a teenager.

'Twenty-three.'

'So that would make Mr. Penpolney twenty-four, logically?' She nodded and grabbed her glass of wine. 'You must have one hundred and one questions running through your mind, and

I'm sure that Mr. Penpolney will have no fewer when I read him the Will this afternoon. Before we get to the main reason we're here, the food, I'll just suggest this. When he gets here at two, I'll see him alone and read him the Will, and then I'll call you in and we can look at precisely what it is that you're inheriting.' Petra shook her head in disbelief.

'I don't know whether I'll be able to keep any food down,' she muttered, then, as her bubbly good humour returned, she added: 'I hope Mr. Penpolney doesn't spill his tea, as well!' They ordered their meal.

Colin Penpolney's reaction to Carruthers' steady, measured reading of the Will was less violent than Petra's, but he was no less confused and surprised. A mild-mannered man, mature for his age, he stared across the desk at Carruthers. Before Penpolney could speak, Carruthers reached for the intercom button.

'Petra, come in now, please.' He looked at Colin Penpolney. 'Miss Zabrinski happens to be my Legal Assistant,' he explained. Colin nodded.

'I saw, I recognised her when I came in. But why us?' That was the burning question in Petra's mind, too. Carruthers had no idea either, but he had already dismissed the notion that a demented Ingram had concocted some lunatic match-making scenario out of a Rossini opera.

'I've handled some bizarre bequests in my time,' Carruthers started, 'but I think this one takes the biscuit! And I can't imagine what you two are thinking. Of course, it's not for me to make suggestions, but I feel that as your executor and lawyer, although you didn't choose me, it would be irresponsible of me not, at least, to offer whatever assistance I can. Free of charge, of course.'

'I'll need all of that.' Petra said firmly. 'And more.'

'I'll willingly accept that, I learned the hard way the stupidity of intentionally refusing expert advice. To my cost,' Colin finished.

'Very well. I understand you have a week's holiday?' Colin nodded. Carruthers turned to Petra. 'Then so do you, starting today.'

'But...'

'No "but-s" my dear! You will need time to assimilate all this. Not least the fact that you are not only now owners of Polmine Estate and Clifftop Farm, but also all liquid assets and the investment portfolio of the deceased.' Carruthers consulted a bank statement. 'No way of knowing what the portfolio holds, but that's my job to investigate, for probate. The current bank balance is fifty-four thousand pounds.' Petra gasped. Colin's face was as hewn from stone, a grave statue staring at the table top. 'That kind of money would buy you a dozen Cornish mansions, with enough left over to furnish them, just to give you an idea of what such a sum means...' Carruthers coughed gently. 'To return to my offer of avuncular advice, as far as handling finances is concerned, I'd suggest that all transactions, especially cheques drawn, be from a new account with double signature. Even if you were a couple I'd advise that, and as relative strangers I'd consider it essential, to avoid potential misunderstandings.' They both nodded. 'In that case I'll draft a document, but no hurry for that.' He opened a drawer, took out a cheque book and rapidly signed five blank cheques which he tore out and placed on the desktop. 'Any interim expenses you can draw from my escrow account...' he pointed to the account name on the top cheque. 'All you have to do is date the cheque and enter the payee, etc. Now... I need to study this file again, for probate details, but I've already gleaned that there are four tenants in the farmhouse, free of rent for life. There's the retired farmer Blackitt, and his assistants Derek and Emma Collingley, and their daughter Sarah Penham. Sarah seems to have been Mr. Ingram's housekeeper, and since his stroke two years ago his helper. I'll come back to them.' In his own legal, precise way, Carruthers had already won over the legatees Petra and Colin.

'As a final suggestion, I'd propose a visit to the Estate tomorrow, and I'll join you with the plans. And I'll try to arrange a meeting with Sarah Penham, because if anyone knows what Mr. Ingram's intentions were when he bought the Estate, she will. For now, to give me time to study this lot...' he lifted the heavy dossier, '... I suggest that you two head off. I'm sure you have a great deal to talk about!' They both nodded. 'So meet me at the bottom of the track to the clifftop, where the lane from Penlyn reaches the village at ... say, ten o'clock tomorrow?' Two more silent nods. 'So, congratulations, and off you go!'

Carruthers pushed the cheques across the desk towards them; Colin gave them to Petra. They disappeared in her handbag. Chairs scraped back and the two young people left Chambers in silence, descended a dark staircase and stepped out into blinding sunlight drenching Polhaven High Street. Colin looked right down the High Street, Petra looked left. Then Colin said:

'Well, you live in Polmouth. I live in Polmouth. Unless you have a better idea, I suggest the ferry across the estuary, and try to work out what on earth Ingram was thinking of. I mean, I hardly know you.'

'No better idea, Mister Penpolney.' Petra giggled, reverting to her bubbly self. 'I can't go on calling you that, it's a jaw-breaker! Will you settle for Colin?' He smiled.

'Zabrinski is barely any better! So it's Petra and Colin, then.' She nodded. They reached the harbour and boarded the ferry as it was about to depart. 'I'm afraid I remember nothing about you.' Petra's impetuous giggle was inevitable.

'Well, you certainly know how to flatter a girl! Nothing? Nothing at all?'

'Uh… you were in the hockey team… whoever designed hockey skirts must have been blind, or a cruel pervert.' He smiled suddenly. 'I do remember you were the only girl with nice legs… in a hockey skirt. All the others were running around on tree trunks.' She giggled again. The white ferry belched black smoke from its smokestack and inched its way at a snail's pace towards the harbour exit.

'That's the best you can do?' Petra's blonde ponytail was dancing in the breeze. 'What about "A Servant of Two Masters"? When you were Head Boy and I was a hockey skirt flirt.' Colin reddened.

'Oh Lord, of course! You were my daughter, Clarice. I was Pantalone. So sorry… hey, you know what? I can only remember the very first line, I had it as the curtain went up. You were sitting on a chair and I was standing half beside, half behind you… d'you remember?'

'So you *do* remember me.' She was playful. 'Do you remember what happened on the first night?' Colin blushed again.

'Unfortunately, yes. As the curtain went up my first line was to you, it was *"Come, come, my dear, not so shy now!"* It's the only line I remember. And at all the rehearsals I'd let my hand hover over your shoulder. But when it was the real performance, I thought "what the hell" and lowered my hand to put it firmly on your shoulder. But you shifted on your chair and my hand came down on top of your head! And all the cast froze… thinking "My God, he's touching her!" For Heaven's sake, it wasn't a screen kiss!' Petra's giggle seemed irrepressible.

'Everyone remembers that. But afterwards, everyone was saying that's how real actors do it. I thought you were brave.' Colin was sitting next to her on deck in the sunlight, the wind across the bay ruffling his long hair.

'I've never been brave in my life. But I have a feeling that, with what Mr. Ingram has thrown at us, we'll need to be. This ferry is hopeless!' he observed. 'It used to take just 30 minutes to cover the 6 miles. But we're hardly moving...'

'You don't read the papers then!' Petra poured omniscience. 'It's the rationing, petrol and diesel. They minimise consumption, meaning minimise speed. You could row across more quickly.'

'I've never rowed a boat in my life, either,' observed Colin sadly. 'If you're feeling like me, you'll probably be wanting some time on your own, after all this. I know I do. But may I invite you to dinner this evening, "Crab and Lobster"? We have a lot to discuss.' She nodded, and tightened the band on her ponytail. Having announced that she would not use the jawbreaker surname, being a woman she now proceeded to do just that. Frequently.

'Well, yes, and no, Mister Penpolney. Dual signature means we go Dutch. Each pay half.' This time it was Colin's turn to laugh, which he rarely did. 'And don't go thinking you're the senior partner, just because you're a man, were Head Boy and are older.' He gave an exaggerated artificial shudder.

'Please tell me you're not a feminist?' Another giggle.

'I don't read that dreadful "Spare Rib" magazine, no. Each to their own. God...' she stared out at the broad waters of the estuary. 'We're barely half way across. I could swim there faster.'

'With fifty thousand pounds, we could buy a helicopter.' Colin suggested drily. She stared at him.

'I'm starting to think I like you...' She left the thought unfinished.

'Dual signature, but don't even think of forging mine.'

'With a name as long as yours, I wouldn't waste the ink.' She gestured to the tiny cafeteria indoors. 'You may also buy me a cup of tea, Mister Penpolney. Dual signature, of course!' Laughing, she led the way inside.

The ferry finally moored in Polport and they crossed the gangplank to terra firma.

'You live in Harbour Lane.' asserted Colin. 'It's on my way home, so may I walk with you?' She stared at him.

'You truly are conservative. And yes, Mister Penpolney, you may.'

'I don't even know our member of parliament's name!' protested Colin with a laugh. 'But if you say so.'

'I do.' she announced grandly. 'But I prefer your style to the libertine proletariat. This way.'

On closing the front door of her tiny flat Petra went to a sideboard and poured herself a large cider, then sat down in the only armchair, grappling with the incomprehensible. What on earth had possessed Ingram, she was wondering. She was aware that he had considered her his star pupil in Latin, and his lessons to a class of just five sixth formers had been superlative. But now, thrown together with the relatively unknown Colin Penpolney… And a huge estate, and a fortune. She didn't dare contemplate what was in the investment portfolio. She drained her glass, kicked off her shoes and went to lie on the bed, then stared at the ceiling. *"Thank God they had Carruthers"*, she was thinking. In the confusion of her thoughts, two words were reverberating: "Carruthers" and "they".

Chapter Seven

Discoveries

At seven Colin was waiting outside the door of the "Crab and Lobster". He had changed into a three-piece suit and a silk tie, knotted with a double Windsor. Petra saw him from a distance, looked down at herself. She realised that she had misjudged. She was wearing a daring, flared purple miniskirt and a blouson that hugged her generous contours. Oh well, too late now. She joined him at the door. Whatever Colin was thinking he kept to himself and followed her in.

'I've reserved a table for seven-thirty, so let's have a drink. You do drink, I suppose?'

'Gin and tonic, please.' She perched herself on a bar stool and tried to pull the skirt down an inch, but it resisted her best efforts. Colin glanced down.

'That's a lot better than a hockey skirt,' he observed quietly. She was privately flattered but determined not to show it. She rather enjoyed teasing him with his conservative responses.

'So I've got nice legs. You told me.' She sipped her drink. Colin glanced down at her skirt, then studied her face.

'You still have. You're very pretty, too. Now.' She jumped on this with relish.

'Now? Now?! So you're saying that by the time I'm thirty I'll be a raddled old bag! "Pretty, for now!" You really know how to flatter a girl, Mister *Pen-pol-nee*!' She examined his face. 'Actually, you're not too bad yourself. Pity about your hair, though!'

'What? What's wrong with my hair?'

'Far too long.' She was definite. 'Needs a cut. And middle parting, brushed back from the forehead. Then you might even look like an intellectual.' He sighed.

'Well, now I'm shaggy Samson, and you're bossy Delilah. You're definitely a woman.'

'What powers of observation, Mister Penpolney! What's that supposed to mean?'

'I spent a year in Germany, for my degree. I had a girl-friend, Helga. Spent half her time getting me to change my appearance, my dentist, my clothes, my shoes... Why do women always want to change a man, as if he's her pet poodle?' Petra was fired up. She took a risk.

'So that was half the time. What was she doing the rest of the time?' Colin looked at her thighs again, and didn't answer. Then:

'You know what we're doing, don't you?' She nodded.

'We're running away from talking about what really matters. What on earth possessed Ingram, and what we're going to do with it. You're right, running away. I think I prefer flirting to fortune.'

'Perhaps Ingram intended they be the same thing.' murmured Colin. 'Let's order.'

They were well into the meal before Colin started the batting again.

'You know why, don't you?'

'Why what?' Petra poured wine into his glass then her own.

'Putting it off. Putting off talking about what we can't handle. Until we've seen the beast. The estate. We both want to see it, but until then it'll all be conjecture. You studied Classics, my degree is in German. Romans and Germans don't do conjecture.'

'The Greeks did. Cassandra, she had plenty of predictions.'

'No, but seriously, there's no point, is there? Until we know what we've got, and we certainly can't work out why.'

'So what on earth are we going to talk about, then?'

'You know,' Colin mused, 'several women I've known have spent a great deal of time talking about themselves.'

'And don't tell me… they're all called Helga!'

'You're doing it again.'

'Doing what?'

'Running away from it. Fine. But please don't run away from me. For one thing, I don't deserve it, and for another, I was rather enjoying flirting on the ferry. With my partner.' She stared at him, tossing her pony tail characteristically.

'Actually, so was I.' She paused. 'Running away from you was the last thing on my mind, in fact it wasn't on my mind at all. But partners going halves means just that. You know nothing about me, nor I about you.'

'So we go Dutch, as long as it's ladies first.' Her face fell.

'Do we have to? Have you no gallantry?' Colin sensed that he had touched a raw nerve, but he persisted.

'Is it boyfriend, or family?' She coughed and put down her cutlery, reaching in her handbag for a tissue.

'I don't think I can eat any more. I'm sorry, pity, because it's delicious. You?' He pushed away his plate.

'Same. Here? Or out by the harbour?' She looked at him gratefully.

'Somewhere where it's dark. Harbour wharf will do fine.' Colin summoned the waiter and drained his glass.

'You don't miss much, do you?' They were standing beside a rusty metal railing, overlooking the darkened boats in Polport harbour, the water gleaming in the reflection of street lights and a half moon low in the sky. 'Family or boyfriend, you asked. Well, you scored a full house there. Do you smoke?'

Colin nodded and produced a packet of Bensons, and a lighter. They lit up.

'We don't have to do this,' Colin ventured.

'It was your idea. At least it's a warm night. And yet I'm shivering… Colin, I promise I'll come back to your question. It's the right thing, but… I'm scared. I've never even owned a TV or a sofa without buying it on the never-never. I know, I know, I'm doing it again, putting it off. Here goes. But we're going Dutch, remember? Your half in return for my half…'

'I wouldn't have it any other way.'

'At school, I don't think anyone ever knew. They for certain wondered about my name, hardly Anglo-Saxon indigenous. No, my father was Polish. Before the war he was a carpenter. He escaped to Britain in 1939 and joined the RAF as a fighter pilot. I understand a lot of Poles, Czechs and others did that. He survived the war, then married my mum here. He was the village carpenter in Polmouth. I was born in 1951. When I was two, there was a fire in the woodstore. I was in the house. The firemen got me out… And that was that. They couldn't get to my parents.' She was staring blindly out over the still, dark waters of the harbour, the occasional reflected gleam visible in her black eyes. 'So I never knew my parents, only photographs, and what Auntie Elsie told me… my mother's sister.' she added.

'I'm so sorry I asked.' Colin felt awkward.

'Don't be sorry. Whether we like it or not, we're stuck with each other. Partners, God knows why!' A tiny giggle escaped her. 'Sorry, don't take that the wrong way.'

'You were adopted then?' He sensed rather than saw the shake of her head.

'I was put into foster care. When I was six, the Social wanted to have me adopted, but I refused. I had to be very stubborn, and very resolute to convince them. But the true reason was that I loved my foster parents, they were all I'd known, and they were brilliant. So the Social gave in, and my dear foster parents kept me until I was 18 and went to university. They're both in a residential home, now, and we have no contact. No family.' She sniffed. 'Your turn now.'

'Well, technically speaking I have a family, but in reality, I don't. The year I went up to university they separated, then divorced. I think they'd been putting it off until I was out of their hair. My mother's in Scunthorpe, I believe, and no idea where my father is. And I don't care. They were both footloose, I'm a bit of a Polmouth fixture. And now with Ingram, the estate... it's as if he must have known.' They were standing shoulder to shoulder. Petra shivered, despite the warm air. The fingers of her right hand were playing with the ends of her pony tail behind her shoulder.

'Well, that gets us half way. Now I want to know all about these multi-Helgas, and your better half.' Colin turned her to face him.

'Believe me,' his voice was stony, 'you don't.'

'But I'm going to, because you're going to buy me a drink, probably several drinks, and I'm going to get drunk, because we've just won the lottery. And bugger "going Dutch", it's your round!' She pulled him back to the pub.

'Helga was an initiation, perhaps not the best.' Colin sipped his whisky. 'Last year I got engaged, here in Polmouth. Girl called April. We were very close. Or I thought we were. Until I found out...'

'Lesbian?'

'Oh, for God's sake, this may be 1974, but do me a favour! No, when we weren't together, and even when we were, she was screwing with some hi-fi salesman in Penlyn. And as if that wasn't bad enough, she was also having it off with a man in his thirties, married with a wife and young child, a bassoonist in some Army Band in Truro.'

'Christ! You must have been mortified! But how did you find out?'

'The bitch took pleasure in telling me. When we were in bed together, of all places! Don't get me wrong, this was before getting up in the morning, not after... I mean when... no, that part wasn't a problem. But she bloody well was. So I told her it was over. She went berserk, started to tear my living room apart, sobbing, hysterical. I understood then.'

'Understood?'

'I was simply her rock, her security, I was her Polhaven, her Safehaven, and she was an explorer, no, a sexplorer bobbing about in search of adventure. The Polhaven human trawler. If the other guys rejected her, she expected to come back to good old Colin. I wasn't having that.' He looked at his feet. 'Even if it hurt. Me, hurt me, I mean.' Petra hesitated. She, too, had been hurt in her time. But she persisted.

'So how did you get rid of her?'

'I have a car in Polhaven. She thought I was driving her to work. But I didn't, I drove her to the bassoon player's place in Truro, parked outside his house. For Christ's sake, his wife was playing with their little girl in the garden. 'I said: "That's where you live, and where you belong. Good bye!" And I pushed her out of the car. Never heard from her again, and don't want to.' He looked at his empty glass and ordered another. Petra also held her empty glass out to the barman. 'Do you always drink gin and tonic? Doubles?' She shook her head, tossing her blonde ponytail defiantly.

'Only when it matters.' Puzzled, Colin paid for the new drinks.

'Your turn...'

'My boy-friend chucked me four months ago. Said I was boring and frigid. I ask you, me?! So I told him...' she had already downed nearly half her double gin and tonic. 'I told him if I was boring that was because he was uneducated, and as for the second bit, that was entirely his fault.' She drained the glass and held it out imperiously to the barman. 'Double G & T.' she commanded. Colin wondered whether this was a good idea. 'Don't worry, I can hold my drink,' she reassured him. But the third glass was downed almost as rapidly as the second, during which neither spoke a word. She looked down at her purple miniskirt.

'I feel ridiculous.' she announced, sounding tipsy.

'I think we're done here.' Colin settled the bill. 'Let me walk you home, Miss Zabrinski.'

'Mister Polpen… I mean Pen-pol-nee, I accept.' When they reached the Harbour Walk, she slipped her arm through his but he was uncertain whether this was because she was unsteady on her feet, or for some other reason. When they reached the tiny sixteenth century cottage she warned him: 'You're tall. The doors are all just five feet high. So mind your head.'

'I'll see you inside.' Petra was not as drunk as she was making out, tipsy yes, but well aware of what she was doing, her intentions.

'Well, you aren't coming in for coffee,' she announced, opening the front door. 'You're coming in to put your partner to bed!' She closed the door behind them and led Colin into the bedroom.

'I'm not sure this is a good idea…' he started uncertainly.

'I said: "put to bed", not "take to bed". If you turn your back…' her impetuous giggle burst out in the dimly lit room, '… I'll just get into something more comfortable.' Colin turned to the bedroom door and examined the ancient mortice lock, then the glass fronted drinks cabinet beside the door. Petra slipped out of her clothes and pulled on pyjamas, her eyes fixed on Colin's back all the while. What she saw was what she had expected. A man, and a gentleman. This made a change. 'Now I need your help,' her voice was husky. He turned to see her pulling back the sheet. 'Will you tuck me in?' she asked sweetly, climbing under the bedclothes. Colin swallowed, staring into her strange coal black eyes beneath her very fair fringe. He pushed the sheet and blanket under the mattress, and she lay there in her single bed like a little girl. 'Just three more things, Mister Penpolney.' The giggle again. 'Lock the front door when you leave, there's a door key under the plant pot outside.' She smiled up at him.

'That's two things.'

'Yes. This Helga… was she any good at kissing?' Colin saw where this was going, and was relieved it wasn't somewhere else.

'I've forgotten.'

'There's an "e" and an "a" in my name, too. Turn out the light.'

A few minutes later Colin left the tiny medieval house and crossed to the harbour wall. He shook his head in disbelief.

Chapter Eight

The Estate

Colin was first to arrive at the junction where Penlyn Lane entered the village and the one mile track up to Polmine Estate started. The sun was already high in the sky, promising a scorching day. Under a tree he perched on a milestone that was of no use to anyone, as Penlyn Lane was unpassable, putting distant Penlyn firmly out of reach. Petra approached, rather unsteadily he thought.

'Heck, what did you give me to drink last night? My head...' Colin stood up and looked her up and down. Just as her girlish pony tail belied her true age, so also today did a clinging red T-shirt and jeans that seemed to have been glued on.

'If we'd gone halves, as you insisted we should, instead of letting me pay full whack, you'd remember.' He was dry. Carruthers joined them.

'Good, good.' he said meaninglessly. He was carrying folded plans of the Estate and a heavy bunch of keys. 'Sarah will join us later. Sarah Penham,' he reminded them, 'farmers' daughter. Right, let's go and see what we shall see.' He started walking. Colin closed in from behind.

'Have you ever been up there? The Estate, or the farm?' Carruthers shook his head.

'If I have it was so long ago, I've forgotten all about it. We'll have to rely on the plans, and Sarah Penham. Keep up, Miss Zabrinski.'

On reaching the top Colin and Petra saw for the first time their extensive clifftop property. Nothing had prepared them for the huge expanse of land, the tall mine workings, pump and lift, the sprawling farm and in the distance the mansion house size Croft House, and the lakes. But what held their attention most spectacularly were the eight giant equine creatures placidly grazing in the jungle of undergrowth only a hundred yards away.

'No idea what they are,' said Carruthers apologetically. 'We'll have to ask Miss Penham. Now...' he unfolded the plan and laid it flat on the gravel.

'I have the keys, but I'd counsel against going down there...' he gestured through a metal fence to an iron door set in the cliff, '... into the mine. I have a detailed report from Camborne School of Mines. They found a ventilation shaft from the cliff face was blocked. They cleared it and repaired the grille. But you'd need powerful torches and steady nerves. Over there...' he gestured to the distant lift mounting and high Pump House, '... you'd need one of the Camborne engineers with you. But the mine is yours. I think you ought to see inside the cottages, all five of them. I have the keys and I'm told the electricity is connected, and the water.' Petra nodded and with due female curiosity led the way to the nearest door.

After their inspection they all welcomed the warm sunlight.

'I don't understand.' Colin was at a loss. 'They're perfectly preserved, fully furnished, even got beds. All that's missing are mattresses and carpets. Even got built-in wardrobes. D'you think Mr. Ingram kept them maintained? Or let them out to holidaymakers? But, without mattresses... If not, what for?' Carruthers shook his head.

'I've read the file on his plans, but I'm pretty sure Miss Penham may have the answer to your question.' They walked to the mine-head and the railway track across the Estate. Unlike Latimer and Hendricks ten years previously, the new owners now had a solid grit track laid by Ingram alongside the rusty railway line all the way to the lakes, the Croft House and the rail head.

Sarah Penham, a no-nonsense forty-year old in an apron, met them. As they entered the Croft House kitchen via the back door, she looked and sounded uncomfortable.

'It feels very strange, being in here without Mr. Ingram. For ten years I was his housekeeper, and... well you can see. This is where he lived. After his stroke two years ago, he needed a lot of help, but he was a wonderful gentleman, never complained. I'll let you look around on your own, if that's all right? There's here, then three reception rooms, and five bedrooms upstairs, two bathrooms. I'd prefer to wait outside. But I can tell you anything you want to know later...' She went quietly out to the sunlight.

'You must have a lot of questions.' They were standing by the tranquil blue water of the larger lake, where the raw undergrowth and wild brambles had been cleared and kept as a strip of grassy embankment. 'And I'm wondering – I guess you are too – what connects you to Mr. Ingram?' Petra shrugged.

'He was my Latin teacher to A level. And he awarded me Junior Latin prize, and the Senior one as well. Otherwise... nothing.'

'He was my Latin teacher too. But I never knew the man. So I'm at a loss. Do you know?' Colin asked Sarah Penham. 'I mean, I understand you were with him a lot of the time?'

'I was. But I never heard him mention either of you.'

'A mystery for now, then. But he must have had a reason,' Colin observed. 'He wouldn't just have picked random names out of a hat. Oh well... when can you tell us about what he had planned for the Estate, why he bought it?' Sarah looked awkward.

'I live with my parents, in the farmhouse. But they're not really used to visitors, especially intellectuals like yourselves. They might feel awkward if we sat down and discussed all this with them present. So can I suggest we meet for supper down in Polmouth this evening?' Petra nodded.

'Great idea. And I think our inheritance might just stretch to offering you a banquet at the "Crab and Lobster".' She giggled, her black eyes gleaming playfully. She glanced up at Colin beside her and laid her hand on his sleeve. Sarah Penham looked at her quizzically.

'I'm beginning to sense a spark of what's going on here.' she said inconsequentially. 'Mr. Ingram never married, had no children.'

'That had crossed my mind, too,' murmured Colin. Petra threw her head back defiantly and turned to face him directly.

'You never told me any of this!' she said accusingly. But her black eyes were sparkling, and Sarah Penham's sudden illumination was growing in intensity. 'Half past seven?' Petra asked. Sarah nodded, they shook hands formally and Petra and Colin turned to leave. Colin turned back.

'Those monsters, look like giant horses out of a horror movie... what are they?' Sarah grinned unexpectedly.

'Tell you tonight!'

As Colin accompanied Petra down the track to the village, he broke the silence.

'I'd stick to wine tonight. Maybe save the G&Ts for after the meal?' She nodded.

'A girl like me ought to be able to get into bed without assistance!' The silence returned. Then: 'On the other hand... Adrian never did that. Me, frigid?!' She slipped her arm through his.

'Let's start with what you saw, in the order you saw it,' suggested Sarah. They were in the "Crab and Lobster", menus on the chair beside them. 'What was the first thing?' Petra and Colin both spoke at once:

'The horse things.'

'The equine monsters?'

Sarah grinned.

'They're the easy part. Great Horses. Outsize Shire horses. We brought them ten years ago from our Equine Sanctuary in the New Forest. Endangered species. They were to be a major attraction in Mr. Ingram's project.' A waiter approached, but they were in no hurry to order. He stared at the menus on a chair beside the table and disappeared in a huff. Petra sipped her wine cautiously; Colin looked on approvingly.

'Did this project have a name?' she asked.

'He would have called it "Polmine History Project". That'll be why there's a whole file on it. I guess the next thing you saw was the metal door set in the cliff top, the Phoenician mine?'

'Don't know about Phoenician, but yes.' Petra again. 'What's with Phoenicia?'

'Better read the file, that was Mr. Ingram's pet element in the plan. Now, the cottages... He planned on converting all five to a museum display, maps, descriptions, section plans of all the mine levels down to two thousand feet... and artefacts. That was principally for school groups visiting.' The waiter approached again, impatient, and this time they paused to order. A bottle of wine was opened and served. 'Mr. Ingram reckoned he could get Camborne School of Mines to collaborate on opening the deep shaft, get the Pump House working and the lift, and if safe take small groups down and into the workings that extend under the sea... But he'd need Camborne to install lighting, and maintain the machinery. And he'd have to provide hard-hats with lamps. He said the accident insurance would make it very costly. But he never gave up the idea.'

'He aimed high, then,' Colin commented. 'In fact, very ambitious.'

'But there's more! He wanted to lease a train from British Railways and run four times a day from Penlyn Junction to Polmouth, stopping off at the Estate, dropping and picking up passengers at the rail head and the mine head. It was a grand idea.'

'I never knew you could lease a whole train!' Petra was astonished. Colin nodded.

'Leasing a train isn't expensive. When I was studying at Royal Holloway, in London, some railway enthusiast groups used to hire a private train at weekends up to Carlisle and the Lakes, or to York, and back in the evening. Tickets were two pounds return, so 400 miles for two pounds! But we've seen the track across the Estate… it'll need maintenance. How did he intend to…?'

'He was a wealthy man. He was prepared to pay for the spur and track across the Estate to be overhauled, and then when entrance money started coming in, using that for day to day upkeep.' Petra glanced at Colin.

'Ambitious indeed! It'd be a huge undertaking! But with sponsorship from Camborne Mines School for the museum… and Polmouth having a rail service again… Did he approach the Village Council?'

'Oh, he was going to, but…' The lobster bisque was served, and there was a short pause. 'That'll be in the file, too. It's all very sad.' But they had to wait to learn what was sad. The main course was being filleted on a side table. A second bottle of wine was opened and left to breathe.

'So the Great Horses were to be a family attraction, and picnics by the lake.' Colin had picked up Ingram's notion. 'That leaves the Brick Croft, and the Croft House…'

'He planned boating and fishing for the lakes, as well. And Mr. Ingram intended to have another museum display inside the Brick Croft baking tower, and he'd give guided tours of the machinery, the brick cutting process. And he had two projects for the Croft House. A Tea Room on the terrace and in one of the reception rooms, and upstairs convert four of the five bedrooms to basic Bed & Breakfast Guest House standard, with continental breakfast in the Tea Room.'

'Good God!' Colin was speechless.

'And Ingram thought up all this?' Petra's astonishment matched Colin's. 'So how come it never happened? He had ten years, you said...'

'That's why it's tragic. It was all so promising at the start, ten years ago. Mr. Ingram was looking for sponsorship or funding from the Department of Education and Science in London, the Local Education Authority in Cornwall and Camborne School of Mines. He started with British Railways, for leasing a train. And that's where it all started to go wrong...' The waiter approached to clear the plates.

'Dessert?' Colin turned to Sarah, unwisely played the male, Head Boy, senior partner. Petra stepped in imperiously.

'Bring us the menu. Please.' This to the waiter. She gave Colin a warning glance, but her eyes once again told the true story. 'What started to go wrong?'

'BR liked the idea, subject to two things. The first was easy, having the track put to running standard, and safety checks, a test run. Ingram was ready to pay for that. But the second was the sticking point. They'd only agree to the lease if Ingram could show funding from the DES and the LEA. So he went to Truro, and then London, and both were happy with the project. But here things went haywire. The LEA said it'd only contribute if the DES said yes first. And the DES...'

'Poor Ingram!' Colin interjected. 'The DES would only chip in if the LEA promised its contribution... Am I right?' Sarah nodded.

'A nightmare. Everyone liked the idea, but none would commit to funding unless the others did first. Same story with Camborne Mines School. He was stymied. And he didn't know where else to turn. He told me he had enough funds for the railway, the track and lease, but that would be it.'

'And the Village Council?'

'He didn't even bother asking, he was sure they'd say the same. And besides, the Council has very limited funds. And the poor man simply didn't know who else to ask... Tragic.'

'What's tragic as well,' said Petra firmly, looking grave, 'is that he was teaching us all at school at the same time, and never showed any of his feelings. Truly, a classicist.' The desserts were finally ordered. The waiter wanted nothing better than to see the back of these tardy diners.

'Well, you've certainly pushed us to read that file in every detail.' Colin reflected. 'And you've been really helpful. Don't know what we'd have done without you.' Petra was eyeing the bar hungrily. This did not escape Colin. They finished their desserts, and he signalled for the bill. And this in turn did not escape Sarah. She tactfully pushed back her chair and reached for her handbag.

'Well, thank you for a wonderful meal, and glad to have been of help.' She stood up to leave.

Colin, ever the gentleman, stood up in deference to good manners.

'Shall we walk up with you?' he asked politely.

Petra's eyes were screaming in the candlelight. **"No, you fool!"** they lanced, **"Why did you have to ask that?!"** To her relief, Sarah shook her head.

'Thanks, but I can find my way from here to the track and all the way up to the farm, blindfolded. Call me or pop in to visit any time. Bye.' Petra relaxed. She had not missed the waiter's incensed reaction to their slow orders. She pulled Colin to the bar.

'You know, sometimes Mister Polpen... I mean Penpolney, good manners please one lady but irritate the girl who's with you.' She turned to look at the bottles suspended behind the bar; Colin was trying to work out why women always spoke in code. Petra ordered the inevitable, Colin cognac. Petra perched her compact form on a bar stool. Colin, already taller than she, remained standing. 'You're doing it again!' she said accusingly. Colin was even more lost than before. 'Me sitting down, Clarice, your daughter, you, Big Daddy Pantalone standing beside and behind me, and next thing, Mister Penpolney, you'll be putting your hand on my shoulder, actually touching me, and saying "*Come, come, my dear, not so shy now!*"' She paused. 'Or something...' Colin gave one of his rare, spontaneous laughs.

'I don't think Goldoni was writing a play about incest...' he started. Petra dragged him down beside her on the next stool, her eyes sending a clear message. Colin was learning to trust her eyes rather than her words. Petra pressed ahead.

'But you forgot something, the shocking part...'

'What?'

'When Pantalone kissed Clarice, his daughter!'

'He didn't!' protested Colin. 'I mean, I didn't!'

'So last night was just a bad dream, then? Wonderful! Honestly, men!'

Colin feigned nonchalance, which was not how he felt.

'Oh, that.' he said vaguely, and put his arm round her shoulders, left it there. The barman served the gin and the cognac. Colin eyed her glass as she squeezed his arm fiercely. He addressed the barman. 'Ice and lemon slice for the lady. You're slipping!' he admonished the forgetful barman. She released his arm. His stayed in place.

'You're doing rather well.' she said. 'I can see why they made you Head Boy.'

'I almost turned it down,' he murmured. 'Felt I wasn't right for it. Not in the heroic mould... Anthony and Cleopatra, Caesar, Dido and Aeneas...'

Petra was fired up with a warmth she had not previously known.

'You're hopeless! Dido was from Carthage, Aeneas from Troy. And things turned out very badly, she died on her funeral pyre because he chucked her and went off to found Rome. If that's how you see things turning out, Mister Penpolney... I'll get properly drunk at home…' her voice tailed away, carrying a double meaning.

'At home,' Colin echoed. 'But if I read your eyes aright… no point in listening to the drone of your husky voice… then "home" is a very moveable feast. Don't you agree?' His arm pressed down around her shoulders. She laid her head against his shoulder promisingly and looked up into his eyes.

'I'm quite glad Mr. Ingram had no children… we could move in next week… but I'm not carrying my furniture a mile up an uphill track. Solution?' Colin drained his glass and paid the barman.

'Oh, that. I have it sorted…'

'What?' Her smouldering black eyes met his gaze. 'What? How?'

'A few Great Horses and farm carts. Just pick a day when it won't rain. Home?'

'No. To my temporary pad, yes. Home's next week.' They stood up and left, crossed to the harbour wall. Petra's arm was now firmly around Colin's waist. It was another starlit night, waves lapping against the stonework.

'I have a bottle of some ghastly French concoction somewhere in the temporary pad… probably gone bad by now…' she giggled.

'Then let me give you an expert cognac testing, as long as you don't keep it under the bed!' She giggled again, her arm tightened around his waist. Her head was once again resting on his firm shoulder.

'Say, this Helga girl… How did Fräulein "e & a" match up?' Another giggle, nervous this time. There was a pause, then:

'I don't know anyone called Helga.' Another silence. 'I do know a girl called "e & a", she's got…'

'Don't you dare!' Petra was into overdrive. 'Don't you start on the legs again, and "pretty now"!' Colin laughed, the second time that night.

'I wasn't going to say that!' he protested. 'In fact... I don't know what I was going to say.'

'I do,' she announced, and turned to face him. 'This...'

While Colin was being very clearly instructed about what he had been going to say, in Paddington station, London, Daniel Mortimer was boarding the night train to Penzance, but his ticket was to Penlyn, and his destination was Polhaven. Documents in his briefcase purported to show that he was Professor Mortimer from the Accounts Department, Mineralogy, at the Camborne School of Mines, but those documents had been fabricated in an anonymous block of offices on Whitehall, where Under-Secretary of State Bonham was working late. His desk phone warbled and he winced. A telephone should damned well ring, he thought irritably.

'Yes?' A voice made garbled noises in his ear. His irritation dissipated. 'So they're out then... Yes, come up. Now.' He rang off. On the floor below Richard Hamlyn picked up a number of documents and left his office accompanied by Cedric Tring. They climbed a staircase and entered Bonham's office.

'They made it, then.' Bonham's voice had a ring of satisfaction. 'And where are they now?' He gestured to the chairs and Hamlyn and Tring sat down facing their superior.

'On a Royal Navy Corvette, sir, making for Malta...'

'What? We agreed that if we succeeded, they'd be housed in a Safe House in Venice.' Tring looked awkward.

'We think the Venice House has been compromised, sir... the Bulgarians...' he ended lamely.

'Again? Another SH compromised? Not good enough. So why Malta?' Bonham sighed. 'All right, brief me fully. Just don't take all night.'

'Helmuth Schiller and Uschi Meissner, code names "Zero" and "Plenty", attended a colloquium in Yugoslavia, town called Split. With it being a coastal town and in relatively moderate Communist Yugoslavia, the East Germans would normally have held human collateral back in East Germany, to prevent any defection, family members usually. But neither has any family, so the East Germans took the risk. Mainly, we think, because Uschi Meissner is the DDR's scientific equivalent of the Soviet Bloc's Olga Korbut...'

'Lost me there!' snapped Bonham. 'Olga who?'

'Teenage gymnast, Olympic Gold medal, massive banner waver for the Communists.'

'Continue!'

'Our people in Yugoslavia gave their guardians the slip, got the two on a motor boat out into the Med, and onto the Corvette "Hampshire". Now en route to Malta. Malta, because the Corvette can anchor indefinitely in Valetta port, many British naval vessels do, and there's no significant Stasi presence there. Libyan, yes, but these people won't interest the Libyans. The initial debriefing will be done on board, "Zero" and "Plenty" will never go ashore, no risk of a chance sighting. Or abduction by the Stasi, or worse... elimination.'

'Where is their SH in Britain?' Bonham looked at his watch. 'I know they can't go direct to Porton Down, although the boffins down there desperately want them. Buckinghamshire as usual, I suppose?' Now it was Hamlyn's turn to share Tring's earlier discomfiture.

'Fraid not, sir. All the houses are occupied, except two, and we can't use them because they may be compromised.'

'Them as well?! MI6 is leaking like a sieve! Need to get their act together over there! So where?'

'That only left Scotland, or Cornwall. Scotland we ruled out as too distant...'

'And Cornwall isn't?' Bonham's derision was manifest. 'Where in Cornwall?'

'If I may show you on the map, sir....' Hamlyn opened a document on Bonham's desk. 'This is the river Pol, East of Penzance, here a little town Polhaven, and here...' he pointed, '...the village of Polmouth. In the war, the War Cabinet requisitioned Polmine estate, here, and its mine and… five miners' cottages. They sold it in '45, but kept a lease easement on two of the cottages. The Beeching Cuts closed the railway years ago and there's no road, so they'll be delivered by sea.'

'From the Corvette? I get it. When?'

'Depending on debriefing in Malta, and the voyage, less than two weeks. Middle of June, then a month in the SH while we evaluate whether they really are defecting, or have been allowed to seem to escape and are really double agents. Porton Down can't afford biological and chemical warfare material getting out. At least a month in SH quarantine.' Bonham grunted.

'And who's the minder, their keeper?' At last Tring took over.

'We chose the "Hampshire" for that reason. One of the Sub-lieutenants, name Katrina Rothmount. Ideal, she'll be with them from now until Cornwall, and delivered a day before them, check the premises, live in the second house, evaluate and send daily reports.'

'That's her real name?'

'Now, yes. Original name Katrina Rothenberger, German Jewess, parents fled to the UK in 1938. The main reason is she grew up in Penlyn, went to school there, less than 20 miles from Polmouth. She won't stand out when she goes shopping and all that. "Zero" and "Plenty" will never leave the Estate, nil contact.'

'And their cover?' Bonham was impressed but also in a hurry.

'That all three are writing a book, supposedly mineralogists from Camborne School of Mining. The mine adjacent to their cottages is the perfect cover. We have a man going out there tonight to confirm the cottage lease with the local lawyer. All sewn up.'

'Makes a change.' grunted Bonham. 'Anything else?'

'Logistics will move in shortly to secure the premises, store supplies for a month. Appearing to be from this Camborne School place.' Bonham nodded.

'Approved.' He pushed the map back to Hamlyn. 'Good night.' He opened his red box and took out the next document.

Chapter Nine

Although Carruthers did not usually work weekends, he was in Chambers by nine o'clock. He had the Ingram file to plough through. But his reading was suddenly interrupted by a ring at the doorbell. Surprised to have a caller on a Sunday he opened to find a short, rotund man in a crumpled three-piece suit and carrying a no less battered briefcase. Not, he decided, a travelling salesman.

'I hope I'm not disturbing...' Mortimer's nasal whine was more than slightly effeminate. 'Daniel Mortimer...' he slipped a visiting card from his waistcoat pocket, 'Camborne School of Mining. It's about Polmine Estate.' Carruthers' eyes widened.

'Come in, take a seat.' Mortimer sat facing the lawyer. 'My word, you people certainly move fast. Word really gets around.' Mortimer was taken aback, at a loss.

'Uh... sorry?'

'I was going to call the School on Monday, to request a new inspection of the mine and machinery, and a report for the new owners.' Now Mortimer was really concerned. With the Germans being impostors, the last thing MI6 needed was a team of real Camborne mining people all over the place... He was forced to improvise.

'Oh, I know nothing about that, I'm accounts. A separate department, know nothing about mining. No, I believe you represent Mr. Ingram, the owner. What's this about new owners?' Carruthers explained. This disquieted Mortimer even more. Carruthers was still confused.

'If the new owners haven't contacted Camborne, why are you here?' Mortimer set aside the potential problem of neighbouring owners to the defectors' cottage. He opened his battered briefcase.

'Well, I came to confirm the easements and you seemed the obvious choice rather than the owner, Ingram. Thought I'd try here rather than trek all the way up to the mine. But you say Ingram's passed away... It's this.' He pulled a document from the briefcase and passed it to Carruthers. 'As you can see, the Ministry of Defence, when they sold the Estate to "Chronos Investments", kept a lease in perpetuity on two cottages of the six. That's the contract signed with the Ministry in 1945, by Chronos.' Carruthers stared at the document. He didn't understand.

'But... I have the Land Registry extracts... there are no easements, no annotations... not for the cottages and lease. Wait, please.' He pulled open the Ingram file and took out two Land Registry extracts. He studied the 1945 document, then glanced at the 1965 extract. 'Look,' he turned them for Mortimer to see. 'Only the farm easements. And yet,' he lifted the Chronos contract, 'I can see this is a legal document in due form. How could this have happened? I'm even now handling probate for the inheritance.' Mortimer shrugged.

'Hmmm... evidently they weren't registered in the LR, then. But as to how that could have happened... it was 1945. This is more your domain, Mister Carruthers. Who would be responsible for notifying the LR in...' he glanced down at the documents, 'Truro?' Carruthers was still shocked.

'Well, the purchasers, "Chronos Investments", as they accepted the change, the Servitude, they owned the property. "Servitude" is a legal term, easement. I can only surmise they were negligent, failed to do so, or they *did*, but in the post-war chaos it wasn't handled correctly. This is terrible. I'll have to notify the new owners. They're half and half for the whole Estate, or they thought they were. So did I!' He stared at the three documents. 'So what brings you here, about the easement? You're from Camborne, but this easement is in favour of the Ministry of Defence.'

'Ah, that's why I came in person. The Min of Def has no use for the cottages right now, and they're being sub-let to the School of Mining. And we *can* use them. I'll explain... We have three potential tenants, affiliates from Stuttgart on secondment to Camborne, mineralogists writing a book. They could be put in student accommodation, but that isn't really on.' His nasal whine indicated that would be beneath them. 'And with the sub-lease and mine alongside... it's perfect.'

'Not for my clients, the new owners. I'll have to tell them.' Carruthers was not enthusiastic. 'Is this a long term residence?'

'Well, I'm neither a mineralogist nor an author, so as long as it takes.' Mortimer peered at the contract. 'Lease in perpetuity.' Carruthers picked up the contract and studied it in detail.

'Thirty pounds a month. You're an accountant, can you find out whether this sum has been paid every month since 1945? But I suppose that's my responsibility, for probate...' Mortimer interrupted him, looking relieved at being the bearer of good news at last.

'There I can help you. I was in London last week, sorting this out. The Min of Def held their hands up. Not only did "Chronos Investments" never receive any rent payments for the lease – things must have been really chaotic back then – but nor did Ingram. I understand Chronos went into liquidation ten years ago, so I'd surmise that the entire sum due now accrues to these new owners? As it's an inheritance, you say?' Carruthers nodded. He normally spent Sundays gardening. And even on a weekday this would have been a very unusual event.

'Do you know the sum due?' Mortimer gave a rare smile.

'Better than that.' He drew out a cheque from Her Majesty's Government for nine thousand pounds. He handed it to Carruthers.

'This is made out to Ingram. Can you endorse it to my escrow account?' He scribbled the account number on the back, Mortimer wrote two lines and signed it. 'Well, at least that bit of today's news is welcome.' He filed the cheque, looking thoughtful. He adopted his favourite reedy, nasal tone which he always used to intimidate clients whose behaviour seemed dubious and steepled his fingers in imaginary prayer, looking for all the world like a judge about to pass the death sentence.

'Bear with me, if you please, for this is not directly your responsibility... Mmmm... this document...' he tapped the lease contract between the Ministry of Defence and "Chronos Investments", '... was signed in August 1945. We are now June, 1974.' Carruthers made some calculations in pencil on a jotter; he detested the new-fangled calculators which had only one outcome, the dulling of any ability in mental arithmetic. 'You being an accountant will help you to keep up.' he commented, still scribbling. Mortimer, who was nothing of the kind, was feeling distinctly uncomfortable. He had not foreseen this eventuality, and MI6 left the mathematics to those qualified, which he was not. Carruthers continued in his dry, legal voice.

'1945 to 1974... well, that gives us whole years for 1946 to 1973, 27 years times 12 months per year is... 324 months when rent was due,' he peered at Mortimer penetratingly, 'but rent was not paid, as it contractually should have been. Now, if we add five months August to December for 1945, and January to June for this year, the actual rent payable for the entire period of unpaid funds will be £30 times... 333 months, which would render a net income of... £9,990 pounds.' He opened the file again and took out the cheque dramatically, holding it to the light as if the better to see the sum paid. 'But this... seems to have been rounded down to £9,000. Hmmm...' He paused theatrically. Mortimer was already totally lost and Carruthers was about to confound him completely. 'But there is more. This is not just an underpayment of £ 990, there are two further complications.'

Mortimer dreaded what was coming next and forced his face into the MI6 manual's "stone faced" response, but a tic below his left eye belied the strain. Carruthers, who had practised not just as a solicitor but also as a barrister, did not miss it. Even while making more calculations he was wondering what, precisely, Mortimer really was.

'In 1946, a four bedroomed house in Cornwall sold for £1,750, believe it or not. Today's value is, on average, £28,000. So an increase in venal value of 17 times that of 1945. Which, if applied to the supposed monthly rent of £30 would put the monthly rent today at £510.00.' He peered at Mortimer. 'I am sure that you, as an accountant will have had no difficulty in following... so I suppose you agree with my calculations?' Mortimer hadn't a clue, just swallowed and nodded wordlessly. 'Good. But there is the second complication...'

Oh, no! Mortimer steeled himself, feeling like a total dunce, which in this situation is what he was. 'By my calculation, the annual rent payable today should be £6,120 per annum. Two-thirds of what the MoD considers the sum due for...' He adopted a tone of incredulity, '... *28 years.*' He paused. Now he served the *coup de grâce*. 'I have not the slightest doubt that a Tribunal would find in favour of the MoD's annual rental liability being indexed annually since 1946 to the base rate of savings accounts which would have benefited the lessors, both in net income and in savings earning that level of interest. My clients, by inheritance. D'you see?' He peered artificially across the desk. 'Because government salaries, and more importantly *procurements*, have always been indexed to the base rate since the war. And inflation has been rampant...' Mortimer clutched at the only straw in sight.

'But you did say that Camborne is not responsible...' His voice tailed away as he saw Carruthers' stern face.

'No. I said Camborne is not ***directly*** responsible. But as sub-lessees Camborne needs to know that I shall be writing to the MoD with a codicil to this contract, as follows. My clients will, at their pleasure and without prejudice extend the lease to the MoD on an annual basis, with the right to cancel for the end of each calendar year. If the MoD refuses, my clients will take the case before the Rents Tribunal, demanding the arrears as calculated by the Tribunal and immediate termination of the lease on the grounds of breach of contract. I assume you must have lines of communication with the lessees, the MoD?' Mortimer nodded, greatly relieved. At least, then, the use of the Safe House would not be compromised for the duration of the Germans' quarantine there.

'It would be courteous of us to inform them, and say that as sub-lessees we accept that condition.'

'Good.' Carruthers looked at his watch. 'Well, I'm in regular contact with the new owners, in fact one is my Legal Assistant and secretary. Will you notify me in good time of the arrival of your mineralogists?' Mortimer nodded. This conveniently brought him to the final hurdle for MI6, security checks on these owners.

'If you give me their names, I'll have them put on file in the School of Mines. And we'll certainly let you know in good time. Oh, and there's something else you should tell them. The Min of Def told me there's no road access to the Estate from Polmouth, in fact none to Polmouth either. They said it's our responsibility to check furniture, bedding, whatever's needed. We'll be bringing it in by helicopter.' Carruthers did not find this unusual.

'They got that right. I'll warn the owners. Plenty of flat land. Oh, and it may help to know that the cottages are fully furnished, all that's missing are mattresses and carpets. If that helps...?'

Mortimer was relieved. This just left the problem of the real Camborne School being called in to inspect the mine when the Germans were living in the cottages. It would be risky in the extreme to have three impostors living beside the mine, purporting to be from Camborne Mining School with a dozen Camborne experts inspecting the mine. But how to avoid it? He had an idea, his training in subterfuge providing the perfect cover. Carruthers handed him the two owners' names "c/o Carruthers and Charteris, Polhaven". Mortimer invented cold-bloodedly.

'About these three Germans…' he seized Carruthers' notepad and scribbled the three names, 'as I said they're affiliated with my School, but they're not on the payroll.' He shrugged. 'Frankly, we couldn't afford them, hence the free accommodation. They're from Stuttgart University, West Germany. Would it be possible to ask the new owners…' he consulted Carruthers' paper, 'Mr. Penpolney and Miss Zabrinski, whether our German guests may accompany our engineers when they inspect the mine for the owners? Be very helpful…' his voice tailed away. A meeting between the East German scientists and the mining experts was the last thing he intended to happen, but the request seemed eminently logical to Carruthers, if overly polite.

'I don't see a problem with that.' Carruthers nodded. 'Well, you've given me quite a handful, today.'

'Sorry about that.' Mortimer feigned the apology. 'Took me by surprise, as well. And sorry to have disturbed you on a Sunday.' Surprisingly, Carruthers grinned.

'Nine thousand pounds in favour of my clients, it was worth the interruption. And the financial matters are not Camborne's direct affair. And, of course, you've simplified my completion of probate. God forbid I should have learned of this after completion, that would be a thorny one. So thank you. Don't forget to let me know when these mineralogists are arriving, and the helicopter, so they can be given the keys then.' Mortimer left and went to the nearest phone box. He called

London, requesting immediate security checks on Zabrinski and Penpolney, then caught the bus back to Penlyn.

Carruthers looked at his watch. Midday. He sought a slip of paper in the folder, and called Colin Penpolney. After a short monologue during which Colin listened silently, Carruthers said:

'D'you want to come in with Miss Zabrinski to hear this face to face? Or will you tell her?'

'I'm seeing her this evening. I'll tell her. These tenants must be important, if Camborne's using a helicopter...'

'Not as grand as it sounds.' Carruthers corrected him. 'I hear it's the School's, to access distant mine workings. And they're all Germans, University of Stuttgart.' Colin looked pleased.

'Then I'll be able to practise my German. Fine. I'll tell Petra. Have a good weekend.' The two men rang off and Carruthers went to lunch. He had already elected to spend the afternoon gardening. Colin, on the other hand, swallowed a sandwich before calling Renwick Removals in Polhaven and leaving a message on their answerphone to book their services. Then he sat down at his dining table and started to write.

'A helicopter?!' They were seated at the bar in the "Crab and Lobster". The waiter, who had seen them from his station in the adjacent restaurant, sighed. 'Must be VIPs then.'

Colin shook his head, then looked at Petra's glass.

'No, I think it's furniture and stuff they can't get up the track. In fact, they can't even get whatever it is to Polmouth. Makes sense.'

'Then we should hire one as well, for all our furniture, to get it up from the village.' Colin shook his head.

'We've got to get Mr. Ingram's stuff out and down to the village before we bring ours up. I suggested Wednesday, to Sarah. Can you be ready by then?' Petra nodded.

'I still say we can afford a helicopter...'

'That's one dual signature I shan't be signing. Great Horses and farm carts, more romantic.' He looked at her mineral water again. 'Have you gone off G&T?' She pulled a wry face.

'Tell you later. Which bedroom d'you want? In our new home...' Colin shrugged.

'You choose first, still leaves me four.'

'Let's go up again tomorrow, have a closer look, And I can be packed by Wednesday midday. Will that be enough time, to move in?'

'We'll be camping the first night. By the way, I'm hopeless at interior décor. You do the furniture placing and all that.' He had a thought. 'We're going to have two of most things. Two colour TVs, for example.' Petra waved a nonchalant hand.

'We'll put your stuff in the Tea Room, and on the veranda. You can keep your bed, though.' Colin gave a broad smile.

'We're on the same wave length.' He held up a sheaf of papers. 'I'd like you to have a look at these... shall we eat?' With feminine curiosity Petra almost pulled him to their table. Stony faced, the waiter brought menus. He was discouraged to see Colin place them on a spare chair and spread papers over the table. Petra shuffled rapidly through a dozen neatly handwritten sheets. Wide eyed, she said:

'We *are* on the same wave length. When did you do all this? Today?'

'This afternoon.'

'Well this time, I can truly see why they made you Head Boy.' She picked up the menus, handed one to Colin. 'I'm hungry. Will you order wine, white, to go with fish?' Colin signalled to the waiter.

'The sole?' suggested the waiter impatiently. Both nodded and Colin named a wine. This time the waiter's eyes widened with anticipation. There was a huge mark-up on that vintage. He hurried away.

'On the same wavelength,' Petra repeated. She glanced at the top sheet. 'We agree on this, the railway has not only to come first, but be absolutely established. But what if British Rail prevaricate again?'

'We need to know what's in that investment portfolio, its value. But whatever it is, if we get trains, well *a train* running from Penlyn to Polport station and back, every day, I'm sure we'll get a contribution from the Village Council, and all the ticket money, of course. A blessing that the station, line and all that belong to the village.'

'Head Boy, indeed.' murmured Petra, her black eyes fixed on Colin's face. The waiter brought the wine, performed an elaborate ceremony on the bottle and presented the label to Colin who shook his head.

'My partner will do the tasting.' This was a request that the male chauvinist waiter had never heard before. A twitch of a smile teased Petra's lips as she lifted her glass. She nodded and wine was poured.

'Cheers, partner!' She raised her glass and leant across to kiss Colin briefly on the lips. 'So you think we should put in the money for the railway, get it running anyway, whatever becomes of the project?'

'Polmouth desperately needs that railway. Everything is there, station, points, rails and track, it all belongs to the village. I'm thinking of us creating the "Felix Ingram Foundation", and getting a service going as soon as possible. If British Rail won't play ball, we'll ask the West Cornwall Light Railway Society. Steam'd be really good to attract the public, but with the miners' strike... And once we know the value of the portfolio... we could inject funds, keep the fifty thousand for immediate expenses, and as a safety net... d'you think?' Petra nodded, her eyes glistening.

'But Ingram's problem was funding. Don't tell me the pupil has surpassed the mentor?'

The waiter arrived and started expertly to fillet two huge sole on a side table.

'Later. Let's eat.' Colin reached out his arm to the bottle to replenish the glasses but Petra got there first, her eyes still sparkling.

During the meal there was no further mention of the "Felix Ingram Foundation", nor the project, but it was preoccupying both diners. It was only after dessert that Petra plucked up the courage.

'About those bedrooms...' she began hesitantly.

'One for you, one for me. Where's the problem? We'll choose tomorrow.'

'Well, I was thinking, for the Guest House one day... if the Great Horses and carts are fetching and carrying all day Wednesday... we should get some beds up and install them at the same time, for the future.' she finished ambiguously. 'And bedding, sheets...' Colin looked at her curiously, then he understood but he continued in an off-hand voice.

'The big bedroom could be a king size. I'll let you decide all that, I told you, I'm no good with interiors.'

'So that's one cheque you'll countersign?'

'Buy really good bedding for really good beds. Don't skimp for my sake...'

'No risk.' Petra lit a cigarette, her heart thumping. 'There's a clearance sale at Polbeds Ltd in Polhaven. I'll go tomorrow, test some. And then...' she hesitated, 'We'll need carpets...' Colin was still smiling.

'Whatever, just don't buy a piano, as well.' He thought for a moment. 'How will you get them across the estuary?'

'I'll try to book them on Wednesday's morning barge to Polport. We can pick them up at the harbour with the helicopter-horses.' She looked at the bar. 'It's time for my G&T. Come on.' As they were crossing to bar stools, Colin spoke.

'About that...'

'About what?' They sat down.

'Have you always drunk that much of that poison? Or what?' Petra reddened and looked embarrassed.

'You truly don't miss much, do you? I never drink the stuff, normally, just kept a bottle at home for Adrian. The toad!'

'Is that spelt "my ex"?'

'Right first time.' The barman approached but Colin waved him away.

'So why...?' Petra shrugged.

'It's been a big shock... I mean us, Ingram, the Estate, the mine, Brick Croft, farm, horses... I went over the top. And by the way, sorry about tucking me in and all that, I had no right...'

'On the contrary.' Colin smiled. 'I'd do it again, any time. So what do you usually drink?' Encouraged, Petra persisted.

'Give you three guesses.' He studied her face, then unashamedly her figure, ending with her legs. 'Uh-uh! Don't go there again!' She was playful.

'I've seen all I need to know. Cider.' She looked surprised.

'How could you possibly know?'

'Oh, those rosy cheeks, and of course the Apple.'

'I do **not** have a red face. And what Apple?' He let his gaze come to rest on her generous bosom and now Petra did go red.

'You know... the Apple of Discord, in the Garden of Eden... surely you did basic Theology?' Petra's face cleared and her giggle returned.

'Piffle!' she exclaimed gaily. 'I reckon you took a peek in my drinks cabinet while I was getting undressed!'

'As a pretty girl with nice legs, called Fräulein "e & a", said recently, you don't miss much. I admit it. No rosy cheeks, no Apple of Discord.' He thought about this, glancing again at her breasts. 'Then again... well, no discord anyway. Will you be cancelling the lease on your little cottage, when you move?' The switch had her fazed.

'Uh… hadn't thought about it, suppose so.' She stared at him. 'Why?'

'What's the rent?'

'Where are you going with this? Three pounds a week. But why?'

'I think you should keep it. Might come in handy…'

'Oh, no!' Petra groaned theatrically. 'Don't tell me you're planning on installing another Helga in there! I'm not countersigning that!'

'I told you, I don't know anyone called Helga. I was thinking of where to store Ingram's furniture from next Wednesday, when we move it all out, and keep it there until the train's running. Then it can go to Penlyn, for auction.' The barman moved in impatiently. Petra nodded to Colin and he ordered her cider and something she had never heard of. Petra was searching for the right avenue in his maze.

'You took a degree in German, right?' Colin nodded. 'What did you get?' He shrugged.

'Upper second. I was happy with that. I hated the Literature, so I neglected it. My own fault.'

'I reckon you deserved a first. Ever thought of taking the test to join "Mensa"?' Now Colin gave a rare laugh.

'Well, if we did, you'd beat me hollow, you studied Latin.'

Petra was having a hard time keeping up with the suddenly ethereal Colin Penpolney. The waiter finally served the drinks and she seized her glass greedily, then paused, staring at his tiny glass and some green liquid in it. 'What's that?'

'A special brew, not everywhere stocks it. They get it for me specially.'

'But what is it?'

'Try a sip, first. But just a sip, 55% proof…' She tested it on her lips and winced.

'Heck, it burns! So…'

'Chartreuse, French liqueur, made by monks in the mountains.' She stared.

'You're having me on!' Colin waved a nonchalant hand.

'Remind me, when or if we ever get a holiday, to take you there. Hope you don't suffer from vertigo, though. They live in the sky.' Petra finally got to taste her cider, half-emptying the glass in one draught. 'Now, about Ingram's furniture...' Colin returned to earth with a bump. Petra made a final effort to take the upper hand.

'Yes, about that.' She inspected Colin's arms. 'You're not an all-in wrestler, and two litres of cider is all I can carry... Solution?' Colin was still strangely nonchalant.

'I have that sorted.' he said vaguely. 'So we move on Wednesday?'

'I wish it was tomorrow.' Her voice was wistful, and her dark eyes were fixed on his face. 'I don't remember you being like this at school...' her voice was hesitantly admiring.

'That was six years ago. And besides, you only knew me as Pantalone, me, a bearded old git marrying off his daughter. You. I think I prefer this arrangement.' Petra drained her glass, signalled to the waiter.

'Tonight's on me, fair's fair.' She thrust money at the waiter with a dismissive gesture. 'Largesse of the landed gentry,' she giggled to Colin. 'Now you can walk me home. Unless you have anything better to do...' He coughed gently.

'Fact is, I'm not very good at flirting. Never was...'

'You bloody well are, liar!' She had her arm through his as they left the inn and turned up the narrow cobbled streets to Harbour Lane.

'So why did no-one ever tell me this before?' Colin adopted a plaintive, injured tone.

'Glad they didn't! You'd have been unbearable.' They had reached the low door to her cottage, and she retrieved her key from under the plant pot.

'And I'm bearable now?'

'Come in, and find out!' He shook his head.

'Just for a minute or two, then I'm off home.'

'I told you, home starts next week.' She pulled him relentlessly inside and closed the door. 'Little Clarice wants Pantalone daddy to tuck her in again.' She made for the bedroom door. 'You did say "any time"...'

'And I meant it. So I'll study the locksmith's expertise on your bedroom door, while you prepare for...' There was a long silence during which she prevented either of them from completing the sentence. Then she gently released him and he dutifully turned his back to examine a masterpiece of nineteenth century engineering. Five minutes later he placed her front door key under its plant pot, and walked to Cliff Rise Mews. But he did not go to his apartment for long, he spent only two minutes there, then made his way through the narrow cobbled streets towards the track to Polmine Estate. Under the light of a generous three-quarter moon he strode up the slope. He was indeed going "home". Better, he was "coming" home and he had the keys in his hand.

It was after midnight when Colin reached the plateau. The farmhouse was in darkness, but the whole Estate was bathed in pale, silver light. He advanced to the mine workings then turned left onto the track alongside the railway line. It took him only minutes to walk to the Croft House, the moonlight setting the waters of the adjacent lakes sparkling. Colin mounted the two steps up to the terrace, then turned to survey their Estate. Only now was the enormity of his and Petra's inheritance sinking in. His gaze crossed the rough terrain to the distant mine workings, then further, over the cliff edge to the grey sea where a number of trawlers' glowing lights indicated that they were indeed trawling. Colin walked round the side of the house, pulled the keys from his pocket and went inside. He tried the light switch and a naked bulb illuminated the kitchen. He crossed to the sink, turned on the tap, but the water spurted out deep brown and unpalatable. Upstairs he entered the late Ingram's spartan bedroom, the bed neatly made, and everything in place, as if Felix Ingram might return at any moment, and berate him and his class for messing around with "dog Latin", such as *"ego sum imperator"*, to which he would snap: "Verb at the end! ***Imperator sum***! How often must I tell you?!" Colin walked down a corridor to the remaining four bedrooms, paused in each, switching on the lights, leaving them burning as he passed from room to room. He was finding the burden which Ingram had placed on his shoulders and Petra's increasingly heavy.

Downstairs again, he repeated the pilgrimage through the reception rooms, the intended Tea Room, and back out to the terrace, the moonlight and the distant sea. His mind was made up. He was home.

An hour later, all lights extinguished, he lay down fully dressed on Ingram's bed, scenting the essence of an elderly man's handicap, his increasing bitterness, his defeat. And increasingly conscious of that extraordinary man's battle, his resolve, and now his final gesture of defiance, the legacy. Colin stared up at the ceiling in the darkness.

'This time,' he muttered into the darkened room, 'this time it *will* work.' He closed his eyes, and envisaged the completed project, groups of school children, a puffing steam train chugging across the Estate, the rowing boats on the sunlit lake... Home.

Chapter Ten

Monday dawned grey and cloudy, the moist Atlantic air a harbinger of rain to come. Petra took the early morning ferry across the estuary to Polhaven. Although beds and carpets were on her list, she first called in at Chambers. She knocked and walked in to find Carruthers at his desk. He looked up in surprise.

'I told you to take a week's holiday,' he said, 'so unless you've had a row with your new partner, or are here as a valued client...?'

'May I sit down? I'm here as a client, I suppose.' He waved her to sit down at the desk. 'If you have a moment?' He nodded and closed the file on his desk.

'I'm all yours...'

'Actually, I have quite a lot of questions. We have several major plans in mind, Mr. Penpolney and I, so we were wondering if you can find out the current value of the investments?' Carruthers reached to one side of the desk and pulled the Ingram file in front of him.

'I called Ingram's broker first thing this morning. He seems to have invested for more than ten years in Unit Trusts.'

'Never heard of them.'

'A brokerage company selects a palette – in simple English, a basket – of investments, stocks and shares, that are known to be good performers, or seem promising. Middle class investors use them because returns are modest but risk is very low. Well, Mr. Ingram was involved with several. All of them performed well, particularly those with a holding in Nestlé, Boots, the high fliers. According to Samuelson, the broker, the current value, if sold, stands at...' He opened the file and leafed through the top papers. '...four hundred and eighty-three thousand pounds.'

Petra's mouth opened involuntarily and she had to make a conscious effort to close it.

'Half a million pounds?' she said incredulously. 'My God!'

'An impressive sum, for a Latin teacher,' murmured Carruthers. 'I'll be transferring the Deeds to your names today, so you have immediate access. Samuelson will advise on which to sell for the best return, and which to keep as longer term investments, if you wish to release some liquidity.' Petra tried to compose herself.

'If I act as your Assistant for a moment, may I make you... us some tea, sir?'

'Willingly. A pot and two cups, then.' He paused. 'This is getting to be a habit... By the way, as an esteemed client, please drop the"sir".' She smiled and went to boil the kettle. Half a million pounds... What had possessed Ingram to name her and Colin as sole beneficiaries?

In his office Carruthers was asking himself the same question.

In his tiny apartment in Polmouth Colin was at work early. He first called Penzance library and asked to speak to his friend Jake Richards. After a short conversation which satisfied him he steeled himself for the next call to Rodney Hastings, the owner of Polhaven book shop. This call lasted considerably longer and was singularly acrimonious. Colin waited for Hastings' flood of irritated comments about the unreliability of the young generation, how he had hoped for better things from Colin, to abate. When Hastings finally paused for breath, Colin jumped in.

'Mister Hastings, I have found a replacement, someone much better qualified than I for the shop. Name's Jake Richards, my age, he was Assistant School Librarian at Penlyn Grammar, took a degree at the LSE and he lives in Polhaven but is working as a voluntary librarian assistant at Penzance library. He can start immediately, and he'd be really pleased if he could take my place...' Hastings was mollified on learning that "the young generation" had at least a spark of decency.

'When can he start?' His voice was still aggressive.

'I suggested next Monday.' Hastings was in a corner, and he knew it. He had no contract with Colin Penpolney.

'Tell him to come in at eight.' Hastings rang off, putting down the receiver with a bang. Colin called Penzance again and told Jake the good news.

'We have plans.' Petra informed Carruthers. 'Ambitious. Can we authorise the sale of one hundred thousand pounds of the Unit things, and can you open two bank accounts in our joint names, one current with two cheque books and a savings account with the best interest? Say, half and half to each account?' Carruthers was scribbling notes rapidly. He sighed.

'If only all my clients could be so clear and concise. It'll be done by the end of trading today.' He looked at her speculatively. 'May I know the general gist of these plans?'

'Well, for starters, we're moving into the Croft House. On Wednesday. So we'll need furniture and stuff.' Carruthers started to revise his dismissal of demented Ingram having concocted some lunatic match-making scenario out of a Rossini opera. 'And we're determined to open the railway as soon as possible. Mr. Penpolney is contacting British Rail today, and if they're reluctant, we'll try the West Cornwall Light Railway people.' Carruthers pen was speeding across his note pad. He put down the pen and looked at Petra admiringly.

'Well, you certainly don't hang about! That's two major undertakings... Ahh, I think I see what the next question will be. Well, yes is the answer, electricity, gas, water are all connected and I'll change the billing details forthwith. I believe the telephone has been cut – not sure about the cottages – so I'll register that in joint names today as well, have it reconnected tomorrow.' Petra looked diffident.

'Many thanks for all that, but actually they were lower down my list.' Absent in this conversation was any sign of a list in her hand. Carruthers knew that appointing her had been one of his best decisions. He just hoped she wouldn't contemplate leaving.

'So... next?'

'We'll need to know all the annual outgoings... rates, water rates, Council tax, anything else like that, but it's not urgent. When you can get round to it.' Carruthers had reached the third sheet of his notepad. 'And the last thing is, can you give me five more signed cheques to draw on our funds for some urgent expenses?' Carruthers opened a drawer and took out the cheque book. He handed the five cheques to Petra.

'And that's all?' He glanced at the wall clock. 'Good Lord, a record! Client's orders, given, received and noted in less than half an hour! Now, unless you're in a hurry to be out of here, I have a few questions for you, as Legal Assistant, as a friend, and as a client. I'll try to be as concise as you.'

Colin's morning consisted of a seemingly never-ending series of telephone calls. If Carruthers had covered three pages of notes, by midday Colin had scribbled ten. But his morning had been far more rewarding than he could ever have hoped. Petra covered a lot of ground as well, but on foot. Having bought three beds, a quantity of Bassetti bedding and carpets for the bedrooms and reception rooms, she finally reserved the Wednesday morning barge for the furniture and carpets and took the midday ferry back to Polport for lunch in the "Crab and Lobster".

They met at the bar. Colin was looking quietly self-satisfied, Petra smug. They carried their drinks to a reserved table. The time-server of a waiter looked on in dismay.

'You go first,' Colin encouraged her, laying the two menus flat on a spare chair. The waiter had expected nothing else. He rolled his eyes.

Petra's report was as concise as her requests had been to Carruthers. Colin wasn't sure whether he appreciated the more her sharp, precise mind, or the fact that it served to highlight the dichotomy with her bubbly, effervescent nature socially.

'I think we'd better order, because my news may take a little longer. I'll keep my good news for after lunch.' He handed her a menu. She looked at him quizzically.

'Does that mean your news is so bad it'll spoil my appetite?' He laughed, reached across the table and covered her hand.

'That's my answer!' Her face cleared.

'Good enough for me, you never laugh! Oh, and I learned something we didn't know before, about the farm and Ingram's plan.'

'Food!'

'In a minute… there's a forge on the farm, where they make horseshoes. And a smelting furnace, to make iron.' Colin looked astonished.

'I thought it had been a dairy farm? And how can they make iron?' Petra shook her head sadly. Colin's hand was still firmly over hers and she made no attempt to remove it.

'Colin, I thought you were high IQ! The entire plateau is iron ore deposits… they have a trench, opencast mine. That's how.' He gulped.

'Food…'

Over coffee Petra could no longer contain her curiosity.

'Your turn.'

'I may not be as brief as you, there's a lot of technical stuff for the railway. I'll condense. British Rail: they passed me to the guy who handled Ingram's request ten years back, and that helped. Since British Railways became BR, they've improved their customer service...'

'In brief?' Petra nudged him forwards.

'Sorry... Well, there's still a water and coal facility at Penlyn for the summer steam trains from Falmouth to Penzance run by West Cornwall Light Railway. That was the first tick. Second, BR will unconditionally lease us a two coach diesel all year round for four trips a day, seven days a week, Penlyn to Polport and back, one passenger coach, one freight...'

'I need more than coffee!' exclaimed Petra and signalled to the waiter urgently. 'Unconditionally?' Colin reddened.

'Nearly... provided we pay each year's lease up front, linked to inflation, and they'll run trains as soon as we can have a positive engineer's report for the track, eighteen miles of it.'

'I'm listening.'

'It gets better... West Cornwall will lease us their steam train, locomotive and two passenger coaches, all year round on request, but not weekends in the high season...'

'Which is?'

'Weekends July to end of August. That's when they use it.'

'Go on...'

'Better still, they have two retired BR drivers who are hankering after the Good Old Days, and they'll stoke and get steam up, and replenish the boiler and coal at Penlyn. One of them has a daughter here in Polmouth, so they agree to leave the train overnight in Polport and he'll stay at his daughter's. Poor old duffer never gets to see his grandchildren, he'll welcome overnights. And he'll get steam up in the morning.' Petra's glass was still full.

'Good God! And they say pensioners are a burden on the state. I thought my morning had gone well. Is there more?'

'You haven't touched your drink.'

'Don't tease! More!'

'West Cornwall will send their engineers out tomorrow to verify the track from Penlyn to Polport, and then the spur to the Croft and on to the mine.'

'Eighteen miles? On foot?!'

'Not my problem. Just let's hope they don't find any major items. Because BR can start the service the day after we get the engineers' all clear.'

'Like this week?' Colin nodded. Petra suddenly looked serious.

'And can we afford all this?' He nodded.

'British Rail must really be in difficulties, financially I mean. They're asking peanuts, but I told you chartering trains isn't expensive. The man who handled Ingram's request, today's man, told me the company hates having rolling stock sitting idle on the sidings when it could be earning revenue. So we keep any ticket revenue, BR gets the lease money up front.'

'Uh-huh. And West Cornwall?'

'They're a registered charity, so the amount they can charge is capped. Well within our means, and now you say the investments are that big...'

'So we need to meet the Village Council President, tell him. Ask what they'll contribute.' But Colin shook his head.

'Let's get the track given the all clear, then tell him. Oh, and by the way, I've given up the job in the bookshop. Forthwith.'

'I'll bet that went down well!' He shrugged.

'Wasn't best pleased. But it's necessary. One of Ingram's mistakes was trying to launch his project while still working full time.'

'The major problem was funding. Ideas?' Colin looked awkward.

'I'd rather broach that when we have more time.'

'We have time now!'

'No, we don't. We have thirty-six hours to pack up everything we possess for the removals men on Wednesday morning. That's how I'll be spending my afternoon.' Petra looked astonished.

'Removals men? What removals men?!'

'I told you, I have it sorted.'

'You're too good for "Mensa", the IQ people. Can we meet tonight, dinner?'

'I'd be very disappointed if we don't. Have you brought an umbrella?' He pointed at the window. The rain was pelting down, gurgling in the drainpipe.

'No.'

'Then it's as well I thought of that.' He pointed to the coat stand. 'It's big enough for two.'

'"Mensa",' she muttered again and drained her glass.

By seven that evening the rain had stopped and the clouds were clearing to the East, but Colin was taking no chances. He folded his umbrella and crossed to Petra at the bar of the "Crab and Lobster". He had opted for casual dress, jeans and a T-shirt, but Petra, after her embarrassment at the previous meeting in clothes that clashed, was wearing a silk Laura Ashley confection that floated to ankle length, but clung promisingly to her bosom, which was why she had bought it. When she saw him approaching she realised she had misjudged again.

'I'll get it right one day.' she said gaily, eying him up and down.

'I'd rather you didn't,' remarked Colin. 'Must have cost you a fortune. Excellent taste. What shall I... silly question.' He turned to the barman and ordered a cider. The barman looked at Colin questioningly. 'I'm thinking. Serve the lady.' He perched himself on a bar stool beside her. 'D'you think Ingram knew?' His voice was soft, very bass, gritty almost. Petra sensed that he was emotional; it touched her without knowing why.

'What?'

'That we're destined to succeed, you and I, to achieve, to realise his dream, his project? But there's more.' The cider was served and Colin ordered a bottle of a special red vintage, to be decanted, not poured. The barman had never decanted a bottle in his life and signalled wildly to the waiter who, seeing his least favourite guests at the bar, approached unwillingly. The barman muttered in the waiter's ear. The latter's face cleared, and he dragged the barman to the wine cellar. Minutes later the waiter reappeared without the barman and took his place.

'What's tonight's meat special?' Colin asked. The waiter, who had by now realised that these two had more money than most of the villagers put together, glanced furtively over his shoulder. In a low voice he said:

'We have a saddle of venison, with red cabbage and chestnuts, pasta. Only accept orders for two or more, and it'd be about forty-five minutes. Oh, and all the trimmings…, peach slice and cherries…' Petra nodded and Colin gave the order. The waiter hurried to the kitchen.

'More?' Petra prompted, sipping her cider. Colin looked deep into her black eyes, then at her blond ponytail. She looked like a well-dressed debutante at her first ball.

'I think… I think he's adopted us *in absentia*. In fact, I'm certain of it. He never had any children, never married. But that does present me with a slight problem… potentially.'

'Which is?'

'Well, that makes you my adopted sister, who just happens to be the girl whom I've kissed passionately three times in as many days… you see?'

'It's four, actually. Times. *I* did it that time. And it's not a problem! Cleopatra married her brother, so there's an excellent precedent.'

Colin decided to overlook the marriage part of the precedent.

'Hardly a very helpful analogy. She proceeded to murder her husband, I mean brother, and after his assassination started screwing around with Julius Caesar, and when she got tired of him, screwed his best friend Mark Anthony. Not a very promising comparison. And she finally committed suicide by clasping an asp, a poisonous snake to her naked breast...' Colin's eye fell involuntarily on the generous bosom in front of him. 'And incited the serpent to bite her there with fatal snake venom. I don't think Ingram saw things turning out like that... And to cap it all, you're blonde, and far prettier than the raven-haired bitch Cleo. You see my problem? What, I'm wondering, am I getting myself into? Or rather, into what has Ingram plunged us?' Petra grasped at the nearest, the only straw.

'I thought you studied German, not Ancient History?'

'Oh, that was just General Knowledge. And by the way, Adrian "The Toad" was certainly wrong in what he said.' Colin looked for the barman, but it was the waiter who approached carrying a carafe of the precious vintage as if it was the centre piece of the Crown Jewels. He poured a soupçon into a tiny tasting glass. Colin sniffed it, tasted and nodded. The waiter poured one glass then looked at Petra. She shook her head.

'Later.' He put down the carafe and left. 'Go on about "The Toad". What was he wrong about?'

'About you being boring, you're not. Wrong, too, about whatever else he said.'

'I didn't think so either. Remind me what this "whatever else" was.' Colin looked over his shoulder, verifying that the restaurant was sparsely populated. Petra giggled, turning the tables. She adopted a deep, gravelly voice: '*Come, come, not so shy now!*' Colin placed his hands on her shoulders and stared into her black eyes from a distance of inches. When he spoke, his throat was dry.

'It was this...' The embrace seemed to last an eternity. It was perhaps fortunate that the waiter and barman were deep in gossip at the other end of the curved bar, out of sight. Colin released her. 'I'm sorry... I told you, I'm no good at flirting.'

Petra burst out laughing and seized his arm, led him to their table. The waiter brought the carafe and two new glasses.

'Saddle of venison, twenty minutes.' he announced. He knew he was in for a long evening with these two, but the wine cost the "Crab and Lobster" forty-nine pounds wholesale and was priced at one hundred and eleven pounds in the wine list. He felt the platform shoes of imminent promotion to sommelier; a late finish to his shift was a small price to pay. Petra returned to the immediate issues.

'Half a million will go a long way. But Ingram's mistake wasn't only teaching full time, not having enough time for his project. It was funding, or rather insufficiency. I asked you "Has the pupil surpassed his mentor?" Has he?'

'He may have, time will tell. Ingram targeted only three sources, the DES, the LEA and Camborne School of Mines. We need a far wider net. I have a list of possibles... take a look.' From the back pocket of his jeans Colin pulled a crumpled typed sheet. Petra studied it.

```
        Felix Ingram Foundation Consortium
            Polmine History Project
             Own funds: £ 100,000


                British Council
               National Heritage
                Exeter University
       Department of Education and Science
      Cornwall Local Education Authority
            Cornwall Tourism Board
              The National Trust
           Camborne School of Mines
            Polmine Village Council
```

'Good Lord!' she muttered. Her black eyes met his again across the table. 'I see what you mean about Ingram... his

intentions, his determination to find two people who...'
She did not complete the sentence of what two people were
destined to do. Together. 'D'you think we should add Devon
LEA and Tourism, now we have the trains? Year round.' Colin
nodded, suddenly animated. 'I can see why you quit your job,
following up all these'll be a full time activity. A lot of calls to
make, presentations to prepare and deliver. Showing visitors
round...' She studied his T-shirt and jeans with a critical eye.
The waiter arrived pushing a trolley on which were plates,
cutlery and the saddle of venison with "the trimmings". He
started to carve the juicy, red meat. Petra hadn't finished.

'You'll need a new suit, preferably two. And so shirts
and matching ties, a selection, and shoes of course. A whole
wardrobe. I can help you with that...' Colin groaned theatrically;
the waiter paused in his carving, listening.

'Oh no! I knew it, I knew it was too good to be true! You *are*
Helga Mark II! Here we go again! New man Colin, in fact you're
worse, she never insisted on suits, just... well...'

'If you compare me to your bloody Helga one more time, I
swear I'll go back to G&Ts and join Hogarth's vagrants on Gin
Lane!' She giggled. 'Am I really like her?' Colin reached out his
arm and covered her hand. The waiter, embarrassed, returned
to his assiduous carving.

'Not in the least, you're as pretty as your brain and wit is
sharp, and if you look in the mirror you'll see that's no mean
feat.' Petra reddened and toyed with the ends of her ponytail.

'That's the nicest thing anyone's ever said to me...' she
mumbled.

'Sorry,' said Colin absently, 'I promise it won't happen
again.'

'Give over!' She was playful. 'You didn't even throw in that
dreadful "pretty now" bit.'

'If a barrister questions me on that, I'll deny I ever said it.'
It was perhaps fortuitous that the waiter finally tore himself
away from this real life Punch and Judy show and served the

steaming plates. Silence now reigned, a strangely amicable harmony verging on the amorous.

'If food be the thingummy of love,' remarked Petra, her mouth full, and wiped her lips.

'It was music, the food of love,' Colin corrected her.

'When we're together, I don't need music.' Her black eyes once again held his across the table, and they were moist. She looked down. 'This is very good.'

They were walking to her home in Harbour Lane, Petra's arm firmly through Colin's and her head resting on his shoulder.

'What are your plans for tomorrow?' she asked him.

'I have some questions for the engineers from W.C.L.R. I'll meet them.'

'If they're walking eighteen miles, how?'

'If they can walk eighteen, I can walk nine, I'll meet them half way. Learn something about railways.'

'I'd come with you, but I'm still packing for Wednesday. But please come in tonight, I have a present for you.' She looked up into his eyes again, compelling him.

'Just for a ...'

'For a minute, I know! Well, here we are. The last time for the flower pot man and his key. Would you?' Colin retrieved the key and let her in. He refrained from saying so but it seemed that she had made very little progress with her packing for the move. She tugged him to the only soft chair, sat down beside the kitchen table on a wooden stool. 'I've got you some of that green French poison, the stuff the monks in the sky brew up... in the cabinet there. And pour me a cider will you?' Colin obliged, handed her the glass and sat down again. 'Oh Colin, tell me this is really happening, I mean, that we're not dreaming. Pie in the sky? I keep thinking I'll wake up and be really disappointed that... I know you understand,' Colin shook his head.

'Nine square miles of land, multiple properties, income from the lease of two of them, a farm that makes horse hooves for ten Great Horses, a railway and half a million in funds… not to mention a stunning sea view. No, they're real, we're real.' Petra drained her glass in satisfaction.

'You've convinced me. Now it's T-I-T.' Colin tried to cover his inner feelings.

'The only tit I know is a bird indigenous to the British Isles and which frequents bird tables and nesting boxes… Oh,' His face cleared. 'Tucking-In-Time. Come on then, lead the way.' In the bedroom he turned to face the door. 'You know, I'll be glad to see the back of this Victorian locksmith's handiwork.' Petra was already between the sheets.

'T-I-T, then,' she whispered. He turned but did not approach the bed. 'If I asked nicely, would you stay? The night?' Colin's mouth twisted strangely as he made a supreme effort.

'You once asked me: "Have you no gallantry?" I try. And you know, that bed is very small and narrow, and I have size twelve feet. But didn't you say we're getting a King Size brand new bed on Wednesday, at home? You do realise that I'll have to test all the beds, at least once each, to make sure they're fit… for purpose?' She giggled, seeing where this was going.

'And *you* do realise that, as business partner, I'll be obliged to do the same?' He nodded, said nothing.

'So come closer, partner, and tuck me in, please.'

Chapter Eleven

Last Mile to Polmouth

Tuesday was another scorching day, the heatwave showing no sign of abating. Petra was up at dawn, stacking crockery, cutlery, knick-knacks, pillows, in fact everything portable into banana boxes from the greengrocer's. Then she turned her attention to the hi-fi unit, the LPs and cassettes. Meanwhile, Colin was already up at the Croft House. The first thing he did was to run the water from every tap in the building. Within minutes the brackish, brown coloured supply was running crystal clear. Next he tried the telephone and was relieved to hear the dialling tone. Everything was coming together. He boiled a kettle of water on the gas stove, then threw the water away and boiled a second. He was starting to feel like a home owner; it was an unnerving sensation.

An hour later he pulled the last of the ground floor furniture through the Tea Room and out to the stack already on the terrace. When he inspected the now empty rooms, the kitchen especially looked bleak and forlorn. All the rooms needed Petra's interior design. Finally, he pulled his diary from his pocket and called the West Cornwall Light Railway office in Falmouth. It was the General Manager who answered, confirming that the engineers were already proceeding along the eighteen miles of track from Penlyn, and should be at the Spur Junction to the Estate around midday. But there was one item of information which he withheld from Colin, news that would have delighted the new owner. Colin decided to walk to meet the men. He unlocked the gate that blocked the railway line out of the Estate, passed through and after locking it again walked briskly between the rails towards Polheath.

His layman's eye could detect no anomalies on the track other than the dried wood of some sleepers. As he reached Polheath and the expanse of gorse, heather and bracken, he stopped to get his breath, stared out over the endless olive green land with purple patches of heather extending to the horizon and the cloudless blue sky. He remembered this view from his countless traverses on the train to and from Penlyn Grammar, but teenage boys are not subject to pantheistic sensibilities unless there are mountains and snow. Now he was seeing the heath through adult eyes. He continued on his way.

At eleven o'clock he saw three men in the distance. One man was walking between the tracks, his head down, visibly inspecting the rails and the sleepers. A second man was carrying a heavy toolbox, the third had a strange, six foot long pole. The first man stopped and crouched down, apparently checking something on a sleeper. He signalled to his colleagues; Mr. Toolbox set down the metal chest and took out some indistinguishable item, while Mr. Pole started twisting his spanner on the object that had caught Number One's attention. The work completed, they resumed their slow walk towards Colin. Minutes later they were introducing themselves.

'Peter Tenworthy, Senior Engineer, my son Paul, and the invaluable bag man, Jerome Penland. You must be the owner of Polmine?' Colin nodded, impatient for an interim report, but his hopes were dashed. 'Well, we're over half way, too early for anything useful to tell you. What's this about Spur Junction, some track through to a mine?'

'I'll tell you as we go. What were you doing back there, when you stopped and worked on something?'

'Here and there we found a loose bolt on a chair.' This had Colin foxed.

'Chair?'

'The nut and bolt fitting holding the rail to the sleeper. We replace a loose nut as we find them. Only three so far.' Peter Tenworthy was slowly advancing, his eagle-eyed inspection unrelenting. 'We'll stop at this Spur Junction, and I'll give you an interim appraisal. For now...' So Colin had to wait to learn whether investment would be necessary before trains could run again. It wasn't that funds were lacking, but the longer it took to get the line operational, the longer he would have to postpone his approach to possible sources of financing.

They finally reached Spur Junction where the rails divided between the last stretch downhill to Polport and the mine extension through the Brick Croft railhead. Colin unlocked the gate and Tenworthy was about to resume his inspection alongside the platform and onwards, but Colin's patience was exhausted.

'This stretch of line's a bit different...' he ventured. 'The main line was in daily use until ten years ago. But to the best of my knowledge, this extension last saw a train in the War, when the Army sequestered the Estate. Not since. More to the point, we shan't want to run trains through beyond the platform here until next year. Other things have priority...'

Young Paul Tenworthy and Jerome Penland looked relieved, easing their knapsacks off their backs, but Senior Engineer Peter Tenworthy was truly driven by his enthusiasm for railways.

'Perhaps just another hundred yards...'

'Dad, we're starving.' his son interjected. 'Is there somewhere we can sit down?' he asked Colin. 'We've brought a packed lunch.' He hefted his knapsack in one hand. Colin pointed to the two lakes fifty yards away.

'There?'

'Perfect... you have a beautiful place here.' They headed for the grassy embankment beside the nearer lake, but Peter

Tenworthy was staring at something between the tracks ahead of him.

'You go on, I'll join you...' he murmured and started to walk slowly along the line, staring at the ground between the rails. Colin accompanied the younger men to the lake.

Tenworthy walked a good deal further than a hundred yards, he had advanced a quarter of a mile when he finally straightened and crossed the rough ground to join his colleagues.

'Well...' he said, and his forehead was wrinkled in a frown. 'Hmmm...' He opened his bag and took out a bottle and sandwiches. Colin was impatient for news but good manners won. He waited while the men munched and drank in silence. Finally:

'So how are things looking?' Peter Tenworthy grinned.

'Better'n I expected, seeing it's been ten years since... We've replaced a few of the nuts on the chairs, expected more, to be honest. Sleepers are heavily weathered, but they're perfectly viable. Need re-impregnating, a tar mixture. But it's not urgent, we can do a few miles at a time in the coming months. No, the main line's perfectly useable. The old limit was 40 miles per hour. I'll authorise that to British Rail tomorrow, no problem. We'll check the final stretch to Polport differently.' A smile flashed across his face, but he quashed it for fear of spoiling the surprise. 'But I'm puzzled by this spur, the extension...'

Colin's relief at the news that trains could start running that same week was suddenly tempered with this last statement.

'As I said, we don't expect to use it for maybe a year. And any repairs are well within my means...' Tenworthy shook his head, looking puzzled.

'It's not a question of whether it's useable... It's almost *too* useable...' He was scratching his head. 'Last used in the forties, you said? The Army? So that's thirty years ago... Never since?' Colin shook his head.

'Not to my knowledge. Why?'

'Well, setting aside the obvious and inevitable growth of thistles, weeds, and that, the section I just checked is in even better condition than the main line, which was used as recently as ten years ago. The Army, you say... Have they been back since?' Colin shook his head, not seeing where this was going.

'They have a lease on two of the miners' cottages. That's it.'

'Do they?! This is beginning to make some sense...'

'What is?' Colin was irritated.

'Did they open the mine, back then?'

'I believe so... but no-one ever knew what they were doing down there. What's all this about?'

'It's this. Those sleepers have been so heavily tarred and impregnated... and the bolts and nuts on the chairs aren't standard issue, they're stainless steel... military would make sense. Royal Engineers, perhaps. No, this railway line hasn't been deserted. It's been mothballed. As if for future use.' He looked at his watch. 'A bit of a mystery, maybe nothing.' He stared around the vast expanse of the Estate, and he noticed ten immensely tall Great Horses wandering lazily around in the rich undergrowth. 'Do they roam free over the whole land?' Colin nodded. 'In that case you should have the line fenced in on both sides, the whole distance to the mine. Problem?' Colin was frowning.

'I can see why, but it'd be terribly unsightly, when the place is open to visitors. Is there no other solution?' Tenworthy reflected.

'Are you intending to run trains here in darkness? Or just daylight hours?'

'Just daytime, shuttle up from Polmouth and back for tourists. Does that make a difference?'

'A big difference. In the early days of steam, when all the trains were slow, most of them used a system called VLR, Visual Lookout Reference. When the train was subject to VLR, the stoker had to climb back onto the coal tender and stand on top, acting as lookout for obstacles, warn the driver in the cab. I could authorise use up to 20 mph using VLR. No fencing needed for that.' Colin looked relieved. The engineer took a last look around. Then: 'Listen, may I use your bathroom over in the house?'

'Of course. We're moving in tomorrow, so it's a bit Spartan. Bathrooms are upstairs.'

But it wasn't the bathroom that Tenworthy really wanted.

'A bit of a liberty, but… do you have a phone? There's a call I need to make.'

'Connected today. In the kitchen. Help yourself.' Tenworthy stood up and made for the house. His son Paul and Jerome Penland knew why and were having difficulty in keeping a straight face. Colin did not know. Innocently, he continued:

'How will you get back to Penlyn, and Falmouth? Not another 18 mile walk?' Jerome squared his jaw.

'That'd be one way. Or we could take the ferry to Polhaven and the bus. We'll see…' But Jerome knew that the three would neither be walking back nor taking the ferry. He changed the subject. 'How'd you come to own this place? It's stunning…'

While Colin was explaining, Peter was on the phone to Falmouth. He put down the receiver. This was like nothing he had ever done before.

In the Falmouth sidings and the locomotive works of the W.C.L.R. the Foreman was beaming.

'Listen up, folks. We've got the green light and you've got an hour. Hose down the coaches. David, the engine for you, and Charlie, you'll be seeing your grandchildren tonight, so get up a good head of steam. Now!'

Everyone working at the W.C.L.R. was a volunteer, almost obsessed with steam engines and railways. None was ever paid, other than a take from the summer season ticket sales, and none worked for money. But the prospect of their pride and joy running all year round in their beloved Cornwall animated them all; the dual prospects of satisfying their passion and receiving some income from it fired them up.

Peter Tenworthy crossed the rough terrain and sat down beside his colleagues.

'Well, lads,' he said and his voice smacked of satisfaction, 'we shan't be walking back!' He looked at Colin. 'We have a surprise for you. Our locomotive "Land's End" will be leaving our depot within the hour to baptise your line. All the way to Polport. Now you have a choice… either you hurry down on foot to bring the good news to the villagers, or you join us and take the train from Spur Junction the last mile down to Polmouth and surprise them. Which is it to be?'

There was a long silence, then Colin stood up and walked to the water's edge to hide his emotions. A train. Today. But only one word was ringing in his inner ear: Ingram.

An hour later the four men were standing by the points at Spur Junction. Colin saw the approaching train in the distance, a plume of white smoke and steam trailing from its chimney as it advanced at a steady forty miles an hour. There was a lump in his throat. The dark green locomotive came ever closer. Its red stripes along the sides and the bronze plaque "Land's End" on the front gleamed in the sunlight. Behind it were two passenger coaches, freshly washed with the gold livery of "WCLR" on the sides. The engine slowed as the drivers saw the men waiting and came to a halt beside them, steam hissing from the pistons.

'You're in First Class,' called Charlie, the retired BR engine driver, holding the inevitable greasy rag in one hand. 'Front coach.'

'Take this last mile slow,' warned Peter, 'should be fine, but it's unverified track so keep to maximum ten mph, okay?'

'You're the boss!' Unable to formulate any coherent thoughts, let alone words, Colin followed the three men into the First Class compartment and closed the door, waved one arm through the open window. The locomotive groaned and the train started to roll. This is surreal, he thought, staring out through the polished glass.

It was a glorious day down in Polmouth, the sun blazing down from a cloudless, blue sky. Janet Magnusson, the greengrocer, was replenishing the boxes of vegetables and fruits on the pavement stand in front of her shop window when she lifted her head, cocked it to one side. I must be mistaken, she thought. In the stillness of a village without cars, sound carried a long way. It can't be... she was thinking, and yet she was hearing the unmistakable puffing and chuntering of a steam engine some distance away, a sound not heard these last ten years. Now came definitive proof, the long whistle of a steam locomotive. She hurried into the next door hairdresser's.

'Millie, come quick! Listen!' She dragged her neighbour out onto the pavement, and put her finger to her lips. 'Listen!' They both now clearly heard the approaching steam train.

'It's a train!' screamed Millie, and dashed off town the steep lane towards Polport station, shouting at everyone that she passed. 'A train! It's a train! Coming in now! Hurry.'

Within minutes more than twenty stupefied villagers of all ages had congregated on the platform of Polport station and were staring expectantly up the line towards the bend where the phantom train must surely soon appear. Other villagers, alerted either by the rumours running from house to house, or by the sound of the steam locomotive getting ever closer, joined the first arrivals on the platform. Soon, half the village seemed to be crowding onto the single platform. Charlie, the engine driver, obeying orders, was advancing at a paltry ten miles an hour on unverified track.

In her bare kitchen with everything packed up and ready for the removals men next morning, Petra heard someone knocking urgently at her door. It was her neighbour.

'A train!' the woman screamed semi-hysterically. 'It's a train, coming in now. You have got to see this...' She ran down the cobbled lane. But Petra did not run. She listened, heard the unmistakable puffing of a steam engine close to the village, and getting closer. She went inside and shut the kitchen door, leaned against the sink with her back to it. She was softly crying, her cheeks moist with tears. 'How the hell, Colin, did you contrive this?' she was wondering. Four days ago Carruthers had shocked them both with the Will, the inheritance. And today... four days and the train running. Now the face of her Latin teacher was superimposed. His name rang in her ears, too: Ingram. Her tears were gentle, but they would not stop.

Down on the station platform the crowd now exceeded fifty. At last the majestic green painted boiler of the engine "Land's End" appeared on the bend into Polmouth. Someone let out an involuntary cheer and within seconds this was taken up by all present, shouting and waving their arms high above their heads in welcome. No-one had the slightest idea what was going on; gossip of the most ridiculous kind was already pulsing through the excited crowd.

The locomotive slowed to a halt, steam escaping from unknown mechanical parts, and the door of the front compartment in the First Class coach opened. A man stepped down onto the platform, staring at the crowd. Everyone had suddenly fallen silent. He advanced a pace. A man's voice called out:

'That's Penpolney. Colin Penpolney!' The crowd surged forwards, all talking at once, surrounding Colin. He was tempted to retreat to the First Class compartment, but he stood his ground. He raised his hand, trying to look imperious, but he felt ridiculous.

'Just a test run...' he said but it was not loud enough. Those at the back were pressing forward, a real crush.

'What did he say?' was on everyone's lips. Word was passed over shoulders, children's heads. A dog barked joyfully. Colin tried again, raising his voice.

'The Grand Gala Opening will be announced shortly. Now please, make way, please!'

The uncomprehending crowd relented, not dispersing but spreading along the length of the train. Colin pushed his way through the throng. Petra was waiting for him in the ticket office hall.

'We can't go yet,' he muttered, taking her head between his hands and staring into her black eyes. 'Soon, yes, but until then...'

'If you go on like you have today, Colin,' she whispered, 'I'll wait for ever. You'll find me here. When you're through.' She leaned up and kissed him, then pushed him away. 'Later...' she said softly. 'Go.'

When Colin made his way back onto the platform the throng had not diminished. On the contrary, people were now questioning him from every side. He shook his head and went in search of Peter Tenworthy. He pulled the engineer back into the First Class compartment.

'Two questions. Do you have freight wagons at Falmouth as well as passenger coaches?' Tenworthy nodded, sat down.

'Several. Why?'

'Question number two... can we have the train tomorrow, all day, with the freight wagons?' Tenworthy's face cleared.

'Ah, I see. Quite a haul up to the Estate without a removals van, eh? I'll fix it. What time?'

'Here by nine? Until six?'

'Shouldn't be a problem. Good thinking. Now I must save the engine drivers before the cab is mobbed... Come on.' Satisfied, Colin was rapidly revising his plans for the move next day. But before he could marshal his thoughts, the elderly

President of the Village Council, Percy Teague, approached him. His lined face was creased with emotion.

'Mister Penpolney...' he started, but his voice cracked and he fell silent, speechless. He gripped the younger man's arm in a vice-like grip. 'When can you brief me?' Teague, like Temeritus Tennent the Headmaster, had been an Army Officer. The crowd milling around on the platform had now grown to one hundred and fifty, well nigh the entire village population, and it was pandemonium. Colin forced a grin and raised his voice to be heard.

'I'll call you, sir, and make an appointment. But we do have a lot on our hands...'

'We?'

'Miss Zabrinski and I.'

'Oh, Mister Penpolney...' Teague's voice was now almost a sob. 'You mean the Estate, as well? Polmine? And Clifftop Farm?' Colin nodded. 'At your earliest convenience, then, please.' Teague stared at the gleaming locomotive still gushing smoke. 'It's a miracle! A miracle!' He stumbled blindly away. Colin went to Petra in the ticket office. Their silent embrace spoke volumes. Then:

'What's next?' Her voice was husky with emotion, and a deeper underlying desire which she had no wish to quash.

'Is your telephone still connected?' he asked. She looked at him in wonderment.

'Of course. Why?'

'Let's use it, and you'll see.'

At six o'clock Petra entered the "Crab and Lobster" and crossed to join Colin at the bar. The waiter's reception was now markedly different from previous days. Word carried swiftly in the tiny village and he was apprised of the extraordinary event that Colin had contrived, the incipient rebirth of the village conjured up overnight, seemingly, by this mysterious couple who had appeared from nowhere only days previously. Petra sized Colin up as she approached.

'I got it right, for once.' she said, indicating his open shirt and jeans, matching her green T-shirt and slacks. 'Jeans suit you.'

'You do realise that that T-shirt is highly revealing...'

'It shrank in the wash... anyway, why else d'you think I'm wearing it?'

'I wasn't complaining.' he said affectionately, putting his arm on her shoulder. 'Not surprised everyone's staring at us.'

'It's not my tits, for once. No, it's you, Mister Penpolney. Where's my cider?' Colin signalled to the barman who brought an ice cold glass within seconds. 'It's been in the fridge, awaiting Cleopatra's arrival.'

'Don't start that again!' She attacked her glass. 'Is there anything you haven't done today? Track checked, train running, arrived safely, getting the entire village to turn out, reorganised the removals people and cancelled the horse carts for tomorrow, booked the train instead, telephone connected in the Croft House...'

'There is one thing. I haven't sat down with my partner for a meal. Let's order.' He accompanied her to their table. The waiter's transformation was complete, hardly had the two taken their seats than he was at their side, menus in hand.

'Would madam, sir, prefer the menus on the table, or on a chair?' He was sickeningly unctuous. Colin smiled and pulled back a spare chair. The waiter had expected nothing else.

'We know the menu by heart. What's today's special?' The waiter beamed, but his eyes were on Petra's revealing T-shirt. There were times that he regretted that he was a man's man.

'Grilled turbot, sautéed potatoes and broccoli, madam, sir.' The waiter had his priorities right. Colin had caught the direction of the man's fixation. Petra nodded, Colin nodded.

'But leave the menus for the dessert, please.' The waiter hesitated.

'The wine...?'

'The vintage white, please.' Now the waiter's heart was thudding. The vintage again!

He felt promotion crowding in around, and with this couple now the Village Masters, running the lifeline train... He was gone in a flash. Colin was laughing.

'What's so funny?'

'Good thing that guy's gay, else he'd have torn off your T-shirt to guess what size you wear. But that'll never happen, his "friend" works at the tobacconist's.'

'How can you possibly know that?' Colin shrugged.

'I thought everyone knew.' He looked at her admiringly. 'You're a walking power house, in that outfit.' Petra frowned.

'The Toad once said I was a walking minefield.'

'I told you, he got everything wrong. Just jealous, probably.' The wine arrived and was served with due ceremony. 'So, is everything packed up and ready to go for tomorrow?' She nodded.

'Except the bed obviously, and the percolator for the morning, and the bathroom essentials, of course. You?' Colin smiled and didn't answer. He veered off on another tack as the waiter brought the huge turbot and started to fillet it.

'You any good with figures, money, accounts?'

'Never tried. Why?'

'We need to keep track of income and expenditure, especially when we start getting funding, and then even more so. A gift is a gift, but the donor has a right to know where the money's going.' Petra was staring at him in wonderment.

'Is there anything you haven't thought of, Mister "Mensa"?' She reflected for a moment. 'Maybe one of the members of the Village Council?' But Colin shuddered.

'Last people on my list. None of them got elected through transparent good practice. Can you ask Carruthers if he has any names, impartial?' She nodded. There was a pause while they ate. Then Colin made his move.

'So all your stuff's packed?' She looked at him, puzzled.

'I told you, except the bed. A girl needs a place to sleep.' Colin sipped his wine.

'Yes,' he said thoughtfully, 'yes, she does.' He continued eating. Petra wondered where he was going with this, as so often in recent days. 'But it's a very small bed... I mean, I know you're very slender, but still... You deserve a special night for the last before we go home.' His baritone voice was very deep. He stared into her dark eyes.

'We go...' she repeated softly, '... we go home...'

'They have rooms here, in the inn. Single rooms, no problem there.' Petra was trembling, and when she lifted the wine bottle to replenish their glasses, she had to hold the wrist of her right arm with the left to hide it. She stared at her full glass for what seemed an age.

'I don't have any nightclothes,' she ventured finally, 'toothbrush, toothpaste...'

'Nor do I,' said Colin encouragingly. 'Anyway I never wear pyjamas.'

'*Quelle surprise.*' she muttered. Then in a small, timid voice: 'They also have double rooms.' and left it like that, the ball in his court.

'You could get your toothbrush from home up the lane.' he suggested. She giggled.

'And my pyjamas...'

'That's not fair, I don't have any. But do you remember where you've stashed the cider, and the French stuff, the Chartreuse? That'd be more use.'

'Colin, this is a pub!'

'With licensing hours. So do you?' It was just past seven o'clock.

'If you come with me, help me find it, we'll have it in no time.' But he shook his head. She emptied her glass, and seemingly accidentally nudged the menus lying flat on the spare chair so that they fell on the floor. 'Oh, well, there goes dessert. I'll go, you book the rooms.' He stared at her, wondering just what they were getting into.

'So it's "yes", then?'

'Of course, I'm not turning down a full English breakfast, served at table.'

'Single rooms, then?' She stood up, stooped to whisper in his ear.

'Don't be silly!' she murmured dreamily, and remained standing facing him. The waiter misinterpreted her evident imminent departure, but he was too far away to overhear. She drew herself up to her full height and adopted a severe, reprimanding mien, wagging her finger at him theatrically and tossing the fair ponytail. Now the waiter had every reason to fear the worst. 'Who'd have thought it? Pantalone seduces young daughter Clarice, who also happens to be his adopted sister...tsk, tsk, tsk!' She shook her head. Colin reciprocated with the amateur dramatics, spreading his arms out as if remonstrating.

'Please! Even the Ptolemys didn't take things this far. But as long as you don't hold a venomous snake to your naked breast and invite it to bite, I'm fine with the rest.' He paused. 'Don't forget to bring the cider and the Chartreuse, and a spare toothbrush.' She turned and left. The waiter was thoroughly disquieted. The idea that she had left her partner would make big, and very bad, headlines. He approached with the bill. Colin saw that there was no-one more senior in sight.

'Can I reserve a room for the night?' he asked. The waiter's worst fears were confirmed. She'd left him. He nodded.

'A single, then, sir?' Colin decided to ham it up.

'Good God, no! Your best double! And breakfast for two, at eight o'clock, please. Oh, and a bottle of champagne in the room, on ice. Do you stock the Roederer Cristal?' The waiter swallowed. The Roederer cost £300 retail, would carry a one hundred percent mark-up, and they did not stock it. He was unable to hide his relief that the saviours of Polmouth were still partners. And apparently more.

'I'll get the Manager to show you the room, sir, as soon as it's ready. And I'll send out for the Roederer.' He took the bundle of bank notes, staring at them, payment for the meal and the wine.

'I'll be in the lounge bar. Keep the change.' Colin was on top of the world. And as she hunted in packed banana boxes for the bottles, so was Petra.

Chapter Twelve

Wednesday, June 12ᵗʰ 1974

The June heatwave continued unabated. Carruthers opened the morning mail, read through a letter from the Midland Bank, and reached for the phone. It was ten o'clock. He telephoned Colin Penpolney but there was no answer. The same when he called Petra Zabrinski. Then he tried the Croft House, but before the phone had even started to ring, he remembered. Wednesday, they were moving in today. He put down the receiver and thought, then decided to try his friend the Harbour Master at Polport as a last resort.

Trevor "The Pirate" Benson's nickname went back years, the result of the huge man's stature and swarthy appearance, he stood six foot six tall with a commensurate bushy black beard and Neanderthal eyes. He answered the phone in his gate box at the entrance to Polport harbour, but his eyes were fixed on the extraordinary events unfolding a hundred yards away at the station.

'Hello Carry, hey you should be here to see this! Sorry... what can I do for you?' Carruthers explained. "The Pirate" grinned.

'That won't be a problem... they're just over there on the platform. And it's a pity you can't see this, in fact someone should be filming it! What? What can I see? It's like something out of Victorian England... or a film set! And it's been going on for over an hour... first the morning barge dumped three beds and carpets on the quayside, but no-one seemed to know why. Then the woman from Clifftop Farm brought one of her nine foot tall Shire horses pulling a farm cart, and it was piled high with furniture and boxes. Three men put all that on the platform and went away. They've just come back for the fifth time, it's far more than one person's... And during all that, the steam train came in again, and now they've nearly finished loading the whole caboodle into wagons... I mean the train. Do *you* know what's going on?'

'They're moving into the Croft House today. Is Mister Penpolney still there?'

'Uh-huh, d'you want me to call him to the phone?'

'No, but can you give him a message? Just tell him I've opened the accounts and transferred the funds, will you do that?'

'I'll have to move, they're all getting into the train... on my way. Call you later.'

He hurried the hundred yards to the train where he saw Colin and Petra standing in the open doorway of a freight car. He spoke to Colin, then stepped back as the locomotive gave a prolonged hoot and the train started to roll backwards out of the station. The eleven o'clock ferry from Polhaven sounded its siren on entering the port.

Up at the railhead of the Brick Croft the heavy lifting and carrying continued. But before the three removals men could install the furniture in the Croft House, they had to remove Ingram's belongings. Leaving the new owners' furniture and the three new beds on the platform they followed Colin and Petra the short distance to the house.

'Can we have a break?' asked the foreman. 'Nearly midday.' Colin nodded.

'Take all the time you want. It's nice over there by the lake... you have food?' The man nodded to the train.

'We're fine in the train there. Thanks, we'll see you back here later.'

Colin took Petra's hand and gently led her towards the grassy embankment beside the lake. They sat down, soaking up the warm sunshine. He gazed around the miles of what was now their land to the mine workings in the distance and beyond, the blue sea of the English Channel sparkling to infinity.

'Well, we're home.' He put his arm round her; Petra rested her head on his shoulder, then flipped her blonde ponytail to one side to look up at him.

'Home...' her voice was a murmur. Then: 'What did "The Pirate" want?' He told her Carruthers' news and her eyes were moist. 'So it is real, then... Every day it seems more and more like a dream, and I'm scared I'll wake up and find nothing... Home...' she murmured again.

'Aren't you hungry?' he asked. She laughed and shook her head.

'After that breakfast, no way. We can get something when we take down Ingram's stuff to the cottage. But we'll have to buy food for the evening, and breakfast...' Colin shook his head.

'I have that sorted.' he said, but that wasn't good enough this time for Petra.

'Tell me!'

So he did, but he did not tell her everything.

'I've reserved a table at the "Crab and Lobster".' She hugged him.

'That's perfect!'

'By the way, I hope the bed you've bought is as good as the one we had last night?'

'I bought beds. Plural.'

'And I said *"the bed"*. Well?' Her giggle was impossible to suppress.

'Oh, Colin! Honestly! We agreed we'd both have to test it...'

'I hadn't forgotten. A promise I shan't regret.' Her eyes misted.

'Nor I.' She glanced at the train where the removal men were on the platform again. 'Back to work, then.'

The train finally made its last journey of the day down to Polmouth, where the indefatigable men set about carrying all the late Ingram's furniture to Petra's cottage. Colin and Petra could only watch. But shortly after the train's arrival from the Estate, they had a visitor, right there on the station platform.

Carruthers stepped off the ferry from Polhaven and saw the gleaming train just a hundred yards away, then Colin and Petra assisting the three removals men. He was carrying an expensive camera. Relieved that he would not have to make the climb up to Polmine Estate, he crossed to meet them. He raised his camera and gestured to the couple to move to stand beside the shining green boiler of the locomotive.

'I really had to see this,' he said, 'and although I hardly knew the man, you've really done Ingram proud! But that wasn't the only reason I came... it's to do with the Camborne School of Mines. They've got your number and will call to fix a date for the deep mine inspection and report. But they're sending a couple over tomorrow to do a survey of the shallow Phoenician mine, the one with the slope and an iron door, and they'd like you to go with them. Apparently there are some installations for ventilation and lighting that date from the War years, and if they're working they'll show you how to use them. I'd explained you'd like one day to open the shaft for visits. Can you be there tomorrow at ten with the keys? They're coming over via Polhaven.' Petra nodded.

'We'll be there.' She took Colin's hand believing she was being discrete, but Carruthers didn't miss it. He broached the topic that was uppermost in his mind.

'You've achieved miracles!' he said admiringly. 'I'm beginning to see why Ingram thought... well, anyway. Do you have further plans, next step, steps...?'

'I've quit my job, so I'll be able to do promotional work, looking for financing.' Carruthers looked grave. He glanced at Petra.

'And your role in this?' She understood.

'I'd like to go on being your Legal Assistant, if that's all right? And I was going to suggest, in return for your offer of advice on legal matters, we should suspend the salary for three months, or simply pay you for your help.' Carruthers swallowed, pleased that she would be staying, and moved by the sincerity of the suggestion.

'Very noble, I appreciate that, thanks, but I wouldn't dream of it! I can't imagine a more able... euhh... colleague.' Colin's lips twitched with pleasure at his partner's new status in Chambers.

'I'll be there on Monday, as usual, then.' Petra was also touched. At that moment the removals men returned for the next load to carry. Carruthers left.

When the three men had finished, Petra and Colin accompanied them to the ferry. They were about to board when Colin produced three envelopes, distributed them. The Foreman looked inside. A fifty pound note. He touched his forelock respectfully.

'Sir.' They boarded.

'I need a drink.' Colin set off down the street.

'Too early for me... for you, too.'

'Tea. "Polly's Tea Room", scones. Come on.'

Seated at a highly unstable table on the pavement outside "Polly's Tea Room", protected from the afternoon sun by an awning, the two were served a true Cornish Cream Tea. There was an abundance of clotted cream and wild strawberry home-made jam. The steady stream of scones overwhelmed the wobbly table. Passers-by frequently paused, and then, moving a few yards away, indulged in conversations in low tones, studying the new Lord and Lady of the Manor. Colin feigned complete indifference, but Petra was less restrained.

'I think they've appointed you Lord Colin Penpolney of Polmouth.' Colin, his mouth full of scone, jam and cream shook his head, swallowed.

'Wrong. It's the beautiful Lady Petra they're all imagining on the front cover of some women's magazine, entertaining her butler. Afternoon tea and all that. Or... no... perhaps the horse cart chauffeur.'

'Lord and Lady Polmouth of Polmine Manor! How grand!' She looked at her watch. 'We need to make a shopping list, go shopping for the morning, coffee, tea, bread, butter, all that...' Colin gave a nonchalant wave of his hand.

'I told you, I have that sorted. We'll go shopping in the morning, after the barge has come in.'

'The barge? What are you on about? And I haven't even made up the beds...' Colin tut-tutted theatrically.

'I didn't notice you complaining about *our* bed last night.'

'Colin! You haven't...?' Colin looked apologetic.

'Well, I know it's not the Ritz, but I felt entirely... comfortable, last night.' She stood up, walked behind his chair and leant over him, hugging him.

'I should have met you years ago.'

'You did, you were wearing a hockey skirt and were about thirteen.'

'Not the bloody hockey skirt again, it's a fetish with you, and anyway that doesn't count... oh, no!'

'Now what?'

'My pyjamas are up in the Croft House.'

'Not those damned pyjamas again! You didn't need them last night.' She looked at him tenderly, swinging her ponytail.

'I might just survive another night without, I suppose.'

'You've hardly eaten anything. Tuck in. We have a busy day tomorrow.'

'I'll need to walk this lot off first. But only if you come with me down the mine.' She spread a scone liberally with jam and cream, bit in hungrily. 'What's this about the barge tomorrow?'

'Please. You wouldn't want to spoil a surprise. By the way, can you ride a bicycle?'

'A bike? Oh, no, you haven't bought bicycles! Up that hill, no way! Please tell me you haven't.'

'No. I mean, no I haven't. And you wouldn't want to spoil a surprise.' She took his hand.

'No, no I wouldn't. But you do bring them on at ten a day, you know!'

'Dynamic, that's me.' She squeezed his hand more firmly.

'No arguing with that.'

At ten o'clock that night they had retired to their bedroom early, were sitting in armchairs at a small table at the foot of a four-poster bed that looked almost as old as the sixteenth century low, black beams that traversed a white ceiling of wattle and daub. It was unique, and uniquely romantic. Each had a glass of champagne in one hand and a cigarette in the other; the window was open but the night air was hot and still. Petra was staring at the huge bed.

'Don't know whether I'll sleep tonight, I'm so wound up. Aren't you?' Colin was serious.

'More than you know.' He covered her hand. 'I'd be a dead loss at all this without you.'

'I was thinking exactly the same thing, about you. What did Ingram know that we're just finding out? It doesn't make sense...'

'Doesn't have to,' said Colin firmly. He sipped at his glass. 'Tell me about your degree. York, wasn't it?' She nodded. 'Plenty of Roman history there.'

'The best parts were the visits abroad twice a year. One to Italy, the other to Greece, each for a month at a time. There were about twenty of us in my year, but a surprising number were absolute prats, God knows how they ever came to be offered places on any course.'

'Classics is a rarefied field.' remarked Colin. 'Why were they prats?' Petra sniffed in irritation at the memory.

'We went to Rome four times. When we were supposed to be visiting the Colosseum, or the Forum, in fact any research on the ground, there'd be five of us actually there, and the other fifteen were studying...'

'I don't understand?'

'In the "University of Shopping"...' Colin smiled.

'Now I understand.'

'German's quite specialised. How many on your year?'

'Fewer than twenty... German is a minority subject at school. I spent the whole of the third year in West Germany, not studying. For my thesis I persuaded the *Goethe Institut* – like the British Council – to let me visit twelve of their residential adult language schools all over the country, observe every aspect of teaching and students' social life. I promised them a separate report at the end summarising students' views on each *Institut*. To my surprise, they offered me accommodation in little family-run historic *Gasthäuser* in each village or town and free meals for four days and nights at every one! Which meant I spent many hours on long distance trains, met scores of Germans from every part of West Germany, and West Berlin, and only had to pay the train fares. Learnt to speak very fluently. But it was quite funny, all the teachers called me *"Herr Inspektor"* and looked terrified of my class visits. Heck, I was only twenty years old!'

'Did you go into East Berlin?' He nodded, then laughed.

'I'll never forget that day! There are only two places to cross from West to East; Check-Point Charlie, and Friedrichstrasse. That's the one I used. The contrast was shocking. Houses destroyed by bombing in the war still total wrecks, untouched for thirty years. The people all seemed strangely grey, drab and somehow forlorn. And the steak I ordered in the best restaurant was inedible leather. It was there, in the restaurant, that I got the shock that made the day unforgettable.'

'Don't tell me you were arrested as a spy!'

'That came later.' Petra's eyes widened. 'No, when I opened my wallet to pay, I discovered I'd lost my passport!'

'Christ! That must be the worst thing a westerner could do in Communist East Germany...' He nodded.

'Yup. A westerner's passport is worth gold dust to people organising escapes. I was shocked.'

'I'll bet! What did you do?'

'Had two choices... try to retrace all the route I'd walked... but I'd taken a tram to the Alexanderplatz, so that was no good. Or beat it to Friedrichstrasse, tell them, and ask them what to do. But that backfired badly...'

'You mean they wouldn't help?'

'Worse. Far worse. I told you I'd spent months travelling all over West Germany, hours of conversations with Germans. And my base was Munich, Bavaria, I'd even picked up a Bavarian accent... it's distinctive, a bit like a Cornish accent is in England. I wasn't just fluent, I didn't make any mistakes, grammar and all that. In fact, I spoke like a native speaker. I stupidly thought my fluency in German would be helpful, move things along, no need for an interpreter. I was wrong.'

'But it must have helped.' Colin shook his head.

'It was my Achilles' heel. They bundled me into a small room with no windows and no handles on the inside of the doors, and left me there alone for an hour. Then an officer in a green uniform came in, sat down opposite me and started shouting, screaming almost, and swearing at me to stop wasting his "effing time" and tell him the "effing truth"! All in a very marked East German Berlin accent – it's even more distinctive than Bavarian.'

'Good God! I'd have been terrified... weren't you?'

'All of that... it turned out that they refused to believe I wasn't a West German, and were accusing me of being a western spy, and said I'd used a stolen or fake British passport and given it to someone to be used for an escape. "Who?" he kept screaming, "Who did you give it to? Name, his name?!" You can see why it's impossible to forget.' She was staring at him fixedly across the small table, her black eyes indicating fascination and something else. But Colin was lost in his reminiscing.

'Remember I said you brought on ten surprises a day? Well, you've just made today's total four score and ten. Obviously they let you go or we wouldn't be here now. How?'

'That's when melodrama turned into farce. Some uniformed minion walked in and muttered in the officer's ear. He stood up dramatically and left the room. I was alone again. Then the minion returned and handed me my passport. "Follow me!" he ordered. And he escorted me wordlessly to the crossing point and walked with me as far as the barrier on the West German side. He stopped, I stopped, it was like a spy movie exchange of westerner for Communist. And then the prat saluted me, military style, heels clicking together, and he said: "*Auf Wiedersehen*", turned and left for the East German barrier. I can only suppose I must have dropped it just after leaving the crossing on going in… anyway, someone had obviously found it and handed it to a border guard. So…' he sipped his drink nonchalantly, 'here I am.' He took her hand again. 'Here we are.' He looked thoughtful, then hopeful. 'I don't suppose you have any true stories about being arrested by a Roman Centurion?' She leaned across to kiss him briefly.

'The Sabine Women thing was a long time ago. I understand now, though, how you came to meet so many Helgas.' Colin stretched, leaning back in his chair.

'If we last a thousand and one nights, I can probably manage to beat Scheherazade. So for tonight…' He pulled a face. 'Ingram would kill me for this, he used to hate us messing about with "dog Latin". But this explains a lot… my father, just before the divorce, came with me to the station when I was leaving for the year in Germany. He'd lived there before the war. The very last thing he said to me, in fact for ever, was a sentence in German... here goes in your department: *"mulieres germanorae subjectae ad enthusiasmi ardentes sunt"*. Get it?' Petra's face was a mixture of imminent laughter and astonishment.

'I get the picture, but just to be sure... in English?'

'"German women are prone to sudden ardent enthusiasms." What my father actually said was: *"Deutsche Frauen leiden an Schwärmerei."* He never spoke a truer word. I met several who proved him absolutely right.' Her impetuous giggle made him smile.

'Are you trying to make me jealous, or something?' He stood up.

'If you were, it'd be a no contest. We're here, you and I, and they're still chasing chimera in Germany.' He looked at the bed. 'Are you going to condemn me to another study of locksmiths' perfect work? Please not!' Again the giggle. She suddenly turned out the light. She whispered in the darkness:

'No, I need your help with a tricky zip. And I'm over here.'

There was nothing romantic about another darkened room at that hour, in the depths of Whitehall, where dyspeptic Undersecretary of State Bonham was once again working late. His irritating phone warbled and he seized the receiver.

'Bonham!' A distant voice rattled metallically and a smile flitted across Bonham's ascetic face. He pressed a button on the underside of his desk beside his knee and rang off. Within minutes there was a knock at the door and his assistants Hamlyn and Tring entered with a sheaf of papers. Tring tried to be funny, the last thing to do at eleven at night with the irascible Bonham. In a servile voice he said:

'You rang, sir?'

'Don't mess about, siddown!' snapped Bonham impatiently. 'So brief me, what's new? What's going on?' Hamlyn opened the sheaf of documents.

'The East Germans Helmuth Schiller and Uschi Meissner, on board HMS Hampshire... the Corvette's left Malta for Gibraltar, be there before dawn. They'll be on a military flight to RAF Plymouth, arriving mid-morning. But they've only got what they were wearing when they defected. Once they're in Polmine they'll never leave the quarantine area, and their keeper will buy whatever's needed. But they can't go shopping, buy clothes, just like that in Plymouth tomorrow, even if it isn't an obvious Stasi hit list surveillance spot. They'll go with their keeper, this Katrina Rothmount, all three dressed in naval uniform, hats, sunglasses, unrecognisable.' Bonham glanced at his watch, it was evident he had only been half-listening.

'Go? Go where? Explain!' Tring, however, had been listening.

'Shopping, sir, in Naval disguise, with their watcher.'

'Got it. Why didn't you say that?! And then?'

'To get them to Polmouth with supplies we needed a heavy, Army transport helicopter, twin rotors, and the RAF have repainted one white, changed the registration to a civilian one. It's loaded with mattresses, and provisions, tinned food, washing powder, everything for a month. When Schiller and Meissner have got their clothes, they'll dress as civilians and travel tomorrow afternoon with the provisions on the helicopter. They'll be installed by nightfall, all three of them.'

'Three? Oh, yes, of course... the Rothmount naval girl.' Bonham mollified. 'Sorry, gentlemen, it's been a long day.' He tried to concentrate. 'These new owners of the Polmine Estate, I suppose they've been given security clearance? Their names?'

'Penpolney and Zabrinski. Affirmative, they're clean. Village folk, tucked away in a remote corner of Cornwall at the end of the earth. Which is good, as it means there's no harm in contact between them and the Krauts, and anyway, as they live on the Estate and own it, contact's inevitable. Might even be desirable, get them used to British society.'

'Stop waffling, man! I assume they've been told? Of the time of arrival. For the keys and just so they know? Haven't they?' Tring looked awkwardly at Hamlyn, who was looking at his feet.

'Well, the MOD have always had the keys, so that's taken care of...' he mumbled. Bonham exploded.

'The MOD? Keys? That was forty years ago! Supposing the locks have been changed? And answer my question, have you informed the owners of... Polmine? Have you?' He was increasingly aggressive. 'Jesus Christ! All that cover, well planned, well executed, and you expose the whole mission not only to public scrutiny, but to public ridicule at the same time! The only reliable keys are in the hands of the Estate owners, and no, I do not want James Bond to break in and steal them in the night! What were you thinking?! What was the name of the contact Mortimer visited? The lawyer?' Hamlyn shuffled through his papers.

'Carruthers, sir. I have the details here.'

'Right, call him first thing in the morning. You're from Imperial College, partner university to Camborne School of Mines organising the visiting Germans, you need access to the cottages by... what time will they arrive?'

'After three in the afternoon.'

'... at or after three o'clock, can he get the owners to be there with the keys then. Stress the importance, helicopter from the School of Mines, urgency and all that. If he can't, you, Tring, will fly to RAF Plymouth from Northolt to be there by midday. You have my authority to override any other commitments Northolt may have. And you'll go with the three and find the owners, however long it takes, and get them into the cottages, incognito and unseen, by nightfall. Do I have to write it down?' He glanced at his watch again. 'It's midnight, you won't get home and back by eight. Bed down in the nuclear shelter bunks. Keep me informed.' He dismissed them peremptorily and reopened his red box.

Chapter Thirteen

Thursday, June 13th 1974

It was just eight o'clock. Carruthers was opening the door to his Chambers when he heard the ringing of his telephone in the office. He hurried through, took the call standing up.

'Carruthers and Charteris.' He walked around the desk and sat down. 'Yes, go on...' Tring was relieved; it was at least a step in the right direction.'

'My name is Robert Tomlinson, Imperial College, London University. I believe you're acting for your clients... Penpolney and Zabrinski? I think a Mister Mortimer was in touch, about tenants of cottages in a place called Polmine?'

'I can confirm that. What about it?'

'Camborne School of Mines is our partner college, and Imperial College is handling the visit of German authors from the University of Stuttgart... and I've been asked to contact the owners of Polmine to alert them to the arrival of the tenants. Do you have any contact with them?'

'Well, on and off. I can try... when are the Germans arriving?' Tring relaxed; this was promising.

'That's why I'm calling so early... today. This afternoon. It'll look really sloppy, on our part, if they can't get in, you understand. The MOD passed the old keys to Camborne, but just in case the locks have...' Carruthers interrupted.

'Yes, I see, in case the locks have been changed. Well, I'll try now.'

'Much appreciated, many thanks. But if you can't reach them, I'll have to make other arrangements, so if you contact them, their tenants will arrive some time after three this afternoon and need the keys for the cottages. Can you call me back within the hour?'

'If I can't reach them by then, assume you'd better make these "other arrangements". Give me your number.' Tring rang off. Everything depended on Carruthers now. Otherwise... Tring had a dread of flying. Unsuspecting, Carruthers first tried the Croft House. When the ringing went unanswered, he put the phone down and reflected. There was no point in trying their previous homes. Then he remembered Petra's surreptitious hand-holding, the ambiance between the couple. He smiled; of course. He rang the "Crab and Lobster".

Colin and Petra were tucking in to a full English breakfast when the waitress approached timidly. She spoke briefly and Petra signalled to Colin to take the call. He listened, nodded, said thank you and rang off. Carruthers dialled the London number that Tomlinson had given him. Both men were satisfied, a successful early start to the day.

'But how did he know we were here?' Petra was blushing. Colin wiped his lips and didn't answer. He looked at his watch.

'Come on,' he said encouragingly, 'eat up. The barge arrives at nine, and we need to be there.' And they were.

The barge nudged its way into Polport harbour and unhurriedly advanced to its quayside mooring. There was the usual assortment of packing cases and provisions for the retailers of Polmouth, and today something stood out that was not typical cargo. Petra was scouring the decks for bicycles, but the two-wheelers that held her attention were red, shiny Mobylette mopeds. Brand new.

'Colin! It's a great idea, but I don't have a driving licence! In fact, I've never driven a car in my life...'

'Irrelevant!' His arm was round her shoulders in the crisp, morning air. 'It's just like riding a bike, only you don't have to move your legs.'

'But the law...'

'No law. I checked with the Council President, Teague. Because no motor vehicle exists in Polmouth, never has, all the streets, and our track, are classified as private roads, exempt from road traffic laws. Let's get them ashore, and I'll show you how to drive... Oh, and by the way, he's convened an Extraordinary Meeting of all the villagers for tonight, seven o'clock, asked us to be there.'

'Be where?'

'The Primary School hall. Should be interesting. Come on.'

Half an hour later Petra was sitting astride her gleaming red Mobylette while Colin hefted two olive green jerry cans into the basket attached to the front of her bike, then the remaining two onto his.

'What's in those?' she demanded, and before he could answer, 'If you leave those in there, there won't be any room for the shopping.' Colin sighed. Women! he was thinking.

'Two-stroke petrol. There's fuel rationing, I've used up a whole month's coupons. But these things do a hundred miles just on one half gallon tank. And we've got four gallons.' She precariously climbed unsteadily off her moped, put down the stand and crossed to him.

'Bloody hell,' she murmured, pressing against him, 'is there anything you haven't thought of, Mister "Mensa"?'

'I told you,' he mumbled, 'I couldn't do any of this without you... and anyway, I'd look pretty stupid, trying to ride two mopeds at once...' He put both arms round her and held her close. The deck hand on the barge was looking at them sourly, spat over the side into the dark water. By Christ, he was thinking, she must really have the hots for him, it's only nine o'clock. He lifted two more packing cases with the hoist and swung them over the side onto the jetty.

Colin looked at his watch over her shoulder and gently released her.

'It's half past already, we have to go. Mustn't be late for the mine visit and we'll need the keys. From the Croft House.'

'But… the shopping…'

'Later. Come on, try to get yours going, but don't, **do not** turn the handle bar until I show you how it works, or you'll end up in the dock…'

It took several minutes of short trips along the quayside and back before Petra felt ready for the traverse of the village to the track up to the plateau. At the top Colin drove ahead of her along the rough path that passed in front of the entrance to the Phoenician mine, the cottages and the lift for the deep mine before turning left onto the track alongside the railway. Petra, unnerved by the bouncing and bumping, twisted the handlebar accelerator to slow down. But she twisted it the wrong way and the moped leapt forward like a red stallion. She narrowly missed Colin who had been in front of her and raced past, her blonde ponytail flying.

'Wheee!' she shrieked joyously, and sped ahead. 'Slowcoach!' She arrived at the Croft House well ahead of him, and just managed to throttle back and apply the brakes at the last moment, narrowly avoiding flying headfirst over the handlebars. Exhilarated, she climbed off her bike but forgot to put the stand down, the moped toppled over on its side and the two jerry cans of fuel fell out of the basket. Colin finally arrived. He dismounted and helped her right the bike.

'Baptism of fire,' he remarked drily, 'and with two gallons of fuel, it could have been some conflagration!' She shrugged, spoke in a little girl's voice of contrition:

'Didn't mean… couldn't help…' and fell silent, her face expressing a very different emotion.

'Leave the bikes, we'll get the keys.'

'I need the loo first!'

'Makes two of us, you had me really worried there...'

'Men! No faith!' She seized his hand, held it in a firm grip. 'Come on! What are we waiting for? Got a mine to visit.' Colin swallowed and accompanied her inside, watched from afar by an astonished Sarah beside the hen huts at the farm.

Just before ten they left the Croft House.

'Walk? Or bikes?' Petra asked.

'Don't be silly. We didn't buy them for them to rot in some museum. Bikes, of course, but please...'

'I know, I know...' Petra saw two people appear at the top of the track and look around, uncertain of the direction to take. 'Come on. They're here.' And she raced off again, regardless of Colin's caution.

Seeing two bikers apparently hurtling towards them along the track from the mine head and the cottages, the two visitors from Camborne waited, surprised to see as the hosts approached that they were riding modest mopeds. Colin dismounted and advanced, followed by Petra. This time her moped did not fall over.

He introduced himself. The shorter of the two mining experts, a dark swarthy man in his thirties spoke first.

'Well, congratulations on your new property. David Evans.' He was unmistakably Welsh. 'Delighted to be of service...' He turned to the very blonde young woman beside him. She was holding a bundle of folded documents in one hand, extended the other in greeting, but her eyes were on the comparatively juvenile and equally blonde Petra.

'Helga Rasmussen, Chief Engineer.' She nodded at Evans. 'He's just my apprentice. Doesn't know a thing. Yet.' Evans laughed cheerfully.

'You'll get used to her. It took me a while. Do you have the keys?' Colin handed over the gate key and the one for the iron door.

'Over to you.' He allowed the two to advance to the gate. 'They're very young,' he murmured to Petra, 'I'd expected some wizened old goat.'

'Well, you got another gorgeous blonde Helga. Happy now?' But her eyes were sparkling and betrayed no sign of jealousy.

'Come on.'

Helga Rasmussen, accompanied by diminutive David Evans, led the way onto the gravel track that descended steeply to the iron door. At the door, Rasmussen gave Evans the key.

'See if he can manage that.' She was clearly in a good mood, and this was professional sparring, not animosity.

'Where are you from?' Colin enquired. 'Your accent...'

'Quit flirting!' hissed Petra playfully. Colin replied out of the side of his mouth as the two visitors wrestled with the lock.

'How often do I have to tell you? I'm useless at that stuff... Shhh!' The engineers had wrenched the door open and a waft of cold stale air drenched them in malodorous vapour. It was a frozen steam bath.

'Denmark... We're not going in yet,' announced Helga Rasmussen, spreading the plans out on the ground. 'Look, we're here.' She pointed to the entrance on the very right hand edge of the paper. 'The main tunnel descends for a mile.' She stood up and looked over the cliff edge to the sea. 'The cliff here is two hundred feet above sea level. This long tunnel descends to just twenty feet above sea level. You'll see why in a while.' She pointed to tunnels branching off to right and left along the artery of the main shaft. 'These are mine workings, as you can see there are at least ten on each side. The ones to the right, the short ones, could only go as far as the cliff face. The ones on the left, they go well underneath the estate, almost a mile, some of them, so I guess half way across?' She looked at Petra, ignoring Colin, wrongly assuming that in this world, as in hers, the women wore the trousers. Colin was amused and let Petra reply. She nodded wordlessly. Helga Rasmussen continued.

'When our people examined the mine ten years ago, they found a store of explosives in one of the side tunnels. They called in the Army. Who said, "Sorry, we must have forgotten these were still here…". I ask you! What kind of army forgets ten tons of high explosives when it pulls out? And you know what they did?' She started to laugh. 'They just carried the boxes across the mine to a ventilation shaft, and threw the whole lot into the English Channel! It's all in the report, which is how I know. I guess whatever it was is now fish fodder. Just don't buy cod from Poldeep Channel!' Her face straightened. 'Normally, we'd need hard hats, lamps on the front, but for this bit we shan't.' She pointed to a rectangle drawn on the plan close to the entrance. 'Here. This is what the Army was doing in the War. Well, the bit that we know about, there must have been a lot more down the deep mine. That's not my area of expertise, deep mines. This you have to see, we think it's unique.'

'But what is it?' Colin was puzzled. 'It's symmetrical, yet all the tunnels look like rabbit warrens…'

'Correct. But actions speak louder than words. Let's go inside. I'll lead, I have to find the box, and in the dark…' She led the way through the iron door and into the black tunnel, the floor sloping steeply down. The tunnel was surprisingly wide, five feet or more. In the dim light that reached them from the open doorway they saw she was feeling along the right hand wall with her arm at shoulder height.

'Couldn't you use a lighter, or a match, to see better?' asked Petra, wondering what "the box" was.

'A naked flame and mines don't go together.' Helga Rasmussen's tone was dismissive. 'Four thousand years ago oil lamps were all they had, methane gas or not… Ah, here. Wait there…' They heard her finger nails raking over something metallic, then she exclaimed: 'Got it, the button. Now, it's been ten years, so I'm not expecting miracles, but fingers crossed…' She pressed the metal button firmly into its mounting and waited. Nothing. 'Trying again,' she called over her shoulder and pressed again sharply. This time she elicited results. They all heard a strange mechanical coughing from the bowels of the mine, the sound echoing eerily through the numerous tunnels, bouncing back off a dozen walls. It reminded Colin of the sound of the crank handle used to start the his grandfather's pre-war Ford Six. And now the coughing was replaced by the unmistakable clunking of a diesel motor starting up from cold, then roaring into life before settling to a steady unstoppable growl. Helga Rasmussen reached across the metal casing attached to the wall, feeling for a mains handle. She grasped it in her left hand and pulled it down. The tunnel around them for as far as they could see was suddenly illuminated in white light from a seemingly infinite chain of light bulbs suspended from the ceiling overhead. The rough-hewn stone walls were moist with little rivulets of water running down to the ground and into a narrow central gulley. The electric light reflected off the mirror-like surfaces to provide a shimmering pathway into the unknown. A trickle of water flowed down the sloping, makeshift drain.

'I bet the Phoenicians wished they'd had that,' remarked Colin. Petra kicked his shin.

'Quit flirting!' But she was giggling, as surprised as Colin at the unexpected lighting. Helga Rasmussen turned to face her colleague David Evans.

'I told you it'd work.' But inwardly she admitted to herself that she had been far from sure after all these years. Then to Colin and Petra: 'At Camborne, we think you're the only people in Britain to own a mine, any mine, deep or shallow, with lighting installed courtesy of the Royal Engineers. Come on, I'll show you.' They all moved forward at normal walking pace now that there was light. Colin took Petra's hand, she squeezed his gratefully. He noticed that the hewn floor had been smoothed with some twentieth century mechanical device, but the walls and ceiling were pitted with pockmarks, untouched for a thousand years. They reached the first of the branch tunnels to the right; it was also illuminated and led them to an unlocked door.

'This is the first of the bunkers,' announced Helga and they entered to find daylight from a hole in the cliff face with open air, sunshine and the sea beyond. But what held their attention was a large, squat metal housing in the middle of the rectangular cave, the diesel motor and generator. The diesel was purring confidently, surprising as it had probably not been activated since the last Camborne inspection ten years previously. The powerful generator was soundless.

From the top of the housing two broad pipes were attached to the ceiling all the way to a solid grille set just inside the cliff top opening. Helga Rasmussen tested the solidity of the metal grille by attempting to shake it with both hands.

'This is so no-one can fall out. Or jump,' she added sombrely. 'But it lets air in, exhaust out, and no infiltration from nesting birds,' said Helga succinctly. She pointed at the roof just in front of the door. 'And cables into the mine. A masterpiece, and just to think, it was built and installed in the 1940s. The Royal Engineers, without a doubt.' There was silence while they thought about this. 'Well, there's only so much of a good thing you can get out of a mine, so let's press on, I'd hate to bore you. Next stop is right down at the bottom. We should have light all the way.' She stepped out of the bunker and turned right down the main shaft. 'Come on!'

During the mile long downhill walk in the tunnel with electric light bulbs every twenty yards, they noticed a score of narrow tunnels leading off to left and right but these were much narrower and all in darkness. Helga Rasmussen seemed to be in a hurry to reach her next showpiece, so Petra and Colin kept their questions until later. Over her shoulder Helga called:

'I hear you may be planning visits to this part of the mine one day, tourists, enthusiasts, school groups... that right?'

'We're considering it.' Colin was cautious. 'Rather depends on your assessment.'

'For the main tunnel, and the generator room, no problem. This entire tunnel, and a handful of the branch off-shoots, were reinforced by the Army in the 40s, no-one knows why. But you'll need solid wooden barriers to all the secondary tunnels, the dark ones. Don't want some daft schoolkid playing hide and seek in there, and some are very low and narrow.'

'So are they unsafe? I mean rock falls and things?' Petra called.

'No, they were all declared safe ten years ago, each and every one of them, and that can't have changed. Besides, there's no seismic activity here. Just they're impossible to patrol, with twenty of them. Ah, we've arrived, Level Seven!' She stopped and turned to face them. 'Four thousand years ago men worked and toiled down here, for tin. Once they'd exhausted the main vein along here, they drove the shafts under the estate and there they found plenty of ore. But has anything struck you about where we are? Two hundred feet underground, a mile from the entrance, anything?' Colin cottoned on.

'Air. It's ventilated. And that trickle of water, it has to be going somewhere. I noticed there's no pump, whereas the deep workings have an immense Pump House.' Helga grinned and turned to Petra.

'You've got yourself one bright partner here!' Petra blushed with pleasure, but Helga continued. 'Air. There are three sources and outlets. They were bright, four thousand years ago, the Cornish...' She turned to Petra again, still smiling warmly. 'I bet your guy's Cornish, hey?' Petra smiled back timidly, nodded. 'I knew it! Anyway, this last branch to the right explains it all. Come on, but it's dark, mind your step, take it slowly, stoop down and stay low...' She led the way into the narrow black tunnel. But it wasn't black for long. After a sharp bend to the right that took them all by surprise they saw daylight ahead outlined in a rough circle, another round opening on the cliff face, and a broad, short cave hewn out of the rock. But here there was no metal grille, just a view of the outside world. 'So four thousand years ago, they weren't daft... natural drainage for seepage water here, straight out over the edge and into the sea. And air in and out not only here, but also from the main entrance, and what is now the generator room. But here was even cleverer... no-one wants to drag iron ore up to the cliff top and then down to Polport when it's all going out by sea. No, this outlet is just fifteen feet above sea level at high tide. All the signs are they lowered sacks of ore out through this opening to boats below. No effort, speedy despatch. Like I said,...'

'Bright people.' Petra intervened. 'Wow!' She cautiously approached the opening in the cliff face. Timidly standing on the very lip of the aperture, she peered over and down to the sea twenty feet below. 'Colin,' she called. He joined her, standing just behind and holding her in a vice-like grip. He had no head for heights. 'Look...'

The waters just below them at the foot of the cliff were deep blue, indicating that the Phoenicians probably had sailed their boats to this spot for the sacks of ore. But only thirty feet from the cliff a mound of black rocks rose from the water like a parallel barrier to the open sea.

'They must have been bloody good sailors, getting into this tight channel under sail right against the cliff without hitting the *Polfelsen Rocks*. In fact, even to have identified the deep channel right here, Poldeep Channel...'

'The Phoenicians were extremely intelligent and resourceful people.' Helga Rasmussen was just behind them. She peered over Colin's shoulder, then pulled him gently backwards, sensing that his vertigo was doing him no favours. They all retreated to the centre of the cave. Now in the dim light Colin saw not one but two red and white life belts attached to the walls with ropes, one on either side of the aperture. He looked questioningly at Helga Rasmussen. But she did not answer immediately. 'So, are we done here? I could do with a drink. And David here is Welsh, no point in asking him.' It was clear that there was more affection involved here than professional partnership. 'I'll tell you what we know about those lifebelts in a while. But if you want groups down here, you'll need to fence off that opening.'

She led the way back to the main tunnel. Ten minutes later Helga had turned off the generator, after showing Petra and Colin how to activate it, and they walked out into warm sunlight and birdsong.

'We're still moving in,' said Colin apologetically, 'but please join us for lunch down in Polmouth.'

'Do they do vegetarian?' David wanted to know.

'Pescatorian o.k.? Fish in abundance.' David nodded.

'Lead on.'

They locked the door and the gate and, leaving the mopeds where they were, the four set off down the track to Polmouth.

'I hope you don't mind me mentioning this, and please don't take it the wrong way…' They were seated at the bar in the "Crab and Lobster" '… but that's a massive estate, with the mine, a farm, and whatever the buildings are at the northern gate… I mean, you seem quite young…' Her voice tailed away uncertainly. Colin glanced at Petra to his left, handing her this one. She tossed her ponytail characteristically.

'We're not just "quite young", we're *very* young! But we'll make a go of it. And Mister "Mensa" here has an IQ of over 150, so there's no chance it won't succeed. About those life belts, two of them… was there an accident? Someone went over the edge. Or suicide?'

Helga smiled.

'I wasn't involved in the assessment ten years ago, but I've been through the files. Henry Baxter, Chief Engineer at the time, wondered that too. So he contacted the Army for any information they might have.' She sipped at her glass. 'Got him nowhere, they clammed up. But Henry persisted. ***Something*** must have happened for the Army to put the lifebelts there and he was determined to get to the bottom of it. He reasoned that a suicide or accident would have been registered in the Penlyn Registry Office. But it was the Penlyn Coroner's Court that provided the answer.' The waiter approached deferentially but Colin waved him away. 'There was what British law quaintly calls "an affray". Down the mine, at the bottom.' Another sip. 'British Army Squaddies are not the most docile of creatures when angry, and many seem to be angry a lot of the time. And violent. The Coroner's verdict shows that two Squaddies got into a fight down in the cave and either pushed one another or fell together over the edge and into the sea. There were no lifebelts then, and probably no reliable witnesses, knowing how Squaddies think. The water's over forty feet deep, there.' She paused. 'It was war time. No lifeboats around then. They both drowned. Only one body was retrieved. You can see why the Army clammed up.'

'Good God!' Petra was horrified. Colin decided enough was enough. He glanced at their reserved table.

'Forgive the pun, Miss Rasmussen, you're a mine of information, and today looks like being Mines Day. We're expecting another group from Camborne School of Mines this afternoon, and they're coming by helicopter.' Helga Rasmussen looked surprised, raised a querying eyebrow to David Evans. He shook his head.

'Well, it's not the deep mine team, they're all up in Doncaster this week. Could be anybody. We have a lot of sections at Camborne, and what everyone regrets is that the left hand never knows what the right hand is doing.' Helga drained her drink.

'Actually, people think it's the Accounts Department that like it that way. No-one knows the other departments' budgets.' She looked meaningfully at the tables behind them. Colin took the hint, and stood up.

'Shall we?'

As they crossed to their table Colin stepped alongside Helga Rasmussen.

'When we reached the diesel room, you called it the first bunker. So there must be...'

Helga stopped beside their table. The waiter had hurried over and pulled back her chair but she did not sit down. She turned to Petra, put her hand on the younger woman's arm in a girlish fashion.

'Miss Zabrinski, if only you knew how gratifying it is just for once to note that someone has actually been listening to what I was saying.' Now she sat down, followed by the others. 'I'll explain over lunch.'

They parted as the harbour clock on the dockside nudged its way to two o'clock and the visitors boarded the Polhaven ferry. Colin and Petra waved to the departing engineers on the ferry making for the port exit. A man in a blue uniform rushed out of the nearby Coastguard Hut and ran towards the huge boathouse with the inscription RNLI painted on the side only yards from them. Beside it was a tall thick pole, a good twenty feet high. He lifted a flap on some metal box and inserted a key, then pressed a button. There was the deafening explosion of a petard in a basket high up on the pole. It echoed throughout the entire village. Then he ran into the boathouse and seconds later the ear-splitting wail of an air raid siren alerted all within earshot to a nautical event needing immediate assistance. He stepped out of the boathouse and stood in the doorway, waiting. In less than two minutes three men wearing orange lifejackets and waterproofs had arrived and were releasing the lifeboat from its mounting. With a roar the red, thirty foot lifeboat rolled down the rails on a trolley and entered the water in a cloud of spray. The twin motors ground into life and the boat zoomed through the harbour and out into the estuary.

'For those in peril on the sea,' murmured Colin, then looked up at the cloudless sky. It was another scorching hot, serene Summer's day. 'I reckon it's a drill, an exercise.'

'Whatever, they were very quick. Less than two minutes. Impressive!' Petra paused, tugging at his sleeve. 'Shopping now?' She sounded plaintive but he shook his head.

'Not yet. This is new...' He pointed to a huge display panel protected by a sheet of glass, the entire structure mounted on two solid supports. Inside was a single item, a chart three feet long and two feet high. He studied it. 'This is the navigation chart for the estuary and the coastline to the East...' Petra examined it.

'It even shows the water depths, like Poldeep Channel here... I'm trying to relate it to the mine. A mile from the entrance,' she examined the scale drawing then pointed with her finger, 'here are *Poldeep Felsen* rocks, so this must be where the shallow mine opening was used to load the boats with ore.' He nodded, comparing the deep blue tint of the water at the foot of the cliffs with the table in one corner.

'Deep blue, thirty feet or more. It looks as if Rasmussen was right. How big were the Phoenician boats?'

'They'd be sailing ships, big. Twice the size of a modern trawler, at least that. Phoenicia was at the eastern end of the Med. They had to make it all the way to Gib, out into the Atlantic, North through the stormy Bay of Biscay... They must have been very sturdy, and to carry ore... Big, in a word.'

'Incredible. Thousands of years ago... this is new. This is the Village Council's work, it wasn't here two days ago. I think President Teague is expecting a great deal from us.' She stared at him.

'Colin...' her tone was lightly reprimanding, 'what have you done now?!'

'Well, I had to call him some time...' He sounded vaguely apologetic.

'Who? Call who?'

'President Teague, about the trains, and well,... things. I think he's as ambitious as we are, but we won't know until this evening?' Petra was lost.

'This evening? What, this evening?' Colin sighed extravagantly.

'The Village Council... tonight's meeting? I think we're in for fireworks.'

'So I'll have to wait to find out what you've done.' She paused. 'Aren't you scared? I know I am.' He gazed blindly over her head and out to sea.

'I feel we're carrying the entire village on our backs. So, yes I am.' He released her, looked at his watch. 'Come on. We have to be at Polmine by three... the helicopter. Remember?'

'But the shopping...'

'Naff the shopping! I promise you, you won't go hungry. I have it sorted. But we mustn't be late. These people are paying us rent, after all.'

'Oh, yes, I'd forgotten.'

'I hadn't! Just to add to the burden, we're now landlords.'

Chapter Fourteen

Princess Triple-OS

On reaching the mine they retrieved their mopeds and returned to the Croft House at speed. On entering Colin paused.

'I know you've got your percolator, it's on the sideboard. Did you pack any coffee?' Petra nodded.

'It'll have to be black. Sugar?'

'Please. Lord and Lady Polmouth of Polmine Manor will take afternoon coffee on the veranda while waiting for their tenants. Don't bother with saucers.' He rummaged in one of his own boxes, pulled out a small leather case and arranged two chairs on the terrace overlooking the Estate. "*Carrying the whole village on our backs...*" He was wishing he hadn't said that, but the thought would not go away. Petra arrived with the coffee, sat down beside him.

'We haven't unpacked a single box yet.' She stared out over the Estate.

'We have a whole lifetime for that. Tomorrow, we'll start tomorrow.' Petra did not relent.

'And we still haven't done any shopping...' Colin smiled broadly.

'Oh, for God's sake, this fetish with pyjamas and shopping is too much!' He took her hand reassuringly. 'I told you, I have it sorted. Tomorrow, I said. Besides, it's Thursday, early closing. All the shops are shut. We have other priorities, and I can hear one approaching.' Petra cocked an ear to the sky and detected the unmistakable sound of a helicopter nearing the Estate.

'So now what?'

'We wait until the Serfs come to her Ladyship for the keys. This coffee's very good.' She shook her head in wonderment and took his hand.

The roar of the twin rotor helicopter hovering above was deafening.

'My God! It's huge!' Petra had to shout, her mouth close against Colin's ear. The helicopter descended slowly and landed gently on the rough land just in front of the cottages. The motors died and the rotors slowly stopped turning.

'I guess it has to carry heavy loads, mining machinery.' Colin was relieved that the ear-splitting noise had stopped. He opened the battered leather case beside his chair and took out a pair of powerful binoculars. Petra stared at him as he raised the black metal to his eyes.

'Mister "Mensa".' she muttered and fell silent. Then, overcome with feminine curiosity, 'What can you see?'

'Four men have got out, they're opening the hold. Pilot's still at the controls. Now one of them's going to Cottage 1, the end one. He's opening the door. So they *have* keys already! We needn't have hurried!'

'And now?'

'Mattresses, two of them. They're taking one into Cottage 1, putting the second in front of door 2. Now they're opening Cottage 2. What a waste of our time! They're coming out again, helicopter... packing cases, loads of them. Now... there's a woman. Young, our age, jet black hair...'

'Not another bloody Helga! Give me the glasses!' Petra seized them playfully, adjusted the focus. 'I can't see any woman... oh, yes I can... she's looking this way... oh my God! It can't be.' She pressed the binoculars more firmly against her eyes. 'It is!'

'Can't be and is what?' Colin was amused at her running commentary. Petra lowered the glasses, stared at him.

'But she joined the Navy. I thought.'

'But who? Who joined the Navy?'

'Her. Princess Triple-S! The bitch...'

'Please...'

'Princess Triple-S, we called her. Miss Smug Self-Satisfied. She was in the Sixth Form with me. I'm trying to remember her name... Jewish, was excused Morning Assembly and Prayers, and Religious Knowledge lessons. Like the Catholics. What was her name... You must have known her... Katrina something.'

'As I remember it, there wasn't much mingling between Year Groups,' ventured Colin, reaching for the binoculars but she had them glued to her eyes.

'Well, there well and truly is now.' She giggled irrepressibly. 'Head Boy flirts with Hockey Captain...'

'What's happening now?'

'Princess Triple-S is directing the Plebs to carry about fifty packing cases into Cottage 2. What on earth can be in them? When I travel, I use a suitcase. Anyway, I'm glad they have keys. I'm in no hurry to meet the bitch again. I was sure she'd joined the Navy.'

'Obviously not. Any sign of the Germans?'

'Wait... yes, two people climbing out now. That'll be they, in their forties at a guess, both fair-haired. Yup, definitely Germans. Going inside Cottage 1. Here.' She handed him the glasses but he put them back in the leather case.

'So you're not in a hurry to go over and welcome your tenants, then?' Petra shuddered.

'Not if she's one of them! Couldn't stand the bitch, no-one could. But it makes sense, her parents are Jewish refugees from Germany. So she probably speaks German. No, I'm in no hurry to see her again. I'll make more coffee. Let the Mountain come to Mohammed, and let it be a long time before it gets here.'

'That bad?'

'Wait until you meet her!' She disappeared into the house. The helicopter rotors started to spin.

'They're leaving!' he called into the Tea Room. 'Anyway,' he continued, 'we have a full evening ahead.' She hurried out without the coffee.

'What? What?!'

'The coffee?'

'Help me make it!' She dragged him inside, a welcome relief from the din of the departing helicopter.

An hour later they walked out into the afternoon sunshine and mounted their bikes. But Petra's wish to avoid Katrina Rothmount was in vain. At the corner from the railway onto the track past the cottages and the descent to Polmouth they saw Katrina standing in the middle of the gritty path staring across the huge Estate. They were obliged to stop. Katrina threw her head back and looked down her nose at them as if they were specimens of some low quality mineral rock. She blenched when she realised that the blonde girl, Petra, was her contemporary from Penlyn Grammar. And Colin, she recalled, had been Head Boy in the year above them. MI6 hadn't mentioned this. But she covered up well.

'Good Lord, well, well...' she drawled haughtily. 'Little Zabrinski. Hockey was your thing, wasn't it?' She stared with unrestrained jealousy at Petra's clinging, revealing green T-shirt, and sniffed disdainfully as if there were a smell of cow dung hanging in the air. Colin began to understand why she had alienated her peers.

'I believe you were into boxing.' suggested Petra mischievously. 'Last I heard, you joined the Navy?'

Katrina was obliged to invent. This was a pain in the neck. Why hadn't MI6 done their job, why hadn't they warned her? She sniffed condescendingly.

'I lasted a week at Portsmouth Naval College. For Officers.' She added malevolently.

'What happened?' Petra really didn't want to know.

'All these butch women parading up and down in silly uniforms and hats. Intolerable. I quit. Joined Camborne, I did Sciences at Penlyn. You were Classics?' Petra nodded.

'Surprised you remember.' There was an awkward silence. Katrina unwisely tried to score points, but it backfired badly. She pointed to the distant Great Horses.

'What are those Eohippus things?' Petra went in all guns firing.

'They're not. Not Eohippus, they were **pygmy** horses, and anyone can see those are anything but pygmies! No those are Great Horses, and they roam the Estate. But they're shy, won't trouble you or our other **tenants**.' She relished the last word. Colin coughed gently.

'We have an appointment… down in Polmouth, so if you'll excuse us.' He paused, studying Katrina Rothmount intently. 'I remember you now… your parents are German, name of Rothenberger. I met them once, a Parents' Evening. But Rothmount? Your name?'

Katrina was instantly defensive, hackles rising.

'We're Jewish. Wherever Jews settle, we're persecuted. There's antisemitism everywhere. We changed our name, Rothenberger to Rothmount. Like the Royal family, Battenberg to Mountbatten. So?'

'I see. Well, we're still moving in here, so maybe we can meet in a few days' time?' But Katrina wasn't ready to take the hint. She stared penetratingly at Colin's face, head back and down her nose again. There was an awkward silence while she insolently studied his firm jaw, the crows-foot creases around the eyes, then slowly ran her eyes over his broad shoulders, his slender waist, his hips… It was almost indecent. He looked very mature for his age, and reminded her of the First Officer on the Corvette, clean-cut military officer material. Her arrogance infuriated Colin.

'You did languages. German wasn't it?' Another unforeseen. Damn the idiots at MI6! Colin nodded.

'If the German authors are agreeable to the suggestion, I was looking forward to some practice, chatting with them?' Katrina shrugged offhandedly.

'Up to them.' She looked meaningfully at their mopeds. 'Well, mustn't keep you.' But Colin now took his time in responding to her tacit earlier challenge. He was wondering whether her distinctly embittered face had been formative in shaping her vile character, or whether it had been the other way round. He held her eyes coolly. During a long, pregnant silence, he studied her face with matching insolence, taking up the gauntlet. Petra held her breath. It was a tacit *Bataille Royale*.

Although of the same age as Petra, Katrina Rothmount's compact, athletic and not unattractive body was let down by her fixed sourpuss scowl. Her mouth, unflatteringly on the small side, with downturned lips at the corners, underscored the overwhelming impression of a sulky, spoiled little girl. She stood her ground at first, as if on parade, but then the duel was won and lost, and she turned wordlessly and went inside. Petra looked at Colin in admiration.

'Wow! Another four score and ten day of surprises from you! Don't know how you do it. But you see what I mean?' Before he could reply she zoomed past him and raced to the downhill slope to Polmouth.

With it being early-closing for the shops, the narrow streets were only sparsely populated as the two putt-putted cautiously through the cobbled lanes at slow speed. Nevertheless, there were sufficient nosey bystanders for several eyebrows to be raised at the sudden arrival of the only two motor vehicles in all of Polmouth, inciting a tide of gossip to surge like wildfire to every pair of ears ready to listen.

It was just before six in the evening, with Polport harbour bathed in golden sunshine, when the two riders parked their mopeds in front of the "Crab and Lobster" and went to the bar. Petra grasped Colin's sleeve.

'What are you planning now?' she demanded. 'You certainly made it game-set-and-match against the bitch, wow!' They arrived at the bar. The waiter was at their side in seconds, carrying two menus.

'Will madam, sir, be dining again tonight?' He held out the menus but Colin waved them away.

'Yes, but later, much later. We're attending the Extraordinary Assembly called by the Village Council in an hour. After that, certainly. But there is something you can do. Please inform the Manager we'll be taking the same room as last night, and put another bottle of Roederer Cristal on ice. Thank you.' Petra was now clutching his arm more tightly, the waiter was already half way out of the door on his way to buy the champagne.

'My pyjamas....' she wailed, but he could see that she was laughing. Colin signalled to the barman, ordered.

'You'll be reunited with them one of these days. I'm wondering what President Teague has come up with. Should be interesting.'

'You're not fooling me with that! Whatever he's going to say, *you'll* have made it happen. So come on, what am I going to hear?' Colin raised his glass, shrugged extravagantly.

'Whatever it is, it's quite out of my hands. Cheers!'

They arrived at the Primary School hall at five to seven. There were already over one hundred villagers seated and impatiently awaiting the evening's announcements. Percy Teague met them at the door.

'Reserved seats,' he murmured, 'front row.' As they advanced the length of a side wall the chatter of conversation in the hall fell to a low hum, conjecture and rumour rippling through the audience. Seated on the central chairs in the front row Petra turned to Colin accusingly.

'You knew about this!' He shook his head.

'Complete surprise to me,' he murmured. 'Sshhh!'

President Teague opened the meeting with ceremony and panache. Once that was out of the way, he drew himself up to full stature, a military officer announcing a great victory to his troops.

'Ladies and gentlemen,' he began, 'ten years ago I presided over this Assembly with a heavy heart, presaging the Decline and Fall of Polmouth. I am sure many of you will recall that fateful day, the closure of the railway and the liquidation of Polmine Estate.' He paused for effect. It was a mistake.

'Get on with it!' called a voice from the back. Teague reddened.

'Today we meet under much happier circumstances! Thanks to the extraordinary generosity of Mister Colin Penpolney and Miss Petra Zabrinski, the new owners of Polmine Estate and Clifftop Farm, Polmouth will, as of this coming Sunday once again enjoy the service of seven, yes *seven* trains a day to and from Penlyn, four using British Rail rolling stock and three with the West Cornwall steam train. seven days a week, three hundred and sixty-five...' The remainder of his sentence was drowned in a sudden burst of applause which became deafening as the entire audience gave a standing ovation. The villager to Petra's left dragged her to her feet and she in turn signalled to Colin to stand beside her. They turned to face the crowd, both blushing and looking at the floor. Petra spoke to Colin out of the side of her mouth.

'You might have warned me!' But he had to lip-read the words, such was the din. They sat down quickly, and Teague raised an imperious hand.

'Seven trains, the first at eight a.m., so reinstating the school service to Penlyn Grammar as it used to be. All trains will have a freight wagon, so retailers and all other users of goods can also return to the former system. We hope rail supplies will replace the barge from Polhaven within six months.' Another voice called out:

'So will the Council reduce the Council Tax when there's no more need to subsidise the barge?' There were both approving and dissenting voices to this interruption. Teague made an effort to sound understanding.

'We certainly hope so! But by precisely how much will have to be calculated and set against the rampant inflation of recent years... 25% this year, I remind you...'

'So you won't!' The distant voice was bitter. 'I knew it!' Teague played the politician's card to dig himself out of a tight corner.

'There is more good news!'

'That wasn't "good news"! It's a rip-off! You should be ashamed...' called the voice bitterly, but the assembly had lost patience with the heckler.

'Be quiet!'

'Pipe down!'

Teague beckoned to Colin to join him on the stage, but Colin firmly shook his head. He nudged Petra.

'This is your show.' She disagreed but stood up anyway and whispered to him.

'Not mine, not ours. This is Ingram's show!' She mounted the steps and stood beside Teague. Another wild burst of applause. She waited, then took a deep breath. She dispensed with niceties.

'Mister Penpolney and I are but the messengers here today. If there is good news to announce, then it is sent, no, it is **brought** to us, by a silent partner. A silent leader.' She hesitated. 'Colin...' she signalled to him and he joined her.

'We are but a couple, and we hope that our endeavours will realise a dream. Yet it was never *our* dream. Our strength lies in being part of a triumvirate, an invincible trio, namely Miss Zabrinski, I, Colin Penpolney, and essentially, the fount and the foundation stone of this undertaking, the legendary spirit of Mr. Felix Ingram. We shall shortly be naming this the "FIF", "The Felix Ingram Foundation" for the "Polmine Project".'

During a renewed standing ovation Colin signalled clearly to Teague that they were done, over to him. But they remained standing beside the President. He announced the train times, the Gala Opening of the new service the coming Saturday afternoon, and that plans for the development and sponsors of the "Polmine Project" would be published shortly. Now he turned to the table behind him and picked up a number of scraps of paper, leafed quickly through them.

'Some of you have shared your disquiet with me...' he held up the handwritten notes, 'about just how the re-opening of the railway, and the potential development of Polmine Estate, may affect the tranquillity, the village harmony, which has reigned in Polmouth for a thousand years. Have no fear!' he announced grandly. 'The Village Council will work entirely in the spirit of the late Felix Ingram's vision! I can assure every single villager, and... yes, all villagers yet to be born, that we shall maintain Polmouth's status of a picturesque, miniature village steeped in History and never, I repeat *never* a village drowning in the mire of commercialism and cheap entertainment.' To the astonishment of all present Teague was interrupted by a silver haired gentleman in the audience rising to his feet and crying out:

'Bravo! Bravo to that!' at which applause rang out. It was old farmer Blackitt. He sat down. Teague continued, while Colin and Petra stood like dummies in a shop window wanting nothing more than to sit down and be lost in the crowd.

'That means that there will be no debauched Med-Style holiday camps, no apartment blocks, no second homes, no amusement arcades and the like... no, Polmouth will remain the kernel of the peach that is the very heritage of England. An example... the Village Council will immediately deploy the Council gardeners to clear Polport station, platform and track, of weeds, and plant flower beds and window boxes. And trees will be planted the length of the Esplanade. Starting tomorrow!' Wild applause. Colin nudged Petra and they hastily descended the steps to their seats while Teague was winding up the Assembly, inviting all to the Gala Railway Opening on Saturday. The crowd rose and dispersed noisily. Several of the audience seemed to hesitate, considering having a word with the unknown benefactors, but when they saw that Petra had both arms around Colin's neck and that the two were standing face to face, they all seemed to change their minds and filed out of the hall.

For the millions whose working day is nine-to-five, five days a week, some routines would be unthinkable. But there is a hidden army of valiant workers without whose contribution the daily nine-to-five schedule simply could not function, and their routine is set in distinctly anti-social hours. Yet they have no Trade Union and their pay is pitiful. They appear on the streets between ten p.m. and midnight, disappear into countless blocks of offices and administrative buildings scattered around the country, and beaver away until around six a.m. when they scurry out into the cold light of incipient dawn and hurry home to bed. The generic name for this "valiant army" is "cleaners". But occasionally, valour is a quality that is conspicuously lacking in recruits. One such was fifty-four year old spinster Thelma Wilkins, and although she would never have recognised herself under the denomination "a liability", it is what she most certainly was.

Thelma's employers would not merely have been shocked if they had known what she was really up to in the darkened rabbit warren of corridors and offices, she would have been thrown in gaol for a very long time indeed. But for both employer and employee, ignorance was bliss, albeit in very different ways. Blissful ignorance had induced Thelma's employer, Her Majesty's Government, after carrying out intensive security checks, to award her a very high level of clearance to work in government offices. That same blissful ignorance ensured that she could perpetrate her nefarious activities with impunity.

For Thelma was not just a cleaner, she was a traitor. In plain English, she was a spy.

Thelma had two established routines: The Tuesday-Thursday-Saturday Schedule, and the Monday-Wednesday-Friday-Sunday Schedule. For the latter, she confined her activities to simple, standard cleaning. But on the 3-day schedule she had an additional activity. And today was a Thursday. It was eight in the evening when she showed her security pass to the guard at the door of the anonymous Whitehall building and started on her innocuous activities. The others would come much later that night.

As Thelma was showing her Whitehall security pass to the doorman, many miles to the West in Cornwall another door opened in far-away Polmouth and Colin and Petra entered the "Crab and Lobster". The number of drinkers in front of the bar and diners at table was more than usual for a Thursday, but then it had been a highly unusual not to say memorable day. Conversation fell suddenly to a muted mumble of whispers and lowered voices. All eyes were on Petra and Colin.

'I feel kind of conspicuous,' muttered Petra, embarrassed. Colin took her hand as they advanced to the bar.

'If you will wear that green T-shirt, what can you expect?'

'Haven't had time to unpack properly, yet. You never give me a minute!' They reached the bar. Three wizened trawler-men in appropriate roll-necked knitted pullovers pulled their stools sideways to make room. Before Colin could speak, the barman hurried over, a folded piece of paper in his hand.

'Message for you, sir.' He handed Colin the paper, but Colin seemed in no hurry to order drinks.

'Well, you certainly exceeded your previous record of four score and ten surprises in one day. You're at 92 and counting.' said Petra. She reached across to seize the folded note from Colin's hand but he lifted it out of reach. 'What does it say?' she insisted. Colin finally read the brief message.

'From Carruthers. Camborne again. They're sending a team tomorrow to inspect the deep mine, it'll need all morning to get the pump and lift working. We can go down in the afternoon with them.' Petra shook her head in wonderment.

'Four score and thirteen and counting! How d'you do it?' Colin ordered the drinks.

'I haven't done anything,' he said plaintively like a little boy. 'It's everybody else keeps on...'

'Piffle! So it'll take all day. Pity.'

'Why? I mean why "it's a pity"?'

'I'd planned on some long overdue housekeeping. There are boxes to unpack, beds to make...' She paused and looked at him meaningfully. 'Shopping, food for dinner. Lots to do. You never give me a spare moment!' she repeated mischievously.

'You any good at cooking?' Colin changed the subject. 'I'm a dead loss. Just about do a boiled egg for breakfast, and a tin of beans...'

'I can manage scrambled eggs on burnt toast for breakfast, and Spaghetti Bolognese for supper. But not out of a tin. I make it myself,' she announced virtuously. 'A sandwich in my lunch break in Polhaven is the best meal of my day. Or a pasty. In fact, I was hoping to buy a recipe book tomorrow.'

'Then we'll continue eating here until you feel comfortable with cooking for Lord and Lady Polmouth. Instead of paying ourselves a salary. That's decided.' He sipped his wine. Then: 'Good God! Why didn't I think of it before!?'

'Don't tell me! You've reached four score and fourteen? Surprises. Now what?' Colin nodded absently, not really listening.

'The W.C.L.R. Company. Of course!'

'What about them? They run trains, not restaurants.'

'You're wrong. They do, in summer, to and from Falmouth, on the excursions train. A full-blown 1950s dining car, rescued from the Orient Express in all its finery. A galley kitchen down the end for two cooks, A la Carte meals for lunch. Why didn't

I think of it before?' He drained his wine and signalled to the barman. 'And the steam train can be rescheduled to do the ten-thirty from Falmouth to Polport, bringing the Orient Express dining car and a chef. Stay every day until 2.30 in the afternoon, serve lunches like a restaurant. And best of all, they have a drinks licence! Seven days a week! Just think of it...'

'I am! That'll go down really well with the "Crab and Lobster", us offering luxury dining competition. Besides, Colin, no-one works in Polmouth because there are no jobs. Everyone works in Polhaven or Penzance.' She waved to the barman, her cider glass empty. But Colin shook his head.

'Uh-uh. Not everyone. There are lots of pensioners who for certain are tired of cooking for themselves every day. Young housewife mothers, doting relatives visiting, and later tourists. And we can set the prices far lower than the "C & L", no competition, more a complementary offering. And when it's an overnight stay, evening meals as well, A la Carte. Same on the tourist specials to Polmine Project, when it gets going. And then there'll be the weekend dinner train... on Saturdays. Leave at 6.00 p.m., dinner in the Orient Express dining car to Falmouth, and we'll charter one of the St. Mawes ferries for the return to Polport around ten. That'll bring in some money...'

'All right, you win. Four score and fourteen. Next surprise?'

'Coming up. I must be getting old! The train comes from Falmouth each time, goes back there. And Falmouth has a Hotel School, training, among other people, professional chefs. We invite a couple of trainee chefs, waiters and waitresses too, so that the students can take it in turns in a real environment.' Petra groaned theatrically.

'This has got to stop. That's 95 today. Please...' Then: 'I'm hungry. Come on.' She tugged his arm until they reached their table. The jaundiced waiter looked at his watch and sighed. However, the value of their order put a smile back on his face.

It was nearing eleven o'clock when they pushed their chairs back from table and looked at each other. The ambiance and the message were unmistakable.

In her Whitehall overalls, wearing latex gloves and disposable blue slippers over her shoes, Thelma was diligently completing her dusting and cleaning of the corridors and outer offices of the enclave which was her domain, Bonham's section. Big Ben chimed eleven times in the distance. Aware that Tring, Hamlyn and Bonham habitually worked into the small hours, she had devised a system to suit all involved. A box of keys was suspended from the wall outside Bonham's office. Usually, all staff handed their keys to the Security Officer at the entrance, but for the purpose of Thelma's night duties Tring and Hamlyn would hang their keys in the box for the cleaner. It was her responsibility to lock the rooms on leaving and hand the keys in as she left. But Bonham's key was absent, so he must still be working. Thelma had a solution to this eventuality as well. And this part made the whole activity fool-proof. She knocked at Bonham's door and waited. A barking noise came from within.

'**In!**' She entered, closing the door. One of Bonham's many pet hates was the door being left open. 'Well?'

'Reporting for the night round, sir. Mr. Tring and Mr. Hamlyn have left, so I'll start there.'

'Fine.' Bonham was only half listening, but this nightly charade was mandatory. 'I'll be here another half an hour, so do mine last. Thanks, Thelma.' She left and went down a level to the large office shared by Tring and Hamlyn. Here she also had a fool-proof procedure. Before starting she locked the door, as she was supposed to do, then took a vacuum cleaner from an unlocked cupboard, plugged it in and hoovered half the floor. Leaving the motor running, she turned to her capacious handbag and took out a bunch of more than twenty keys provided by her paymaster. These were not just any old house

168

keys. They could open practically every cupboard and drawer and filing cabinet in the northern hemisphere. Next Thelma took out a 1950s child's toy, an Ekta-Sketch tablet.

Measuring eight inches by five it consisted of a plastic frame across which a transparent plastic sheet was stretched, and underneath was a grey surface. Hanging from the tablet was a short, leadless pencil on a string, and at the bottom corner of the frame a plastic knob, attached to a slider. Thelma could write a good deal on the grey surface with the magic pencil, but if surprised or interrupted, wipe the entire surface clean by swiping the slider across it. The text disappeared instantaneously and irretrievably. If questioned by security about this object in her handbag, which had never happened yet, Thelma would say it was a toy for her grandson.

There were three drawers in each of the men's desks. Now came the sensitive part. The magic keys opened each drawer and inside she found a number of folders. Before touching any of them, she studied their configuration, their position, memorising which lay under which, and finally looked for the "stray hair" trick. A classic tell-tale of documents being illegally touched was for the owner to leave a hair in an almost invisible position before locking the drawer. If in the morning the hair was gone, or had moved, security had certainly been breached. She found no hairs that night. Finally, to minimise any chance of suspicion if she were interrupted, even with a locked door, she placed the first folder on the desk, closed the drawer and using skim-reading sought any tit-bits that could interest her paymasters. It was to prove a fruitful night.

Chapter Fifteen

Friday, June 14th 1974

The midnight magic of Polmouth cast a silent spell over the bay, the estuary and the miniature harbour of Polport. Nowhere were beauty and tranquillity better in fusion than under the Cornish deep blue night sky, the planets preternaturally bright. A Midsummer Night's Dream. If some might rue the lost opportunity to indulge themselves in the velvet mystery of soft, starlit stillness, one young couple regretted not a jot their sole presence beside the stone wall of Polport harbour. Nothing stirred, and the silence was a commodity as rare in the modern world as Polmouth was destined to be, in Teague's words: *"the kernel of the peach that is the very heritage of England"*. Leaning against the low wall neither Petra nor Colin seemed ready to breach the beauty of intimate silence. Then, in a very soft, gentle voice, slightly husky, Petra said:

'I don't want to sound argumentative, not tonight of all nights...' she glanced up at the firmament of tiny glowing stars and galaxies, '... but there was something you said earlier, about...'

Colin pressed his finger against her lips to stop her.

'I know. It hit me as I said it. I was crass. I'm so sorry, it should never have happened. Above all, not to you, from me.' She turned to stare up at him, wide eyed in the silver night.

'You know? How can you know?' He snorted in irritation with himself.

'Because I'm not an insensitive blockhead most of the time, and this time I was actually ashamed. I'm so sorry, Petra.' There was a catch in his voice. She spoke in a whisper:

'Just to be sure, will you...?' He interrupted her, holding her close.

'Will I say it again? No, but I'll say it the way it should have come out. Here goes: "Then we'll continue eating here until *we* feel comfortable with cooking *for each other*." Is that better?' Her eyes were wide in wonderment.

'Is there anything you don't presage, you don't get right?' She giggled. 'In the end, anyway. Just don't argue with me about what constitutes a cup of flour...' Then, staring up at the starlit sky: 'It's nearly mid-summer's day, the solstice. The sun'll rise before five. I'd really like to see a sunrise over Polmouth... with you...' her voice tailed away. 'We could stay out.'

'And freeze!' Colin rejoined firmly. 'But a sunrise over Polmouth you **shall** see, sorry, *we* shall see, very soon. And it'll be so spectacular, it'll last a thousand days and a thousand and one nights. Put the Arabian Nights to shame.'

She kissed him, then turned to stare out across the picturesque harbour and bay, the dark waters of the estuary. Although the night air was warm, she shivered.

'Take me to bed,' she murmured. 'And hold me tight. For ever.' They crossed the road to the inn. 'And show me the eternal sunrise.'

Sunrise in Whitehall was singularly unromantic. Shortly before six in the morning Thelma handed in the office keys to the yawning Security Officer and left the building. Her breakfast ritual was equally unromantic. She walked in the growing light to the all-night Lyons Corner House overlooking Westminster, bought an early edition of the Daily Express at the tube station entrance before taking her habitual table near the pay telephone in the corner. The waiter approached. She nodded wordlessly. All the staff knew Thelma and her daily fare without her even ordering. She rose and crossed to the telephone booth, closed the door, put £1.00 in coins in the slot and dialled a number in West Berlin. As always her call was answered by a machine, tape recording her intelligence.

'W4 from UK 21,' she started, her usual code. She drew the magic writing tablet from her bag and in a clear, slow voice said: 'Zero, Plenty, Polmine Safe House, Quarantine, destination Porton...' and then read the second line of her Ekta-Sketch tablet, and in the same slow, clear voice, the remaining five lines of data gleaned from various files. She had not the first idea what she was saying actually meant, nor whether it was important. On ringing off, she pulled the plastic knob on the bottom across the screen and the words disappeared for ever, she believed. But it was not truly for ever. In Berlin they would shortly be deciphered and cause consternation, of which she was unaware.

At her table she picked up the newspaper and started to read it while her Full English was served, and continued reading as she ate. Not only did Thelma never know what use, if any, her intelligence would be to its recipient, her knowledge of world affairs was so meagre that she did not even know that Berlin was a city divided by a wall of death, the West half a thriving, capitalist enclave, while East Berlin, the so-called capital of East Germany was a drab and unconvincing showpiece for the Soviet Communist Bloc. Berlin was the focal point of the Cold War, where Communist Eastern Europe came into immediate contact with Capitalist Western Europe. All that Thelma cared about was the anonymous brown envelope that mysteriously appeared through her letter box at the end of every month with a sizeable amount in used bank notes. Nor could she know that her tape recorded intelligence would be passed to East Berlin and distributed later that day to places as far as apart as Moscow, Bulgaria, Romania, Czechoslovakia... in fact to whomever needed to know who was an enemy of the West.

'What time are the Camborne deep mine people coming?' Petra asked. They were finishing a copious breakfast in the otherwise deserted dining room of the "Crab and Lobster".

'We're to meet them at nine off the Polhaven ferry, open the Pump House and the lift workings. They'll get everything up and running and in the afternoon they'll take us down. Should be exciting. But that leaves us the morning...'

'I can use that time finally to start unpacking, making the Croft House look like home...' She paused, staring at her empty coffee cup. 'Home...' she repeated softly. 'My foster parents were magnificent, I adored them. But I never really had a place I could call "my home".' She wiped her eyes. 'Oh, Colin, I promise I'll make it really nice, for us. I promise I will!' He put his arm round her shoulders.

'You can count on me, all the way.' was all he said. The waitress had been approaching with a fresh coffee pot for them, but as she neared their table, she thought better of it and beat a silent retreat.

The Polhaven ferry was still a mile out in the estuary when Colin and Petra arrived at Polport landing stage. Petra had been strangely silent for some time, but now she spoke.

'Of course, Rome wasn't built in a day. So I can't see us moving in definitively today...' Colin took the hint.

'I thought you liked the bed in the "Crab and Lobster"? And the food's excellent... besides we can't move in until we've bought a cook book, and that won't happen today.' She giggled.

'I knew you'd cotton on. D'you really think we can authorise visits into the deep mine? What if it's too risky?'

'That's one of the things I want to find out from today's experts. We'll have to walk up with them, pushing the mopeds.' Petra looked mischievous.

'You can if you like. I'll ride ahead on mine, get the keys!' A sudden thought occurred to her. 'What'll you be doing while I'm building a castle in the sky?'

'I thought I'd call on our German writers, invite them to a tour of the Estate. I could show them the shallow mine. Should be of interest as they're mineralogists.'

'Brilliant. But... sandwiches for lunch? Not very hospitable for our deep mine guests!' Colin looked across the Esplanade.

'Go and buy half a dozen pasties, the big ones. We can reheat them for lunch, and they can join us on the terrace if they want. Or they may have brought their own lunch.' Petra was already on the other side of the road, entering the small shop. Colin smiled. By the time the ferry had docked and the gangplank was in action, Petra was riding swiftly up to Polmine Estate with supplies for lunch in her basket on the moped. Colin greeted the three Camborne engineers, identifiable by the miners' helmets they were carrying and their two large travelling bags the size of suitcases. The tallest and visibly most senior was a grey haired man in his fifties. His face bore the ravages of a great deal of time spent in dangerous, confined spaces deep underground where scrapes, bumps and bruises were the least of a miner's worries.

'Mike Novak, Head of Faculty. This is Harry, doesn't have another name, he's "just Harry"!' Harry was as short as Novak was tall, clearly a valuable asset when squeezing along tight, low tunnels. 'And this is our deep mine specialist, Jenny Pacton.' He looked around the harbour and across the estuary. 'What a charming place, it's a gem! I never knew it was this pretty. Well, which way do we go?'

'I'll walk with you. Just have to collect my moped on the way.'

They were nearly half way up the track to the mine when Colin had a sudden recollection.

'The team inspecting the shallow mine said something about you all being up in Doncaster this week. We didn't expect you so soon...' Novak paused in his stride.

'The Dean of the School, Sir Robert Maxton, insisted we return early. Just for this visit.' Colin was astonished. Before he could query this, Novak continued, resuming his uphill walk. 'Sir Robert was also Dean ten years ago, when Mr. Ingram made his request for support, funding. The School has limited financial resources, but Sir Robert was strongly in favour of the project. He was mortified when none of the sources that Mr. Ingram approached would offer sponsorship or financing. And the railway wouldn't launch a service without that.' He paused to get his breath and Colin saw a solitary figure advancing towards them down the track. It was Katrina Rothmount. Even at a distance it was apparent that a silent mutual decision was instantaneous. When she passed the group, neither Katrina nor Colin made any sign of recognition, still less greeting. Oblivious to the crossing of two gladiators, Novak continued. 'I was a lowly faculty member back then, but Sir Robert discussed it with me at length. Now that you've taken over, and the clincher being the train… well, after we've got the mine going this morning, and you've seen the essentials this afternoon, we need to talk about the whole project and the Dean's proposal for Camborne involvement. It was because he takes it so seriously that we were called back at short notice.' At this point they reached the top of the track and Colin was obliged to pursue this promising development in depth later. The three engineers were enthusing loudly about the entire estate and in particular the distant Pump House and lift structure.

Petra came hurtling towards them without a helmet, her ponytail flying behind her in the breeze, and very nearly destroyed Colin's manhood as her front wheel skidded to a halt almost embedded between his legs. She climbed off her moped and Colin disengaged himself from the spokes of the front wheel, introduced her. She held out the keys, two for the deep mine, two for Colin's guided tour with the Germans.

'See you later!' she called gaily over her shoulder as she sped away. The engineers stared after her through the cloud of dust she was enjoying raising behind her. Harry grinned.

'Not sure how safe she'd be down a mine!' But he was laughing. They reached the row of terraced cottages, and Colin paused.

'Here,' he gave Novak the Pump House key and the one for the mine shaft workings. 'You go ahead. I have a call to make. But do join us for a simple lunch over there in the Croft House when you're through with the hard work.' Novak shook his head.

'Much appreciated, but we brought our own rations, if that's all right?' Colin nodded and watched the three walk on to the mine, then turned to Cottage Number One. He was not sorry that the detestable Princess Triple-S had gone out. He decided to test the Germans' level of English before revealing his fluency in German and knocked. It was a full two minutes before Helmuth Schiller opened the door, looked at Colin in surprise. Then his face cleared. Of course, the owner of the Estate.

English was scarcely taught in schools in the DDR, East Germany, but Helmuth considered he had a sufficient smattering for basic conversation. The principal foreign language taught in the DDR was Russian in which both Helmuth and Uschi Meissner were proficient, as they used it regularly at work. Colin spoke very slowly, enunciating clearly and avoiding any abbreviations.

'Good morning. My name is Colin, I am the owner of Polmine. I hope that I am not disturbing you?' It was evident from Helmuth's blank face that even this was beyond him. But he was not ready to give up. He called over his shoulder:

'Uschi, *wir haben Besuch!*' Uschi Meissner appeared behind him. Colin tried the same introduction again. Uschi at least gleaned the gist.

'Good mornink. My name… Uschi Meissner, this Helmuth. You want?'

'Can I show you the mine? Polmine…?' Colin waved his arm expansively indicating the whole Estate. Uschi nodded.

'Yes. We see… all… I get light.' She went into the back room.

Helmuth raised a hand, frowning and mimed picking up a telephone receiver to his ear and dialling a number.

'Vee haff problem. Telephone, not *verbunden*… can work?' Colin nodded. He had forgotten that each cottage had a telephone. He kept the answer short and simple.

'Yes. I do it.'

Understandably, lack of contact with the outside world had been a major concern. Helmuth's response to this welcome news prompted him automatically and unwittingly to respond in the only foreign language that he knew:

'хорошо, идеальный!' Uschi was still in the other room so she missed her colleague's blunder. Colin showed neither surprise nor incomprehension at this strange noise that most certainly was not German. Although as a linguist he recognised the words as Russian, he had no idea they meant "good, perfect!". He feigned nonchalance and led the way to the gate and the shallow mine. They entered the black tunnel.

'You wait here!' He made a sign to stop, and advanced to the metal switch box, and within less than a minute the corridor was fully illuminated. He signalled to the two Germans to join him. 'Perhaps we can speak German?' he suggested.

Such was Helmuth's relief that he unconsciously recidivated; he responded again in Russian:

'Хорошо!' This time Uschi Meissner heard him. She stared at him angrily and, realising what he had done, he bit his lip and tried to cover up by saying in German: 'Magnificent, I have never seen a mine tunnel like it! Please show us more.' Colin gave no sign of having recognised that the word was Russian, and presented "his mine" with panache, impressing both the Germans with his faultless accent and fluency.

Meanwhile, Petra was hard at work putting their home into shape, a dwelling fit for Lord and Lady Polmouth of Polmine. It gave her intense satisfaction, nothing more so than when it came to making up the king-size bed in the bedroom, and arranging all the furniture tastefully. For a young woman who had never had a place to call "home", she had the woman's touch to perfection.

In the mine they had reached the first bunker. Helmuth stared around in surprise while Uschi went to the grille and looked out over the English Channel. The diesel engine and the generator were performing almost silently. Colin gave them time to examine the installations and the rough-hewn walls of the vault, and used their inspection to think about what he had heard. When they resumed their progress down the main tunnel, he had decided to probe a little deeper, and Uschi provided him with the perfect opportunity. They continued to converse in German.

'You speak German perfectly, you could even be a German... I suppose you've lived there?' Colin made his first move.

'I lived there for a short while,' he lied. 'Mostly travelling. A beautiful country, so much variety. Unforgettable was the approach on the ferry from Harwich up the river to Hamburg!' Helmuth unwisely took the bait.

'The River Rhine is indeed a beautiful river.' Uschi's scarce knowledge of West German geography could not correct the blunder.

'Yes,' agreed Colin thoughtfully, 'yes it is. But I think I remember most a walk up the Feldberg one Spring morning and taking coffee at the cafeteria on the top. The Harz mountains... breath-taking!' Uschi in her turn stepped into the open jaws.

'I've been there. You're right. But then I'm from just a bit away, the Black Forest, *Schwaben.*'

'Yes, of course. Swabia. And you Helmuth?' Colin was now sure that something didn't add up here. They had nearly reached the bottom of the tunnel and the ventilation and drainage shaft to the sea.

'Würzburg. Have you been there?' Colin shook his head.

'No,' he lied, 'no I haven't. Maybe on my next trip.' He warned them to lower their heads as they entered the final spur and Uschi at last had a use for her torch. Once again Colin allowed them time to wander around the cavern. He had decided not to divulge that he had spent not "a short while" but a whole year based in Bavaria, not far from Würzburg, and had actually lived for a week in the town during his Goethe Institut research. He had not the slightest doubt that these two scientists were intellectuals engaged in something that approximated to the profession of mineralogy, but he needed time to draw conclusions that weren't impossibly far-fetched. Something didn't make sense here.

On reaching the outside world and welcome sunshine, Colin locked the gate and made a suggestion.

'Please feel free to roam the estate and explore. But your colleagues from Camborne School of Mines are down the deep mine right now, doing an inspection, so I'd recommend we leave that for another time.' Colin could not know it, but meeting anyone who truly was from the School was the last thing that Uschi and Helmuth wanted. 'And if you wish to visit the farm, let me know first, please. The farmers don't know you're staying here, and I really should introduce you for that...' To Colin's relief the Germans agreed and they went back to their cottage, leaving Colin to mount his moped and drive to the Croft House, where he found Petra in tears in the kitchen, seated at the table and sobbing. Now what?

'Hey, hey, hey!' He hurried to her and took her shoulders, standing behind her. 'What's all this? What's the matter?' She stood up and hugged him, her cheeks wet with tears.

'Oh, Colin, I'm sorry... it's just... I told you, I've never had a home to call my own, and... oh, it's just so nice, so very, very nice! Home?... It's a mansion... And not a dream?'

He shook his head.

'Not a dream! Or rather, yes, a dream, but a real-life one! Come on, show me our new home.' She wiped the tears from her cheeks with the back of her hand.

'You always know how to say the right thing!'

On returning to the kitchen Colin looked at his watch.

'It's twelve o'clock and I'm hungry. Where've you put the pasties? How many d'you want? I'll have two.' He turned to the stove. 'Oh good, it's gas, not electric.'

'What's the difference?'

'All the best chefs use gas, because it's analogue, whereas electric stoves are digital.' Petra was mystified.

'Uh... in English?'

'You can adjust gas instantly to any setting and heat you want. Electric you only have the pre-set six heat levels.'

'Oh... does it matter?'

'When we start cooking, we'll see.' He opened the oven door and lit it with a match. Petra was watching him suspiciously.

'You sure you've never cooked anything more than a boiled egg?' She took the pasties out of a cupboard, then two plates. 'Here, or the terrace?' Diplomatically, Colin remembered his promise.

'You decide.'

At two o'clock two of the three engineers met them as they approached along the railway line.

'Good timing,' said Novak approvingly. 'Well, you're in for a surprise, in fact several surprises! You'll see at last what the Army was doing down there during the War. What we don't know is why. Looks like a work still in progress... we'll start in here.' He led them into the pump room where the immense, gleaming pump piston was slowly pushing down into its cylinder then slowly rising again to ceiling height high above them. There was a constant, distant gurgling noise and malodorous, dirty, grey water was being pumped out of a pipe and down a drain.

'Where does the water come from?' wondered Petra. Novak led them across the cavernous Pump House to an immense chart he had pinned to a wall. It was a three dimensional plan of the entire mine workings on four levels.

Level One showed a broad tunnel feeding palm-tree configurations of much narrower, subsidiary branches. The Level Two plan was similar, and the two lowest levels showed very long tunnels extending far under the sea bed for at least a mile.

'The water's down here, Level Four.' Novak pointed to the tunnels extending under the sea. 'Levels One to Three are what we call a "dry mine", no accretion of water. Level Four is a "wet mine", seepage through the sea bed a mile away, draining into the pit of the lift shaft. Stagnant sea water, which is why it smells so brackish.' He led them into the adjacent lift workings and machinery. Greased cables led from the engine housing up at an angle to exit via a hole in the ceiling through which they could see the tower, tapered at the top.

'That's the "hoistway" where the lift cage rises to ground level.' He moved to a prehistoric looking metal box with a number of buttons of different colours set in the surface and a telephone handset to one side. 'Harry's still down there. He'll call when he's ready to come up. By the way, we'll need the outside line connecting to this. Come over here.' He led them behind the rack and pinion machine to an equally ancient metal housing inside which some mechanism was whirring softly. A number of armour plated thick cables led from it to the outside. 'This is something very rarely found in any mine, be it coal, copper or gold. You're really spoiled here...' At that moment the phone rang and the woman Jenny Pacton answered it. Then she rang off and pushed a red button on the control panel. The cables started to run in and out of the building and looking up they all saw the immense wheel at the top of the tower turning rapidly. 'Well, if you're ready, we'll leave Jenny and Harry up here to keep an eye on the smooth running of things while we go down. You're in for a surprise!' he repeated. A bell rang and automatically the cables stopped turning. 'Come on!'

Outside he stopped beside one of the travel bags and took out two helmets, each with a lamp on the front above the forehead. Next he took out what looked like armbands with a lamp attached. 'Ankle lamps,' he announced. 'Switch them on, at the heel.' Finally, he took out chest belt lamps to strap around the torso. He helped them into the belts. 'Leave the lights on at all times underground. And all visitors have to wear this gear. But the School has a plentiful supply for loan. Right!' He led them into the cage. There was no sign of Harry. The cage could hold eight people. Novak pressed a button and the cage started to descend. They were immediately plunged into complete darkness as the lift entered the shaft, the only light coming from their lamps, their ankles lighting the floor and the chest lamps powerfully shining ahead. The lift seemed to be descending at an unhealthily rapid pace.

'How deep are we going?' Petra's voice sounded distinctly uneasy.

'Level One first, eight hundred feet below the clifftop plateau, five hundred below sea level.' The lift slowed, and first their feet, then their bodies and heads were gradually lit with white, neon light. 'Surprise number one.' said Novak with satisfaction. 'And truly a rarity, thanks to the Army and the Royal Engineers, in the 1940s,' The lift stopped and he slid open the concertina door. They stepped out into a cavern with several neon strip lights attached to the rough-hewn roof. Novak stopped talking to permit the two to get their bearings and take in the size of the place. They saw several tunnels leading off like blades of a fan; only one was lit and looked as wide as the shallow mine main shaft. 'Someone mentioned possibly bringing groups down here.' Novak continued, leading them towards the illuminated, broad tunnel. 'Perfectly possible, if aged 14 or above, and all the lamps are issued and worn correctly. But I'd like to come to that later, back up topside. This way…' They walked in silence for about thirty yards, with the tunnel curving to the left. Then Novak stopped in front of a metal door identical to the one in the first bunker in the shallow mine. 'Here is what the Army was doing.' He opened the door into a long, broad room. 'Here we're under the sea, but it's shallow over this stretch, and we're well below the seabed. No water here, be a good place to bring the groups of visitors to. Give 'em a thrill. And look at the ceiling, the walls…' They looked, squinting against the bright white neon lights. The ceiling and walls were of reinforced concrete. There were long metal shelves attached to two of the walls. 'So this is what the Army was doing. But we haven't a clue why. Broadening the tunnel, excavating this. They dumped all the excavated rock in the disused tunnels we passed. Let's go down to Level Two. We'll give Level Three a miss, and Level Four, with the long under-sea tunnels, is mostly stagnant water.'

Half an hour later they stepped out of the cage into warm sunlight and divested themselves of the lamps. Still neither Petra nor Colin spoke. It was three o'clock. Harry came to meet them with Jenny Pacton.

'Impressive, innit?' Harry's query brought Colin down to earth with a bump. He nodded and made an effort.

'Would you like to come over to the Croft House for coffee? We don't have much of a selection of anything stronger…' His voice tailed away when he saw Novak shaking his head.

'With your permission, and many thanks for the offer, but we've had a dusty morning, I'd like some sea air. Is there anywhere by the sea, a park or a café, where we can discuss a number of issues?' Now Colin remembered the Dean's urgent recall of his deep mine crew.

'I understand perfectly.' He glanced at Petra then said to Novak: 'If you'd like to walk down, we could meet at "Polly's Tea Room", on the Esplanade, in an hour, say at four?' He looked questioningly at Petra and she nodded. Novak looked satisfied and was already making his way out of the lift house.

'Before we go, one thing.' He hesitated, gestured to his colleagues. 'You go ahead, I'll find you.' They left, carrying their helmets and the bags. Novak locked the lift house door and then made for the Pump House, locked it as well and gave the keys to Petra. 'Sir Robert insisted that I stress that he doesn't want to appear presumptuous. This is 100% your project, and yours alone. But he does so want to support it. To support you.' He looked diffident. 'It's this... he assumes that, like Ingram, you'll be looking for sponsors, financing, yes?' They nodded. 'And he supposes the LEA and the DES are top of your list?' Two more nods. 'And that, if you can find possible sponsors, you'll be doing presentations of the project, here, on site?' He didn't wait for their response but pressed ahead. 'When do you intend to hold the first, the first presentation to possible sponsors, I mean?' Petra shrugged.

'We haven't talked about it, yet. Things are moving so fast...' She looked at Colin. He nodded.

'I was hoping that, if we can get enough of our list to come down, we could go for next Thursday.' Petra gasped, but bit her lip. Now for the first time, Novak's creased face split in a broad grin.

'Can you tell me, here and now, that you'll have it ready next Thursday? It's a simple yes or no...' Petra squeezed Colin's hand and nodded, pre-empting Colin's reassurance that it would take place, whoever came, with free train transport on the W.C.L.R. steam train for the guests from Penlyn, and back. Times to be fixed. Another grin from Novak. He turned to leave. 'In an hour then, Tea Room, Esplanade... I'll find it.

Oh, and bring your list with you!' He strode off, leaving Colin and Petra staring after him. As soon as Novak reached Polport harbour he looked around for a telephone box.

In the East Berlin suburb of Grünwald, in an office not dissimilar to Hamlyn's and Tring's in Whitehall, three men were sitting at a conference table. Each had an identical open dossier in front of him. At the head of the table, Oberleutnant Maximilian Traub looked disparagingly at the two secret service officials seated to his right and his left. He despised anyone not in uniform, but was obliged to tolerate these two, one a retired officer. Besides, it was the best that the DDR could muster, and in his more objective moments he had to admit that their success rate was high, but principally because their work load was low. Today, Traub was in a particularly subjective mood. He now knew for certain that his wife Karin was frequently unfaithful to him in the most graphic terms possible, and he was impotent to do anything about it. Maximilian Traub especially loathed impotence in anything, perhaps because where it had mattered he had been found wanting. He opened the proceedings.

'Well?' he barked. 'Do we... do *you* know who they are, these "Zero" and "Plenty"?' The man to his right in a shabby grey suit, Dieter Karling, looked uncomfortable. He swallowed.

'Helmuth Schiller, Uschi Meissner, scientists at the chemical warfare research centre in Dresden... They defected from a colloquium in Split, Yugoslavia, a few days ago. The Royal Navy lifted them, so it must have been prearranged. Our men are looking for the leak, the mole. Now they're in England...' Traub interrupted him savagely.

'You mean there was no collateral here in the DDR? No family members, nothing to make them return? So why were they allowed into Yugoslavia? We know the Yugos are liberal, have a porous frontier?' Traub's irritation was growing. The third man, elderly Peter Rüther, who remembered better times in Germany's colonial paradise of Namibia in Africa, was growing heartily tired of Traub's choleric manner. He decided to put him in his place.

'Oberleutnant,' he began with artificial deference, 'may I remind you that you are here to help us resolve the matter, not waste time on useless rhetoric?' Traub, who recognised that ex-Colonel Rüther, retired, carried far higher rank, had to cede to his superior.

'All right,' he grunted, 'moving on. What and where is Polmine?' Here Karling was on safer ground. He drew three maps of Southern England and Cornwall from his dossier, distributed them. He proceeded to explain in detail precisely what Polmouth and Polmine were like. Then he surprised his colleagues. Considering that the DDR had no official links with Great Britain, his information was comprehensive.

'Polmouth was actually on the national news in England just two days ago. That won't worry MI6, nothing to do with their Safe House at the mine. Apparently the rail link to the main line was cut ten years ago, and is to reopen this weekend.' Traub's choleric day was just getting more and more intolerable. He exploded.

'*Um Gottes Willen*! We have urgently either to get these two scientists back, or eliminate them before they get to the British Biological and Chemical Warfare centre at Porton Down, and you're waffling about *railways*?! Explain, or shut up!' This time, Colonel Rüther intervened more severely.

'Oberleutnant, it is significant, and you are wasting valuable time! If you have nothing constructive to say, please...' he unleashed his strongest rebuke so far, '... hold your tongue!' Traub reddened. His position at the head of the table suddenly felt considerably diminished.

'Well, get on with it!'

'Even if we could get them back,' Karling continued patiently, 'which we can't, they'd never work for us again. Speaking to their colleagues in Dresden it's clear they've defected on principle. Even if they never actually work for the British at Porton Down, and they probably won't, they've taken the decision out of our hands. No choice. Elimination.'

Colonel Rüther looked at the papers in his dossier.

'How will it be done? Do we have a *Jäger* in the U.K.?' Karling shook his head.

'Not enough missions to make it worthwhile. But we have a base in Kensington, London. For this mission our best man will travel from Berlin. The English have given us Meissner and Schiller on a plate with their standard quarantine procedure. They always take at least a month to evaluate cases like this… there was a Bulgarian who defected last year, they kept him two months in one of their Safe Houses. So we have time on our side. But we are taking it seriously. I refer you to document three in the folders.' They all shuffled papers, finding a single sheet with a short biography and a photograph of a man. Traub, already incensed at his treatment, made a come-back. Or rather, he tried to.

'Who is this creature?' he snarled aggressively. 'Looks like a schoolboy, or a cherub on a Baroque church fresco! Well?!' Colonel Rüther had had enough.

'His name is Zoltan von Horváth, Hungarian, age 40, one of our best marksmen, and utterly cold-blooded, ruthless. I don't think he has a spark of humanity in his entire body. He has an outstanding record of missions accomplished…'

'But that means he is not unknown to a number of security services,' Karling interrupted. 'If you will look at the photo, you will see that he has no facial hair, is very blond, and thus stands out in a crowd where a spy should normally mingle unnoticed.' Traub tried to regain territory.

'Why? I mean why not, I can see he looks like a schoolboy, 40 or not, so what's wrong with him? Is he castrated, or what?' Karling sighed.

'Oberleutnant, it really would be very unwise to ask him that. Your days would be numbered, whatever your rank. His outstanding virtue is, he's tenacious. Cautious, but determined. If a mission looks to be in jeopardy, he'll pull back and give it another go when it's safer. And he's resourceful.' Traub nodded reluctantly. 'And he's waiting outside. May I bring him in?' He was asking Colonel Rüther not Oberleutnant Traub, and the latter's ire increased. Rüther nodded and Karling went to the door. An extraordinary figure entered behind him as he returned to his seat. The newcomer stood stiffly to attention at the foot of the table, but did not speak. The three seated men stared at him. Von Horváth was diminutive, scarcely five foot nine even standing to attention, and his fair hair topped a cherubim physiognomy with glinting blue eyes and a face that had never been touched by a razor. It was clear that, despite his being short for a man, his physique under the casual clothes he was wearing was testimony to a very fit man indeed. Karling gestured to von Horváth to sit down.

'Here is your schedule.' He slid a document down the table to the assassin. 'You'll leave by train on Tuesday night, the "Ost-West Express", Moscow-Oostende direct train. You'll join it at Berlin Ostbahnhof. So collect your papers and passport from Central Office, transit via Berlin Friedrichstrasse to West Berlin, out of the DDR at Helmstedt into West Germany, and for the Belgian frontier at Aachen and again at Oostende. And of course papers for the UK. You're travelling as Thorsten Magnussen, Danish, age 24, postgraduate student. Any problem with that?' he queried. But before von Horváth could reply, Traub made a final attempt to make his presence felt.

'Why the train?' he demanded. 'There are direct flights from West Berlin to London? Why?' he repeated. Karling sighed again, addressed all those present, trying valiantly to remain patient.

'Passengers from West Germany, particularly Berlin, are scrutinised at Heathrow very carefully, even sometimes pulled from the line at passport control for checks.' He looked meaningfully at von Horváth. It was clear that he meant such a face would hardly go unnoticed. 'We have chosen the rail and sea ferry route. Dover is the usual port for cross-Channel ferries, but at Dover the checks, although less rigorous than Heathrow, are still risky. We've chosen the night train "Ost-West Express" because that particular ferry crossing lands at Folkestone, where passport controls are far less stringent.' He turned to von Horváth. 'The boat train goes direct Folkestone-London. You have the Kensington address in your notes. Go there, await further instructions. The weapon will be provided when you're there. The rail service all the way to this Pol-place makes things easier. Questions?' Zoltan von Horváth shook his head, stood up, gave a stiff Prussian bow with clicked heels to the seated men and left the room. Colonel Rüther, now thoroughly in control of the meeting, closed his file.

'Well, gentlemen, that's that.' He looked at Karling, ignoring the apoplectic Oberleutnant. 'You'll provide frequent updates?' Karling nodded and Rüther stood up. The meeting was over.

Chapter Sixteen

Petra and Colin were sitting in the shade on their terrace, out of the burning sun and mid-summer heat.

'Well,' said Petra. 'You're full of the four score and tens. Another surprise, presentation next Thursday, hey?' She stared at him critically. 'I told you you'd need suits. Shoes, shirts, ties, and you've done nothing about it! Honestly, men! Hopeless!' She giggled. Colin shrugged.

'What do you suggest?'

'Penzance. Next week. No good clothes shops in Polhaven. We'll have to go to the bank there first...'

'I'm not expecting Prince Charles' tailor...' Colin protested. He made to leave. 'I'm going to get changed. By the way, you pick one of the bathrooms and I'll have the other. Luxury living. Then I'm impatient to hear what Novak has to say. Oh, and you'd better grab those damned pyjamas you're always on about.' Her eyes widened, moist.

'You mean... another night in paradise?'

'Well, you can hardly wear them in the street. We'll do the main moving in on Sunday.'

'Why not start tomorrow?'

'Busy day, Gala Opening of the railway. So two nights in paradise.' Petra's eyes were now really shining with imminent emotion. She looked around the estate then at the terrace.

'Colin,' she murmured, 'we've got our own paradise. Right here.' There was a long silence, then Colin scraped his chair back and stood up.

'And you know what the best part of it is?' Petra frowned.

'No. What?'

'There are no apple trees, and no serpents!' He went into the house.

They arrived at "Polly's Tea Room" before Novak and selected an indoor table. Novak appeared in the doorway and joined them.

'Good idea,' he said pointing to the air conditioning unit on the wall above them. 'Far too hot out there. I pity those poor gardeners…'

'Gardeners?'

'I counted eight of them spread along the Esplanade. Looks as if they're planting palm trees. And there are more men with wheelbarrows of earth and what look like boxes of seedling flowers, in the station.' He looked at Colin penetratingly. 'Don't suppose you'd know anything about all that?' Colin looked awkward.

'Well… I did hear talk of something planned for tomorrow. Gala Opening of the railway, I think. But it's nothing to do with us…' His voice tailed away unconvincingly. He looked around. 'Miss Pacton and Harry not joining us?' Novak shook his head.

'They've taken an early ferry to Polhaven. They've been away from home, their families, all week. I have no family, and this is the prettiest village I have ever seen, with or without trees and flower beds.' A waitress approached and they ordered. Colin was impatient to discover what, exactly, was motivating the Dean of Camborne School of Mines, but before he could broach that, Novak continued enthusing about the village.

'In fact, it's so pretty and tranquil, and as I said I have no family. Is there a hostelry of any kind where I could put up for the night?'

'We're staying at the "Crab and Lobster" while we get moved in at the Croft House. It's excellent. And the food is superb. We could show you where it is?' Novak nodded.

'Sounds perfect. Now, to business.' But at that moment the young waitress served copious plates of cream teas then returned with teapots. Finally: 'As soon as I got down to Polport this afternoon, I called Sir Robert in Camborne. Now, as he said, this is your project, and only yours. And Camborne can't provide direct funding, we have to scrabble around to find enough for ourselves. But what he does want to provide is maximum support. It's very difficult to find anyone who has a real interest in mines and mining. So here's what he'd like to do... Ingram failed because he didn't know which names to contact and he didn't carry any clout when he found one. Sir Robert has access to all the names, and he carries a lot of clout. So he contacted Cornwall LEA, and the DES in London. I called him a second time just before coming here. So refreshing to find a phone box that's not been vandalised.' Petra was on tenterhooks and stared at this admirer of British values. 'He doesn't hang about!' continued Novak admiringly. 'Both his contacts remembered Ingram and his impasse ten years ago. Now that you've secured the train service, the LEA will provide funding, and also subsidise school groups as soon as you're open for business. On hearing that, the DES said it would equal whatever the LEA puts in, and distribute material advertising the educational value of a visit to schools. And not just "schools"! Nationwide! Not bad for an hour's phone calls, hey?'

'Not bad? Not bad?! It's miraculous.' Colin could not contain his excitement. He stared first at Novak, then Petra. But before either of them could grasp the enormous step forward, the security it provided financially, Novak flattened them with what he had to say next.

'Another of Ingram's problems would have been the high insurance premiums for groups visiting either mine, but especially the deep mine. Camborne has a number of mines which it maintains; it insures all staff and visitors against accidents in them. He suggests extending the cover of the policy to include Polmine. It'll hardly increase the existing global premiums, and he'll also guarantee that Camborne provides maintenance of the deep mine and for the pump and lift machinery. If that sounds all right?' Without waiting for the obvious answer he industriously buttered a sliced scone with a liberal coating then added an even heavier spoonful of jam.

Colin and Petra were staring silently at their clean plates, the cutlery untouched. Then, like twin robotic automatons, they took a scone each and started to eat as if it were a duty, not a feast to be savoured.

'Actually, there's more...' Novak continued imperturbably. He couldn't remember when a conversation had given him so much pleasure. 'Quite a lot more...' Colin gave a kind of confused groan.

'Mr. Novak...' his voice was a croak and he reached for his tea cup. 'Please! There's only so much a man can take!'

'*I'm* keeping up!' Petra announced virtuously, her arm around Colin's waist. Novak was gaining a better understanding of Ingram's bizarre bequest of the entire estate to these two. But he seemed to veer off at a tangent.

'Miss Zabrinksi mentioned that the restaurant is very good at this "Crab" place?'

'"And Lobster".' Petra was radiant. 'It is.'

'Excellent! Then, unless you have anything else on this evening, may I invite you both to dinner, courtesy the Dean of Camborne School of Mines?' Petra was on top form.

'Mister Novak,' she said gravely, 'even if we had an audience with the Queen this evening, we'd stand her up in favour of...'

'And anyway, we don't, so yes, many thanks.' Colin cut her short. 'We'll take you there when we've finished this, and then meet again at...?'

'Seven thirty all right?' They nodded and the remaining scones were eaten in a strange, electric silence.

'We have two and half hours,' said Colin to Petra as they left the Tea Room, having given Novak instructions to find the "Crab and Lobster" on the Esplanade. 'Hardly worth going back up to the Croft House. Besides… oh Lord! I'd clean forgotten!'

'Forgotten what?'

'I'm an idiot. We have the Gala Opening of the railway tomorrow, and I've forgotten to call the W.C.L.R. to arrange the train for two o'clock, not to mention I've also not booked the BR diesel to follow just behind so we have them both at the same time. Hell!' He looked at his watch.

'Not to worry.' Petra was calm, jovial almost. 'I have it sorted.'

'Please! Don't *you* start on that. Anyway, that's my line!'

'Well, I have. I called President Teague this morning when you were with the Germans, and he's fixed the trains. For two o'clock, as you said. I told you, I have it sorted.'

'Teamwork,' muttered Colin. 'All those hockey practices, I suppose?' He took her hand and firmly led the way alongside the harbour wall to the jetty and the pier.

'Where are we going?'

'I need your help on this, and a classical dose of Latin logic is required. We'll take a seat on the end of the pier where no-one can hear us, and I'll explain.'

'I told you I spent a year in West Germany, and met scores of different people, from all over the country. And they have as wide a range of regional accents as Britain. As varied as Scots and Devon, Essex and West Yorkshire. And I quickly learned to identify them.'

'Example?'

'Well, everyone at school learns *"nicht wahr"*, like *"n'est-ce pas"* in French. But the colloquialism used everywhere, which no teacher ever tells us, is *"geh?"*, but that's Bavaria. In Hessen it's pronounced *"gel?"*, like "get" in English, hard G. And elsewhere they say *"gelluh?"* I learned to identify a lot of nuances...'

'All right, I'm convinced. Where is all this going?'

'I'll take the anomalies in the order they happened this morning. The first was at the door of the cottage, I'd just introduced myself and the man Helmuth asked to have the telephone connected. We were speaking English at that point, or rather he was trying to but he doesn't have any English, and when I said I'd fix it, he unconsciously blurted out two words in... Russian! Something like *parasho*.' Petra's eyes widened.

'It's not *parasho*, although they make it sound like that. It's *harasho*. Means "good, excellent". They say it all the time...'

'How on earth do you know that?' He was astonished. Petra gave her inevitable giggle.

'You aren't the only one to have flirted with foreigners as a student. All your Helgas, for example.'

'So all yours were called Sergei?'

'Something like that. Refugees working for Radio Liberty, an American propaganda radio station, and studying in York at the same time. So go on, Sherlock.'

'During the whole year I spent in West Germany, no-one ever spoke Russian. Everyone seemed to speak English, but never replied to me in Russian. So... I thought I'd investigate, find out more. I started with the approach to Hamburg on the river Elbe, one of the great attractions for visitors to Germany. Every Primary School child knows Hamburg is on the Elbe. Well, Helmuth doesn't, he thinks it's on the Rhine, which actually flows into Holland! And as if that wasn't enough, I tried the Feldberg mountain, in the Black Forest. Also school kids' stuff. And I threw in the magnificence of the Harz mountains all around it. Uschi Thingummy jumped right in. What she said was: "Yes, magnificent. I've been there, and come from a bit away, the Black Forest..." Well, the Feldberg isn't "a bit away" from the Black Forest, it's the most central and highest point *in* the Black Forest. And the Harz mountains lie 300 miles to the North. I haven't even come to the accents yet...' Petra was looking confused.

'Which means you're going to one of these days. So they're ignorant.'

'Ignorant university graduates in mineralogy from Stuttgart University? Uh-uh, I don't think so.' Petra was intrigued and impressed but she enjoyed teasing Colin. She sighed.

'All right. Now give me the accents.'

'Starting with the Uschi woman. Says she comes from a region called *Schwaben*, Swabia. Well, I had a girl-friend in *Schwaben*...'

'Another bloody Helga?' Colin laughed.

'That was her name, yes, but it was purely platonic. She had two sisters, beautiful girls, Roswitha and Karin.' Petra opened her mouth to make some acid comment, then thought better of it. Colin was clearly deeply preoccupied by something. 'I stayed at their house for a few nights, on my travels. They were a lovely family, so welcoming. The father was a train driver.' He laughed despite his concern. 'He used to jest, saying I was the only man he'd allow to sleep in his house without marrying one of his daughters first! A lovely family.'

'*Please*! Get on with it!'

'I am! They were all pure *schwäbisch*, Swabian, born and bred. And the accent there is a bit like English spoken by a person from the Welsh valleys, very sing-song, up and down, an attractive lilt. But this Uschi, not a hint of it. On the contrary her accent, not one I've heard before, is harsh and metallic, monotone. Wherever she's from, she's not *schwäbisch*.' Petra was frowning, she saw that this was not just some simple misunderstanding, and she trusted Colin's knowledge completely.

'Which brings us to Helmuth.'

'Yes. He's worse! Says he's from Würzburg. I was based in Bavaria, not very far from Würzburg. Spent a week there for my research. And the accent there is even more specific to the locality. Germans always pronounce the letter R rolled in the throat, not using the teeth like the English. But the Würzburgers have an oddity unique there. They tongue the R like the Spanish, a trill with the tip of the tongue, a bit like the Scottish do. Not Helmuth. And now the clincher. I visited West Berlin, I told you. And the accent there has its own idiosyncrasy. Everywhere else all the letter Gs are pronounced like "get" in English, hard G. But the Berliners always pronounce it Y. So "tomorrow", *"gestern"*, they pronounce *"yestern"*, *"gut"* pronounced *"yut"* All the Gs are Y. And Helmuth is 1000% Berliner, I'm certain. Not from Bavaria, and certainly not Würzburg.' He stopped. 'I need a drink. "Crab and Lobster"?'

'With all haste.' They held hands and walked back the length of the pier in the evening sunshine, both deep in thought.

If either Petra or Colin was struggling to digest the events of that Friday, Novak's injection of promise, security and rapid progress for the Polmine Project on the one hand, and the strange circumstances surrounding the two German tenants on the other, neither showed any sign of it on entering the "Crab and Lobster" at seven o'clock. They headed for the bar. Before either could order the barman produced draught cider and a glass of white wine. Clearly the two celebrities merited accelerated service. They sat down.

'You'd better steel yourself, *we'd* better steel ourselves... What was it Novak said, about this evening?'

'He said there was more, "quite a lot more" were his words.' Petra shivered. 'Not sure how much "more" I can take tonight. You'd better make a list.' Colin raised a querying eyebrow. 'Of everything we talked about today. And if we add the German enigma...'

197

'About that,' said Colin, sipping his wine, 'I was meaning to ask you. You any good at writing a diary? A lot of girls do that, I know.' Petra wrinkled her brow, then smiled.

'Oh, I see! So that one day, when we're old and wizened, and no longer very attractive carriers of the banner of the *"peach that is the heritage of England"*, we can supplement our old age pensions with sales of our memoirs. But you're right. This is special enough to merit at least a daily record. All right. I'll start tomorrow.'

'Better get it out of the way in the morning, then. The Gala Opening will fill most of the rest of the day.' Colin put his arm round her shoulders. 'You're shivering!'

'It's the thought of standing next to you for hours on end, in that tatty old grey suit of yours. I'll be embarra...' Her voice tailed away, and she blushed deep red. 'Oh, God. You'll never embarrass me, not in a million years. Sorry, that came out all wrong.'

'You've got a sartorial fixation.' It was perhaps fortunate that Novak joined them at that moment, sat down on a bar stool beside Petra.

'Well!' he said in wonderment. 'If the village is a gem, this place is... how old is the "Crab and Lobster"?' he asked.

'1576.' Petra signalled to the barman who appeared as if on roller skates.

'It's like something out of Beatrix Potter,' enthused Novak. 'And the room... low beams, walls looking like wattle and daub, a bed fit for a king... How many rooms do they have here?' He was suddenly down to earth.

'A dozen or so, I think. Why?' Colin was taken aback by the sudden switch. Novak ordered a beer.

'Well, this presentation, next Thursday. Not everyone coming will necessarily be able to get home that evening, if they come from London, or the North. You could reserve a few rooms here, and the Dean can add the enticement of a rustic night, and the chance to explore the village.'

'It's started...' muttered Petra sotto voce, and squeezed Colin's hand.

'Sshhh!' Colin turned to Novak. 'It's a brilliant idea. We'll reserve all the single rooms, and see how many are finally occupied. And we could offer dinner here for the group, however many there are, and I could invite the President of the Village Council, Mr. Teague, as well.' He emptied his wine glass in one draught.

'Four score and sixteen, and counting!' Petra hadn't given up, and was giggling.

'Sshhh!' The unctuous waiter was approaching carrying three menus.

'On the table, sir, or on the chair as usual?'

'The chair will be fine.' They followed the waiter to their table, where he ceremoniously placed the menus on the fourth chair. Novak stared after the disappearing waiter, then the menus lying flat on the chair.

'Uh... is this some kind of Polmouth tradition?' He was foxed. Colin pulled back Petra's chair and she sat down like the Queen of Cornwall.

'He thinks we like it this way, Heaven knows why.' Colin waved a nonchalant hand. 'I hope you like fish, because the beef is from Argentina and tastes like it came out of a tin of cheap goulasch.' He picked up the menus and handed them round.

They were waiting for the waiter to clear the plates from the soup when Novak opened the encyclopaedia of surprises for the evening. As the waiter deftly set new cutlery for the main course, he started.

'To come back to the Dean's proposals..., as we're effectively a science university by another name, he has extensive links with schools, particularly in Devon and Cornwall, for obvious reasons. Cornwall and the entire western peninsula are effectively remote from the body of England. But his contacts reach much further than that. The School of Mines would add to the LEA's and the DES sponsorship of school visits with further subsidies and sponsorship of study tours from any of the forty-four of the universities in Britain. Publicity, pamphlets, maps, plans of the mine workings sent to all of them… I don't doubt he can elicit a positive response. And, of course, it would put the Camborne School firmly at the forefront of that domain.' Colin grinned. It was a stroke of genius.

'Please convey our sincere thanks to the Dean,' he said formally, feeling rather stupid. The waiter served the plates of poached haddock with sautéed potatoes and spinach. Novak inspected it with interest.

'I'm looking forward to this! The last time I had haddock was last year, in Bognor Regis. It was dreadful!' He lifted his knife and fork but with due decorum waited for Petra to start first.

'Perhaps the Bognor haddock lacked the "Regis" touch,' she suggested playfully. Novak smiled.

'Anyone can see you studied Classics, Miss Zabrinski. This is superb!' There was an expectant silence. Novak felt two pairs of eyes surreptitiously looking at him, and wiped his lips.

'The Dean mentioned too that as the LEA and the DES will for certain get groups coming, once the Project is up and running, there will be the question of adding to the current timetable of trains from Penlyn. And perhaps from further away, and so he was thinking of chartering excursion trains, or a reserved coach on scheduled services for groups from London, the Midlands… and then a special from Penlyn to the Estate, to fit the main line schedule. What do you think?' He smiled again. 'Or is that a silly question!'

'At the risk of being rude, Mister Novak, it would be a very silly question!' Petra was radiant, and refilled the man's glass from the wine bottle. 'There's the answer.'

'Miss Zabrinski always has the last word,' murmured Colin and stared at Petra with an unmistakable look in his eyes. Novak paused, allowing the two to savour a very special moment. With delicate timing, and looking at the empty plates, he murmured:

'You two are something else! I can see why Ingram...' He left unspoken what he could see and continued in a normal voice, 'It would be a crime to order ice cream after that delicious dish.' Colin nodded and signalled to the waiter who arrived in a flash with the speed of Aladdin's genie.

'What's Chef's best dessert? His speciality?' The waiter beamed.

'The apple crumble, sir. For three?' Another nod.

'Will it take long?'

'Twenty minutes, sir.' Colin looked at his fellow diners and raised a hand in acquiescence. He had a feeling that Novak would have no problem in filling twenty minutes. Novak did not disappoint.

'Now we come to what I, personally, think is the Dean's master stroke. It's all about that dreadful modern jargon word, "inclusion". In brief, encouraging tourism in general in Devon and Cornwall with groups from London, the Midlands, the North. In fact most groups won't be able to do the trip and back in a day. So he'll arrange with Cornwall Tourism, and the Devonshire Tourist Board to arrange accommodation, anything from three nights up to a week, in Guest Houses, Hotels or whatever else, even Youth Hostels to fit the charter train schedules. Not in Polmouth, too small, nor Penlyn. No, Penzance, Newquay, Falmouth, Plymouth, Torquay... the list of possibilities is endless. With the day's visit to the Polmine Estate the centrepiece. I mean, you've got the mine, the Brick Croft, the beautiful lakes, the train right to the door, and a lot more. The farm...' Petra's chair scraped back suddenly.

'I'm sorry... would you excuse me...?' She stood up abruptly and hurried to the door, but not before both men had seen the tears on her cheeks.

'Oh Lord!' Novak looked horrified. 'Is this my fault?' Colin shook his head firmly.

'Heavens, no! She's got this obsession with lipstick.' He thought for a moment. 'Actually, it's probably mascara, this time.' Novak stared.

'But… she isn't wearing any lipstick, nor mascara.'

'That explains it, then.' said Colin. 'But while she's gone, may I?' He extended his right hand to Novak and the two men shook hands with a firm grip, their eyes meeting and each holding the other's gaze. Novak felt a sudden hitherto unknown paternal urge, and was loath to release the younger man's hand. They saw Petra returning, and both stood up. Colin eased back her chair. 'You'd better buy two diaries for 1974,' he muttered. 'One won't hold everything.' He sat down again. Petra was back on form and now it was her turn to surprise Novak. The waiter served three enormous plates of apple crumble, and set down a dish of whipped cream in the middle of the table.

'You're right about the farm,' she said to Novak. 'It'll certainly please the younger groups, what with the hens, and the Great Horses. And then, of course, the opencast mine, the foundry, the smelting furnace, making tin. And the anvil where they create horseshoes…'

'What?!' Novak had been lifting a spoonful of crumble to his lips but now he suddenly put it back on the plate. 'Say that again?' he demanded. Petra didn't understand.

'Smelting furnace, foundry, horseshoes on the anvil. And Sarah makes ornaments, jewellery, pendants…' She looked at Novak anxiously. 'Why, what's the matter?' Novak swallowed, staring at her.

'The matter? My dear, nothing's "the matter"! They do all that? On the Estate?'

'Of course. The farmers only have the hens otherwise, the cows all left years ago. They have an opencast trench mine, dig out a wheelbarrow full of ore, and take it back to the farm…

Something's the matter!' she repeated. 'Your face...' Colin didn't understand either, and now Novak seemed to be talking to himself.

'Wait until the Dean hears this!' He seemed oblivious to his guests' presence. 'He'll never believe it.' He looked incredulously at Colin. 'Let me get this straight. Up at Polmine, there are people actually mining ore, smelting it, fabricating iron, and then beating it into horseshoes for the Great Horses? Truly?'

'That's what Miss Zabrinski said. After all the entire plateau is sitting on reserves of iron ore.'

'Oh my Lord!' Novak suddenly started to eat at high speed, savouring each mouthful rapidly before lifting his spoon again.

'Shall I call a doctor?' queried Petra solicitously. 'You sound distressed.' Now Novak put down his spoon for the final time and pushed his plate away.

'No. And I'll tell you. It's this...'

Before Novak could finish explaining why this development would be so significant, the waiter approached carrying three small glasses of Apple Liqueur.

'Compliments of the management,' he announced and cleared the empty plates. Now Colin and Petra shared Novak's excitement.

'Do you realise,' Novak concluded, 'that your Polmine Estate is probably the only working mine in Britain mining ore, smelting it, and making something with it? And if Camborne School of Mines, all the students... My God, you're unique!' Colin shook his head.

'I'm very ordinary. But as regards Miss Zabrinski, I can hardly disagree...' She kicked his ankle under the table, wiping her cheeks meaningfully and he stopped before the tears rose again. 'Well, there it is. Now you know everything.' His heart was beating with a rapid thumping in his chest and he realised that something quite out of the ordinary was taking place this night in little, insignificant Polmouth. Novak could not possibly miss the emotion in the air between the two, and signalled to the waiter.

'This is on me, tonight.' He turned to the waiter. 'Can this go on my bill?' The waiter nodded but his face fell. Not for long. Novak slipped him a ten pound note as a tip. The waiter smiled and left. Now Novak tactfully did the same. 'Off to my Beatrix Potter room then, I'll say good night. Hope to see you at breakfast...' Neither Colin nor Petra seemed capable of speaking coherently, so they just nodded and Novak discretely took his leave. There was a long silence, then:

'I fancy another of these Apple Liqueurs, you?' Petra nodded and Colin signalled. The silence continued for several minutes, after which they rose, still wordlessly, and went out into the warm air of the night, a panoply of stars overhead and the moon nudging its orange path towards the horizon.

'Now where?' whispered Petra, her arm around Colin's waist.

'This way.' He led her onto the jetty and the long pier.

Neither spoke as they strolled the length of the narrow jetty with a group of moored yachts just inside the harbour rocking gently on invisible baby waves. Their tall masts stretched skywards like slender sentinels, striving to reach the stars. Both knew that one of them would have to speak first, but both were loath to be the one to break the magic stillness of this most memorable of days. Finally Petra ventured:

'I thought I'd found the "eternal sunrise" last night,' she tightened her grip around his waist meaningfully, 'but today... the sun suddenly seems to rise in the East, the South, the North and the West all at the same time. And we've reached four score and eighteen, ninety-eight surprises in a day. The question is, will you break through the hundred mark tonight?' Colin's expression was invisible in the darkness but it was not a smile.

'There's a strong possibility.' he said tersely and they walked on in silence. When they reached the bench at the end of the pier and sat down, Petra tried again.

'Is it the Germans?' she asked tentatively. Colin had been hoping to avoid precisely that topic.

'I keep trying to push them to the bottom of the list of all the things churning around in my mind. But they keep coming back. Well, as you've asked, I can see a pattern, but it doesn't make any sense.'

'So tell me.'

'We know that neither comes from where they say. Neither has a clue about West German geography, impossible for intellectuals born and bred in the Bundesrepublik. In itself, that makes no sense and it leads nowhere. But listen... the cottages are actually leased to the Ministry of Defence, have been for decades. They say they're sub-let to Camborne. But *they* told Carruthers the Germans aren't on the Camborne payroll, just affiliates. Again, leads nowhere. Until we think of two more things. You were sure that Princess Triple-S joined the Navy although she denies it. Who is in overall charge, who has responsibility for the Navy? It's the Ministry of Defence. But...'

'I don't think I like the way this is going.' Petra sounded very unhappy.

'You think I do? What does that leave us with? MoD cottages housing strange Germans who are certainly German, but not from where they say they are, and Princess Triple-S who supposedly only joined the Navy for a week. And I think she's the link.' Petra sighed.

'Shakespeare didn't have this in mind when he penned "On such a night as this".' She looked up at the stars then at the lowering moon. 'Go on, then.'

'Her parents, the Rothenbergers, were Jewish refugees, just before the war. From Germany. Fair enough. But this is 1974. What Germans, if any, would want to flee Germany today, from *any* part of Germany, in whom the Ministry of Defence and the armed forces might be interested?'

'Oh my God! You're thinking East German spies! Aren't you?'

'I'm thinking East German, but that's as far as I've got. Now d'you see why I wanted to put it to the bottom of my list? It leads nowhere.'

'Whatever...' Petra made an effort. She slid from her place on the wooden bench to sit on his lap, her arms around his neck. 'Four score and nineteen. One more to go, before midnight.' She kissed him and remained sitting sideways on his knees. But when in the moonlight she saw that his face was grave, strangely drawn, she let him continue.

'Did you know,' he began, 'that there are only six Grammar Schools in the whole of England that have boarders, with a small boarding house as part of the school, and that Penlyn is one of them?'

'No to the first part, but yes about Penlyn. It's boys only, about twenty boys of the 600 pupils. So?'

'D'you remember a boy called Kelworthy, Paul Kelworthy?' Petra shook her head. 'He was a lot younger than us, when I was Head Boy he was just 13, in the Third Form. He was a boarder. And he hated it.'

'How d'you know?' Petra shifted on his knee and pressed her chest against his, sensing that he needed not arousal but reassurance, not passion but compassion. He did not push her away or lean backwards. They stayed like that.

'One reason I was tempted to refuse the position of Head Boy was that I wasn't a major sports player. Head Boys were always big, hulking lads, Captain of the rugger team beating some other player to a pulp in a match every Saturday afternoon. Or Captain of cricket. The only sport I was any good at was swimming, Captain of the school team. No-one gets beaten to a pulp swimming... My strengths were the Arts. Leader of the school orchestra at the front desk of the first violins, major roles in drama… But it was in my final year, as Head Boy, that I began to realise that quite a few of the younger boys, as young as 12, 13 and 14, were really unhappy. One of them was this Kelworthy. I only found out because as a Lifesaver with a certificate, I was put in charge of supervising groups of boys after school for free swimming. One day, Kelworthy turned up with about four friends.' Colin paused. 'They were all his age, Third Formers like him, but they were no friends of his. He was standing on the edge of the pool in his trunks, and I was up on the first diving board surveying the whole pool for risk, for accidents… And then I heard these four boys in the water, his "friends", and they were calling to him on the side, taunting him with an exaggerated stammer: "C..C..C..Come on, K…K…K…Kelworthy! G…G…G…et in!' I got off the diving board and went to him. He looked terrified. I said: "You go and get back into uniform. Then go outside and wait for me in the quadrangle. I'll give you five minutes to get there, then I'll clear the pool and join you." It was tragic, Petra, me in my smart shirt and whites, and plimsolls and this little boy, puny and scared, and I so much taller than he. He looked up at me like a grateful dog, and hurried to the changing rooms.' Petra tightened her grip around his neck.

'Is there nothing you've not done, Colin?' Her voice was a whisper.

'Listen. I met him outside and we walked once all the way around the perimeter of the playing field. He told me the most terrible story. He said there were six boys in his dorm, and at night when they were all in bed the other five would throw their outdoor shoes at him as he lay there in his bed, and mock his stammer all the time. Then, when they came to retrieve their shoes, they used them to beat him through the blankets, all five at once. He said it had got so bad that he'd slept every night for the past two months *under* his bed, using the pillow and blankets as a barricade, to protect himself.'

'That's dreadful!' Petra's face was only inches from his and her face was strained.

'I was appalled. Another boy, Billy, told me an identical story, in more detail, but he'd been bullied in a previous school. I'd always thought Penlyn had a good record on bullying. I learned a lot from Kelworthy. But that's nothing compared with...'

'Oh, God! There's more?! How can anything be worse than...?' Colin gently eased her off his knee.

'Can we walk back? The bar'll be closed, but we have cider and Chartreuse in our room, don't we?'

'We do.' They walked, and Colin talked.

'I didn't learn the full extent of this little boy's tragic life until the next time. He agreed to meet me in the lunch hour next day, and we'd do the perimeter again. But I'd learned another lesson that afternoon. I'd learned that the Head Boy's role wasn't maintaining the reputation of the school in the Inter-School Rugby League on the sports field, it was caring for every member of the school community, except the teachers, especially the vulnerable ones. And my God, if ever there was a vulnerable lad it was Kelworthy.' They were walking slowly back along the pier, very close.

'How bad does it get?' There was a catch in Petra's soft voice.

'This bad... He'd been put in a Prep School as a boarder when he was six. Six? I ask you! Anyway, he hadn't had a stammer then, he said. But he could hardly remember ever not having one. Petra, darling, this has a way to go yet, but I really want it out in the open with you tonight. Because it'll need your agreement.'

'This "it" concerns young people?' Petra had already divined this much. He had never called her "darling" before. 'Then we have all night, and many more to come. Take your time.' They had walked another hundred yards and were nearing the point where the jetty joined the Esplanade.

'When we get in, then. Oh, and I roped in the Head Girl, Helen Watts, for the younger girls.'

Sitting at the small table at the foot of their giant bed in the "Crab and Lobster" with two bottles and two glasses beside them, Colin resumed.

'This is where your department comes in.' Petra stared at him blankly as he poured her a glass of cider. 'It was a small Prep School for boys somewhere in Sussex. The school motto was Latin, *"Dexter non Sinister"*. Of course, the Headmaster must have been quite deranged, a lunatic. You can see why.' Petra nodded.

'I can. It doesn't mean anything. The English is "Right, not left". Meaningless.'

'Not to the crazy headmaster, it wasn't. *"Dexter"* gives us in English, "dexterity", agility, ability, correct, right. And *"Sinister"*...

'... indicates not only "on the left hand side" but also menacing, dangerous. So how did this barmy Head translate it into school life?' Colin drained his tiny glass and refilled it with green Chartreuse.

'You ever heard of Albania?' Petra stared at him.

'What are you on about now?'

'Go on, have you?'

'Of course, a small Communist country on the Adriatic, hard line, part of the Soviet Bloc. But what on earth?'

'Light relief, I need some. What do you know about Albania?' Petra thought, trying to see where Colin was going.

'Uh... closed society, reclusive, primitive and poor... that's it.'

'There is more,' said Colin thoughtfully. 'Hard to imagine but the following three things are punishable with an immediate prison sentence... Being in a possession of a Bible, growing a beard...'

'What?!'

'And being left handed. Being *"sinister"*, left handed, disparaged in the Roman Empire, wasn't allowed at all at this mad Prep School, *"Dexter non Sinister"*. Poor Kelworthy.'

'Oh, no!' Petra's voice was almost a strangled sob. 'He wasn't... please tell me he wasn't.' Colin looked at the wall.

'I can't do that, because he was. And it was left to the sadistic PE teacher to "correct" him. Aged six, for Christ's sake!' He sounded angry and Petra felt his ire too.

'Please tell me they didn't...'

'They did. The boys wore short trousers, of course, and belts. This PE teacher pulled Kelworthy's left arm behind his back on getting up in the morning, every morning, and tied it firmly to the middle of the boy's belt, behind his back. He had to eat, drink, write... everything like that until bedtime. Do everything one handed, *right handed*, when he wasn't. And imagine the public humiliation, in class, in PE lessons, at lunch in the dining room, all the boys seeing this and sniggering... That wasn't when the stammer started, though, according to him.'

'Oh, Colin, I'm really not sure I want to...' Petra's pretty face was distraught, and she reached up a hand to release her pony tail, letting the blond hair fall over her shoulders.

'I think the ending may be much better. If I have anything to do with it, it will.' Colin encouraged her. She nodded reluctantly. 'After four weeks, they released his arm. He immediately reverted to being fully left handed. So the sadistic PE teacher tried his last vile technique. He took the boy, alone, to the school swimming pool, fully dressed in short trousers, shoes, and socks, and shirt. And strapped his left wrist again to the belt in the middle of the boy's back. Then he threw him into the pool.'

'Oh, Christ. Colin! Please...'

'Happy ending very soon,' Colin promised. 'Kelworthy couldn't swim, and anyway, one handed, with shoes, fully dressed... He told me he started to drown, and I had no cause to doubt his version. I suppose realising the folly of his actions, the teacher jumped in and saved him. They stopped the hand tying then, but the stammer started that day, and I don't think he'll ever be rid of it. And of course he's still left handed.'

'So now do I get the happy ending?' She poured more cider into her glass and drank it rapidly.

'I was thinking this… supposing we don't use the five cottages for the mine display, as Ingram planned to. Supposing we get the sub-lease transferred from Camborne School of Mines to Polmine Estate and later try to buy its annulment from the MoD. We have the money. And we open a Holiday Activity Centre, in reality a Sanctuary Camp, in the school holidays, half-terms as well, for children aged ten to fifteen who've been identified by LEAs as damaged, or in need of emotional support. Mild handicaps as well, why not? With two qualified adult Monitors to supervise 24/7? Four rooms to a cottage, one bed to a room, four children per cottage. Separate cottages for boys and girls, obviously. Around fourteen per group. Adult monitors, one woman and one man in Cottages 1 and 5 in the downstairs rooms, and they make their ground floor into bedroom and lounge, with the kitchenette. Just imagine being ten again, exploring the rough terrain, seeing the train, going into the shallow mine, to the farm and the hens, the Great Horses towering above them, playing by the lakes… And the highlight, a day out. Excursion train from the mine to Falmouth, in the Orient Express dining car, lunch served there, then a ramble, and after a cream tea we'd hire one of the St. Mawes ferries that cross the River Fal, all the way back to Polport by sea. What d'you think?' There was a long silence during which Petra drained her glass and closed the cider bottle with care. It was not that she had nothing to say, she was unable to speak, her chest heaving with emotion and her face wet with tears. Silently she stood up and crossed to the bed and started to undress. Wearing only her bra and panties she finally spoke. Her voice was husky.

'I'll find those damned pyjamas tomorrow. Are you coming?' And she switched out the light.

Chapter Seventeen

Saturday, June 15th 1974

Perhaps understandably, Colin and Petra only made it down to breakfast well after nine o'clock. Novak, who had long since finished his, was nevertheless waiting for them, reading a newspaper. When they had eaten, he approached.

'May I...?' Colin and Petra nodded and he pulled back a chair. 'Well,' Novak started, 'you really gave me something to think about last night! My word...' He stopped because Colin had burst out laughing and seemed disinclined to stop. Not only Novak but also Petra stared at him. Colin never laughed. 'I'm sorry... have I said...?'

'Us? Give *you* a lot to think about? Mister Novak, you're the expert in that domain!' His laughter subsided. 'You mean the smelting, the ore, all that?'

'Yes, "all that". I'm eager to broach my ideas with the Dean at the earliest possible moment.' A smile flickered across his face and was gone. The "earliest possible moment" would be sooner than either Colin or Petra could imagine. And then... 'Actually, this is a bit of a cheek, but... if I stay on for the Gala... I suppose the train will be going back to Penlyn after the event?' Novak already knew very well that it would, to return a number of visitors coming for the Gala Opening. But Colin and Petra knew nothing about any visitors, for they were to be a surprise.

'Both of them. There'll be two trains. And as *we* lease the trains, if Miss Zabrinski says you can travel, then you can.' He turned to Petra as if asking permission from the Gala Queen. She nodded gravely.

'Many thanks, then. It starts at two? I look forward to it.' He stood up. 'I'll see you there, I suppose?' This mattered, and not just because it was their event. There was someone he wanted them to meet.

'I shall escort Miss Zabrinski to her throne on the platform.'

'My Equerry,' she explained, giggling. Novak shook his head and left with a wave from the door. She turned to Colin. 'We'll have to go to the Croft House, get changed for the afternoon. I suppose you'll wear that dreadful drab three-piece?' Colin shrugged.

'I might just surprise you.'

'Colin, you passed 100 last night! Could you give me a day, just one, without surprises?'

'I can't promise you that. So, off to the Croft House?'

When Colin came out of his bathroom at half past twelve and descended the staircase to the lounge of the Croft House he stopped and stared. But Petra, who was standing by the window, turned and saw him and she, in her turn, stood there transfixed, her jaw slightly open.

Colin, for his part, had never seen Petra looking so radiant, so beautiful, dressed in a closefitting sheath dress that was a kaleidoscope of colours and more. Gold, yellow, red and orange predominated, shining, pure silk. Petra for her part was as taken aback by the utter transformation that Colin had achieved. He was wearing what looked like brand new, white Levi jeans and a new pair of blue and white trainers. A black leather belt was topped by a black shirt with sunlight rippling across the immaculately ironed cloth, and the top button open. Petra crossed the room silently to him, took his hand and they went onto the terrace and sat down. There was everything to say and nothing to say.

At one-thirty they left the Croft House and mounted the mopeds. Petra was giggling.

'We'll look ridiculous!'

'Nonsense! You're just self-conscious. Anyway, it's a tight fitting skirt.' Before Petra could formulate an appropriate retort, he continued. 'Come on, we're due there before two.' They roared off to the track down to the village. Just before reaching the junction with the defunct Penlyn Lane they had to slow on seeing one of the Clifftop horse carts descending ahead of them drawn by a tall Great Horse with Sarah holding a loose rein alongside. They joined her at walking pace.

'Going to Scarborough Fair?' quipped Petra. Sarah shook her head.

'I wouldn't want to miss today for the world, and Magnus here…' she gestured to her horse, 'will be the showpiece. Sorry! Second to you two of course.'

'See you there!' They zoomed off to the foot of the track.

They parked the mopeds in front of the "Crab and Lobster" and walked the remaining fifty yards past newly planted palm trees around the headland to the Esplanade. They had only just reached the port when Petra stopped abruptly.

'Oh, my Lord!' Her voice was a whisper. 'Look!' But Colin was already looking. In the harbour a dozen yachts and motor boats were all gaily decked out with multi-coloured bunting from the mast head to the bow. And the sailor of each boat was already standing or seated at the helm, ready to cast off. Now they saw out in the estuary a dozen other boats in line, led by the Polhaven ferry, heading up river towards the village. They too were bedecked with bunting flapping in the breeze.

'My God.' Colin too had lost his voice. 'Who on earth arranged…?' Then he turned to Petra. 'This is your doing! You said you called President Teague. Oh, Petra...' He stopped then and turned away to hide his face from her.

'I promised I'd make it really, really nice for you.' Petra murmured. Then she saw what had caught Colin's attention. Where the station platform sloped up at the end from the road, there was a serried row of flower beds in full bloom, pansies, geraniums, a flood of colours. The ballast between the rails had been cleared of vegetation, and the buffers painted black and red. They saw Sarah and her Great Horse standing on the platform surrounded by a group of admirers and what looked like a TV crew.

'I didn't arrange *that*. Come on.' She pulled him to the end of the platform and up to join the others standing there. First to approach was Carruthers from Polhaven. He stared at them, then put his arm around Petra's shoulders, shaking hands with Colin at the same time.

'Who called the Press, do you know?' Colin finally found his voice. Carruthers looked sheepish.

'Ah, well, that was my...' The rest of his answer was drowned out by the deafening chorus of klaxons, sirens and horns from the twenty boats now out in the estuary in single file, turning in a 180° curve to face the open sea. And the sirens and klaxons gave no sign of letting up. The TV crew hurried past Colin and Petra to the pier and jetty to film the flotilla of small boats, led majestically by the white Polhaven ferry as they stationed just off shore. But neither Petra nor Colin had time to take in the grace, the majesty of this show of local patriotism for at that moment another loud whistle echoed eerily down the line from Polheath. The crowd of villagers on the platform were all looking expectantly to their right hoping to be the first to glimpse the approaching steam train. The TV reporters ran back to the centre of the platform and the TV cameraman unwisely jumped down onto the tracks to get a once in a lifetime shot of the locomotive as it rounded the final bend and slowly rolled into the tiny station. A young woman, apparently a reporter for the West Cornwall TV News was recording urgent text into a microphone. As the train hove into sight a mighty cheer went up from the hundred villagers, and with good reason. The "Lands End" steam engine was covered in a panoply of flowers of every hue on the buffers, the ledge at the front and suspended in baskets on either side of the boiler. Engine Driver Charlie was leaning out of his cab waving the inevitably oily rag while his stoker attended to the brakes. The cameraman was backing adroitly away from the advancing locomotive. Charlie reached into the cab and sounded a mighty whistle that lasted fully ten seconds. Everyone heard the echo returned from across the waters and Polhaven. Colin and Petra were joined by Novak.

'There's someone I want you to meet!' he announced and pulled them towards the front coach, the classic Orient Express dining car where doors were opening and the Gala's guests were alighting. But the TV crew were looking for the same man, and by the time Novak and the two had pushed through the mélée, Sir Robert Maxton, Dean of Camborne School of Mines was already being plied with questions by the young female reporter. None of the other fifteen guests was known to either Colin or Petra. 'I guess we'll have to wait a few minutes. That's the Dean, and he hasn't come to be interviewed by the Press, he's come to meet you two.'

'Who are all the others?' Petra had to raise her voice for the flotilla out in the estuary was once again giving vent to a joyous celebration of the rebirth of Polmouth.

'We'll be joining a few of them later...' Now a new voice was to be heard, the throaty clarion call of a diesel train approaching. But the British Rail train that was drawing round the final curve and slowing to halt buffer to buffer behind the W.C.L.R. gleaming steam train was unlike any that any passenger in the British Isles had ever seen. This was no grimy, blunt ended commuter train with the appearance of a 1950s design typical of most services. This was a prototype of which only two had been built for testing.

The cab had a panoramic raked windscreen, giving every impression of a high speed train, another cab at the other end of the three coach unit made the train into a self-contained vehicle for luxury travel. Equally striking was the new livery in yellow and dark blue. A further novelty was hydraulic doors which now all slid open in unison. The Press was in a quandary; where to film first?

For some obscure reason, perhaps he had had his fill of boats and trains for the day, the TV cameraman was soon filming the Great Horse in close-up while the journalist interviewed Sarah. Novak pushed his way optimistically through the crowd towards Sir Robert Maxton, closely followed by Colin who had Petra's hand firmly in his. But the eagle-eyed third member of the TV crew, the editor, had seen them now standing beside Sir Robert and ordered his colleagues back to surround the Dean. Novak tried to introduce Petra and Colin but the reporter was once again making fatuous commentary remarks into her microphone, wondering who the Dean's new companions were.

'This is impossible!' exclaimed Sir Robert. He turned to the chattering journalist. 'If you want to film us, or have any questions, then in here.' He gestured to the Orient Express dining car behind him. He led Novak and the two others to the open door. The TV crew crowded in after them and started to film the opulent historic interior while Sir Robert's group sat down at a Pullman table laid with a white table cloth for dinner, gleaming wine glasses and the silver cutlery catching the light.

Novak tried again to complete the introductions, but again he was interrupted. They heard a tapping on the outside of the window and saw a tall man of military stature, silver hair neatly crimped backwards across his head, mouthing something inaudibly. Sir Robert signalled to him to join them and the man made for the door at the other end from the TV crew.

He approached the length of the aisle; it was Headmaster Temeritus Tennent. He stood towering above Petra and Colin, smiled at Sir Robert whom he evidently knew.

'Well, well... Zabrinski and Penpolney. My word! Hockey Captain and Senior Latin Prize, I recall, and Head Boy,' he explained to the Dean of Camborne. 'Two outstanding alumni of Penlyn Grammar.' There was an awkward silence, then with strange deference he addressed Petra. 'May I have the honour of shaking your hand, Miss Zabrinski?' Automatically Petra rose to her feet and extended her hand. Before she could resume her seat Tennent paused. 'Wait... wait, wait!' he exclaimed. He looked down at Colin in his aisle seat and then Petra standing in front of him. The TV reporter with her microphone sensed that she wanted to record this and pressed closer, the cameraman filming over her shoulder. 'You two have worked together before.' Now the reporter was hanging on every word, the human aspect surging to the fore. 'Wait... 1968, Goldoni, the School Play. Yes...' He chortled unexpectedly. The only ones who had a clue as to what he was talking about were Petra and Colin, the latter looking distinctly discomfited. Petra, on the other hand, elated by the entire day's events was on a high. Tennent stared at Colin again, and the cameraman framed the two in a vertical shot, the tall, military Tennent looming over Colin below. 'Surely you remember?' prompted Tennent. 'Just after the curtain went up!' Colin reddened, and hung his head. Now the cameraman humiliated him thoroughly, providing a close-up zoom on Colin's face.

'Uh... I really don't remember, sir.' he muttered, addressing his former Headmaster in bygone terms. Petra saw her opportunity, resisting the temptation to laugh. She adopted a deep, throaty tone. The cameraman was seeing his best material of the day, and she was very attractive, which helped. He framed Tennent, Petra and Colin while the reporter advanced the microphone at the full extent of her arm. Petra placed her hand in the air over Colin's shoulder.

'Come, come, my dear, not so shy now!' and lowered her hand affectionately but firmly on top of his head. Novak and Sir Robert Maxton evidently thought that there was a whiff of insanity in the air. Tennent's laughter increased. He looked at those seated.

'I'm sure he remembers now!' he exclaimed jovially. 'Colin, dear boy, you nearly decapitated her!' Colin looked thoroughly miserable. The young woman with the microphone was now also convinced that Polmouth-madness, a hitherto unknown syndrome, was manifest, and started to speak softly into her microphone in medical terms, suggesting that inbreeding over generations living in outlying villages could cause genetic insanity. The cameraman, however, persisted with his close-up of Colin and this paid off. Petra sat down on Colin's lap and kissed him with unmistakable passion. The reporter's medical analysis went into overdrive. Colin seemed to recover. Before anyone could speak, the reporter pushed forward to ply them with a barrage of questions, but Colin got in first.

'We'll happily answer a few questions later... we live on the Estate so we shall be here all evening. A little later, then?' He added meaningfully: 'This is a private conversation!' The reporter had the good grace to redden and signalled to her cameraman to stop filming. She nodded and they left the dining car.

Half an hour later Novak climbed down to the platform to go in search of the TV crew, inviting them to put any questions they may have now. They followed him with alacrity, seeming to have run out of any more flower beds to film.

There were the obvious inane questions which Colin was happy to let Petra parry. Then came the one he had been expecting. Could the TV team come up to the Estate, today, and film there? Petra too had been expecting this and looked at Colin. He was firm.

'Not today. Miss Zabrinski and I are only just moving into the premises, and besides, today is not the moment. What we can suggest, however...' Petra appreciated the "we" and squeezed his hand encouragingly. The cameraman, whose lens seemed fixated by the clinging rainbow silk dress and Petra's bosom, finally managed to focus on Colin. 'We shall be giving a detailed presentation to potential sponsors and partners next Thursday, at the Estate. So...'

'And I and Mr. Novak, Chief Engineer at Camborne, will be present.' interrupted Sir Robert.

'And I!' Colonel Temeritus Tennent was not going to be left out. He introduced himself, then added a few remarks about his now celebrated alumni.

'If you will give me your card, I shall make sure that you receive a formal invitation.' Petra intervened. 'So, will that be all, for now?' Once again the reporter took the hint and all three crew members retreated to the platform. At that moment the cameraman saw something that made him hurry alongside the coach towards the harbour, and those seated in the train heard an unexpected new noise, a children's choir singing in unison. Tennent put his finger to his lips and listened intently. Then he exclaimed:

'Good Heavens! It's the "Polmouth Trawlermen's Refrain"! Haven't heard that for forty years... come on!' He rose rapidly and led the others to the door. Thirty young children were standing on the end of the platform, catching the afternoon sunlight in their hair and each holding a song sheet. Petra held Colin back so that the others unwittingly moved ahead. When the song ended, she nudged him towards the ticket office and the open air in the lane outside.

'I think this is where we take our leave, for now. Do we still have a room in the "Crab and Lobster"?' Colin nodded and they slowly made their way to the left, taking the long way round to the little street that led back to the seafront and the pub.

When they descended to the bar at seven o'clock they were again wearing the same attire as for the afternoon Gala, for the simple reason that all their clothes were a mile away in the Croft House. However, the multi-coloured, silk dress and the white jeans and black shirt were entirely fitting for the relaxed atmosphere that greeted them as they entered. The barman had never seen so many guests in the bar and restaurant. At least forty villagers and several visitors were filling the intimate dining room and lounge. As soon as Petra entered followed by Colin a round of applause started and increased in volume as they approached the bar. Petra blushed and looked at the floor as an elderly villager vacated his bar stool for her.

'If they start on "For *he's* a jolly good…", I'll walk out!' she muttered to Colin. Fortunately, no-one did. But it took a while for the clapping to die down. The barman brought their drinks without even asking them, and before they could take a sip the waiter approached accompanied by the Manager. 'Now what?' she wondered, aloud.

'Good evening, Miss Zabrinski, Mister Polpen… I mean Penpolney. The Management would like to offer you both a special tasting menu, on the house, with accompanying wines idem, in recognition of today's most memorable events.' He looked around the full room. It was clear that he was not referring to the Gala *per se*, but the huge amount of revenue it was providing for the "Management". 'Chef has been keen to offer it for some time, but we have never had guests who would truly appreciate its exceptional culinary grandeur… until very recently.' He looked meaningfully first at Colin, then Petra, laying on the superlatives with trowels. 'May I present the tasting menu for perusal?' He gestured to the hapless waiter who was looking, in vain, for a chair. Colin helped him out and pointed to Petra who took both menus, then handed one to Colin. The two men retreated.

'Good God! Five courses? I'll look like a Great Horse if I eat all this!'

'And they each weigh over one ton,' remarked Colin inconsequentially. She looked at him maliciously.

'All right, Mister "Mensa", let's test your general knowledge. The starter is standard fare, "*Bisque de Homard*". Comments?'

'I's a lobster soup, thick consistency.'

'I know that!' She was scornful. 'I was wondering why it's not "*Bisque d'homard*", like "*l'homme*", apostrophe to remove vowel before H?'

'I can help there.' Colin sounded knowing, but in truth both of them were on a high that would not wear off, elated by Ingram's victory that afternoon, as they considered it to be. 'There's a very small number of words in French beginning with H that don't follow the rule of elision. The most famous is the Paris equivalent to Covent Garden market, "Les Halles", and they don't pronounce the S, and they aspirate the H. Now, there's a more contentious word, beans, which is "haricots", so you expect to hear French for "the bean", "l'haricot", but not so. The Académie Française has decreed...'

'All right, you win!' Petra studied the menu. 'I guess I can manage: "*simmered halibut, winkles, cockles and razor clams "marinière*", I'll have the soup and that.' Colin nodded. But Petra hadn't given up. 'Next course: "*lobster with truffled chicken quenelles*". They're meat balls, aren't they?' Colin didn't answer, because he didn't know either.

'Lobster again? I can miss the meat balls... You?' She nodded and turned her attention to the dessert. A wicked smile crossed her face.

'And this? "*rose and raspberry bhapa doi and pistachio burfi*". Go on! What is it?'

'I'll ask the waiter, bet he won't know either. Three courses all right?'

'No, let's try the lobster and truffled thingummies as well. I want to.' Colin acquiesced, and they ordered, then turned to how to occupy Sunday. It was a no contest that Petra easily won. Finally moving in and installing themselves in the mansion.

'So our last night in the "Crab and Lobster"?' she said regretfully. Colin looked dubious.

'Oh, I don't know...' he started. 'I'm sure we'll find a few anniversaries across the months to bring us back... As a boy, I always wanted to celebrate my birthday every week, not every year.' There was a hint of a smile on his face as the waiter impatiently approached.

Chapter Eighteen

The renaissance of Polmouth, Week 2

Sunday, June 16th 1974

As the season neared the mid-summer solstice, the heat wave gave no sign of abating. The sun rose before six in the morning, shining promisingly through the thin curtains and waking Petra. She looked at the clock, then shook Colin awake and pointed to the tray on the sideboard. He wiped his eyes blearily and climbed out of bed, crossed the room and filled the filter machine with coffee.

'I really don't want to wear that dress again,' she announced, sitting up in bed, naked. Colin, also without pyjamas, yawned and spoke over his shoulder.

'You made it through the night without wearing it...' She threw a pillow at him playfully.

'You know what I mean! We've got a long day ahead of us.' She slipped out of bed and crossed to the en suite bathroom. 'One sugar, no milk, please.' The door closed behind her, and Colin heard the shower running. He decided to surprise her and, leaving the coffee filtering, dressed quickly then scribbled a note on a paper serviette.

"Gone to buy a newspaper".

He quietly left the room and walked out into the sunlit lane. There was a strong smell of hyacinth bloom and lavender carrying on the sea breeze from the Esplanade, an underlying tang of salt and seaweed the emblem of midsummer Polmouth. He walked the five minutes to the newsagent's, but when he saw the rack of Sunday newspapers displayed outside he stopped and stared at the range of headlines. Then he selected not one but six newspapers, carried them into the shop. The vendor knew Colin by sight.

'Morning, well you certainly made the headlines! In a big way! Good for you, putting Polmouth back on the map.' He accepted the money. Colin was still in shock.

'It never was,' he said abstractedly. 'On "the map", I mean.'

'Well, it bloody well is now, thanks to you and Miss Zebra...'

'Zab...' corrected Colin, 'Zabrinski'.

'Yeah. Nice photos of her. Pin-up standard.' Colin was more and more disturbed and left, but on the pavement again he stopped and looked at the headline on the first paper, "The News of the World". He blenched.

"Schoolgirl's kiss seals Polmouth's Renaissance!" "Is Romance in the Air?"

shrieked the headline above a full page picture of Petra's passionate kiss in the Orient Express dining car.

"Full story and Gala photo-spread, pages 22-23"

Colin gulped and glanced at the newspaper below. It was the "Sunday Telegraph" but was scarcely more restrained.

"Lovers' Tryst ensures Polmouth Rebirth!"

above an excellent full page photo taken at ground level through a flower bed on the Esplanade, the foreground a panoply of multi-coloured flowers with the focal point in the centre of the estuary, the flotilla of the twenty boats led by the white Polhaven ferry. Shaking his head, Colin tucked the heavy bundle under one arm and strode back to the "Crab and Lobster". But there was no escaping the newspapers here either. Three trawlermen, just returned from a night's fishing, were drinking mugs of tea, a paper laid out in front of them. One of them nudged his companions.

'It's 'im!'

Colin hurried through the restaurant to the stairs and returned to their room where he found Petra drying her hair, dressed only in a bath towel. He put the papers down on a side table and fetched a mug of coffee from the machine.

'You took your time?' she said questioningly. Then, seeing the bundle of newspapers: 'Christ! You've bought the whole shop!'

He sat down and showed her the "News of the World" cover picture and headline.

'I had good reason,' he said bleakly. 'Look. And if you've got the courage, explore pages 22 and 23. I haven't.'

'Oh my Lord!' Petra's attractive Cornish accent was very pronounced. She glanced through the covers lying beneath, hesitated, then pulled out the "Sunday Express". 'Well…!' She was speechless, showed the paper to Colin.

"Refrain of a Comely Cornish Maiden!"
"Come, come, not so shy now!"

and below was another full page picture of her passionate kiss. She put the paper back in the pile.

'That just leaves one question, then.' she said calmly, waving the hair dryer from side to side across her blond hair.

'Try me.' Colin was bleak, totally unprepared for anything like this. Petra switched off the hair dryer and stood up, letting the towel slip to the floor.

'Is there, or isn't there?' she asked, giggling. 'Romance in the air?' Colin smiled.

'Don't be silly,' he said, and stood up to take her in his arms.

After a long silence Petra released herself, quickly slipping into her underwear and the only dress that wasn't in the Croft House.

'I'm hungry! Come on, and leave that drivel for later.'

It was only eight o'clock when they reached Polmine Estate and parked their mopeds in front of the Croft House.

'You do the clothes, get the boxes upstairs. Take the three bedrooms I've carpeted. Leave all my clothes on the bed, I'll store them in cupboards and wardrobes later. You wouldn't have a clue!' Petra was on magisterial form, commanding. Colin opened his mouth to protest, then thought better of it.

'What'll you be doing?'

'Downstairs, of course. I know where I want things. You wouldn't...'

'... have a clue. All right, I give in.

'And about these bedrooms...' she continued softly now, 'one for me, one for you, and...' she blew him a kiss, '... one for us. I leave it to your imagination as to what to put in there.' They each went to change then set to work.

Petra and Colin were not the only ones to work on Sunday. In London, Tring and Hamlyn were contractually employed seven days a week. As the Croft House was slowly being transformed into "home", Hamlyn presented his security pass at the anonymous building in Whitehall and descended to the office that he and Tring could justifiably call "our second home". Tring was already there, catching up on overdue filing. No sooner had Hamlyn put his hat on the stand than the phone rang. Both men knew that the only caller on a Sunday had to be their superior from his house on the Ashdown Forest in Sussex. Hamlyn took the call and put it on speaker-phone for Tring's benefit.

'You seen the papers?' Bonham was annoyed and his voice was brittle in the tinny speaker. 'Headlines? Well, have you?' Hamlyn was obliged to answer truthfully but he did his best to mollify Bonham.

'Tring was just leaving to fetch the Sundays…'

'Well tell him to run. And as soon as you've gone through them, not just the headlines, but the inside coverage as well, call me back. You have an hour!' Bonham rang off and Tring was on his way. Neither man had a clue what Bonham was talking about. But when Tring returned minutes later with a wide range of papers, both men understood immediately. They each took a different title and opened to find the "inside story".

It did not take them long to see the source of Bonham's concern. The Polmouth Polmine Estate, indeed the entire village was the major headline of all the Sundays. Tring held up the "Sunday Mirror" for Hamlyn to see.

'She's a cracker!' he said, referring to Petra. But the headline dampened any such enthusiasm.

"Polmouth orphan saves village!"
"Polmine to re-open next year."

'Bloody hell!' exclaimed Hamlyn. 'We didn't reckon with this! Question is, does "next year" mean what it says?'

'There's a line in the "Telegraph" about a visit and presentation on Thursday, for sponsors. We'll have to move them… And fast!' But Hamlyn disagreed with Tring.

'No. All we have to do is ring Rothmount, warn her to get the two Germans to stay indoors all day on Thursday with the door locked, curtains drawn. They probably do that every day, anyway. The Estate people know the tenants are in, and won't disturb them. And they've still got three other cottages to show. But I'll call Plymouth RAF base, request an Air-Sea rescue helicopter on 24-hour stand-by, to scramble immediately if called. To lift them out, and the Rothmount woman, if their cover's blown. And to listen out on her frequency 24/7 in case she thinks they're blown. That'll be enough.'

'You sure?' Tring sounded doubtful. 'And you'll tell Bonham... ask him, first?' Hamlyn shook his head.

'Fait accompli, and he can enjoy his Sunday lunch.' He stood up. 'I'm going to the radio room. She's supposed to be keeping a listening watch on short wave.' He gestured to the phone on his desk. 'I really don't want to use an open line on that, not with a message like this to an MI6 operative.'

At midday Colin finally joined Petra on the ground floor and looked around in astonishment. His first impression was that he was in a Show House for luxury residences, specially prepared by expert interior decorators and caterers. Even the ironed table cloth on the kitchen table was laid for a meal, right down to wine and water glasses, cutlery.

'Well, I'm all done here,' she said cheerfully, pulling off her apron. 'You?' He nodded.

'Perhaps not to your standard of perfection, but...'

'And I need a drink. We still haven't done any shopping, nor bought a cookery book.' Her inevitable giggle burst out. 'So we can't stay here tonight! Do you by any chance know where we can find food, and a manger for the night?'

'We can stretch to fish and chips down by the harbour, on the terrace, and read about ourselves in the newspapers? And there's always that "C & L" place down on the seafront...' She nodded, then held up three dusty albums.

'I found these in the cupboard under the stairs. Ingram's old photo albums. We can look through them over lunch. You bring the papers.' She made for the stairs.

'Where are you going?'

'To pack some clothes, of course! Normal people need a change of clothes and I have to go to work tomorrow. Eight o'clock to Polhaven.'

'Oh, yes. Pack something for me, too, will you?' She was already on the staircase. 'I'd forgotten you'd be back at work tomorrow.'

'I hadn't!'

The consternation in the *Staatssicherheitsdienst* office in East Berlin far surpassed Hamlyn's tranquil response to the news that Polmine Estate had become a focal point of interest in Britain and would within days be visited by a large number of VIPs. In East Germany, university and school authorities represented VIPs, even if in Britain such a description of an LEA official would have been considered laughable. Oberleutnant Traub was particularly incensed that Sunday morning. He had gone to great lengths and considerable expense to charm his errant wife back into the marital fold the previous Saturday evening with flowers, an Army cook to prepare a special meal, and the only champagne available in the Soviet Bloc, the red champagne from Crimea. It had been in vain. She had left in the morning, slamming the front door, and had not returned all night. He was uncertain whether she ever would, and was thus thoroughly indisposed to convene a meeting with his two secret service colleagues. But it was essential.

Retired Colonel Rüther arrived with Karling and all three sat down at the long table.

'Well?!' Oberleutnant Traub was aggressive, his jaw thrust forward pugnaciously. 'You've heard? We need a response. Do we bring the mission forward, over and done with by Thursday?' Colonel Rüther had been expecting this question.

'That would be precipitate, in my view. We know that Schiller and Meissner are kept out of sight, incognito, and as usual, there is a watch-dog, some Jewish woman name of Rothmount...'

Karling intervened, as unhappy at his Sunday being ruined as Traub was at the disintegration of his marriage.

'Rothmount?! Rothmount, my eye! **Verdammt**, she's the daughter of the Rothenberger swine who escaped in 1938! The Jewish gold merchants. Only blessing was they left all their fortune behind, got out with only the clothes on their backs. Good riddance!' Rüther held up his hand severely.

'Irrelevant, gets us forward not one iota. Please, gentlemen...' He frowned. 'I was thinking as I travelled in this morning... MI6 read the headlines. This Rothmount woman is military, not sure which branch. Her instructions will be the same as for the Bulgarian I mentioned. Incognito means they never go out and her job is to make sure they never do. Give MI6 credit where it's due, the choice of this out of the way hiding place was a stroke of genius, and they couldn't have foreseen any of the sudden furore... No, I was thinking as I came in, if we're perturbed, what must MI6 be thinking, how will they react? Will they pull Schiller and Meissner out? And if so, to where? And why would they? A group visiting premises like that are there for the mines, or whatever else there is, not houses with doors locked and the curtains drawn. And you can bet your lives that MI6 has ordered precisely that just for the visit. Only for a day after all, and the headlines talk of "opening next year".' He smiled benignly. 'Von Horváth will take them out on Friday.' His smile faded. 'Whether whatever this Polmine thing is will actually ever open after that... well, that's a British problem.' He pushed his chair back. 'That is my assessment. Proceed on schedule.'

Oberleutnant Traub wanted nothing more than to be out of there and to get drunk. He nodded.

'I can sign a Directive to that effect, but it'll need your countersignatures. Gentlemen.' he added, choking on the word. 'You, Karling?' Karling nodded. 'Right, we'll go to the ordnance room, and I'll get the requisite form.' The three men stood up and left, on their way to sign the fate of Helmuth Schiller and Uschi Meissner. Or they thought that they were.

Seated at a table for four on the terrace of the fish and chip shop, glasses of lager on the table in front of them, Petra and Colin were soaking up the midsummer sun. On one of the spare chairs the pile of newspapers, now thoroughly creased and dishevelled, lay in the shade. On the other were Ingram's three photo albums. Neither Colin nor Petra seemed in a hurry to look inside them.

'It feels like prying,' said Petra, 'and he was such a private man...'

'Perhaps if he'd been a little less private, we might have some idea of why us?' They fell silent while the waitress cleared the plates, looked at them questioningly.

'Got a lovely Apfelstrudel, made this morning...' she suggested. They nodded.

'Oh well, here goes.' Petra reluctantly placed the top album on the table, opened it and they looked together at a private man's life in pictures. The first photo made Petra gulp.

'Oh my God! It's him as a baby! Look!' Colin was looking, unable to drag his gaze from the little baby in a pram. 'And he's got fair hair! When I knew him...'

'When we knew him he was iron grey!' Colin said. 'Oh, Petra, this feels all wrong. But we have to do it, and you know why.'

'Yes.' she said firmly. 'We shall need some of these pictures, enlarged and mounted, in the exhibition. I hadn't thought of this. It's private, yes, but it's a treasure trove in his honour.' She wiped her eyes. 'A very special man.'

'All of that.' Colin agreed, and turned the page. 'Grief, this must be his parents, and the little girl must be his sister, d'you think? I wonder what happened to her?' He leafed rapidly ahead through the album. 'She never appears again... And I suppose he's the child in the sun hat?' Petra was astonished.

'God knows what year that must be taken! I didn't think they had cameras back then!'

'Well, it's not a Daguerrotype.' Colin grinned. 'So obviously they did. We need to take good care of these, get them to Carruthers for safekeeping. And ask what he thinks.'

'I'll take them with me tomorrow. When I have to go to work…' she added meaningfully. 'This is excellent, gives you an excuse to come with me, you can carry them.' At that moment the Apfelstrudel arrived and Colin closed the album as a precaution against flying whipped cream and seagull guano falling from the sky.

They leafed through the albums for half an hour. The first was the only one to provide useful material for an exhibition selection of Ingram's early years, for the other two volumes were exclusively of events in various schools in which he had worked. There was not one of Polmine Estate. Finally, Colin closed the third album and riffled through the pile of papers on the other chair. He pulled out the Sunday Mirror and held up the title to Petra.

"Polmouth orphan saves village!"
"Polmine to re-open next year."

'What d'you make of that?' he asked Petra. She grimaced.
'Which bit?' she asked bleakly.
'The top line, second word.'
'Someone in the village must have blabbed. I didn't think anyone knew… the damned Press must have gone through all of Polmouth like a horde of locusts to find this. The bastards!'
'That's rather my point.' Colin put the paper back on the chair. 'If this… *that* is the best, or rather the worst the Press can do, I'm not sure we want them at the Presentation. So I'll have Teague notify them that they won't be invited but we'll issue a Press Communiqué at the end… no, the next day. You ask Carruthers to put them off, and I'll handle Teague. What d'you think?'

She leaned across to kiss him.

'Perfect. But as we've agreed you'll be seeing Carruthers with me... you can tell him.'

'We didn't! Agree. You decided.'

'You didn't say "No".'

'Petra, it'll be many years before you hear me say that to you.'

Ost-West Express

Chapter Nineteen

Tuesday June 18ᵗʰ - Wednesday, June 19ᵗʰ 1974

There is a Belgian seaside resort with the unprepossessing name of Eastend, Oostende. In 1974 it was in its heyday. The Summer season saw Belgian families and lovers flocking to its beaches, its promenade, its amusement arcades, finding there a cross between Blackpool and Bournemouth. Some went as day-trippers while the lovers tended to stay a week in Bed and Breakfast establishments of highly dubious quality. The staple diet in Belgium is greasy chips, and in 1974 Oostende vied to be the country's top consumer of potatoes. But the season was short, and the Autumn, the Winter and even Spring brought the full force of North Sea gales and storms and Oostende was subject to a battering that would have made even the hardiest tourist turn and run. There had to be another reason why this unattractive little town was a major hub for people and passengers all year round, regardless of the weather.

Twenty years before the advent of budget airlines and the commensurate explosion in the number of people flying around Europe, continental travel relied principally on the European rail network. Britain considered itself to be a part of that network, but foreign visitors to the UK rapidly came to consider British Rail's offering as the poor relation in Europe. Having done away with dining cars and offering only pre-packed, notorious "British Rail sandwiches", that impression was reinforced. To a continental European a "dining car" offered just that; a galley kitchen at the end of the carriage was manned by a qualified chef and experienced waiters offered diners full A la Carte menus cooked to order, complemented by a selection of decent wines. A British Rail passenger returning from a journey on the continent only had to look at the national joke, the "British Rail Sandwich" and feel that service was deficient. Moreover, the longest journeys in Britain were London-Inverness and London-Penzance, whereas these two routes were dwarfed by trans-continental trains travelling three times as far with couchette cars and sleepers, traversing several countries en route. This was truly international travel. There was, however, one post-war barrier: the Soviet Union's "Iron Curtain" across Europe.

There was an odd anomaly to the Soviet Union's policy on international travel. The Iron Curtain that divided Western Europe from the USSR-dominated Communist Bloc was the reason for the truncation of routes that had previously crossed from Paris or Calais to far-flung destinations and were now cut off from Westerners. Trains with famous names travelled barely half the distance that was covered before 1961. The USSR tried everything within its power to separate Eastern Europe, over which it imposed hegemony, from what it considered to be decadent, capitalist Western Europe. In 1961 it even went to the lengths of urging its puppet President of the DDR, East Germany, Walter Ulbricht to construct a barbed wire death-strip the length of Germany from North to South and further across the Czech and Hungarian frontiers, with mines and machine guns. This was, if one believed their propaganda, ostensibly to prevent Imperialist, subversive infiltration or overt invasion from "contaminating" the "purity" of the Communist ideal society, the Utopia of the working class. But it was no secret on either side of the Iron Curtain that the sole true purpose of this death-strip frontier which even extended to a secondary line around and through the middle of Berlin, "the Berlin Wall", was to prevent citizens of East Germany from fleeing the drab, primitive, state-controlled way of life in the DDR to the land of milk and honey where every street was paved with gold beneath neon lights, West Germany. Many tried, and many died in the attempt, machine gunned as they attempted to cross the minefield or scale the barbed wire fence that was East Germany's last defence against defectors, their festering bodies left lying in the "death strip" for days as a deterrent to others.

Tightly controlled entry and exit to and from the DDR was paramount. The journey from West Germany to its enclave deep inside the DDR involved travelling over 100 miles of East German territory from the Inter-German "death-strip" frontier to a parallel deterrent prior to entering West Berlin, a far-flung, lonely but prosperous extremity of the Bundesrepublik and NATO.

Since the opening of the world famous "Orient Express" in 1883, linking Paris to Constantinople, the number of famous, long distance trains had multiplied, and by 1974 there were dozens running daily carrying sleeping cars and dining cars immense distances. Among the most popular were the "Tauern", the "Rijeka", the West German luxury train "Rheingold" and the truncated "Orient Express", limited to western Europe since the forcible partition of Europe. And the one providing the longest uninterrupted transit, despite the need to cross into or out of the Soviet Communist bloc in Berlin, was the "Ost-West Express", covering 1,700 miles in 44 hours and running from Moscow to Paris and back seven days a week, 365 days a year. This was the Soviet anomaly.

Having cut all other routes into Communist territory by arresting trains at the Iron Curtain frontiers, it was the USSR itself which proposed and set up the "Ost-West Express", transiting Russia, Poland, East and West Germany and finally Belgium and France to Paris and the North Sea. Understandably, Western Intelligence Agencies viewed this sole East-West transit with deep suspicion. Russia strictly controlled who entered or left East Germany, Poland and Russia but the "Ost-West Express" provided the easiest, indeed the only route, for nefarious Communist activity targeting the declared enemy, the West. It was little wonder, then, that Colonel Rüther and Karling had chosen to send their assassin on the "Ost-West Express" to the North Sea ferry and the porous Folkestone passport control for their mission.

By the 1970s, Oostende was the terminus and boarding point for the majority of express trains fanning out across Europe, including the "Ost-West Express". One of the thousands of passengers to transit Oostende onto the Sealink ferry to England in 1974 was Zoltan von Horváth.

There were three main line stations in Berlin, one in East Berlin, "Berlin Ost", one on the dividing line between the two sectors of Berlin, "Berlin Friedrichstrasse" where rigorous exit and entry formalities took half an hour between arrival and departure, and then, in West Berlin the "Berlin Zoo" station where West Germans and Westerners could board the "Ost-West Express" without any inspection for the frontier.

Technically, East Germans leaving to transit West Berlin and travel to Western Europe were only allowed to board at "Berlin Friedrichstrasse" where they were subject to intense scrutiny. "Berlin Ost" was usually used only as a *disembarkation* point for passengers from Poland and Russia. Zoltan von Horváth's instructions, however, were to join the train at the supposedly forbidden "Berlin Ost" station. The problem was that, although he could have joined the train like everyone else at "Berlin Friedrichstrasse", there he would be subject to intense scrutiny by East German and West German authorities along with numerous other passengers. The "Berlin Ost" solution relied on him mixing with the Poles and Russians alighting there and then surreptitiously boarding the train. Von Horváth had done this before and he had an infallible ruse to get away with it.

At 9.45 that Tuesday evening von Horváth arrived at "Berlin Ost" and went to the platform where, as he expected, there were no passengers. However, as a Danish national who had ostensibly been working in Berlin legitimately, he was not prohibited from joining the train. He was carrying a Samsonite British suitcase and wearing a light summer coat with the designer label "Canali" sewn into the lining along with the tailor's label "Hollwarth, Vienna". His beige suit was also from a western designer label, "Ermenegildo Zegna", as were his shirts. Indeed, everything down to underwear, socks and shoes had been bought from expensive fashion outlets in the West. Mingling with families waiting for relatives from the train, he sat down to wait. Timing would be everything.

With the efficiency of German punctuality the long train drew slowly into the station at 9.59, with twenty minutes before its departure. Von Horváth stood up and advanced to the nearest carriage door. Intentionally blocking the first passengers to dismount, he turned in a 360° circle as if pushed by the disembarking passengers, then turned to the door again. He stopped the next man descending.

'Please... sorry, I've forgotten my scarf!' The man unwillingly stepped back and von Horváth climbed quickly into the coach. 'Many thanks!' He waited by the lavatory door until the queue of departing passengers were all on the platform then strolled casually to the nearest empty compartment and sat down. Suddenly all the doors closed, although the train would not depart for another 18 minutes. Zoltan von Horváth knew what this meant, and it would not threaten his mission. Indeed, this was the outcome for which he had hoped and planned. It was not long before an East German border guard slid back the compartment door and wordlessly held out his hand. It was not von Horváth's ticket that he wanted. Von Horváth met his eyes steadily, and offered his Danish passport with a small white paper loose on top. The guard's eyes widened momentarily as he studied the paper, which carried no name, no photo. He slipped the document into his uniform pocket and saluted, clicking his heels dramatically. Then he opened the passport, flipped a few pages to the fictitious entry visa stamp and beneath it stamped in an exit visa dated June 18th, 1974. The guard left, closing the door. Fifteen minutes later the train started to roll slowly out of "Berlin Ost" for the four minute journey to the central crossing point, "Berlin Friedrichstrasse". By the time that the train slowed and entered the station, von Horváth had moved to his reserved, sole occupancy sleeper compartment, and already had his suitcase and coat on the rack.

As soon as the train brakes squealed the 12-coach train to a halt von Horváth stood up and pulled back the pristine lace curtains and lowered the window. This was an aspect of East Germany, of the entire schism of East-West paranoia and fear, that he hated, and yet it was his raison d'être, his licence to kill depended on it. And von Horváth liked killing.

As the train doors opened, he saw a dozen uniformed border guards come out of a glass walled human aquarium, each pushing what looked a luggage trolley on two wheels with an angled plate at the lower end to support luggage. But these were not designed to carry luggage, and the element attached at 90° just above the wheels was not a metal plate, it was a mirror. And another oddity was that the wheels did not just roll forwards and backwards, they could swivel through 360°.

Each guard pushed his mirror-trolley to the end of a coach; 12 coaches, 12 guards. A whistle sounded, cutting through the dark night air and the neon lighting. Von Horváth watched as the guard assigned to his coach inched slowly sideways from the junction plate to the next coach, staring fixedly at the reflection of the underside of the coach in his mirror at ground level. Such were the lengths to which East Germans would go to escape the infernal DDR that they were prepared to travel underneath a carriage, perched or lying across the axle. And such were the lengths to which the East German government would go to prevent the defection of even one citizen from the socialist paradise, every train from East Germany to the West was examined with this forensic detail. As the guard passed his window, von Horváth heard the door to his sleeper berth open, and turned to another guard, offered his Danish passport. Seconds later he was seated on his bed, and waited for the train to proceed into West Berlin half an hour later. Then there would be the two hour transit of East Germany during which the train was forbidden to stop under any circumstances until arrival at the final East German town of Marienborn, where the mirror inspection would be repeated.

As soon as the train left "Berlin Friedrichstrasse", von Horváth stood up and went to the dining car for dinner.

As the "Ost-West Express" pulled out of "Berlin Zoo" station at eleven at night, Petra and Colin were once again seated at table in the "Crab and Lobster". The wall clock showed ten o'clock, with British time being one hour behind the continent. The subservient obsequious waiter approached with a platter on which were two liqueur glasses and a bottle.

'Compliments of the management, madam, sir...' He had long ago understood that with this special couple, it was required to address Petra before her manservant. He poured two full glasses. 'Apricot brandy, from Switzerland.' he announced, as if there had been a birth in the Royal Family. He placed first the glasses, then the bottle on the table. The bottle was intentionally in front of Petra. 'I am instructed to leave you the bottle.' He withdrew.

'You know what?' Petra sounded abstracted.

'Give me a clue?' Colin sipped his apricot brandy and winced. 'Christ, this puts my Chartreuse to shame! Burns! What don't I know?'

'It's so hard to find a cookery book.' She seemed to be thinking aloud. 'I mean...'

'Well, having worked in the book shop in Polhaven, I know for a fact they don't stock any worthwhile titles for that.' Colin was following her drift. It was not unwelcome.

'And until we do… well, we agreed…' Petra was playing with the ends of the strands of hair on her ponytail. 'I mean, we'll have to go to Penzance, even Truro. And our schedule is full for days…' Colin smiled.

'I'm sure we can find an anniversary for one of us, obliging us to celebrate, get tipsy and not be able to drive home. And this is the only place we can get Roederer champagne. When's your birthday?' Petra looked mischievous. She seized a clean paper serviette from the glass of them on the table.

'Got a pen?' Colin handed her a biro. She wrote two words. 'Besides, it might be ages before we have time to go to Truro…' She pushed the serviette to him. He glanced down and burst out laughing, a rare event in his life. She had written: "Every night!" He lifted the bottle and replenished their glasses, then signalled to the waiter, muttered in his ear.

'We'll need another bottle of Roederer Cristal, please, on ice, in the room.' It was intentionally loud enough for sharp-eared Petra to overhear. A smile of contentment crossed her face.

As the "Ost-West Express" traversed East Germany towards Marienborn at the "death strip" frontier between the two Germanys, Zoltan von Horváth returned to his sleeper carriage. In the end compartment he caught sight of the conductor for the coach and handed him his passport, standard practice for overnight passengers to avoid guards awaking them at Marienborn and ten minutes later at Helmstedt in West Germany.

Wednesday morning promised to be another scorcher. Once again Petra went into the ritual of prodding Colin awake

246

and pointing to the coffee machine. It was seven o'clock. While filling the filter Colin turned.

'You know, you didn't complain once last night about your blasted pyjamas! We're making progress. Another day at work for you?' Petra nodded.

'Oh, I didn't tell you. Carruthers insists that I only work a two and a half-day week. Says we've got to succeed, with the project. Says he'll pay half my salary to the Ingram Foundation. So not only can I be there all day tomorrow for the Presentation, but Friday as well. No chance of getting to Truro until next week at the earliest…'

'I'll tell Simon to stock up on the Roederer, then.' He brought her a cup of coffee. 'One sugar, black.'

'And your day?'

'Getting my text ready for tomorrow. The "Presentation". Unaccustomed as I am to public speaking…' Petra put down her cup and kissed him. The inevitable giggle.

'*Come, come, my dear, not so shy now!* You'll be magnificent. How many are coming, do we know?' He shook his head.

'Sir Robert will phone us, tell us how many rooms to reserve here. Oh, by the way, I've already booked ours.'

The Polmine Project

The Polmine Project

Chapter Twenty

Thursday, June 20ᵗʰ 1974

'Are you nervous about today?' Petra was standing beside Colin on the platform, waiting for the special train bringing guests from Penlyn for the day's presentation. Her right hand was playing with the tips of her hair behind her shoulder. Colin shook his head.

'After the fiasco I created in that Goldoni disaster, the School Play, it'll be an Oscar Winning performance.' He paused. 'The trophy will be awarded to the star of the day, Miss Petra Zabrinski. I've decided.' They heard the whistle of the approaching train. Petra glanced first at his empty hands behind his back, then down at her own. Neither was holding notes, nor carrying any documentation. She took his hand timidly.

'I feel like a little girl on her first day at Primary School,' she whispered. The magnificent steam engine "Land's End" slowed alongside the platform.

'Here we go, then.' Colin muttered and they moved to the front door of the Orient Express dining car where they found fifteen guests grouped at the front tables. Both were surprised at the numbers; they had expected far fewer. Sir Robert Maxton, Dean of Camborne School of Mines was standing, saying a few words. He turned to introduce the owners of Polmine Estate.

'Ladies and gentlemen, may I introduce our hosts for the day, Mister...' He saw Petra's black eyes spitting fire and stopped. 'I apologise… ***Miss Petra Zabrinski***, and Mister Colin Penpolney.' Sir Robert looked pointedly at Petra. 'I hope I got that right?' Colin nudged Petra encouragingly and she stepped forward.

'Welcome, and sincere thanks for giving up your time today to visit our project.' She glanced at the numerous documents scattered across the Pullman tables. 'I see you have all received our Prospectus and the day's programme. Before saying a few words on that, we have two announcements to make.' She cleared her throat, feeling emotional.

'Every time we use the word "we" for this project, or the word "our", we are not referring essentially to Mister Penpolney and myself. No,' she swallowed, in danger of croaking as her eyes pricked. 'It refers to the late Felix Ingram, who single-handedly has made Polmouth's renaissance possible. "We" means the late Felix Ingram and his two disciples. Our deepest regret is that he did not live to see this day.' She paused, and all the guests seemed to be plunged into a collective reverie. She touched Colin's hand and he stepped forward.

'Welcome ladies and gentlemen. Before we invite you to introduce yourselves and the organisations that you represent, we should like to provide a little context. Ten years ago Felix Ingram bought Polmine Estate and Clifftop farm was donated by Farmer Blackitt. Ten years ago. I was fourteen, Miss Zabrinski just thirteen. We hardly knew each other, we were still young innocents on the threshold of adolescence. How could we know, how could ***anyone*** know the portent, the extent of Mr. Ingram's ambitions, his determination to save this small village, our small village, Polmouth? Well, today, we do. Ten years ago he stood in this station, watching a train draw in, much as today. The village was convinced that it was the last train to Polmouth. Thanks to him, it was not.' He looked around the dining car, unable to continue. Petra stepped in and Colin moved back a pace.

'You will, I am sure, all be relieved to hear that, unusually, today's visit will not be seeking any promises of funding, of financing for the Felix Ingram Project...' She paused to let a general murmur of surprise run through the fifteen invitees. Clearly the contrary had been uppermost in their minds. 'No,' she continued. 'Today is not about money. What we shall be doing though is to ask for support and advice on logistics. I know that several of you have already pledged your services. In that way, financial commitment on the part of our associates and sponsors, which we should like you all to be, will be minimal or zero. But the Felix Ingram Project cannot succeed without the support of your advisory services and material assistance. Not in funds, but in human resources which exist already and may be shared with us. Colin...' She pulled him forward.

'So if I may now ask you to identify yourselves and briefly describe the organisation that you represent... Starting at the back?' He pointed to Headmaster Temeritus Tennent who rose to his feet.

The introductions from the fifteen guests took some time, and as the third, Hilary Tonkin from the Department of Education and Science in London was about to sit down, four white-uniformed catering staff approached with cups, saucers and tea and coffee. During this pause, Petra took the lead.

'May we ask the catering staff also to present themselves?' She was interrupted by a spritely dark haired man rising rapidly to his feet from a window seat. Fortunately, he was standing just in front of Petra which allowed her to read the printed name badge on his lapel.

'Lord Kevin Rutherford, Dean of Falmouth Hotel School,' she announced.

'Falmouth Hotel School has already guaranteed chefs and wait-staff seven days a week all year round from our top students. And they in turn will prepare menus, we shall provide the supplies. The food… Revenue from the restaurant goes to the Ingram Foundation. Today I present…' He pointed to a young man in white.

'Henri Mathys, from France. Chef.' Then the pale man to his left contributed:

'Josef Mankowitz, from Poland. Chef' The others took their cue.

'Rolf Jenkins. Waiter.' Jenkins bowed ceremoniously. He was wearing fluorescent white cotton gloves as was his colleague.

'Henrietta Morton, waitress.' She curtsied and all four continued serving drinks.

'At least they have *some* English students, then!' muttered one woman to her companion.

The introductions continued. Neither Colin nor Petra had expected anything like this turnout. The list was prestigious. Colin had been scribbling the names on a clean paper napkin. As the last dignitary sat down he pulled Petra to his side, nudged her to speak.

'Well, as you have probably seen on the schedule, you now have an hour in which to explore the village, our Polmouth!' she added proudly. 'The train will leave at 11.30 for the rail head at the Croft and lunch will be served here in the dining car at midday. At two the tour will start. A Q&A session will then happen here, and finally guests staying overnight travel down to Polport on the train which will return to Penlyn and Falmouth.' President Teague held up a paper and called.

'I have the hotel list. I'll pass it to the "Crab and Lobster". Just one thing…' He stood up. 'Are there any vegetarian requests for dinner this evening?'

There were none and the passengers rose to disembark by the rear door. But Colonel Tennent approached Colin and Petra.

'You got that just right,' he murmured, touching each gently on the shoulder as if he were the King knighting them. 'Well done, very proud of you, what?' His eyes were glistening. An elderly man happy for multiple reasons. He turned and was last out of the coach. Colin and Petra sat down at the nearest Pullman table and Colin signalled to Henrietta Morton who hurried forward. Colin looked questioningly at Petra.

'May I have a black coffee, with a glass of iced water, please?'

'Same for me, please. And do you have any of that famous Falmouth fudge?' Colin added. She smiled and curtsied again before hurrying to the galley. 'Bet it's a long time since any waitress curtsied in a British Rail buffet car.' Colin remarked. He pulled the crumpled serviette from his jacket pocket and studied the list of names.

'She's very pretty,' Petra remarked, a propos of nothing.

'Really? I hadn't noticed... You were brilliant.'

'Well you didn't bash my head in, this time. It's progress!' Petra was on a high. Neither of them had expected a turn-out like this. 'Let me see!' She seized the list and read it through. 'Sir Robert has really pulled out all the stops to attract these people...' The waitress brought the coffee pot and a jug of iced water and two packs of home-made Falmouth fudge. Again the curtsey, it seemed to be mandatory. Petra tore open a pack of fudge and greedily bit into a square while Colin poured the coffee.

'I think the biggest surprise is this man from East Yorkshire Education, also representing West Yorks... All those mines in Yorkshire, I suppose. And Imperial College, University of London.' He sipped his coffee. 'All the nobility as well. Sir David Roaf, British Council, Sir Robert of course from Camborne, and then Lord Rutherford... You'd better learn how to curtsey!' She gave him a withering look and both sat in silence for some time.

The questions started at the first stop of the tour, in the Brick Croft baking tower.

'Well,' was Colin's reply, 'we foresee here a perfect place for rainy weather activities for the children's holiday week. It is most definitely not a "Summer Camp". We'd like to amplify what kind of children we envisage in our final session. But here we have 400 square yards. And a good example of the kind of support we're looking for. A space for a billiard table, and two table football games, no slot machine payment for them, and definitely no one-arm bandit slot machines. Over there...' he gestured, 'two table-tennis tables. Bats and balls, as also cues and balls for billiards, provided. There, some board games, and cards. No gambling!' It was noticeable that the Cornwall and Devon LEA representatives exchanged knowing looks. 'And by the door an Art Workshop space, but only water colours, for obvious reasons...' This time several realised what he meant and smiled. Parents would not easily forgive oil paint smears on shirts and shorts. The group moved on to the farm.

Here Petra explained how the smelting, the beating of horseshoes and jewellery could appeal to adult groups and children alike. After the shallow mine and a brief visit to Cottage no. 5, unoccupied, they reached the deep mine. Here Sir Robert had already had his men deposit lamps and helmets. More than a few visitors had questions about safety, but Sir Robert Maxton said that eventual associate sponsors would all receive full documentation concerning the safety of group visits, especially for children.

As the group walked along the gravel path beside the railway line towards the lakes, Colin was surprised that no-one expressed doubt as to the possibility of children playing on the unfenced line when a train was approaching. He told the visitors that it was a priority to have the path from the Croft House along the line and past the cottages to the descent asphalted and covered with tarmac. James Langton from the "National Trust" queried:

'That track down to Polmouth looked pretty steep. How far is it?'

'A mile to the junction with Penlyn Lane, and another 800 yards to the port.' Petra had been prepared for this. Simon Knowles from Exeter University frowned.

'Hmm... twelve year old children, it's a heck of a climb at that age...' Colin agreed.

'Good news, there. One of our associates is the West Cornwall Light Railway. They're providing the steam engine and all the rolling stock, and will maintain the track. But I had a surprise call from their chief engineer yesterday with a novel idea. His team are absolute experts, fanatics they'd admit, on every kind of railway. The notion is, if the Village Council gives permission, to construct a single track narrow gauge cable-drawn funicular single coach up and down with a flat-bed coach attached, for freight, running alongside the lane to be surfaced. And they'd design, build and maintain it...' Several of the group had stopped walking, were conversing in low voices. It was becoming clear for the first time that this Felix Ingram Project was not some tin-pot fantasy but had real substance. Simon Knowles called out:

'So all-weather transport from this Penlyn Lane junction to the cottages. Any chance of a covered walkway all the way to the railhead at the Croft?' He had intended it as a joke, but as far as the Project was concerned Colin had no sense of humour.

'Unnecessary,' he said dismissively. He pointed to the railway track beside which they were walking. 'The train can stop at the mine, the cottages, practically beside the top station for the Funi.' Knowles reddened and said nothing. This man seemed to have all the answers.

Dennis Trevelyan from Cornwall Tourism spoke up.

'With a project of this magnitude, surely the County Council can be persuaded at last to improve and open Penlyn Lane to two-way traffic. Wouldn't that increase revenue, and also be good for the local economy? Tourists, coach tours?' Colin signalled to Percy Teague. He stepped forward.

'Teague, President, Village Council,' he announced tersely. 'We have discussed this. Not only would the Village Council discourage any such step, we would absolutely veto it!' A murmur of surprise ran through the group. The obvious question was left unspoken.

'Polmouth is, and always has been, a village without cars. The lanes and alleys are totally unsuited for vehicular thoroughfares. And the Village Council is determined to preserve the pristine state of Polmouth as a village bearing the banner of the kernel of the peach of English heritage...' Several hands were raised to cover smiles on the faces of those sharing a sense of ridicule at this Victorian delusion. 'But setting that aside... to open the road would be financially disadvantageous for the Project.' A voice called out:

'Explain that, please. How could increased numbers of visitors not add revenue?'

'It would necessitate a large coach park and car park on Polheath, with pedestrian ways to the village, and to Polmine. At one pound per head entry fee, that would entirely vitiate the advantage of the rail link holding the monopoly. The Ingram Project will derive a great deal of revenue from train fares, dining car meals on the estate and down in Polmouth of an evening... coach tour groups bringing in picnic sandwiches, thermos flasks and litter are the last thing the Project needs. Or wants.' he added. 'Penlyn Lane is perfect as it is.' He stepped back.

After visiting the shimmering blue lakes and inspecting the projected Tea Room, they all convened in the front of the Orient Express dining car where they were served a copious Cornish cream tea. And so, at last, they reached the final Q&A session.

Petra took the floor. The main topic was the proposed children's Summer Holiday Project. There was general approval for the dates of Summer half-term holiday, the long Summer holidays and the Autumn half-term. Cornwall and Devon LEAs would provide two teachers to live in the cottages with groups of up to fourteen children, one man and one woman for the whole season. And a live-in qualified SRN nurse. Furthermore, they would provide Lifeguards for scheduled swimming supervision in the lakes and advice on whether to fence off the lakes. And finally, at Colin's request, guidance on fire regulations, sprinklers and alarms in the cottages, and fire drills for each week's newcomers. It was Headmaster Temeritus Tennent who suggested a security guard on night duty to ensure children did not sneak out of their cottages in the small hours for a secret rendezvous. The suggestion was welcomed. After a short silence a tall, swarthy man with dark eyes stood up.

'Xavier Modeno, Imperial College, University of London,' he reminded them. 'I have a proposal to make, on behalf of the Dean of Imperial, but there is one question first. You said this morning that you are not looking for finance, for funds. But your plans are not only ambitious, they are also expensive. Tarmac tracks, a funicular to the village, sprinklers etc. in the cottages, pedalo boats on the lake... Can your "own funds" really cover that without a sudden shortfall, and either an urgent demand for funds or closure?' He sat down. Colin looked at Petra. She touched his hand in appreciation.

'I am authorised to tell you that we shall be spending one hundred thousand pounds prior to the opening of both the History Project and the Children's Holiday Project next May.' She raised a hand to quell the astonished remarks. Only Temeritus Tennent was not surprised, for he had known of Ingram's intentions and his fortune. 'And...' she waited to continue, raising her voice, 'we have a reserve contingency fund of immediate liquidity of two hundred thousand pounds and as much again in bonds.' She was drowned out by the excited buzz that now hummed through the group. None of the visitors had expected anything of that magnitude of self-sufficiency. The Italian Xavier Modeno from Imperial stood up again. He was beaming.

'That facilitates my news greatly.' The Italian accent was very marked. 'It is clear that Camborne School of Mines is amply covering every technical aspect, which we shall be prepared to supplement on request.' Sir Robert nodded respectfully to Modeno. 'We shall certainly provide student groups between February and November using the chartered trains offered...'

'...by Camborne...' interjected Sir Robert.

'... and we shall greatly appreciate the offer of tourist accommodation in Torquay and Newquay... But to come to the point. Gratifying as it is to learn that the Ingram Project is self-sufficient, Imperial will be drawing on an Endowment fund to provide twenty thousand pounds annually for five years before assessing the status in 1980. And additionally, at your discretion...' he glanced at Petra and Colin, 'and at Imperial's expense construct a five foot high, broad mesh fence the length of the cliff top walk, to Local Authority norms. With immediate effect.' He sat down.

Suddenly the train gave a jolt and started to move towards the junction and the descent to Polport station. Colin stepped to the nearest wall, raised his hand and pulled the Emergency Stop chain. The train jolted to halt, but Charlie, the engine driver had been warned that if he left before the passengers were through with business, Colin would do this. He looked at the fireman stoker.

'Time for another fag, then.'

In the dining car all the guests were looking bemused; they had never actually seen anyone pull the cord, though several had wondered, on a long journey, what it would be like.

Colin and Petra were standing shoulder to shoulder, and as if to reaffirm their solidarity, Petra now put her arm round Colin's waist.

'This morning,' Colin started, 'I said we should finish the afternoon with comments about the kind of children we are inviting here. This is the only occasion on which I shall use the words "I" and "my", because Miss Zabrinski...'

'Colin and I are united on this. We have both witnessed some damaging events in the lives of children and teenagers around us. Sometimes lasting damage... "I" means "we".' she finished.

'We both met children at Penlyn whose formative years were marked by disturbing events, marred by them.' Temeritus Tennent, Headmaster of Penlyn Grammar, was leaning far forward in his seat. He did not for a moment doubt the veracity of their statement. But where was it leading?

'As early as in the Fifth Form, and more so in the Sixth Form as Prefects, Petra and I both encountered children aged twelve, thirteen, fourteen who hated Monday mornings and coming to school. Sometimes, I learned, they had a sick feeling in the pit of the stomach at four in the afternoon on Sunday. Because they told me, told us...' he glanced at Petra. 'When they were scared to tell a teacher, or their parents. I think that, because we were close to their age, but also because we had a certain status, wore Prefects' badges...' He looked at Headmaster Tennent, 'for which we thank you, Sir, for assistance is the Prefect's first responsibility.' Temeritus Tennent wiped the corner of his eye with a handkerchief. Now he alone among all those present knew why Ingram had chosen these two.

'Quite apart from teenage crushes and unrequited love, which was relatively easy to deal with... I believe Petra had contact with a number of thirteen year old girls...' Petra nodded. 'But there is the endemic, perennial, British school pestilence of bullying.' Tennent nodded silently.

'What is not widely known is that there are two distinct types of bullying. There is the well-known one-on-one hatred, with occasionally a few of the bully's peers joining in, ganging up. But there is a more insidious, inbuilt syndrome, which William Golding identified in his novel "The Lord of the Flies", and it is this one that destroys not only the victim, but all those perpetrating the atrocities. For they do not know that what they are doing is wrong.

'Let me take the case of Billy. At eleven, with parents constantly in conflict, he was put in a boarding school not far from here. He only joined Penlyn two years later, in the Third Form.' He looked directly at Headmaster Tennent. 'Billy Hall, Sir.' Tennent nodded in understanding. The boy Hall's education had to all intents and purposes begun at Penlyn Grammar School, aged thirteen.

'Although Billy did not know it, he desperately craved affection, parental affection, maternal, paternal, and scarce though this had been at home, it was now non-existent. I know this because he told me, in his second year at Penlyn, when he was fourteen. But of course he was too young to draw these conclusions. What the boarding school teachers had thought was attention-seeking, was actually a desperate search for affection.

'It started with hide and seek with his class mates outdoors in the dark, the hour before bedtime and lights out. He was the best at hiding. It became so difficult to find him that the "hunters" said he had to give a shilling to the boy who found him first. Billy mistook this attention for affection, being liked, even admired. He paid. But then the pocket money ran out. So the group demanded a penalty in lieu... A punishment for being found, and not a reward, had to be meted out.'

Some of those present looked distinctly uncomfortable, hearing a stark reminder in Colin's words of some of their own experiences at school.

'Initially it was all the chocolate he had in his Tuck Box. Then it spread to the bedroom, being beaten, punished for *"being Billy"*. Until he finally had to sleep under his bed, protected by his blankets and pillow. But still they came after him, fetching a broom from the cupboard and prodding the handle under his bed. It didn't help that in the morning, and all day long, they were all buddies, class mates, feeling no animosity towards Billy. They didn't actually dislike him, as one-on-one bullies do their victim. They were friends by day, but at night they were the pack and he the hunted, the most natural thing in all the world for some species. And that is why they didn't even know that they were doing wrong.' Several of the guests were visibly shocked. Colin had not finished.

'But the worst atrocity – there is no other word for it – was in the swimming pool changing rooms. Now the "pack" dared openly to attack by day. After swimming, when they were all in the shower room and Billy was naked, one of "the pack" announced that Billy's "punishment" the night before hadn't been enough. He incited the others to drag Billy out to the changing rooms, all stark naked, and they used his underpants and vest to tie him to two hooks high above his head. They were shouting the word: "Crucify, crucify!" Where the PE teacher was during this…? Anyway, now the five naked little boys twisted their wet towels with knots and beat Billy as he hung there, before hurriedly changing into uniform for the next lesson. When Billy managed to free himself and get dressed, he was late for class. And punished for being late. Sharing the classroom with the same boys who had tortured him…'

Colin looked at Tennent again. 'I think that was why he changed schools, and became a very fine young man.' Tennent lifted the handkerchief again.

'My point is, when children come to our Holiday Project, all that ends. Here children will be welcomed and appreciated for what they are, not what others make them into. And for that reason, there will be no football matches, in fact no team sports at all where aggressive, violent activity, which is oddly permitted on the pitch but would be illegal off the pitch, will be offered. Nor tolerated. Because that is where the "wimp" is identified, the poor performer, ridiculed. In my Primary School, it was invariably "the fat boy", the Billy Bunter of the class. In our groups, every child will enjoy her or his own status for what she / he is, unblemished by "the pack".' He turned and passed this to Petra.

'Please do not misunderstand us! We hold no truck with the bizarre notion of banning all competitive sports in Primary School because someone might win and make the others feel "humiliated". It is nonsense! But the children are exposed to enough tough situations in school, in the street back home.'

Petra was a small, compact young woman, and her fragile beauty belied her inner force, her passion. At that moment an aura around her set her apart, investing her with enormous presence. Her voice hardened, and she was wholly in command. Tennent's handkerchief was more often near his eyes than on his lap.

'We will not tolerate any situation where a child voluntarily chooses to be victim, mistaking that attention for affection, for being liked, being someone, while others blindly do terrible things.' Blushing at her own intensity she relaxed and smiled.

'And now Colin will take a walk along the side of the train and apologise to the engine driver for delaying the departure.' She sat down. There was a stunned silence. Suddenly Headmaster Tennent stood up, clapped his arm around Colin's shoulders. He addressed the group.

'We shall go together.' he said and the two climbed out and started to walk towards the green steam engine. Neither spoke.

Ten minutes later the guests staying overnight left the train, led by President Teague. The others requested half an hour to have a last look around the harbour area and the Esplanade. Only Colonel Tennent and Petra and Colin remained standing on the platform. There was a pregnant silence. Then Tennent spoke.

'Felix Ingram was a good friend of mine. The day he bought the estate, we lunched together, he told me his plans. I encouraged him, but Fate was unkind to him.' He looked along the platform at the flower boxes and flowerbeds, then towards the harbour, the palm trees. There was a catch in his voice. He gestured at the train behind them.

'You have achieved vastly more in two weeks than dear Felix in ten years. There has to be a reason...' He stopped, but Petra and Colin both knew what he meant. Why them. Tennent extended his right hand, and after shaking hands he boarded the train. Colin and Petra went to "Polly's Tea Room", walking hand in hand. And the day was far from over.

Sunset over Polmoor

Chapter Twenty-one

Friday, June 21ˢᵗ 1974

Friday was another gorgeous Summer's day. Von Horváth made his way to Polmouth by a circuitous route, the bus from Penlyn to Polhaven, and the ferry across to Polport. In a dark green anorak, jeans and a wide brimmed sun hat, he wore heavy hiking boots for rough terrain and had a large backpack with his sleeping bag and ammunition. The rifle, in several parts, and a Walther automatic pistol were wrapped in a towel.

As soon as he stepped off the ferry he struck off to the North along the footpath beside the estuary and the River Pol. A quarter of a mile outside the village he sat down on a bench and waited.

After a while he heard what he had been waiting for, the whistle of the steam engine and train departing on time for Penlyn. It was three o'clock and he had two hours before the next train. He cut eastwards into the woodland towards the railway. On reaching the track he started to walk uphill alongside the rails.

Following the spur into Polmine Estate, he approached the gate cautiously, crouching down among sparse bushes.

He recognised the main elements from his briefing. The nearest building would be the Croft House, and two miles away he espied the mine workings and the cottages. He lay down flat as he heard the throaty roar of two engines starting up. Petra and Colin rode rapidly along the track beside the railway and turned right at the mine, and soon disappeared down the lane to Polmouth. This suited von Horváth very well.

Half an hour later he was lying in dense gorse well to the left of the railway track and distant from the farm. With his camouflage he would be visible neither from the farm nor the cottages. The rifle was now fully constructed, placed on a two-legged support and had a telescopic sight on top and, unusually, a silencer at the end of the barrel. It was a .300 Winchester Magnum, not a weapon he had used before. Its range was over 1,200 yards, but von Horváth was uncertain of the effect of the silencer so had chosen a spot just 800 yards from the cottages with a clear line of fire. He adjusted the sights to point at Cottage 2. His first target would be Katrina Rothmount, the defectors' keeper. He settled down to wait.

Katrina came downstairs from her bedroom to fetch a book from the front room. Eagle-eyed von Horváth saw the movement through the window. It might be hours before he had another chance and he tightened his finger on the trigger, seeing more than half Katrina's chest and waist through the distant window. Such was his concentration that he did not hear the gentle rustle of an approaching intervention in this, the first of his assassinations that day.

A firm nudge in his ribs pushed him left, the moist nose of a Great Horse gently investigating the prone man. Involuntarily von Horváth fired, an uncontrolled, untargeted shot. He heard the distant sound of a window shattering and a shriek from inside the house. He cursed and rolled rapidly to the left. On looking up he saw the immense, nine foot tall Great Horse looking down at him inquisitively and he rolled further to the left. The infernal giant equine interloper neighed softly, liquid dripping from its nostrils, and turned away.

Von Horváth had lost valuable seconds in his precisely timed plan. He placed the rifle on the stand again, aiming now at the door of Cottage 1. It would be only human for Schiller and Meissner to come out to investigate the cause of the shattering glass and the scream. Von Horváth neither knew nor cared whether Katrina was incapacitated or lying dead on the floor, the aim had been to achieve one of these so that her role as "keeper" would be impossible and provoke exposure of Schiller and Meissner. However, neither came to the door to investigate and von Horváth's ease in picking them off one after the other was on hold. Now his meticulous plans suffered a further set-back, a second intervention. He heard the buzz of a moped rising over the top of the track from Polmouth and saw Petra's blond ponytail streaming behind her as she approached. Seeing the broken glass she dismounted and peered through the window. Taking her out was not part of von Horváth's instructions, and with typical Central European mentality he concentrated only on his orders. Petra saw Katrina lying on the floor clutching her arm and hurried into the cottage. There was blood everywhere; Katrina was trying to stem the flow from her forearm. Petra intuitively guessed what had happened. Colin's assessment had been right. She helped Katrina to her feet, and they both went into the back room. Petra was surprised at the extensive electronics and radio installations.

'Help me stop the bleeding...' Katrina stretched out her arm to Petra who picked up a tea towel. Katrina was already switching on a radio with her left hand before reaching for a microphone.

'East Germans, defectors, you *are* Royal Navy, this is an assassination?' queried Petra tersely. Katrina put down the microphone and stared.

'How did you know?'

'Not now. What do you want me to do?'

'Get them out! Down to Polmouth, or hide in the mine...'

'I don't have the keys.' Katrina pointed to a hook on wall. There were many keys, all labelled.

'The Army kept a set of everything. They must be next door, Helmuth and Uschi. Go, go now. I'll call Plymouth!'

Leaving Katrina in front of the radio, Petra hurried out of the back door and through the tiny yard of Cottage 1. Indoors she called desperately.

Von Horváth did not know that each cottage had a back door and tiny yard, so he was obliged to remain where he was, lying concealed in the undergrowth, awaiting his chance.

Petra received no response to her calls, and the Germans were not in either ground floor room. She hurried upstairs, opened a bedroom door and saw the naked couple in a highly erotic moment of what was evidently volcanic passion. Understandably, both reacted with shock which made their reception even less welcoming. They stared at Petra.

'Oh, for God's sake!' Petra had somehow to convey the urgency. 'Killer, gun... *schiessen!* We go, *wir gehen, schnell.'* She was grasping at the remnants of her "O" level German. '*Schnell!'* She physically pulled Uschi from the bed, and she in turn tugged at Helmuth's hand. Both were stark naked. 'No time, *keine Zeit. Wir gehen.'* Helmuth, distinctly red in the face for several reasons, made for door. Uschi, with a scientist's presence of mind, grabbed her panties and Helmuth's underpants from the floor and ran downstairs after them.

'*Hier*, back door! Katrina... *sendet Radio...* Plymouth... *für Hilfe...'*

As they appeared from behind the cottages and ran towards the cliff top track down to Polmouth, von Horváth saw them. At 800 yards it was impossible to see that two of the three were naked. Cursing, he seized a cotton bag from inside his back pack on the ground, and leaving the rifle where it was he ran towards the three people fleeing. He reached for his holster behind his back and took out a Walther automatic pistol. Even as he ran he checked a full cartridge of ten rounds was in place, then pulled a second spare cartridge from the cotton bag, slipped it into a pocket. Petra, looking over her shoulder, saw the unknown man over a quarter of a mile away, running after them.

'Oh, shit!' She realised that the descent to Polmouth pursued by an armed killer would be suicidal, and pulled Uschi left to the gate to the mine. Fumbling with the keys, they passed inside and leaving the gate open ran to the heavy metal door, closing it behind them. If they had locked either the gate or the door, thus barring access to the marksman, the outcome might have been very different. But they did not.

While Petra was groping along the wall for "the box" and the generator button, Uschi and Helmuth pulled on their underwear. The rough stone floor underfoot was torture.

The lights came on and Petra led the way down the main shaft. The large generator room would be a death-trap so Petra ran on past, urging the others to keep up. With bare feet, running for them was agony, a factor with which Petra had not reckoned.

Von Horváth had seen them delve into the shallow mine and slowed to a smart walking pace, a cruel smile on lips. All he had to do now was to follow, to find and to kill the three. And if they managed to hide, he was gatekeeper to their death-row in a four thousand year old prison. He approached the gate and strolled through the metal door into the lit tunnel. Surprised by the lighting, he now had a double advantage; they would have nowhere to hide. But von Horváth was wrong. Potentially they had a score of labyrinthine bolt holes. Von Horváth reached the first of the narrow tunnels to his left, the light barely reaching a few feet before the remainder was pitch black. He stopped, listened, but heard nothing. He was forced to improvise. He raised the Walther pistol and fired three blind shots into the black tunnel, hearing the whine of ricocheting bullets blend into the amplified echoes of the gunfire reverberating through the maze that extended below.

Already half a mile down the long broad tunnel all three fugitives heard the rattle of automatic gunfire echoing off the warren of stone walls. They paused to take breath.

'*Warum schiesst er?*' Helmuth was at a loss. Petra shrugged.

'*Weiter, schnell!*' She led off down the tunnel, only to pause again as a further volley of shots rang out. Now she guessed at the truth, the killer was firing blind into each of the narrow tunnels to left and right, in the hope of scaring anyone hiding there into coming out. Or killing them as they hid there, in the darkness.

The Phoenicians would never have contemplated running a mile downhill deep underground stark naked and barefoot, but Uschi and Helmuth had no choice. Uschi's feet were raw and bleeding from the agonising cuts to the soles. Helmuth, too, was limping.

'*Ist hoffungslos, wir sind verloren!*' panted Helmuth. Petra shook her head.

'It is not hopeless and we are not lost! We have one chance. *Eine Chance... Kommen Sie!*'

She seized Uschi's hand who in turn grasped Helmuth's arm, and they ran on. Renewed random bursts of gunfire echoed and whined throughout the maze of tunnels. And the shots were unmistakably getting closer.

They reached the end of the broad, illuminated tunnel, left only with the narrow entrance to their right, a black hole with no obvious way out.

'*Kopf nieder!*' Petra stooped to indicate what she meant. '*Folgen!* Follow me!'

She plunged into the dark space. Uncomprehending, Uschi and Helmuth followed cautiously. Petra remembered just in time the sharp curve to the right, and felt along the wall with her hand, while saying: '**Achtung, Kurve!**'

But neither of the Germans understood and Helmuth cursed as his bare arm brushed roughly against the hewn stone, paring the skin from his shoulder brutally.

But now all three saw distant daylight and within seconds they were in the final chamber, an open hole in the cliff-face their only escape. Petra peered over the lip of the exit and was relieved to see that it was high tide. The inviting deep blue waters were lapping just fifteen feet below. She seized the lifebelt from the left of the opening, leaving the ropes hanging from the wall, and threw it out into the sea. Helmuth had understood and wished that he had not. His voice was high and panicky. The gunfire was now frighteningly close.

'*Ich kann nicht schwimmen!*' Oh my God, thought Petra, this is all we needed.

'*Macht nichts!* Doesn't matter! In two minutes, you'll find that you can!' She released the second lifebelt and thrust it over his head until it was below his shoulders, then brutally tugged it up under the armpits as if impatient with a recalcitrant child at the beach.

'*Springen!* Jump!' she shouted, and did not give Uschi the choice, for she pushed the German woman violently in the pit of the back, and Uschi felt herself falling feet first for what seemed an age before she hit the water. When she rose she found the spare lifebelt floating right beside her. She heard a violent splash and saw that Helmuth had been given as short shrift as she herself. His red and white lifebelt kept him well above the surface. Now Petra made a vertical dive, came up several feet nearer the outcrop of black rocks than the others, pointed.

'*Schnell, Deckung…*' She started to swim rapidly round the leftmost rock and looked back. Helmuth, who had discovered to his relief that he could swim, after a fashion, had understood. He took Uschi's hand and they doggy-paddled their way round to the other side of the rocky outcrop, where it faced the endless expanse of the English Channel. Here they were invisible to anyone looking out from the ventilation shaft that the Cornish miners had carved out thousands of years ago. And sure enough, von Horváth finally reached the bottom of the main

tunnel then delved cautiously into the only hiding place left
that led to the cave and the open sea. Von Horváth could not
have known that until minutes previously there had been two
lifebelts hanging either side of the cliff opening, and even if
he had seen the loose ropes dangling there, they would have
meant nothing to him. He peered cautiously over the edge, and
realised that there were only two ways the fugitives could have
escaped. Either they had jumped to their deaths in their final
bid for freedom, or they had given him the slip in the rabbit
warren of tunnels and were even now on their way out and
down to Polmouth to raise the alarm. He failed to see the blood
stained stone floor where both Uschi Meissner's and Helmuth
Schiller's injured feet had left testimony to their suffering.

Now von Horváth's only imperative was to save himself.
He scrambled back to the main shaft and started to run up
the slope, cursing the heavy uncomfortable hiking boots that
slowed him down.

Out in the water behind the rocks, Petra pointed to
a convenient ledge on the next black outcrop. The others
understood. They swam clumsily to the ledge facing seaward
and pulled themselves out of the water, shivering despite the
warm sunshine.

'*Und was zum Teufel machen wir jetzt?*' Helmuth vented his
feelings.

Petra shrugged. Like the others, she hadn't a clue what the
hell they could do next.

In her cottage Katrina Rothmount was furious. Not only
was there no response from Plymouth RAF, it was evident that
they were not even keeping a listening watch on her frequency.
The blood from the flesh wound on her forearm had seeped
through the tea towel that Petra had wound round it, and her
head was throbbing with the pain. It was little consolation that
although she recognised that it was not life threatening, that
information did nothing to alleviate the handicap it caused.

With her one good hand she reached for the wall mounted telephone, but had to stand up to lift the receiver off the hook. Her rigorous training made it quite impossible to pass classified information over an open line to a switchboard, but if she could get the radio room to call her... Now she had to find the special address book...

Von Horváth was on the last quarter-mile uphill to the exit from the mine. He was no longer running but moving at a brisk pace, his ankles already blistered from the stiff leather hiking boots. He was clinically assessing the situation and the outcome; there could only be one. He was in no doubt that whether his targets had escaped into the sea and perished or survived, or whether they had somehow managed to evade him and get back to freedom before him, this mission was over, a failure. It made no difference now whether the survivors contacted the authorities or had simply vanished in the depths of the English Channel, as soon as the other owner of the estate, the man, returned and found the mine open, the broken window and Katrina Rothmount dead or injured inside, MI6 would rapidly abandon the compromised Safe House and set up a wide-ranging search, both for the scientists and for himself. Nor was he under any illusions about what his paymasters would do. When they learned of his failure they would cut him loose, deny any knowledge of his existence and want nothing more to do with him. He was alone now and for the foreseeable future; it was a case of every man for himself. And the only man whose well-being had ever interested von Horváth was von Horváth. His immediate course of action was simple, to distance himself as rapidly and as far as possible from the estate.

On reaching the gate to the mine he paused to assess the immediate surroundings. There was no sign of life other than the scattered Great Horses grazing. He hurried along the track to the Pump House, crossed the railway line at the mine-head and continued north-east to where his bag and the rifle were still lying. He slung the heavy rucksack over one shoulder, and with the rolled up sleeping bag under one arm continued north-eastwards to the distant fencing that encircled the estate. He left the rifle where it was. Progress over the rough terrain was slowed by the pain in his ankles where blood was seeping into his socks, the firm rim of the stiff leather biting into the skin. He did not look back but had he done so, he would have seen Colin arrive at the top of the track on his red moped and slow to a halt beside the first cottage. Colin noticed the figure of an unknown man over half a mile away with a hiker's backpack, striding across the heath away from the mines and the railway line. Puzzled, he now saw that both the cottage doors were open and the shattered window in Cottage 2. Thoroughly disquieted he hurried to peer inside and through the doorway to the other room saw Katrina Rothmount seated with her back to him, fiddling with some electronic console. He hurried into the cottage and now he saw her blood-stained forearm. He touched her on the shoulder and she jumped, turned to look at him. He divined what must have happened.

'The East Germans?' he queried, wasting no words. 'You're Royal Navy, aren't you? Are they spies or defectors?' Katrina, despite her injury and her frustration with the radio room in Plymouth RAF, stared at him blankly.

'How on earth did you know?'

'I worked it out. Where are they, and Petra's moped is out there. Is she with them?'

'The mine, I gave her the keys. But the killer's still out there…'

'He's gone, high-tailing it to the north fence. Where are they?' he asked more urgently.

'They went into the mine, to hide. There was shooting, a lot of shooting, went on for a long time. But one way or the other, they're down the mine. Dead or alive,' she added bleakly.

'Christ!' Colin was already out of the door and running to the open gate, then into the main tunnel. He knew that Katrina had to be right; the lights were burning.

Colin had a strong dislike of physical activity that related to any sport, but he came a very close second to Roger Bannister's four-minute mile that day. When he passed the first dark and narrow spur under the estate he did not hesitate. If they had gone in there, they would have been dead ducks, and he had every faith in Petra's common sense. He ran faster, always downhill which made it easier.

In her cottage Katrina had finally made contact with RAF Plymouth. She wasted no words, just gave her code name, then:

'Scramble the helicopter. Scientists on the run, attempted assassination. Land immediately at Polmine. Out.'

In the radio room the operator did not hesitate. He punched a wall-mounted button and the blare of the alarm klaxon resonated throughout the camp. In their barracks the helicopter pilots and four Air-Sea rescue specialists jumped to their feet, reaching for their gear and ran to the waiting helicopter. The pilot was first aboard and seized his earphones. Thirty seconds later he had his instructions and the rotor was turning.

Colin slowed as he reached the bottom of the mile long shaft. What he had been seeing for the last five hundred yards had him deeply worried. The white-painted floor may have been rudimentarily smoothed by some 20th century machine forty years previously, but it was still a very rough surface. And on the white paint he had seen numerous bloodstains. "A lot of shooting..." Katrina had said. He felt sick, and plunged into the dark narrow exit tunnel to the cavern and the open sea. There was nowhere else they could have gone.

When he reached the exit to the outside world he saw more blood stains, and then noticed that the two life belts were gone, just the ropes hanging loose from the walls. So he had been right. Standing on the rim of the opening he stared out, a wave of relief running over him. Sitting on the top rock of the black outcrop of *Poldeep Felsen* that rose out of the sea were three people, two of them naked, which he could not fathom. The third was Petra, fully dressed. The nude man was haplessly waving a heavy red and white life belt above his head in the vain hope that a passing ship might see them. Colin took a deep breath and shouted with all his force.

'P..e..t..r..a! **Pet-rraaa**!' She heard him and turned, then waved in relief. What Colin did next would live with him for a very long time to come. If ever he had given anyone fatuous advice in his life, he now surpassed himself.

'Wait there!' he screamed, turned and ran back to the narrow access and on up the main shaft.

Sitting on the rocks, thankful for the blazing sun, Helmuth stared at Petra.

'*Was hat er gesagt?*' Petra giggled.

'*Er sagte, bitte warten Sie da*! Wait! **Der Idiot**!' All three started to laugh uncontrollably.

Colin made it back to the surface as the helicopter was already nearly half way to Polmouth from Plymouth. It was not routed "as the crow flies" but over the sea, hugging the coastline. There was a good reason for this as it permitted the simplest approach and landing in front of the cottages. From there everything would depend on Katrina's information and the Naval Officer's assessment.

Speeding downhill on his moped, Colin reached the junction to Penlyn Lane and with scant regard for any villagers standing gossiping in the narrow lanes to the harbour, he raced on, one finger on the klaxon, just in case. He skidded to a halt outside the Coastguard Hut and hammered on the door. The officer on watch came out, surprised.

'People in water, one mile east. The lifeboat!' The Coastguard's training went back many years; act first, ask questions afterwards. He ran to the metal pole, brandishing the key and seconds later the blast of the petard was followed by the wailing air-raid siren that howled to every corner of the village and far beyond.

Von Horváth was by now a mile distant and heading north-east across Polheath. The further east he went, the further he was from the railway and the trains, from passengers who might see him. And the further north he went, the closer he came to the main line that cut east-west from Truro to Penzance. Beyond that he hoped to find a sheltered spot to bed down for the night, preferably with a spring and fresh water. Tomorrow he would make for the nearest village and find a barn or a farm outbuilding in which to hide out. He heard the faint explosion of the petard behind him, then the distant wail of the siren, and his lips tightened. The life boat. For the Germans? Or some event in no way connected? He sat down and pulled out the map. The terrain which he was crossing had to be the extensive Polheath, and he was probably nearing Polmoor, he estimated, but he could not know the huge difference that had given the two areas their names. Polheath was a dry expanse of sandy earth with abundant gorse and heather. Polmoor was a marshy swamp of wet ground and soft peat. He stood up and strode on.

Colin had clambered aboard the lifeboat uninvited. The Captain shoved a life jacket into his arms.

'Put that on!' Then in a loud voice to the whole crew: 'Brace, brace!' The boat slid down the rails with increasing speed and entered the water in a huge welter of spray. A sailor fired the engines and with a throaty roar the twin propellors thrust the boat violently forwards. The Captain skilfully navigated through the harbour entrance and looked at Colin.

'Heading?' Colin felt secure.

'South out of the estuary, then immediately East along the coast, one mile. Use the Poldeep Channel close inshore. They're on *Poldeep Felsen*.' The Captain steered the life boat as ordered, but he was staring at Colin. Only locals called the rocks "*Poldeep Felsen*" after a German freighter ran aground there in the Fifties.

'Who are you?' he asked in surprise. 'You're not a mariner, I'd know. And you're not some softy weekend yachtsman... So...?'

Colin looked puzzled.

'Me? I'm just a... well, a nobody, really!'

Within three minutes they were slowing to a snail's pace in the deep water channel between the cliffs and the rocky outcrop. The Captain at the wheel was carefully steering round to seawards, then he approached within a few feet of the rock on which the three waiting to be saved were perched. While the sailors threw ropes to them and started to haul first Petra, then Uschi followed by Helmuth over the side, the Captain nudged Colin. In a low voice he said:

'How the hell did they get *there*?' He sounded and looked incredulous.

'Oh...' Colin pointed to the dark hole in the cliff face. 'I think they jumped out of the mine...'

'Stark naked?!' Colin shrugged. It did sound improbable.

While all three were drying off with huge towels, Petra stood up unsteadily and stepped towards Colin. It was fortunate that it was another day of dead calm, the sea's surface an untroubled mirror of the sky, for she was distinctly wobbly. She sat down beside Colin, her black eyes staring into his. For a while, as the lifeboat puttered back towards the estuary with no urgency, no injured passengers, neither spoke. Then she started to giggle.

'What is it this time?' Colin's voice bore a hint of resignation.

'Well, I mean... there's your favourite mermaid sitting on a rock in the sunshine waiting for you. She can't swim away because her friends can't swim. And besides, it's a long way to France. So then you show up, and what do you say to her? You say: "Wait there", and you bugger off again. Honestly! *Men!*' But her giggle suddenly choked and as she laid her wet blond hair on his shoulder, Colin saw that was crying, sobbing uncontrollably and unable to stop. Her left hand was gripping Colin's as if she never, ever meant to let go.

The Air-Sea Rescue helicopter was already descending and the pilot was gauging when to make the right turn over the mine head and land when the keen-eyed lookout spotted the red lifeboat slowly returning to Polport. He touched the Naval Officer's arm, pointed.

'Down there! We've found them.' The pilot had also reached the same conclusion and he veered left, descending to fifty feet and hovering overhead the boat. The Naval Officer seized a microphone and his voice boomed out of a loudspeaker in the underside of the aircraft.

'Polmouth Lifeboat! Stop! We shall lift off the civilians now. Repeat: Stop!' The Captain dutifully cut the engines, but he was once again looking at Colin. If he had previously been surprised by Colin's nonchalant knowledge of navigation and his reticent responses, he was now thoroughly curious.

'Who are you?' he repeated. 'And who are these people... I know you're Penpolney, the Polmine and railway man, but there's more to this than...' He pointed to Helmuth and Uschi, both naked, who were deep in conversation. 'They're foreigners, ain't English, anyroads.' Colin shrugged. He looked up at the helicopter hovering deafeningly overhead, and the Naval seaman who was being lowered in a harness from a winch in the open doorway.

'That's an Air-Sea rescue helicopter,' he started, 'but look at the markings. It's Royal Air Force Air-Sea, not the Lifeguards.

And the man descending is wearing a Royal Navy uniform. That's about the only clue I can give you.' He was still hugging Petra who was shivering in her wet clothes. The uniformed sailor landed on the boat and unbuckled his harness before helping Uschi into it. It was a delicate procedure, he helping a naked woman into the tight harness. Five minutes later Colin was the last to be hauled aboard the aircraft, leaving the Captain of the lifeboat thoroughly bemused.

Inside the aircraft the noise was deafening. Colin correctly identified the Naval Officer as the man in command. He spoke into his ear:

'The gunman's gone. Rothmount's injured, Cottage 2. Not life threatening. So you can land there.' The Naval Officer stared at Colin, then spoke into a microphone attached to his headgear, something unintelligible to Plymouth. The pilot descended over the flat land in front of the cottages. As soon as the rotor stopped turning the Officer assisted Petra and Colin out onto terra firma. Katrina, who had been expecting them, hurried past and into the helicopter. The Naval Officer slammed the door from the outside and ducked as the rotor whirred into life.

'I'm staying for a while, Ronald Jamieson.' They shook hands as the helicopter lifted off and immediately veered eastwards towards Plymouth. Inside the aircraft Helmuth was protesting.

'*Unsere Kleider! Wir haben keine Kleider!*' A seaman stared at the nearly naked duo and guessed what was on the German's mind.

'We'll get you new clothes,' he said, but neither Uschi nor Helmuth understood, and made the short flight naked.

'I'm soaked and need a hot bath to warm up. And dry clothes.' Petra was addressing Jamieson. She pointed to her moped a hundred yards away. 'I'll go ahead.' She indicated the distant Croft House, and seconds later zoomed past the two men. They started walking. After a short silence, Jamieson looked at Colin.

'What do you know about the Official Secrets Act?' he asked. Colin shrugged.

'Never heard of it.' Jamieson smiled, pulled a sheaf of documents from an inside breast pocket.

'Well,' he said, 'you have now, and you're both about to sign it!'

The sun was low in the sky when von Horváth reached the unmarked line that separated Polheath from Polmoor. But he immediately noticed the change in terrain and in vegetation. The gorse and heather were replaced by vast expanses of olive green moss and clumps of coarse grass. What he could not yet see was a different colour, a light pea-green inviting sward of soft velvet seemingly laid like a carpet, randomly placed on the moor as if to create a work of modern art. Patches such as these lay some way ahead.

Dartmoor is renowned for its treacherous, hidden bogs, a muddy soup as dangerous as quicksand, hidden under greensward, invisible death traps for hikers and the ill-informed. Polmoor was, if anything, worse. Locals were made aware from very early childhood of the dangers of these pea-green patches, and how to identify and to avoid them. But strangers to the area were blissfully unaware of the danger, and their blissful state could turn in seconds to panic and fear. And von Horváth was a stranger to the area.

Not all such greensward traps were lethal. In some cases, about five feet down a firm stone plate covered the region, and after the initial impression that being sucked ever lower into this abyss of death was to be inevitable, the victim's feet suddenly touched a firm, secure surface, while the glutinous liquid mud was already up to his neck. Such salvation depended entirely on not being alone, and having others outside the man-trap to organise rescue, pulling the hapless victim out and to safety.

But the mud beds with solid rock beneath were the minority. Many such patches of turf were bottomless quagmires, and a solo hiker had no chance whatsoever of ever coming out, the cadaver left deep in the preserving coating of peat for all eternity, invisible to any eyes surveying the tranquil landscape after the event.

Von Horváth saw a bright yellow notice board on a pole to his right and made for it. Printed in black was a menacing skull and crossbones, and beneath in big print:

DANGER!
Army firing range!
Keep to footpaths.
UNEXPLODED ORDNANCE

Von Horváth was not afraid of unexploded shells left lying on the ground, for he knew what artillery and tank ammunition looked like. But he now proceeded very slowly, scanning the ground ahead before every step. He was forced to reassess his night out in the open. This would slow him down and when the light went, about ten in the evening, he would have to stop and sleep where he was. He looked up at the sky and estimated he had about two hours' daylight left. He tramped resolutely on.

At Polmouth's only alternative to the "Crab and Lobster", the tiny "Waterside" bar, the lifeboat Captain was still trying to get his head around the day's events. He sipped at his second pint of the evening, seated at a wobbly table on the pavement outside the pub. A chair scraped back and Jerry Kent sat down heavily beside him with a full glass.

'Heard you had a call-out today?' Kent was inquisitive. 'Was it a big do? Tanker gone down, Russian trawler man overboard again?' Peter Billington, the lifeboat Captain, wiped his lips and shook his head.

'T'were a rum do, to be sure.' He paused. 'That Penpolney from the mine, you know, got the railway going, him. Turned up at the Coastguard cabin. Gave a perfect nautical description, and course heading, the works. We got the boat out. He came with us, which is against regulations, but being who he is, I couldn't refuse. We get to these people, on the *Poldeep Felsen* they were. Two of 'em were stark naked, a woman and a man, and that girl from Polmine. She weren't naked.... So we got them aboard. I asked how the hell they ended up there. Mister Penpolney said he reckoned they'd jumped out of the mine in the cliff face. But naked?! Didn't end there, though!' Jerry Kent looked at his friend's face, then the glass on the table.

'That your first pint tonight, Peter?' His voice was guarded.

'Give over! I'm telling you… stark naked, and no other way they could've got there! Dishy blonde, and they was German! What happens next? An Air-Sea Rescue helicopter orders me to send them all up, but the helicopter wasn't Lifeguard, it was RAF, and the guy they sent down was Royal Navy! I can't make head nor tail of it!'

'I reckon you need a week in rehab, Peter. Give the beer a rest.' Billington shrugged.

'I knew no-one'd believe me.' he said sadly, and drained his glass before going inside for another.

Von Horváth's slow progress was matched by the lazy, relentless descent of the ever more fiery, red ball that was the sun. The lower it sank, the larger it seemed to become. Von Horváth saw ahead what looked like a good place to rest for the night, and prepared to unsling his sleeping bag from his back. He never did.

He stepped unwittingly onto the inviting light green surface of a mossy resting place. It was to be a resting place, but not like any he had ever imagined. After three paces, he felt his heavy walking boots being sucked inexorably downwards as if some monstrous creature of flubber was devouring him inch by inch. By the time the quagmire was up to his knees he had realised the danger, and feared the inevitability. Not for the first time that day his heavy boots were the worst footwear imaginable. Like heavy lead weights, they refused to obey his orders to either leg to lift, to push him back up. Now panicky, he tried to unstrap the heavy bag from his back, then stopped, realising that every movement he made caused the slimy, lethal mud bath in which he was mired to envelope him further.

The setting sun on the horizon curdled his vision, blinding his eyes. He closed the eyelids but now the blood added its own blend of purple to the fiery, angry evening light. The mud had reached his shoulders. He looked around in desperation. Von Horváth had killed many men, but had never once considered what death felt like for the victim. This evening, for the first time, he realised that there is something sickeningly chilling about facing the killer's gun, seeing the finger tightening on the trigger and then the sudden, awful return to the eternal blackness from which every living being briefly emerges, just once, to see the light. And tonight the light of the world, the sun, was bidding him farewell. As the last red glow of warmth, of life, slipped below the horizon the cold grey cloak of night hurried in from the East. When shortly afterwards the rising full moon lit the ghostly expanse of the moor in a silvery sheen, nothing visible remained of the man who had so recently held sway over his victims. There would be no more victims; the von Horváth lineage ended there, the final victim Horváth himself.

Polmouth Sunrise

Polmouth Sunrise
1975

Chapter Twenty-two

'Well, here we go.' Colin and Petra were sitting in their lounge in the Croft House. It was five to six. 'The moment of truth. Let's see whether they trash us...' He switched on the television for the week's "New UK", a series of documentaries on innovative projects around the country.

'And now,' announced presenter David Brierley in close up, 'this week's "New UK" is the most exciting project we have covered in the five years of this series. Tonight we explore...' he consulted a paper on his desk, '..."The Felix Ingram Foundation, Sunrise Estate." So now over to Jackie Rotundo and her report.' Jackie Rotundo's magical sex appeal was considered by many to be the reason for the programme's popularity, not least by the calculating schedulers. Her fetching outfits had men salivating in front of the TV sets, their wives fuming.

During the two minute music and visual programme titles and name lists, Petra stood up.

'I'll fix drinks...' she murmured and went to the cabinet. Now they saw delectable Jackie Rotundo standing on Polheath just outside the entrance to the rail head with the Croft House in the background. It was clearly filmed in the light of the early morning rising sun in Summer. Overhead to her left was a glowing, golden sign spanning the railway line into the estate. It read:

The Felix Ingram Foundation
Sunrise Estate

'Today I'm at what is truly a Pandora's Box of treats and surprises for young and old,' she enthused. 'This is one of the two entrances to Sunrise Estate. Before going any further, this is a "New UK" with a difference, in many ways. There is so much to find here, to explore, that for the first time in five years we shall be broadcasting a one-hour Special next week, such are the merits of this outstanding project...'

'Christ,' muttered Colin, sipping his Chartreuse.

'Sshhh!'

'In fact, fully to appreciate the extent of what Sunrise Estate offers, we shall be taking our helicopter.' There was the deafening sound of a large glossy helicopter landing beside her.

'My God...' breathed Petra, 'a Special Broadcast... Colin! What the hell have we done?!'

'Sshhh!'

Now Jackie's shapely behind in close-up was visible climbing into the rear of the helicopter, followed by a jolting shot of rough terrain as the cameraman with his Steadicam on his shoulder followed her. There were jumbled pictures of the interior of the aircraft, then a window shot of the rail head and the golden sign across the tracks.

The helicopter rose a few feet into the air before hovering, ten feet above the ground. Filmed through the open door, the picture was now a beautifully framed view between the posts supporting the sign. At first it was angled to zoom in on the Croft House to the right, then, as the helicopter slowly swivelled to the left and rose above the golden sign, the camera swept across a panoramic view of the two shimmering lakes and the vast extent of the gorse and heather covered estate seemingly going on for ever behind them.

'Christ! So that's our home...' Colin sounded emotional. Petra again had his hand in hers.

'I told you I'd make it really, really nice,' she murmured. Now Jackie Rotundo resumed her commentary.

'The key to Sunrise Estate's future lies in the railway. So we shall now follow the tracks and join the "Land's End" steam train that runs four times daily from and to Penlyn Junction and Falmouth. It also serves the estate.'

The helicopter rose dramatically to five hundred feet and the camera picked up the distant smoke and steam trailing behind the W.C.L.R. three coach train, drawn across Polheath towards them, the gleaming green steam locomotive at its head. The TV crew flew alongside the train for several miles until it crossed the rail head spur junction and started its descent on the last mile through the woods to Polport.

The helicopter pilot was no novice; his handling of the aircraft brought it down to just twenty feet above Polport harbour, allowing the cameraman to film through the open door with a close-up of Polport station and the train slowing to a halt. The platform was lined with flower beds and window boxes. Jackie Rotundo picked up her sound track.

'This is the tiny Cornish village of Polmouth. Behind me you see the Pol river estuary, and the town of Polhaven...' The camera extended the zoom to a distant shot of the waters and the hill behind Polhaven. '... And to the South, the English Channel.' The cameraman obeyed, then the helicopter slowly turned 45° to the left, showing the viewers the cliffs towering above the village nestling in the nook of land in which the tiny port and the railway station were the central elements. Now the camera picked up the brand new British Rail prototype, the sleek three coach train, standing in the station at a new, second track alongside a white concrete platform by the water's edge.

'A year ago, this station, a single track with one platform then, was, as they say, "nothing to write home about". Today... it is a vital hub, central to the success of the "Sunrise Estate" project.' The helicopter positioned itself twenty feet above and alongside the yellow and blue prototype gas turbine train. Jackie Rotundo was audibly a railway enthusiast.

'Now this is what makes BR's contribution to the renaissance of Polmouth unique. It is the only train of its type anywhere... in the world! Powered by an almost silent gas turbine engine with low exhaust pollution, it is testimony to BR's commitment to innovation. In a statement provided to "New UK", BR said...' The text appeared in a bar at the bottom of the screen.

"BR is fully committed to "The Polmine Project" and the rebirth of Polmouth. This prototype train, the only one in service, places BR at the forefront of Polmine's associates and sponsors."

While the cameraman lavished attention on the gleaming train, Colin was critical.

'She makes BR sound positively philanthropic! Didn't mention that we lease it, and pay for it!'

'Sshhh!'

Jackie was speaking again.

'So now to our first guest today...' The helicopter descended and landed just at the end of the platform between the station and the harbour. Palm trees were blasted by the draught from the rotors. Jackie Rotundo pushed open her door and climbed out with another tempting close-up for devotees of that kind of thing, her behind. On the platform they approached a tall gentleman with silver hair, a little bouquet in his button hole. Behind him was the gleaming blue Orient Express dining car, which preoccupied the cameraman.

'You, sir, are...?'

'Percy Teague, President of Polmouth Village Council.'

'And tell us in your own words what this rejuvenation means to the village? And how it came about?' It was clear from the wording of the questions that Jackie Rotundo's research had already informed her thoroughly on both answers. Teague launched into platitudes about *"the kernel of the peach that is*

English heritage" while the cameraman roved around, filming whatever he could see outside the station that smacked of "English heritage", finally alighting on "Polly's Tea Room". Then Teague started on Jackie's second question.

'Eleven years ago, Polmouth was hit by two calamities. That was the year of "the Beeching cuts" to secondary railways across the country. The service to Penlyn Junction, and thus connecting with the London to Penzance main line, was cut. And the train was the village's only lifeline. There was and is no road. However, the line was built in the 1890s, unusually funded entirely by the Village Council. So although Beeching stopped the trains, the tracks were village property and were never removed. The second calamity was a direct result of the first; the only asset in the village was up on the cliffs, Polmine Estate, nine square miles of prime building land for housing and development. The owners were "Chronos Investment", and it was their only asset. The closure of the railway meant that overnight the Estate was rendered worthless...

'In June 1964, I stood on this platform with a dear friend beside me, the late Felix Ingram, and we watched a tragedy unfolding. The arrival of the last train to Polmouth. But Felix had other ideas... and now it is time to allow you to explain to your viewers how "The Felix Ingram Foundation" was born, and how it has saved Polmouth from annihilation.'

Jackie Rotundo sounded relieved as she expressed thanks that were audibly not sincere, for Teague had stolen her link-line. She climbed back into the helicopter. It lifted off, permitting truly rustic, rural shots of the hamlet's roofs as it approached the junction to the defunct Penlyn Lane. Here the pilot dutifully hovered.

'Now this is the only road link to Penlyn from Polmouth...' Jackie Rotundo was back on the air, consulting her notes. The TV picture zoomed in on a tiny, narrow track overgrown with vegetation, bushes and tree branches that obstructed any useful passage. 'We shall be asking why, if the "Ingram Foundation" is truly set on opening contacts with Penlyn and the outside world, this lane is still, after all these years, unpassable, even on foot.' While the cameraman held the shot over the overgrown track, Jackie did not miss her opportunity.

'You can find out the answer to that conundrum, and many more, by tuning in next Friday at the same time for our one hour Special...'

Colin sighed and rolled his eyes.

'However, the state of the lane does explain one peculiarity about Polmouth; it has not, and never has had, any motor vehicles, for the simple reason that none can get here.'

On cue the helicopter rose to 200 feet and stationed itself to the left of a new small building at the foot of the tarmac covered track that rose steeply up the side of the cliff. Jackie was now fully into her artificial reporter's mode.

'Why, one may wonder, has this new construction been built, and indeed who by and for what purpose...' The cameraman lifted the shot to show a gleaming green and silver funicular car slowly descending into the village station housing, rolling on narrow gauge tracks with a cog-rail in the centre and a solid steel cable attached to the chassis. The funicular ran parallel to and alongside the track uphill. 'And where, one may wonder, does it go? And for what purpose...? Let us find out...'

The helicopter lifted into the air and while it advanced a mile towards the mines, the cameraman took pictures of the glistening blue waters of the English Channel.

'Heck, they've really gone to town on this,' muttered Colin fetching refills from the drinks cabinet.

'Sshhh!'

The helicopter rose dramatically, and the fenced-off sloping track into the shallow mine came into shot, with the cottages behind and to the left, and in the distance the Pump House, the lift workings and the tower above the shaft to the deep mine.

The helicopter landed and Jackie introduced Novak who spent several minutes explaining that it had been used during

World War II by the Army, and then mothballed. Filming continued inside the shallow mine, but nothing like the full extent of the one mile shaft.

'I don't think I ever want to go in there again,' muttered Petra. 'Not if I have to jump out of a ventilation shaft into the English Channel and then be told… "Wait there"!' But there was a mischievous look in her eyes. Colin looked sheepishly at his shoes and said nothing.

A few minutes later there was a third explicit shot of Jackie's anatomy as she advanced along the smooth asphalt track to the cottages, where she was met by a stocky, rotund man in his fifties in a crumpled suit.

'Our third guest is Prep School teacher Maurice Monkton…' Maurice answered her questions on the planned Youth Holiday Centre, explaining the principles, the practicalities. There was nothing here that Colin and Petra did not know, it was their creation. But…

'Maurice is bloody good!' exclaimed Colin. 'He's only been here a day. I can see why Hampshire LEA recommended him for the season. Just hope he won't jack it in half way through.'

'The way he's enthusing it doesn't sound likely.' Petra said reassuringly.

'Sshhh!'

Maurice was still speaking.

'My colleague Tricia Harriman is even now checking laundry supplies with the resident Nurse, Helen Tremayne. The first group of twelve children arrives on Sunday, so in three days' time. Let's go and see their accommodation.'

It was clear from her tight lipped expression that Jackie considered he had just stolen her next line. There followed a brief inspection of the four single-bedded rooms per cottage for the children, the kitchenettes, and the cottages reserved for staff accommodation. Maurice led the way past the deep mine with a cursory comment.

'Camborne School of Mines will maintain the pump and the lift. And escort visiting groups of adults and students for the History Project, simplified for the children, on explorations of the deep mine.'

'He's certainly done his homework!' Petra said admiringly. 'Sshhh!'

'Now this is new...' Maurice pointed to a secondary short spur from the rail line that served the mine workings. 'This track and the coach on it...' The cameraman zoomed in on a pre-war carriage with dark blue livery and the inscription *"Wagon Lits SA"* on the side, '... will be a fixture. Come aboard...' Jackie and the cameraman climbed up the steps after Maurice, permitting a fourth explicit shot of the day. Five years ago the cameraman had been thoroughly briefed by his director, and the public seemed to appreciate the fleeting suggestive glimpses. They were even a frequent topic on radio chat shows, and viewer figures were in the millions for every broadcast, however boring the week's subject.

Maurice explained that the coach had been converted by the W.C.L.R., the Project's associate, as staff leisure quarters and the surgery and accommodation for the full time nurse, appointed and paid for by the Cornwall LEA.

'This guy should be a PR consultant!' exclaimed Petra. 'He's brilliant. But what drives a man like that, of his age...?' Colin was sombre.

'I know what it is. And you're right, he's "driven"... He cares massively about children's welfare, their well-being. A single man, in his fifties, boys' Prep School in the New Forest... He's a man after our own hearts...' Petra leaned across and kissed him.

'Well, he can't have mine. It's taken! And don't you dare tell me to "Sshhh" again!'

'Sshhh!'

Maurice scarcely had time to explain the arrangement, half the coach a lounge with TV for the staff, then the extensively equipped surgery beyond, and the sanitation and power connections to the Pump House, than the helicopter landed deafeningly alongside the *"Wagons Lit"* coach and the TV crew left Maurice standing in front of the mine as it lifted into the air.

Next came the farm, Sarah's interview and the smelting furnace, the anvil for horseshoes and the jewellery that she made. Last was the release of the ten Great Horses to roam the estate at liberty and graze. Jackie Rotundo thought that she had seen pretty well everything in her career as a journalist, but the sight of these immense creatures, nine feet tall and as gentle as lambs, stretched her vocabulary of superlatives to the limit and beyond, for she finally stopped spouting, speechless.

The helicopter flew towards the rail head at the Croft House, the camera picking up Petra and Colin waiting on the Brick Croft platform. When Jackie Rotundo had approached and done the introductions, she nudged the cameraman to film a structure across the railway track. The cameraman dutifully filmed from the base of a metal pole up to the top where an old-fashioned signal arm extended over the track, a metal plate painted white with a black vertical stripe.

'This may be a silly question, Mister Penpolney... That signal... as there's no two-way traffic, and there are no points... what's it for?' It was Petra who had answered.

'You had her foxed here!' muttered Colin, enjoying this bit.

'Sshhh!' But what came next was not quite as she and Colin remembered it.

The cameraman, mindful of his director's instructions, and aware as any man would be that Petra Zabrinski was a vibrant young woman, seemed accidentally to zoom in on her generous bosom, and remain with that in shot until he apparently recognised that she was speaking and pulled back to extend coverage to her face as well. But the bosom was still centre screen.

'The cheeky monkey! Well!' Petra sounded indignant, but the opposite was the truth. A proud girl with a proud body, thought Colin, but did not say so. On the documentary Jackie, unaware of the feminine competition for her glamour spot, looked questioningly at Colin.

'The signal?' Petra had feigned indifference. 'Oh, it's purely ornamental, serves no useful purpose. In fact, I'm not even sure whether the arm's meant to go up or down. Probably does neither. No, it's of no use whatsoever...'

'Then what...'

'It was a gift from the West Cornwall Light Railway. They thought it would look authentic, please the children when they come for a holiday week. But it's utterly useless!'

The broadcast ended with a tour of the Brick Croft baking tower, equipped with a billiard table, table football, ping-pong tables and the Art Workshop in one corner, before moving to the Tea Room and the terrace. The helicopter took off to return to Truro, with Jackie Rotundo eulogising about the huge effort and the prospects for this week's "New UK" project, urging viewers to tune in to the "one hour extended version" in a week's time. She managed to slip in the day and the hour of the transmission four times. When Colin stood up to turn off the set, he was far from sure whether Jackie Rotundo was promoting the "Felix Ingram Project" or the TV programme for which she worked.

'What time are we meeting Maurice and the others?' Petra was playing with the ends of her pony tail again. Colin knew the signs.

'We haven't time for that now! In fifteen minutes, in the "Wagon Lits" lounge. We'd better get ready. What will you be wearing?' Petra grinned.

'Surprise!' She went upstairs.

At seven o'clock they entered the staff lounge in the permanent fixture "Wagon Lits" coach in front of the Pump House to find Maurice, Trish and nurse Helen Tremayne. Helen switched off the TV.

'They gave you a rave review!' she said admiringly. 'So what's the plan for this evening?' Helen came across as a no-nonsense maternal character in her fifties. Neither Colin nor Petra knew why she had been suggested to West Cornwall LEA by the NHS, they only knew that she was a retired SRN. They left the lounge and headed past the cottages to the new gate and Funicular station.

'We'll take the Funi down to Polmouth. We have a permanently reserved table at the "Crab and Lobster"…'

'So you must eat there often?' Maurice looked surprised. He knew what frequent restaurant meals cost, being a gourmand himself. Colin looked sheepish.

'Well, I'm strictly a boiled egg man.'

'And I'm Princess SSB…' Petra chipped in. Maurice was confused.

'Uh…?'

'Strictly Spaghetti Bolognese. At university I actually lived off it. So we have to eat out, you see?' The others laughed and Colin unlocked the Funi coach. Minutes later they were approaching the "Crab and Lobster".

'It's a beautiful little village!' Trish's distinct New Zealand accent with the uptilted lilt at the end of every phrase was attractive. In her twenties, so around Petra's age, after only a day Petra felt a distinct affinity with the young woman.

In the "Crab and Lobster" the obsequious waiter practically ran to the door to greet them and accompany them to their permanently reserved table. The newcomers were impressed to see a bronze label in the middle of the table, "Reserved Polmine". The waiter pulled back chairs for the ladies and brought the menus, placed them ceremoniously on the spare sixth chair and requested drinks orders. Maurice was looking curiously at the strange place to put menus. In his preferred restaurants the waiter opened the menu and handed it to the guest, always from the right. Colin saw his raised eyebrow.

'It's a bit of a tradition,' he explained. 'When we started eating here a year ago, it was the best place to plan, to discuss… we talked for hours. So he'd bring the menus with a degree of impatience, and I used to put them on a spare chair to make space for our notes. *Mea culpa.*'

The waiter took their orders. Colin no longer needed to order the wine, it was always supplied appropriately for the meal.

New Zealander Trish had already been in England for two years but could not get used to the British, two-faced notion of "good manners". To a straight-talking New Zealander two things in particular riled her. One was the way in which they invariably began everything with "I'm sorry, but….", where there was not the least hint of regret, before disagreeing violently and often rudely with someone. There was nothing "sorry" or apologetic about it and she had no time for it. The other was the way the English peppered every answer with "to be honest". It seemed people were too ignorant to realise that what they were actually saying was: "I'm often dishonest, but today, I'm being honest, for a change…' In New Zealand people said what they meant, and asked direct questions, none of this apologia of pussy-footing around. She had been studying the prices on the menu and now opened the wine list. When she saw the prices her eyes widened.

'Kin I ask yew a quistyun?'

'Fire away.'

'Yew don't charge pricy entry fees. Yew seem tuh eat here pretty often. Are yew millyunairs?' Colin smiled indulgently.

'Miss Zabrinski handles all the finances. I just sign the cheques.' Petra stepped in.

'Neither of us takes a salary, we never shall. The "FIF", "Felix Ingram Foundation",' she explained, 'has sufficient funds for the initial launch, i.e. everything so far.' she added. 'Over the past year we allocated one hundred thousand pounds to set up the infrastructure...' She was into her stride, in her element. 'What we had to do, it was imperative, was find enough sponsors to make our expenditure on a day to day basis, and so annually, almost nil. And we managed it.' she said contentedly and looked at Colin. Maurice was astonished.

'How many sponsors do you have?'

'Oh, at least fifteen.' Colin said airily. 'Cornwall and Devon Tourism, the LEAs, the DES in London... Imperial College and the Camborne Mines School, then of course The National Trust, National Heritage...'

'The British Council,' added Petra proudly.

'All right, all right, I give in!' Trish was smiling. 'So they fund it?' But Colin shook his head.

'Not a penny... well, Imperial insist on giving us twenty thousand a year, but we never asked for it...' he added virtuously. 'They insisted!'

Now none of the newcomers understood anything. During the first course Petra explained.

By the time they had reached the dessert they had covered numerous questions. Colin felt it was time to push to more social and sociable pastures.

'As you know, there'll be a brief meeting tomorrow, so I'd suggest...'

'I agree!' Petra intervened. 'But just so you know, our old Headmaster Temeritus Tennent told us that one thing teachers really hate is being given a list of information, and then having to sit on hard wooden chairs in Staff Meeting to hear some pompous Headmaster tell them it all over again at great length in a droning voice for over an hour!' Maurice laughed and nodded.

'Never a truer word!'

'So we'll provide a list, and limit the meetings to a short clarification on points raised.'

Colin looked at the Nurse, Helen Tremayne. His sharp eyes had picked up the fact that there was a marked indentation and ridge on the ring finger of her slightly fleshy left hand, as if a wedding ring had long been worn there. But now there was no ring. He picked his words with care.

'You're a good example of how our sponsors and associates help us. You were recommended by West Cornwall NHS to join us, and we're very glad that you have. And Tremayne is certainly a Cornish name. Apart from your residential work here, do you still work or live in Penzance? Or have you worked as a School Nurse somewhere?' It was the best he could do to disguise the simple question that Trish would have worded as "Tell us about yourself!"

Helen Tremayne swallowed a mouthful of bramble mousse and reached for her water glass.

'I worked in Penzance hospital for thirty years, got my SRN there. Five years ago my husband was diagnosed with leukaemia. Two years ago I retired to look after him full time. He died in February this year, and the Ingram Foundation seemed ideal for me. And you've provided a top notch surgery, state of the art.'

'Not us!' Petra intervened. 'That was provided by University Hospital, Exeter. So you see, everything that we need to make this place work, right down to accountants and a lawyer to handle the Registered Charity status, is provided by our sponsors. It costs them far less than donations of money, and they can see on a day-to-day basis what their contributions actually bring. Ideal!' She paused. 'I'm truly sorry to hear of your loss...' Helen smiled reassuringly.

'In my line, one has to get used to the facts of life. And of death.' she added. There was a short silence.

'What's the procedure if someone's gravely ill?' Maurice wanted to know. Helen warmed to this theme more than to the previous topic.

'In that surgery I can make a pretty quick and accurate diagnosis. If I have the least concern it might be serious, say meningitis, I call in the Flying Doctor...'

'What?' Trish's head jerked up. 'Yew mean... like in Ostraylyúh? Yew have a re-uhl Flying Doctuh?' Helen laughed.

'Yes, a "real" Flying Doctor! Penzance is surrounded by outlying villages with poor road access. Anyone needing hospital attention is lifted out by the Air Ambulance service, and there's always a doctor on board.'

'May I ask which sponsor pays for that?' Maurice was politely curious.

'In the first instance, we do. If we call it out, they invoice us. But then we rely on our insurer. Insurance is on the list for tomorrow.' As for all things financial, it was Petra who answered. Trish looked satisfied.

'Wyill, that sure answers my kwest-yun, thanks.'

The waiter brought five complimentary glasses of a rare blackberry liqueur, and left the bottle. Maurice looked at the unusual brew.

'People must think very highly of you round here.' he remarked. Petra shook her head sadly.

'Between us, sshhh... but they're all simpletons here. I just wrap them round my little finger... I mean...' she pointed at Colin. 'It even worked on him!' She leaned across to kiss him and all present understood that the "Felix Ingram Project" was in the hands of two highly unusual young idealists. As they tasted the sublime bramble liqueur, a noble silence reigned.

'I was thinking...' Maurice Monkton sounded apologetic at what he was thinking. They were walking up through the narrow cobbled streets to the lower Funi station. 'The

Croft House is very big, and you've made the Tea Room very welcoming...'

'That was my work!' Petra intervened. 'He's useless at interior stuff.'

'She's right. But I see what you're getting at... we live there, the two of us, in a mansion. Well, in the early days we planned on keeping two bedrooms for ourselves, and opening the other three as a B&B Guest House. But we've dropped that idea now.'

This was the first that Petra had heard of this. She pressed closer to his side, her arm round his waist.

'Why's that?' Maurice was intrigued. They had reached the Funi station and Colin was opening the gate with his key, then slid the coach door open.

'Well... we've already given up the Tea Room for breakfasts, and snacks for visitors and student groups, school groups too. And built separate washrooms alongside. We hadn't reckoned on our daily schedule being so hectic. Apart from the daily visits and groups, the school weeks in Summer really leave us little time. And if you saw the weekly maintenance check lists for every single installation on the Estate... What I'm saying is, we're reserving the Croft House for our relaxation, what rooms are left. In particular, the three bedrooms. For the family.'

Involuntarily Petra's arm tightened around his waist, her eyes wide. Neither she nor Colin had any family. Colin continued innocently.

'You know, children's bedrooms, a playroom for the electric train, the dolls' house...'

'You never told me any of this!' Petra was giggling again and turned to the others. 'He never told me any of this!'

'She never listens, that's her problem.' Colin was nonchalant.

'Well I'm listening now!' Colin activated the Funicular coach and they heard the reassuring clickety-clack of the cog wheel beneath them.

'Well, Cleopatra married her brother, you once told me, said something about a precedent. They weren't my words.'

This left the others totally fazed, until Trish suddenly pulled Helen to the back of the coach. Her eyes were glistening in the dim light.

'Christ! I think he's just proposed to her!'

Chapter Twenty-three

Saturday, June 14ᵗʰ - Sunday, June 15ᵗʰ 1975

Colin and Petra had a long day ahead. At nine they were already at the mine platform, waiting for a group of students from the University of Durham and any miscellaneous day trippers to the Estate. After visiting both mines, they would be guided to the Farm and the iron ore smelting and then, after an A la Carte lunch in the Orient Express dining car, explore individually. The train passed the redundant black and white signal at the rail head, ignoring the fact that it was a "STOP" sign, and slowed to a halt beside the Pump House. There were eleven university students, all young men, and eight independent visitors. Colin recognised the two Camborne Mines engineers, Derek Compton and Ian Langley. Camborne always sent two on a rota basis from the five volunteers.

As soon as they had given Compton the keys, Colin and Petra headed for the Wagons Lit lounge. There they found Maurice, Trish and Helen, each with a notepad on their knee. Trish would have been less than human not to have shared her observation of the previous evening with the others, and all three were trying, in vain, to hide the fact that they were looking, expectantly, for an announcement. None was forthcoming, but all three quickly noticed a certain radiance about the couple which seemed to indicate that Petra had not been slow in responding. Once seated, Colin looked at Petra who set the ball rolling.

'Any of you can call a meeting urgently if anything untoward crops up. Otherwise, we should meet here again in a week's time to assess the first visit, and make any alterations. Now, as Colin said, we'll expedite this by limiting the list to what you want to know about.' She passed the lead to Colin.

'All right...

Point 1: Contact. All our telephone numbers are listed here.

Point 2: Insurance. All staff are insured against accident, illness necessitating the Air Ambulance, damage to property, loss and theft, legal assistance in the event of litigation against us or the children. And injuries sustained, other than self-inflicted.' Colin smiled thinly. 'As you can see, this was drawn up by our lawyer. The premises are insured against fire, water damage etc. The list is exhaustive, so we'll leave it at that, unless?'

There was no "unless". Petra resumed.

'Point 3: Laundry and cleaning duties. Children make their beds after breakfast each day and bedrooms are checked by Trish or Maurice for girls' and boys' rooms. Children strip their beds on the Saturday morning. The Laundry Service in Penlyn will send someone on the train that collects the children leaving and bundle it into baskets for transport to Penlyn. We shall always have three weeks' clean laundry in stock. Making up the new beds is, unfortunately, our duty. But with a maximum of fourteen beds per weekend... Oh, and Trish and Helen each have a key to the Girls' Supplies cupboard, for the obvious girls' requisites. And a dozen spare toothbrushes, toothpaste, soap, all that.' Maurice interrupted her.

'For young people who've never done this before, I congratulate you! Sounds like you have years of experience in a boarding school...' Colin shook his head.

'A number of LEAs across the country have explained the normal systems that boarding schools use. We've nearly finished...

Last point: As you know, we welcome LEAs' children who are known to have had a bad time, emotional or physical. But we need as many allegedly balanced and happy children in every week's intake. That's why we filter all the dossiers to form a group. You've got all the files, that's your domain, not ours. Finally, every evening we'll distribute the following day's programme with alternatives for wet weather. Any questions?' There were none. On the way out to the sunny heath they found the door blocked by an inquisitive Great Horse. Colin told them to wait, went into the lounge and picked an apple from the fruit bowl. At the doorway he held it out to the Great Horse and then threw it some way away. The horse cantered to find it, and they descended.

'Oh, by the way...' Colin turned before they dispersed. 'If you, Trish and Maurice, take the two o'clock tomorrow from Polport, you'll be in good time to meet the children as they arrive and accompany them here on the "Polmine Special" at four. If any are delayed, call us on our number. Have a nice day!'

Maurice and Trish were sitting by the lake, going over their roles as Monitors to the children. Suddenly Maurice veered off at a tangent.

'You know, that was my shortest Staff Meeting in twenty-five years as a teacher!' Then: 'D'you think they really are? Engaged, I mean? They didn't say anything...'

'Yuh, I'm sure of it. That Cleopatra stuff had me fazed at first, 'cos she married her brother, then poisoned him to put her son by Julius Caesar on the throne. When she got bored with Caesar she conjugated with Caesar's best friend, Mark Anthony. And she finally committed suicide by making a poisonous snake bite her breast. I'm not sure that Colin knows what he's getting himself into... But, yeh. I'm sure of it. They're engaged.'

'Hmmm, well I suppose it's some consolation that Cleopatra had black hair, and Petra's blonde. And that Cleopatra died two thousand years ago.'

- - - - -

At five minutes to four next day Petra and Colin were standing on the rail head platform at the Croft House. Colin held a bundle of papers, the top sheet a name list of the twelve children and their cottage numbers.

'The great day has arrived,' he murmured.

'I can hear the train.' Petra sounded nervous and turned to look at Colin. 'Tell me it'll be all right, it'll work...' Colin put his arm round her. They saw the plume of smoke and steam streaming behind the train, over a mile away. Colin was resolute, his voice deep and convincing.

'I promised I'd show you the eternal sunrise, Petra.' He pointed to the approaching toy train in the distance. 'Here it is.' Her eyes were moist.

'What was all that about the children's bedrooms, the dolls' house, the model railway...?'

'I was just floating an idea, nothing concrete.' Colin was vague. It was evident that Petra didn't believe a word of it, nor did he.

'Piffle. What if we need three?'

'Three what?'

'Bedrooms, silly, for the children.'

'Then we'd have to find somewhere else for the model railway.'

'And the dolls' house... Here it is...'

The gleaming green locomotive was passing through the open gate from Polheath and slowed to a halt. Colin and Petra moved to the front door of the Orient Express dining car, and found Maurice already waiting in the open doorway at the top of the steps.

'I hope Ingram's watching from up there,' whispered Petra. 'Because this is definitely *not* the last train to Polmouth!'

- - - - -

Printed in the United States
By Bookmasters